THE WRONG

LARS EMMERICH

THE WRONG

BASED ON TRUE EVENTS.

IT WAS THE KIND OF WRONG THAT CAN NEVER BE righted. That's why I thumbed off the safety on the .45 in my purse, steeled myself, and gave the ornate door handle a twist.

I didn't have an appointment. I wasn't expected. I didn't arrive during business hours. I didn't use the front door.

Truth be told, I was trespassing. They could easily charge me with breaking and entering, and no doubt it would stick.

But that wasn't even close to the end of it. I was just getting started.

I had no delusions, and I wasn't out to save the world. I'd been around too long to believe any of the fairy tales about justice and the rule of law. I'd spent the first four billion years of my adult life at Homeland catching spies. I'd had no prayer of emerging with my idealism intact.

But I *had* left Homeland with a full bag of deeply antisocial tricks. I chalk it up as one danger of training good people to do bad things. Somewhere along the way, we can't help but lose our goodness. Ends and means, blah blah, but it's hard not to lose your soul trying to serve the higher good using the devil's tools.

"Hello, Commissioner," I trilled, a massive smile on my face, breasts out

1

and prominent, hips doing that thing that tickles the male lizard-brain into instant submission. I marched into Frederick Posner's office balanced atop my ludicrously expensive Jimmy Choos, artificial cheer cranked up to eleven, looking for all the world as if someone had hired me to deliver a singing telegram.

"What…?"

Ruddy complexion, barrel chest giving way to a beer keg around the waist, enough medals hanging on his police jacket to make a third-world dictator green with envy, hands moving quickly beneath his desk, undoubtedly reaching for his service revolver or the panic button mounted beneath the desktop.

I shook my head. I had expected to be a little more impressed by the face of pure evil.

"Please don't," I said, gesturing toward his hands with my "borrowed" handgun, its sturdy heft calming my jangly nerves and dampening the tremor in my hands.

I'd used a gun in anger many times before, but never under circumstances like these.

In the past, I'd been an agent of the state, dispatched to serve justice and comeuppance, or at least to do the bidding of the state. But I'd walked away from the job, even if I was having a hard time walking away from the life.

So this was anything but official duty.

In fact, it was homicide.

The word scorched through my brain like a red hot poker. I blinked and shook my head to clear the thought from my mind, but it left sweaty palms and a metallic taste in my mouth on its way out. It's one thing to contemplate an idea; it's another thing entirely to stand in a man's office with a gun pointed at his face.

I shook my head again. Focus.

"Hands above your head," I said to Posner. "You're a cop. You should be better at this."

Posner's red face had turned pale and his chest heaved. "You're making a mistake," he stammered, sounding nothing like the calm, confident, self-assured police commissioner I'd seen on TV.

"Undoubtedly," I said, aligning the white dot on the gun's barrel between the white lines near the hammer and pointing the whole thing just above a prominent crease in the center of Posner's forehead. "Probably several mistakes. Odds are, at least one of them is important, maybe even fatal."

I talk too much when I'm nervous.

"One chance, Frederick," I said. "I won't ask more than once. Are you ready?"

Posner's eyes closed, his shoulders heaved, and his head shook side to side.

His reaction was all wrong. Way too submissive, resigned… scared.

I got a sinking feeling like I'd seen this movie before and didn't like the ending.

"I don't know who you are, but please, think this through," Posner said. A note of hysteria crept into his words. I took it as a sign that I was doing a good enough job hiding my own nerves. But I was fairly sure that I was mere seconds away from peeing myself.

Murder.

No statute of limitations.

In a death penalty state.

My two decades of federal service might be enough to stave off the needle, but I'd surely get life in prison.

Focus, Sam.

"You have a warehouse," I said, "and at least two co-conspirators."

Posner's eyes squeezed shut. His breath came in gasps. It surprised me again. Here was a career cop who'd cut his teeth on the streets of Philly, one of the most violent cities in one of the most violent nations in the developed world. One middle-aged redhead in a leather skirt and designer shoes wielding a handgun shouldn't have had nearly the effect I seemed to be having.

Maybe, I thought, Posner was having a hard time holding it together because he could see the crazy written all over my face. It hadn't been the best of months and I'm sure I looked unhinged.

"Get ahold of yourself, Commissioner," I said. "I want to know where they are. Right now. No bullshit."

He shook his massive skull and his eyes blinked fast, darting from side to side as the adrenaline played havoc in his brain. The eyes finally settled on me, a little too small for his jowly face and a little too close together to seem entirely trustworthy. How had this man made it so far in life?

Then I saw a semblance of the street cop return, clawing its way to the surface after years of office politics and shady side deals. "Nobody waltzes into police headquarters with a gun," he said. "Drop it now and you won't be shot."

But his performance wasn't convincing. I laughed, harsh and bitter. "Final answer?"

"Jesus," he said. "I don't *know* where they are." I heard panic creeping into his voice again. The man had made a career out of deception and coverups, but I had a strong sense that he was telling the truth.

"Have it your way," I said. I refined my aim and drew a breath.

"Please," Posner pleaded. His first sob caught me by surprise. Big, tough-looking guy like that, breaking down like a bitch. I was disgusted, standing there watching him snivel, thinking about the unspeakable things this man had done just a few hours earlier. The corners of my mouth turned down and there was no mercy in my soul.

His face contorted and his jowls shook. "I really don't know!"

"I'm losing patience, Frederick."

He said the usual things—please, you must believe me, they emptied the warehouse and I don't know where they took the kids, etcetera, but his words weren't compelling.

And I was busy applying pressure with my index finger.

And then my ears were ringing and that unmistakable smell hit my nostrils and Frederick Posner's diseased mind was suddenly spread all over the oak paneling behind his desk. His massive form settled a bit, lost its rigor in increments, wound up a slumped heap of dark blue and deep red. Blood drained in weak arterial spurts from his ruined skull, and I could taste the sickly sweetness in the air.

Done and done. One fewer subhuman littering the gene pool.

Then I had a moment of clarity in which I became keenly and frighteningly aware that my life had just changed forever. Behind me was a clear, bright line that could never be uncrossed.

My instinct was to run like hell, but my job wasn't finished. And I was wearing heels and a skirt. Not conducive to fleeing in panic. I hurried around

Posner's pretentious desk, littered with grinning photos taken with crooked politicians, gangsters, and long-irrelevant semi-celebrities. I used my forearm to shift his heft and ran my finger against the bone behind his ear, taking care to avoid the gaping maw full of muck, noting with disgust that Posner's bladder and bowels had emptied.

I fought nausea. My hand moved on his scalp, fingers pressing, searching. Sweat and dandruff added to the charm. I was looking for something that might not exist, might never be found, already wondering how long I could stand there before panic and revulsion overtook me.

There.

Small bump.

I moved his graying hair aside to look. The bump was rectangular with rounded edges and a small surgical scar nearby.

Bingo.

I placed the barrel of the gun an inch away from the bump, closed my eyes against the splatter, and pulled the trigger again.

I clicked the safety in place and put the gun in my purse. I knelt to retrieve the spent shell casings and dropped them into my purse as well. Then I walked out of the Philadelphia Police Commissioner's office, locked the door behind me, took a left, opened the emergency exit, and calmly descended the stairs.

I'd done the math many times in my head, and I knew roughly how much time I had to exit the building before the guard locked the place down. Six minutes in the best case, and three minutes at worst, assuming in both cases that the fat pencil-pusher at the security desk knew right where to go. Conservative assumption, but optimistic planning had never seemed to pay off in my years of fieldwork.

Sounds assaulted me as I descended the stairs past the door to the fourth floor. Muffled shouts and hard shoes pounding hard floors gave me the urge to kick off my heels and sprint for the nearest exit, but that would have been a rookie mistake, and nobody would look at the lines on my face and the bags under my eyes and mistake me for a rookie. I walked with manufactured nonchalance, even coaxed my face into a soft smile. Just a well-dressed woman descending a few flights of stairs in the Philadelphia Police Headquarters building. Nothing to see here.

The night air was colder than hell and the sting of it caught me off guard as I exited the service entrance. My nose burned and a shiver ran through me. I hunched my shoulders and ducked my ears beneath my collar.

A giant land-barge of an automobile idled at the curb, a Buick/Lincoln/Ford-type thing that spanned several counties, the kind of car owned only by retirees and feds and drug dealers with a strong sense of irony. Its exhaust swirled in white clouds beneath the streetlights. I opened the rear door on the passenger side and climbed inside.

I gave a nod to the driver, a girl of some nineteen years old, and she hit the accelerator.

"One down?" Stacey asked.

"Two to go," I replied.

THE MILES CLICKED PAST IN SILENCE. I'M SURE THE GIRL
and I both had similar thoughts swirling in our heads, but we kept them to
ourselves. It wouldn't take much twisting of the truth to conclude that an
indictment against us was in order.

Because it definitely was.

We'd tried to go through the normal channels, but three things worked
against us. First, the story was far too outrageous for normal people—even
police officers—to wrap their minds around. Second, Frederick Posner and his
cohorts were wealthy and powerful and had taken pains to buy the requisite
loyalty.

Third, Posner was a liar on par with an American politician. He lied
with fearless conviction. He lied with gusto and panache. He attacked the
credibility and lineage and intelligence and competence of anyone who
disagreed with him.

He didn't lie to convince you of an alternate reality. Instead, he lied to
show his dominion over the truth. Posner lied to let you know that facts were
not useful, important, or relevant. He lied to let you know that right and

wrong were inconsequential inside his gravitational field. And he lied to give his entourage plausible deniability.

The result was that the officers around Posner were the worst kind of people: spineless sycophants and hardened criminals. And they protected him with religious zeal.

I smiled a bit as I thought about this. Perhaps if Posner hadn't scared away the last of the competent officers in his department, it wouldn't have been such a cakewalk for me to do what I'd just done.

My smile disappeared as a second line of thinking, one that assaulted me daily, reared its ugly head again. *Who the hell do you think you are? What gives you the right to play god?*

And right on cue came the big one: *You should have burned that fucking password and never looked back. Because you can't be trusted.*

I shook my head and tried to get my insides to relax. *Focus*, I coached myself. *Stay here in the moment. Otherwise you'll get us killed.*

But it was not that easy. My hands shook and a giant rat gnawed on my innards and my thoughts raced.

Two weeks. That's it. Two weeks since I'd escaped the mountain cabin. I'd barely slept since then, my life a series of flashbacks and sudden breakdowns and mile after mile of trying to drive away from myself, trying to get enough space from the nightmares and the voices in my head to get things straight. But that's not how trauma works. There is no getting *anything* straight. You're alone on a raft in the middle of a raging river.

The same two weeks had passed since the largest responsibility on the planet had been forced on me, basically at gunpoint. And I was definitely still in denial.

But what else could I expect?

"Ninety-five south," I said to the girl behind the wheel.

"I know," she said, turning just in time to make the on-ramp.

"Could have fooled me."

She gave me a look in the rearview mirror. Stacey Lamontagne was her name, and she was beautiful by any standard. She had raven hair and icy blue eyes, a perfect face that could easily grace the cover of any magazine, and a trim, athletic body that could easily grace the centerfold. I'm revealing my age a bit because centerfolds are a thing of the past and I'm not even sure a girl Stacey's age would understand the reference.

I admired her. There was steel in the center of her, which was the only reason she was driving the car and not already dead. She'd saved her own life and was now on a crusade to save two dozen more. If she succeeded—if *we* succeeded—we might save hundreds more still.

"There's an accident," Stacey said, looking at her phone. "Almost three hours to Baltimore."

I was instantly smoldering. "Let me see, please."

She handed her phone to me. I rolled down the window, cocked my arm, and hurled the little electronic spy toward the pavement with a grunt. I thought I heard the phone shattering over the tire noise, but I couldn't be sure.

"Do you want to get us killed?" I snapped. "What part of 'nothing electronic' was unclear?"

"It was jailbroken," Stacey said, her expression both angry and a little sheepish.

"Even worse."

"I wanted to make sure I didn't get us lost."

"Ever hear of a map?"

Stacey was full of strength and fire, but she sure as hell didn't follow directions. I shook my head, wondering how long it would take before her lack of discipline came back to haunt us. To haunt *me*.

"Take the next exit," I said, looking at my watch.

"Where are we—"

"Exit *now*, Stacey."

She crossed two lanes, earning a honk and a gesture from a mookish man in a Land Rover.

"Take a right, then follow the signs to the Eastwick Station," I said as we approached the cross street. I took off my heels, tossed them in my purse, and replaced them with a pair of comfortable flats, fighting to keep from cracking my skull against the window during Stacey's erratic turns.

A dozen minutes later, after ditching the car in an alley three blocks from the station, I swiped a prepaid cash card through the ticket machine and punched the buttons for two rail tickets.

"Why are we heading back into town?" Stacey asked.

"Because," I said through clenched teeth, "that's the only way to get to Baltimore from here unless we steal another car."

Stacey's eyes fell. "I'm really sorry about the phone. I don't want you to think I'm ungrateful or whatever. I just wanted to make sure I didn't screw up."

I wrapped an arm around her shoulder. "Forget about it. We'll adapt."

I looked her over, assessing. Stacey was a few inches shorter than me and a few pounds lighter. Her hair was black, in contrast to my red. Her eyes were blue, where mine were green. Other than that, we could be sisters, I thought.

I was flattering myself, of course. The age difference meant that if we were pretending to be related, Stacey would have to be my daughter. And I'd have given birth to her in my late twenties. That nagging thought struck me again: *I'm getting way too old not to have a family of my own.* But that would be more than a little tough. There were two men, neither of whom seemed interested in being with me at the moment. One of them walked away because of my career — which, in the brutal irony that only real life can dish out, I had since given up. And the shadow he cast on my heart had scared away the other one.

Plus, I'd just been through something horrific, something I couldn't yet talk about, and I was in no shape for a relationship. With *anyone.* I was barely functioning, still scared of my shadow, still ready to shoot the first man who came too close.

"Pull your hat a little lower," I said to Stacey. "It's important to keep your eyes hidden."

We climbed aboard the 9:12 p.m. train with seconds to spare. I settled heavily in the seat and stewed. It promised to be a long night, and I wasn't looking forward to what was to come.

I tried to shake it all off and refocus.

Twenty-four hours until the broadcast.

Twenty-four hours to find two more subhumans.

Twenty-four lives hanging in the balance.

THE FIRST TRAIN TOOK US NORTHEAST, BACK INTO Philadelphia. We exited at the 30th Street Station, across the street from the Comcast Center. Next year, the place will probably be named after some other corporate monopoly. I don't know how people keep it all straight.

We had twenty minutes to kill before our connecting train departed, heading southwest this time, and I was nervous. I had taken all the precautions I knew to keep my face from being tagged by a surveillance camera. I wore a set of battery-powered spectacles that featured fifteen small infrared lights to dazzle the IR surveillance cameras. But with technology, you can never be sure. Maybe they'd recently upgraded the cameras.

I also made sure I changed my walking gait. The way we walk is a unique identifying feature that our smart algorithms have learned to use against us. I hoped like hell I had modified mine enough.

I tried to find my zen place as the seconds drifted lazily past. *Breathe in. Breathe out. Clear the mind. Relax the body.* I used to do this kind of thing often when I was a counterespionage agent for the US Department of Homeland Security. Worry and anxiety are a perfect recipe for mental gridlock, which is a key ingredient in most fatal mistakes made by field agents.

I wasn't an agent any longer. If you wanted to put a label on my role at that moment, that label would have to be *vigilante.*

That's another way of saying *criminal.*

It wasn't my fault, really. I'd done my best to involve the authorities. I'd even contacted the FBI. My friend Special Agent Alfonse Archer was on vacation and not answering either of his phones. I got the Class A bureaucratic runaround from the shoe-clerk who answered the phone at the crimes against persons desk. My options were pretty limited by that point. I couldn't just patiently hope and pray that the system would somehow unfornicate itself in time, given how many lives were at stake and how little time remained.

I looked at my watch, then resumed my scan of the sparse crowd waiting for the train to Baltimore. Nobody had that operational vibe and nothing triggered my spidey-sense. Which meant precisely nothing. It's always the tail you don't see who kills you.

Was my paranoia justified? Hard to say. These guys were smart and capable, but they weren't nearly as well-funded and well-connected as the state-sponsored spies I used to track down. But the absence of evidence is not evidence of absence, as they say, and nobody ever regretted staying alert.

I glanced again at Stacey. She was flagging, losing her energy, suffering from the aftereffects of the hideous ordeal she'd endured over the past two days. She needed a good meal and a good night's sleep, though I wasn't sure either was in the cards anytime soon.

The platform rumbled. The train hissed and screeched to a halt. I gave the crowd one last sweep, looking for signs of trouble, and led Stacey onboard.

The train trip took sixty-three minutes. Stacey's eyes grew heavy and she slept. Her body jerked, she cried out, and she awoke once with tears in her eyes and terror on her face.

I understood completely. I'd recently been through pretty much exactly what she had just endured. Extremely recently, in fact. It was a horror that I'm certain will clang around inside my head and heart for decades. It was no fucking picnic. I could certainly understand why Stacey wasn't sleeping soundly, because I wasn't sleeping yet, either. At all.

I used what must have been the last functioning payphone in Baltimore to arrange a ride with one of the ride-sharing companies. It was a risk. It would have been easy for a goon employed by Frederick Posner, may he suffer in eternal, fiery, ass-raping agony, to pose as a cabbie outside the train station. I felt apprehension. The odds of something like that were low, but they weren't zero.

Twenty minutes later a young North African man named Said (he pronounced it sigh-*eed*) picked us up in a small hybrid sedan at the entrance to the station. His eyes lingered on Stacey much longer than on me, which, were it not for my internal Armageddon, might otherwise have made me a little jealous. She *was* a looker, but there was also a time not too long ago when heads turned to look at *me*. Middle age is a bitch.

I didn't give Said an address, mainly because I didn't *know* the address. But I knew where we were going and I offered to navigate, an option I liked much better than leaving an extra digital record of our whereabouts in Said's navigation system. What the spies say is true: paranoia pays.

I only made two mistakes along the way, one flub serious enough to require Said to backtrack, but I didn't mind the detour. It was solid tradecraft, in case anyone was trying to follow us.

Said turned into the Baltimore suburb and I saw the envy on his face as he eyeballed the expensive cars and expansive houses. "It isn't all it's cracked up to be," I said. "Most of these people are up to their eyeballs in debt."

Said nodded, but I could tell that the highly contagious American Dream had already infected him. "Maybe a smaller house for me," he said after a while. "But definitely without the seven roommates."

Seven roommates. How the hell did he manage? I hated having *myself* as a roommate. I couldn't imagine seven other people lurking about. But maybe I'm more misanthropic than most.

"Right here is great," I said, even though we were still a healthy walk from our destination. Said was a nice guy and probably had nothing at all to do with Frederick Posner's posse of dirty acolytes, but I wasn't taking any chances.

Said let us off at the curb next to a perfectly manicured yard in front of a monstrous people-box. I paid cash and included a handsome tip and Said motored off into the night.

We walked the final quarter-mile. Thankfully, I remembered the street name and recognized the house, another McMansion just a few blocks over. I rang the doorbell, then tucked my hand into my purse and wrapped my fingers around my .45.

The man who opened the door was in his early thirties, fit, groomed, and wearing a warm smile and no shirt. He was much as I remembered him.

"I wasn't sure I'd see you again," Fix said. "And I see you brought a friend."

Stacey smiled a little nervously.

"People call me Fix," he said, hand extended. Stacey took it but didn't give her name.

"Ah, the shy type," Fix said. "No problem. It's a big, bad world out there, right?"

"Fix, are you going to let us in?" I said, more of an edge in my voice than I intended.

He looked at me for a moment. "Of course," he said. "I'm sorry. It's just not every night when two beautiful women show up at my door."

I remembered that about Fix. The last time we did business, he subtly let me know that he wasn't opposed to having sex with me. It was obvious now that he was still amenable to mixing business with pleasure. But I still wasn't in the mood—maybe never would be again—and I was sure that Stacey's very recent ordeal had left her feeling anything but frisky.

"You're very kind," I said, stepping into the sparse but tasteful bachelor pad.

"Something to drink?"

I was both parched and starving and I'm sure Stacey was in the same boat, but I declined Fix's offer. His business was entirely black-market, which was an increasingly dangerous way to earn a living here in the People's Federal Republic of America, and I didn't want any of my DNA left behind at his place. I wasn't a federal agent any longer, and I consequently had no plausible deniability.

Plus, I was at Fix's place to make an illegal purchase.

"Straight to business, then," Fix said. "Must be in a hurry."

"I'm afraid so."

Fix led us through his cavernous home. Stacey followed and I brought up the rear. Our footsteps echoed in the sparsely appointed space. I watched Stacey take in the surroundings with a bit of wonder and surmised that her upbringing wasn't privileged.

"My lair," Fix said, opening the door to the basement. Scents of computer hardware and ink and warm paper and cannabis and the damp Maryland earth wafted up. The overall effect wasn't unpleasant, and my olfactory lobes fired up their recognition. Nothing is wired deeper in the brain than smell, and this combination brought back very clear memories of the last time I had needed Fix's services.

Fix's business has two parts. First, he sells fake IDs. It's illegal, but there's nothing wrong with possessing a computer and printer, and he regularly destroys the hard drives containing the digital evidence of his crimes, so he feels relatively safe running that part of his operation out of his basement.

The second part of his business involves brokering other types of questionable transactions. Fix doesn't sell other illegal things, like drugs or weapons, but Fix knows almost everyone on the DarkNet who does.

That makes him extremely valuable because the two most common DarkNet visitors are criminals and cops. If you're looking to make an online purchase that isn't sanctioned by your local authorities, it's very hard to be sure you're not setting yourself up to be the victim of a midnight police raid. You might unwittingly arrange an anonymous, illegal transaction with an undercover vice cop.

Fix applies his encyclopedic knowledge of the DarkNet economy to solve this large marketplace problem. He charges a healthy broker's fee for the service, but I'm sure few people complain. Avoiding jail time is worth a lot of money.

I remembered the setup in Fix's basement very well, and it had changed little since my last visit. Hard to believe it was only a little over eight months ago. Everything important in my life had changed since then. It seemed like eight lifetimes ago.

In the far corner of the basement was a computer table, a photographer's lighting setup, a gigantic printer, and an industrial-sized shredder. There was also a banner featuring a very realistic-looking Maryland Department of Motor Vehicles logo fastened to the wall, and a chair beneath it.

"Where's your friend?" I asked, remembering the thin black man who had worked the computer and produced my fake IDs during my last visit.

Fix shook his head. "New administration," he said. "Efraim didn't come from a country with the right hotel chain."

"They deported him?" I asked.

"Poof. Here one day, gone the next."

"Well, he *was* selling fake IDs on the black market," I pointed out. "Not exactly model behavior."

Fix nodded. "Right," he said. "Score one for the good guys, or something. I could point out that Efraim didn't actually sell most of them. He gave them to fellow immigrants who had barely escaped their home country alive. He fed them and helped them apply for the shitty jobs that we think are beneath us. But whatever. I'm not exactly a moral authority."

"Right," I said. I wasn't sure I had claim to the moral high ground either, given what I'd just done to Posner.

"Stacey first," I said, and she took a seat in the chair beneath the Maryland DMV banner. She did her best to smile, but all the fear and anger and suffering were still churning like a roiling sea inside her head. Her pretty face made something more than a grimace but less than a smile, and the hollowness in her eyes struck me hard in the heart. She was too young for that kind of tragedy.

"Who do you want to be?" Fix asked.

"Pardon me?" Stacey said.

"I have a Jocelyn Rae Rogers, a Penelope Susan Montgomery, and a Karen Michelle Dewitt."

"Are those real people?" Stacey asked, naïve about how the whole thing worked.

"Not any longer," Fix said.

A look of horror crossed Stacey's face. "Those are... *dead* people?"

Fix gave me a look like *help.*

"Let's just say that we want to avoid using the new ID unless it's absolutely necessary," I said.

I didn't want to take the time to explain, so I gave her the Cliff's notes version. If you need access to money, it's important to steal a live person's ID. As soon as you use the identity, especially if you're using someone's stolen credit card or ATM card, the identity becomes worthless. Worse than that, really. It becomes toxic, because banks and police departments and surveillance systems all begin barking up your tree.

On the other hand, if you're just looking to travel around with no one knowing it's you, a dead person's identity is the way to go.

"But *dead people?*" She made a face of disgust and alarm like only a young person can.

"Stacey, look," I said. "If we're not careful, *our* names will wind up on Fix's list of available identities. You barely escaped. You know who they are, and they think you might know where they held you. And because of you, they're now short one very important member. That makes you one hell of a threat to them, and they will come after you. They're probably already putting a posse together. We have no choice but to stay deep underground and off the grid."

Fix looked at me with his mouth agape, but he knew better than to ask me to elaborate.

Stacey nodded quietly, tears forming in her eyes.

"I didn't mean to bludgeon you," I said, placing my hand on her shoulder. "It's just that we have a very long way to go before we're out of the woods, and we need every advantage we can get."

Fix cleared his throat and went back to work. Minutes later, the giant printer whirred and produced a Maryland driver's license with Stacey's likeness above a dead girl's name. Five minutes after that, I had a fresh driver's license and even a military ID, complete with an authentic computer chip embedded in its face.

I paid Fix using cryptocurrency. Eight years ago, it was a curiosity for hackers and nerds. Today, Bitcoin's market capitalization is bigger than PayPal's, and the total cryptocurrency market is over $130 billion. That's more than the combined GDP of the bottom third of the United Nations. At least, that's what I read somewhere.

Crypto scares the US government to death, because the government depends on everyone on Earth kneeling before the Almighty Dollar. But hundreds of millions of people believe they have read the writing on the wall and are busy giving George Washington the finger.

I'm convinced of two things: cryptocurrency won't fade away anytime soon, and government crackdowns are only a matter of time.

And if you want to buy something illegal, you'd better pay for it using crypto. Cash is easily traceable these days.

I pulled a little USB device from my pocket and plugged it into Fix's computer. I pulled up a software application called "Electrum," which almost looks like banking software, even though one of the primary attractions to cryptocurrency is that there are no banks or bankers.

Electrum quizzed my little USB device, which authenticated my payment. Seconds later, our anonymous transaction was broadcast to the global Bitcoin community for cryptographic authentication. It would take an hour for the transaction to confirm, which involved the decentralized crypto community creating a permanent and unalterable digital record of our transaction, but Fix was satisfied and considered our deal closed.

So he returned to hitting on me. "You should give me a little more notice next time," he said. "I could maybe open a bottle of wine and make a little dinner."

I smiled. "You're very kind," I said, feeling no desire to have either dinner or sex with a black marketer who was likely to be arrested at any moment. "But there *is* something you can do for me right now."

FIX LISTENED TO MY REQUEST AND IMMEDIATELY delivered a name, or more precisely, a pseudonym: EvilPhuck. It cost me more Bitcoins, which at the moment were more valuable than gold, but we were in a bind and it would have been a bargain at twice the price.

I didn't know much about EvilPhuck. I surmised that the person either held a Top Secret clearance or was one of the best hackers in the world. Maybe both.

Fix used a DarkNet tool called Beam to place a secure and anonymous phone call to EvilPhuck. Fix vouched for Stacey and me, then left us alone in his basement to talk business.

I wasn't sure what I expected, but it wasn't this: EvilPhuck was female, and she sounded young. She didn't sound evil, but I supposed it took all kinds.

I explained our situation. Evil—her full hacker name felt awkward to me so I dropped the Phuck—was quick on the uptake. "You need Talent Blue access," she said as soon as I had finished. "It will be expensive."

Naturally. What wasn't expensive? But I hadn't heard of Talent Blue.

"RFID," Evil explained. "You said you wanted to find a certain tag.

Talent Blue can find any RFID device in the Northern Hemisphere in under a minute."

"This is a government satellite?"

"No comment."

"NSA?"

"I'm going to hang up now."

"Wait," I said. "I just need to know how big a problem this will be if we're caught."

"Espionage Act," Evil said.

That gave me pause. A conviction under the Espionage Act could earn the death sentence. Stealing a bit of satellite time probably wouldn't warrant the needle, but I sure as hell wasn't eager to test that theory. No alternative came to me though.

"All right," I said. "I need to find two tags."

"Twice the price," Evil said.

Naturally.

"One now, and another one later."

"Give me the RFID codes," Evil said.

"Well, here's the thing," I said. "I don't have the codes."

"So you want me to Harry Potter an answer for you?"

"I have a location where a third tag used to be."

"Used to be?"

"It's been destroyed," I said, recalling the grisly business of finding the lump behind the late Commissioner Frederick Posner's left ear and sending fifteen grams of copper-jacketed lead through the device… and what remained of the vile man's skull.

"And this third tag is identical?"

"I'm guessing all the codes are very similar but differ by one digit."

Evil was silent. I imagined she was thinking about the added difficulty of the job and tallying up the new total for her services, maybe rubbing her hands together and wearing a greedy smile. But we were fresh out of options and time was not on our side. Posner's men were undoubtedly rallying against us, and by then we had a little over twenty hours left before all the trouble would be in vain.

"We don't have much time," I said.

"Okay," Evil finally said. "Five coins."

I stifled a gasp. The exchange rate was a little over four thousand US dollars per Bitcoin. Evil wanted over twenty grand for her services.

"Take it or leave it," she said.

There was no choice to make, but the little accountant in my brain calculated the cost anyway. About $850 per life saved. I'd have paid a hundred times that much, even more if I had it.

"Deal," I said. "I need the first location right away. Ten minutes, if you can manage it."

"It will take an hour for the payment to clear," Evil said, referring to how the Bitcoin infrastructure verified transactions.

"You'll have to trust me," I said.

Evil didn't respond.

"Take it or leave it," I said, echoing her earlier attempt at hardball. "If you're not up to it, then we'll find someone else."

Evil was silent for a moment. "Okay," she said. I gave her the latitude and longitude of the Philadelphia Police Commissioner's office and the approximate time I had blown the device to bits. Evil would use the beacon location and off-air time to verify she found the right RFID beacon. And then she would find the two most similar beacons in the Northern Hemisphere.

Evil gave me her payment address and signed off. I used Electrum and my little USB device to pay her electronically, then did my best imitation of a patient person as Stacey and I awaited Evil's call.

"I'm scared," Stacey said. "I didn't know it was going to be like this. I shouldn't have told you what happened. I didn't know that you were going to do... all of *this*."

I smiled. "I'm scared too. And if I'd known what the hell you were going to drag me into, maybe I wouldn't have stopped my car. Maybe I'd have just let you stumble around naked on the street."

A little of Stacey's worry melted into a weak smile.

I sat next to her and put my arm around her shoulders. "That'll teach me to be a Good Samaritan, won't it?"

"A Good Samaritan who kills people?"

"Only people who need killing."

"I don't want to be part of this anymore," she said.

I took a breath and nodded. "Neither do I. But I have no place to take you where I know you'll be safe. Not until I know what we're dealing with. We have no idea how big this thing is, and who else might be involved. A police commissioner is a big fish, but he might not be the biggest they have."

Forlorn tiredness descended over Stacey's face, like everything behind her had left her too depleted to deal with everything in front of her. I knew the feeling.

Fix's computer warbled. I answered the incoming Beam call. Evil read me the lat/longs, and I punched them into a map.

As the location resolved, my heart sank and my head pounded. The task suddenly seemed light-years beyond impossible.

"Are you positive you have the right tag?" I asked Evil.

"Hundred percent," she said.

"And the right location?"

"Lady, I don't stay in business by being incompetent," Evil said.

Right. I thanked her and sent her back to work finding the next RFID tag. I rested my head in my hands, fighting the midnight exhaustion and the weight pressing down on me, the weight of what I'd already done and what I had left to do.

"How can that be right?" Stacey asked, looking at the red dot on the computer screen map. "It's in the middle of Lake Superior!"

STACEY WASN'T QUITE CORRECT. IT WASN'T IN THE *middle* of Lake Superior.

The second RFID tag was on an island way up in the northern part of the lake, which seemed impossibly far away from Baltimore. Isle Royale, to be precise, was much nearer to Canada than to the United States. The fastest way to get there seemed to be by flying into Thunder Bay, Canada, and then taking a boat or seaplane out onto the largest freshwater lake on Earth.

It seemed impossible. Assuming we arrived in time, and assuming we had no trouble finding and neutralizing the tag's owner, and assuming we somehow managed to escape with our lives intact, how in the holy hell would we possibly get from Isle Royale to wherever in hell the third man might be?

I turned to Stacey. "Are you positive there are three of them?"

Her face was fog and exhaustion, and it was clear she didn't understand my question.

"Three men with the crypto payment tags embedded in their bodies," I said. "I need to know if there's anyone else capable of taking the payment, anyone other than those three."

Tears formed in her eyes and spilled onto her cheeks.

"I'm sorry to make you relive the nightmare, but this is important. I need to know if there's any other way for us to stop this atrocity."

Her diaphragm fluttered, and her tears intensified. She buried her face in her hands. I took a deep breath, doing my best to remain calm and patient, all too aware of how traumatic and devastating my own ordeal had been, but also doing my best not to watch the seconds disappear.

"Stacey, sweetheart," I said, "this is everything. All those lives. It's a lot of pressure, more than anyone should have to bear, but I need you to tell me again. I need to be sure."

I saw some strength return to Stacey's face and spine. She raised her chin, and I saw defiance and determination.

"There were three of them. They chose me from the big room where we were all chained up and they brought me into another room. It had a mattress and… sex things. They bragged about how lucky I was they chose me. They called themselves the 'triumvirate' or whatever. The 'big dick motherfuckers,' they said."

I nodded. My insides curdled.

Stacey took a breath and continued. "I was still tied up. They cut my clothes off and threw me on the bed. They put white powder on my body and snorted it. They gave me a shot of something. An injection. I think it was a muscle relaxer to make my…"

I shook my head and held her face in my hands. "You don't have to tell me again what they did to you. I just need to know what they said."

She wiped tears away and took a deep breath. "I don't know what they were snorting, but they got really high. They joked about something they called the 'Snuff Fest.' I had no idea what they were talking about at first. I'd never heard of anything like it. But as things went on and they got more and more aggressive and talked about all the ways they were going to snuff people, I started to figure it out."

"You're certain that's what they were talking about?"

Stacey nodded her head just a little, her eyes dead and far away. "They slapped me around and choked me and tied my arms behind my back, and then all three of them…"

She trailed off, and I gave her some space.

"After the first time, they kept yelling, 'Payday!' and slapping each other on the ass. Grown men slapping each other on the ass. Then they… raped me again and choked me and high-fived each other. They told me to get used to it, that they would be the last people I ever saw, and if I was lucky, I would get to die during the grand finale."

My jaw hurt from clenching my teeth, and my hands balled into fists. I was ready to murder the other two men. Only I didn't want the next two subhumans to have the undeserved mercy of a quick and painless death like the commissioner enjoyed. I wanted to make them suffer. I wanted them to suffer the pain that my own rapists deserved but never got.

"I'm sorry this happened to you, Stacey," I said, knowing in my bones that for the rest of her life, she would never be the same.

She cried quietly, and I held her to my chest and rocked gently back and forth as if she were my daughter.

"You wanted to know about the payment things," she said after a while. "I'm sorry I got distracted."

"I understand," I said.

"The commissioner guy talked about it most. He told the other two guys they should have gotten their tags put in their cocks. That way they could film themselves getting paid by swiping their dicks against their phones. Then the whole world would get to have the biggest case of penis envy ever. 'Tuesday night penis envy,' they started saying. They thought it was the funniest thing."

"You're sure they meant *this* Tuesday night?"

She nodded her head. "'Two days,' they kept saying. 'Two days to payday.'"

Tuesday night. We were already in the small hours on Tuesday morning. We were running out of time.

"Stacey, is there anyone else who might have a payment tag embedded in his body?"

She shook her head. "They kept talking about how they were going to be the three richest snuffers ever. The whole DarkNet was going to suck it, they were going to own everything. Snuff Fest was going to be legendary, twenty-five in one night, biggest payday ever, they said. Not even the best hacker in the world could ever come close to stealing their money, because they had the tags, they kept saying."

"You're sure? Is it possible they meant something else?"

Stacey rocked her head from side to side. "I suppose it's possible. I mean, I had no idea about any of this stuff, and I was scared and hurting and they were…"

She trailed off, tears making their way down her cheeks. I held her.

"But they were high," she continued after a while, "and they kept saying the same things over and over again. After a while the words sunk in, even though I wasn't sure what they were talking about."

"And you're sure they were planning to *sell* the other kids?"

Stacey nodded again. "Pretty sure. They kept saying that I was the lucky one. The other ones were going to foreigners. Coming in from all over."

"Coming into *where?*"

"I don't know," Stacey said.

"Coming into Philadelphia?"

"I don't *know.*"

"Did any of them slip up and mention where they were planning to transport all of you?"

She shook her head. "I couldn't breathe and they wouldn't stop…"

I wrapped my arms around her. I had nothing else to say. The awful weight of it settled again on my chest, and the despair of living in a world where people could even imagine this kind of atrocity was enough to make me want to stop breathing. Knowing that it was happening inside the country I had repeatedly risked my life for was beyond heartbreaking. I wanted out of humanity. I wanted to be part of a different species.

I'd seen this kind of thing so many times over the years it was rotting me from the center. Our enduring, defining attribute is our bottomless capacity for hatred and cruelty. You even see it in the way we're starting to hate each other over the manure we're fed on cable "news." We lap it up like dogs. We believe that our neighbor wants to destroy our way of life—and his own—because he voted for the other bullshit artist on the ballot. So we fantasize about putting him in his place.

And I wasn't immune. In the middle of my righteous rage, I wanted to torture those other two men to death in the most grisly way possible. I wanted to make them beg for mercy, beg me to kill them, and I wanted to deny them the comfort of death for as long as they could hold out.

Helpless, bitter tears welled in my eyes and I teetered for a moment on the edge of my abyss, dug straight through the center of me by days upon days spent as a prisoner in a cabin in the mountains with men drugging and defiling me over and over again.

Just two weeks ago. I'd spent the time since then wandering aimlessly around the country, unable to sleep or eat or exercise or do much else except run away from everything.

In that moment with Stacey, I nearly fell into the void, nearly fell apart for the millionth time since my ordeal, but I glanced at Stacey and the reminder of her soft strength and her courage and determination held me together. I was the one with twenty years of field experience, and I needed to be strong enough and smart enough for the both of us.

For *all* of us. Because I was beginning to regard all those kids chained in that Philadelphia warehouse as my own. I viewed them as my responsibility. Superhero complex, maybe, but if I couldn't do anything about their situation, who the hell could?

I wiped my eyes. I made a deal with myself, a commitment. I would see this thing through. Maybe I couldn't save every lost kid destined for an unspeakable end, but I was sure as hell going to save *these* kids.

And maybe I couldn't find and punish every pervert and sociopath in every dark corner of the internet whose money funded these kinds of crimes. But I was sure as hell going to make an example of the three men who had organized this whole thing.

"I thought of something else," Stacey said after another minute passed. "I remember that one of the men was called Smokey. He had short hair. Maybe military. He had a cheesy mustache."

"Smokey?"

"Right."

"Another cop, you think?"

Stacey shrugged. "I didn't see a gun or a uniform. He was wearing jeans and some kind of flannel shirt before they started…"

She trailed off, not eager to talk more about the abuse she'd endured. I gave her space and pondered her recollection of the events. This was now the third time she'd recalled the story for me, and the details had stayed consistent.

Consistent enough for me to form a picture of what these three men had in mind, anyway. And consistent enough for me to know that even in the age of cryptocurrency and the DarkNet and anonymous pay-per-view murder pornography, the only way to stop them was the old-fashioned way: up close and personal.

I looked at my watch again and felt crushed under instant exhaustion. It was a little before one in the morning on Tuesday and I hadn't slept in over a day. If Stacey understood the men correctly, the atrocities were due to begin in a mere twenty hours.

"We need help," I said. "We can't do this alone."

Holy hell, I sure missed Brock. He'd have been right with me on this one. We'd have taken these assholes out together. He was perfect and all our jagged edges seemed to fit perfectly together and even though it had been months and months since he'd walked out, my insides still ached for him. *He was the one.*

And I missed Kittredge, too. He was no slouch in a tough situation. And in his own way, he was a beautiful man, strong and resilient and capable.

But neither Brock nor Kittredge was in my life at the moment. And I had grown weary of pining.

I took Stacey's hand and led her upstairs from Fix's basement hideaway. We found him asleep on an opulent leather sofa with a nature documentary playing quietly on the television.

I shook him gently. It took him a minute to come around, but his eyes finally focused on me.

"I must be dreaming," he said.

"Cute," I said with a tired smile. "I have a serious question for you."

"I have a serious answer," Fix said.

"What are you doing for the next twenty hours?"

"YOU'RE SAYING THERE ARE TWENTY GIRLS ABOUT TO BE murdered while being raped on camera?"

"Twenty-four," I said. "Would have been twenty-five, but Stacey escaped."

"From where?"

"A warehouse in Philadelphia," Stacey said.

"How?"

"How what?" I asked.

"How did you escape," Fix asked Stacey.

She looked at me, and I nodded. I didn't want her to have to recount her story yet again, but we needed Fix's help. And a guy like Fix would not help without a damned good reason.

"The three main guys left and there were just a couple of guards watching us. The others and I were all chained up. One of them took me back into the room with the bed in it and…"

Stacey trailed off. "I can't," she said after a minute.

I put my hand on her shoulder. "What you did was courageous like nothing I've ever heard. You don't have to talk about it."

Her eyes moistened. "The guard shoved himself down my throat. I choked and gagged and he laughed and pushed harder."

A look of horror and disgust crossed Fix's face.

"I don't know what got into me," Stacey said. "But I decided I wasn't going to die like that. I wasn't going to be some *thing* for them to use and throw away, like I'm not even a person at all."

I think Fix knew what was coming. He involuntarily curled his body up a little, protecting his groin from the mere thought of what was next.

"I couldn't breathe and I started to see stars. I thought I was going to pass out and choke to death right then. So I waited until he pushed again and then I… I bit down. I bit halfway through it."

"Jesus!" Fix said, doubling over in imagined agony.

"He screamed and fell to the floor," Stacey said, "and I fell down almost next to him. I spit out his blood and then I threw up."

"*Jesus,*" Fix said again, shaking his head. "How did you get out?"

Stacey wiped her eyes on her sleeve. "I just ran. I was crying and scared, and I was sure the other guard would find me. There were so many doors and all of them were locked, but I found a window and got it unstuck and kicked out the screen. I ran as fast as I could. I don't know how long I ran before Ms. Jameson found me."

"You just found her?" Fix asked.

I nodded. "I couldn't sleep. I was just driving around at three a.m. There she was, running like her life depended on it. She had nothing on but her underwear."

"Damn," Fix said. "This was in Philadelphia?"

I nodded. "I took her to a hospital. By the time her story came out, and we figured out that one of the ringleaders was the Philadelphia police commissioner, he had already covered his tracks. He sent one of his lackeys out to take her statement. The guy buried it, obviously. We drove around later looking for the warehouse, but she didn't exactly write down the address as she ran for her life."

"You're kidding," Fix said. "This isn't real. I've heard of this shit happening in, like, Thailand or Russia or some dump like that. But Philadelphia?"

I shrugged. People are people everywhere. Money is money everywhere.

And if it's depraved and stomach-turning, you can bet your life there's an underground market for it somewhere. "You know how people are," I said.

Fix nodded. I knew he had brokered his share of shady transactions, but I hoped he'd never dabbled in anything remotely close to what Stacey had endured.

A long silence settled over the room.

"Fix, I want you to help us save those kids," I finally said.

He had both palms raised at me before I even finished the sentence. He shook his head back and forth emphatically.

"No way. I'm not getting involved. That's not my cup of tea. I'm already in way over my head. You should call the cops or whatever."

I just looked at him. Twenty years of catching spies made me a good judge of character. Despite his sketchy occupation and sketchier acquaintances, I was confident Fix was a good guy.

Of course, I've been wrong about people before.

But I didn't let him off the hook. I just kept looking at him.

"No way," Fix said again. "No way I'm getting involved. I don't need a hundred crooked cops driving down from Philly to bend me over. Not happening."

I said nothing.

"And I have way too much going on right now," he said.

I looked pointedly at the nature documentary droning on in the background and the video game console on the coffee table.

"I mean, how could I even help?"

I chuckled at the stupidity of his question. Fix was one of the most connected black marketers on the East Coast. There was almost nothing he couldn't arrange when he put his mind to it.

"Seriously, this is way out of my league."

I sighed, looked at Stacey, and shrugged. I slapped my knees and stood up. "Guess we'll go somewhere else for help."

Stacey followed my lead and followed me toward the door. "Sorry, man," I said over my shoulder. "I guess I was wrong about you."

I counted the seconds off in my head as I approached Fix's front door. *One. Two. Three. Four. Five.*

"Wait a minute," Fix called from the den.

I turned and looked at him with my eyebrows raised.

"Wait a minute," he said again, standing up now and running his hand through his hair. "Dammit, wait a minute."

Stacey and I just looked at him, tall and bare-chested and groggy and a little red-eyed from the weed.

"Shit," he said, shaking his head. "Damn it. I'll help."

OVER THE YEARS AT HOMELAND, I GOT PRETTY GOOD AT getting people organized and working. I took the reins a bit with Fix, and it wasn't long before he had secure I2P chat sessions going with several people at once.

I2P is one way oppressed people in miserable corners of the globe access the web, and also how Americans access the web when they want to pretend they're outsmarting the NSA's ubiquitous spying operation. I have my doubts about this, and they're very well-founded doubts, but the NSA isn't all that interested in small-time black marketeers. Unless they're Muslim, for obvious reasons. But I digress.

"Airplane, Fix," I said. "Focus on getting us an airplane. And a fast one. A puddle-jumper won't get us there in time."

Fix nodded at me, a little irritated.

"And lots of range. It's eleven hundred miles away."

More nodding. A more irritated expression on his face. More typing into the little chat windows.

"And we need a seaplane to get to Isle Royale. There's no runway."

An annoyed shake of his head. "This will cost you," he said.

I smiled. "Bullshit," I said. "You're doing this because it's the right thing to do."

Fix huffed. "The hell I am. I don't work for free."

I laughed. "I see right through you. Behind all the profiteering, you're a good man at heart."

He stopped typing and looked at me, a protest on the tip of his tongue, but it died before it left his mouth. His eyes met mine and the annoyance dissolved into a smile. There was no small amount of pride in it.

"Our little secret," he said. "You let this get out and ruin my rep, I'm coming after you."

More typing. Then Fix said, "I have a silly question. Why are we flying to Canada instead of just putting a posse together to raid the warehouse full of kids in Philly?"

"Not a silly question at all," I said. "Trouble is, Stacey was running around in the middle of the night in her underwear, and she doesn't remember much about where she was running *from*. And even if she knew exactly where they were holding her, there's almost no chance they're still in the same place. Posner's men have to assume we know the warehouse location, so they have no choice but to move the kids."

Fix nodded. "Plus at least a few Philly cops are in on the thing," he said. "That could be a problem for anyone looking to stop it."

"Right," I said. "So shut the hell up and find us an airplane."

Fix smiled and got back to work.

Thirty minutes later, Stacey, Fix and I piled into his Tesla and wound our way out of the subdivision. Fix lived near Towson, on the north side of the city, and our destination was the Tipton Airport. Tipton sits a stone's throw from the center of the cyber universe, the headquarters of the National Security Agency. I always feel nervous around that place, like maybe they've figured out a way to interpret the electrical signals from my brain and I should put on a tin hat to keep them from reading my thoughts.

Fix drove faster than a man with his lifestyle should ever drive. The Tesla was whisper-quiet and absurdly powerful, and I understood why he liked to stomp on the accelerator—it was like being strapped to a mortar shell. But I didn't appreciate the police attention we were likely to garner. We didn't have the time to waste on a traffic stop.

"I downloaded the bootleg engine control software," he said, reminding me of a high school kid showing off his ride and hoping to talk his female passengers out of their panties. "They call it 'Ludicrous.' Like in *Spaceballs*. Zero to sixty in two-point-three seconds. It's a new record for production cars."

I grimaced. "Didn't you have a new Land Rover before?" I said.

He nodded. "I get a new car every year. Tax deduction."

I left that alone. I couldn't imagine what Fix wrote in the "occupation" box on his tax return. I couldn't imagine it would stand up to even the most perfunctory tax audit, but whatever. Not my problem.

"Just don't get pulled over. I have no desire to learn whether Commissioner Posner had friends on the Maryland force, too."

Fix gave me a cocky smile and pushed harder on the accelerator.

Men.

"Careful," I said, "or I'll think you're compensating for some kind of... *shortcoming*." I held up my thumb and forefinger an inch apart to drive the point home.

That seemed to sting him a little, but he didn't let up on the accelerator.

My concerns notwithstanding, we didn't see any police cruisers on our way to the airport. We exited the Patuxent Freeway onto the 198, then made a quick left onto Airport Road.

I thought maybe Fix had taken us to the wrong place. The runway was tiny. Nothing but bug-smasher airplanes parked on the ramp, the little single-engine jobs that seat half a person uncomfortably and definitely don't fly far or fast enough for our needs.

"What the hell?" I said. "You couldn't stop a jet on this runway with a drag chute."

"Relax," Fix said. "I did the best I could do at two o'clock in the freaking morning. Most of my contacts told me to kiss off until sunrise at least. But I worked it out. We'll take a prop to Pittsburgh, and my guy will have some hardware and a Gulfstream waiting for us there."

"Who's your guy?" I asked.

Fix just shook his head. "You know that's not how it works."

He parked the Tesla and we walked into the little flight business office. Most of the lights were off and the desk clerk was asleep, and it shocked me that the place wasn't locked up for the night.

"They opened just for us," Fix said.

So much for keeping a low profile, I thought.

The desk clerk handed Fix a small, well-worn duffel and a three-ring binder. Fix fidgeted with his phone. He was paying by crypto, I gathered.

The three of us grabbed earplugs and walked onto the ramp. Stacey's face seemed drawn and tight and her skin looked a little pale, though it could have been the lighting on the tarmac.

"Fix," I said, "where is the pilot?"

He gave me that sly smile of his. "Allow myself to introduce... myself."

I shook my head, both at the Austin Powers reference and at the notion of this adolescent child of a man operating an aircraft—especially one with yours truly strapped inside.

"If you fly like you drive, I'm walking," I said.

"Don't worry," he said. "I fly like a *madman*."

Which is exactly what I was afraid of. I considered telling him to get stuffed. But it was nearing three in the morning, our final destination was a thousand miles away, and two dozen lives were hanging in the balance. I filled my lungs with a deep, cleansing breath, shook my head, and muttered the ultimate Zen mantra: "Fuck it."

Stacey wedged herself into the backseat of the Cessna and I climbed into the front. Fix brushed against me as he checked my harness, and I wondered whether it was intentional. I wondered whether I might have enjoyed the attention if everything inside of me weren't a post-apocalyptic wasteland at the moment.

Fix ran through a few preflight checks, opened the window, and shouted, "Clear!"

Then he turned the key. The entire plane shook and shimmied as the prop turned and the engine struggled to catch.

"She's a little frigid right now," he said, and I wondered whether there wasn't a double entendre in the statement. If so, I ignored it. And I wasn't keen on trusting my life to an engine too stubborn to start, which accounted for my vise-locked jaw and white-knuckled grip on the armrest.

Fix tried again, and once more, and at last the overgrown lawnmower sputtered to life. Minutes later I found myself once again relying on a man I barely knew to fly me safely into a deadly serious situation. What could possibly go wrong?

THE SUN WAS ALREADY THREATENING ITS DAILY ASSAULT
on the Western Hemisphere as Fix bounced us to a stop at the Allegheny
County Airport in Pittsburgh, Pennsylvania. He taxied to a stop and
hurried through his post-flight checks, then we hustled to a waiting
Gulfstream.

"You're not planning to fly this one, too, are you?" I quipped as we started
up the stairs to the little hatch in the side of the bizjet.

Fix smiled. "Someday."

A small black man wearing blue jeans and a giant afro and a Fuck
The Man tee-shirt—complete with a clenched fist reminiscent of the Black
Panther logo—met us at the top of the stairs. He and Fix performed an
elaborate handshake and man-hug ritual and lapsed into some sort of urban
cant that I found both impressive and indecipherable.

The display reminded me for the millionth time that there's a nearly
infinite number of worlds hiding in plain sight, dozens of parallel universes
governed by their own laws and customs, and most of the time we have not
the slightest inkling that they even exist. I'm always humbled and amazed.

A tall, skinny white guy with an oversized nose and an undersized tie folded himself through the cabin door and also greeted Fix. They high-fived and then spoke for a minute in Russian.

Freaking Russian.

Fix took the seat next to mine. I stared at him, taken aback by his multi-lingual, multicultural prowess.

"What?" he said, his crooked smile telling me he knew exactly *what.*

"I'm impressed," I said. "You're much more than just a pretty rolodex."

"Very funny."

"Where did you learn Russian and… whatever that other thing was?"

"Jive," he said. "Ebonics. Hoodspeak. Nig Latin. Blinglish."

"Right," I said.

But Fix was on a roll. "Blacktionary. Negronics. Oogabooga. 'Fricanese."

"Okay," I said. "I get it. But where did you pick it up?"

"Nobody lasts in my business unless you're willing to learn from the best. Russians and black people have been perfecting the informal market for centuries."

Informal market. As opposed to the pejorative *black* market. It resonated with the part of me that still didn't buy the idea that the only valid transactions were the ones where the government took a slice, like some kind of mafia don running a protection racket.

It had taken me a long time to deprogram myself from the deep-seated lie that in America, land of the free, legality and morality are the same thing. But I'd seen enough bent cops, bent feds, corrupt laws and lawmakers, and all-around slimy establishment people in my time at Homeland that I no longer held those kinds of quaint notions. People and corporations and governments and criminal organizations take whatever you'll allow them to take. Sometimes more, but never less.

How many people lived like Fix, dancing over and around that thick, gray line where laws and ethics and personal liberty all fought it out daily?

Personally, I couldn't imagine living that way for any length of time. Living under the constant threat of arrest and incarceration would wreck my insides. I've dealt with some horrible people and ruthless organizations over the years, but you can take one thing to the bank: nobody can screw you deeper or harder or longer than Uncle Sam.

And it's another level of misery entirely when you're dealing with corrupt authorities.

Like the late Frederick Posner.

I wondered who else was involved in this inhuman atrocity. Who was Smokey? Who was the third man?

Where the hell were the other kids?

I mulled over the decision I'd made to go after the money men. Would it have been more effective to find and free the captive kids? Was there any guarantee that stopping the payment to the "triumvirate"—Posner, Smokey, and the third man, whose remaining lifespans, if I had anything to say about it, could now be measured in mere hours—would stop the rape and murder? Was I on a fool's errand?

As the pilots ran through their checks, I went back to the beginning. Stacey had escaped from a warehouse in downtown Philadelphia where Posner and a handful of depraved deviants were holding her and two dozen other young adults hostage, molesting them, and, if Stacey's recollection of the conversations she overheard was correct, preparing to sell them for use as victims in snuff films.

Snuffing. Even the name made me retch. A handful of men planned to film themselves killing these kids during the act of raping them. They planned it as a festival. Twenty-five in a single night, offered pay-per-view to those with the money and psychopathy and sociopathy necessary to enjoy this kind of otherworldly cruelty and indifference.

And it would happen at nine p.m.

The tall Russian pilot scampered out of the cockpit, down the ladder, and onto the tarmac. He returned a second later with a large black duffel. It looked heavy. He dropped it on the cabin floor, then secured the aircraft door.

Then the man hefted the duffel over to Fix, who unzipped it and inspected its contents. Submachine guns for all of my friends, Russian Bizons, if memory served. There were also pistols—Russian GSh-18's, I thought, but it had been a while since I'd studied Russian hardware—and what looked to be a healthy collection of knives. 9mm ammo boxes rounded out the kit.

I looked over at Stacey. She stared into the duffel full of weapons and her face lost its color. I renewed my resolve to get her into safe hands as soon as humanly possible.

"Spasibo," Fix said to the Russian-speaking pilot. The man nodded, then rolled back a section of carpeting on the cabin floor to reveal a cargo compartment. A handful of aircraft panel fasteners secured it, and it took the pilot a minute or two to get the panel unlocked. He unceremoniously dropped the duffel bag full of party favors into the secret compartment, sealed it back up, and returned to the cabin without a word.

Fix looked at me with a smile. "Donated by a friend," he said, gesturing toward the smuggler's keep. "Seems I'm not the only bleeding heart out on the DarkNet."

"You guys should hire a PR firm to get the word out about your philanthropy. Then maybe The Man will ease up on you a bit."

Fix smiled. "It'll never happen. Not until they figure out a way to tax us, anyway."

"Might be better than going to jail," I offered.

The engines spooled to life and the aircraft taxied to the runway. A minute later, we were airborne and heading northwest.

"Do you have connectivity?" I asked Fix.

He nodded and pulled out a little netbook with a logo on it I didn't recognize. It didn't boot up with the usual soothing pictures in the background or the usual array of icons arranged on a desktop. It was just a black screen with a pulsing green cursor in the top left corner, like a time-warp to three decades ago when computers were big and bulky and pretty much useless for anything other than playing clunky, rudimentary games.

Except Fix's computer was anything but worthless. As the pilots nudged the aircraft just west of Cleveland and aimed it at the western edge of Lake Superior, Fix typed a few commands and linked up with the aircraft's wi-fi, which linked via a bootleg SATCOM line to an internet access node run by a cell phone company employee with entrepreneurial leanings, who for whatever reason wasn't afraid to violate the employee handbook.

Fix narrated all of this for me as his fingers tapped away, maybe to impress me with his reach and influence. I must admit that it worked.

A few commands later, Fix established a chat session with our new friend, EvilPhuck.

Evil and Fix exchanged a few cryptic jokes, including a reference to "downloading all the chicken" that drew a laugh from Fix but left me acutely aware that I was an interloper in a parallel universe where people spoke a different language using English words.

"The second RF tag is still on Isle Royale," Evil typed after the pleasantries were complete. "I found the third one. Ready for me to blow you away?"

"Blow me," Fix typed with a smirk on his face. "… Away."

Men.

Evil ignored the juvenile humor. "Last stable RF hit was half an hour ago at Allegheny County Airport, Pennsylvania."

The cursor blinked.

I blinked, not believing my eyes. *We* were at Allegheny County Airport half an hour ago.

Another chat message from Evil. "Now it's moving northwest at 500 mph."

Just like *we* were.

I GOT THAT UNCOMFORTABLE FEELING IN MY STOMACH
that I used to get as a child when I realized that I was about to have an
unavoidable run-in with Big Trouble. My mouth grew dry and my mind went
into a temporary state of gridlock, fixating on all the dire consequences Evil's
revelation portended rather than thinking about a smart way to deal with it.

Over the years I've learned not to fight this stage, which is supremely
annoying and counterproductive but something everyone goes through when
things go to shit. I took a few deep breaths and let the mini-panic pass, then
I got busy dissecting the situation.

It wasn't good.

The first RF tag was out of the picture, nothing more than shards of
semiconductor mixed with bone fragments and brain tissue.

The second tag was still on the island in the northwest corner of Lake
Superior.

The third RF tag was following us.

Or it was *on our airplane.*

I looked at Stacey. She had her seat reclined and was fast asleep. Her
slumber wasn't peaceful, though. Her facial expression cycled through worry,

fear, and anger in quick succession. Was *she* carrying the third RF payment tag? Had they planted it on her?

Had she been involved from the start? Was her story all BS? The hospital staff had done a rape kit on her, but that would only prove that she'd had sex—possibly rough sex, but that isn't proof of her state of mind during the act. Perhaps she'd done it willingly. Perhaps it was cover. Perhaps Posner and his people needed outside help of some sort, and a sob story told by an attractive young "victim" might have been just the ticket to get the help they needed.

I shook my head. That theory didn't feel right. I've been fooled more than once by a convincing actor telling a compelling story. But if Stacey was putting on an act, it was worthy of an Oscar.

And there was also the small matter of the way I had responded to Stacey's story. I can't imagine Commissioner Frederick Posner had it in mind to further his unfathomably twisted agenda by eating a bullet. Maybe my killing him was nothing more than an unintended consequence of a plan gone awry. Maybe it was just terrible luck that their mark turned out to be an ex-counterespionage agent with reasonably solid field skills at her disposal. Maybe they should have done their homework on me and picked another mark instead, but someone dropped the ball.

All of that seemed to add up to very thin odds. I couldn't see changing my bet on Stacey's believability based on Evil's revelation about the third tag.

I felt Fix's eyes on me. He was looking at me with a strange mixture of curiosity and accusation on his face.

I took the delicate approach. "If you're involved, Fix, I swear I'm going to twist your nuts off and shove them down your throat."

He shook his head. "*You* showed up at *my* door, remember? Not the other way around."

"Doesn't mean anything. Coincidences happen every day. Could have been an amazing stroke of luck."

He smiled and winked. "For you, maybe."

I rolled my eyes. But he was right. The odds were low that Stacey and I would show up on the Baltimore doorstep of a co-conspirator in a Philadelphia crime operation.

But Fix wasn't just anyone. He was one of the most skilled black-market guys I'd ever met.

And anyway, Stacey had said that all three people with RF payment tags were involved in abusing her at the warehouse. If Fix were one of those people, she'd have recognized him.

But nothing guaranteed that the third tag was still embedded in the third asshole's body. Maybe he heard about Posner's demise and got scared enough to have the tag removed.

Again, given the brief time that had elapsed since I shot Posner, those seemed like long odds.

"How well do you know your boys in the front of the airplane?" I asked.

Fix shrugged. "How well does anyone really know anybody?"

A fair point and an honest answer.

"But I would be very surprised if they were somehow involved," Fix said. "People have seriously deviant fetishes that you'd never know about, but watching kids get raped and murdered? I can't see it."

"Nobody suspected Ted Bundy, either," I said.

He shrugged again. "Like I said, I really have no idea what gets them off, or who else they might do business with. But I would be totally shocked if it turns out they're in the thick of this... madness."

I nodded. I wasn't entirely convinced, but neither did I expect to be.

"Who's paying for the flight?" I asked.

Fix shook his head. "These guys owed me a favor."

"A free charter flight? You must have done them one hell of a solid."

"Must have," Fix said with a coy smile.

I squinted my eyes at him, hoping to squeeze out a little more information about his relationship with the two pilots, but he just looked at me with an inscrutable expression on his face. Then he raised his eyebrows at me and shrugged.

"Get along to get along," he finally said, as if that were some kind of explanation.

I mulled. Friends of Fix's had given us a free midnight charter flight to Canada and free guns and ammunition to use when we got there. I supposed it wasn't entirely far-fetched—if Stacey's story was true, what Posner and his men were planning was light-years beyond the pale, and I could see people from all walks of life rising up to do anything in their power to stop it.

On the other hand, nothing in this universe is free.

I chewed on the other possibility, which was that the owner of the third RF payment tag was going to the same place we were. Perhaps the second guy was on Isle Royale for a reason, and the third guy was making his way up there to join him.

But why would he have left from Pittsburgh? Why wouldn't he have left from Philadelphia, which was his location just a few hours earlier—again if Stacey's understanding of her three rapists' relationship to each other was correct?

Maybe the third man flew out of Allegheny County Airport toward Isle Royale because that's where we departed, and he was tailing us. Maybe I had made a mistake and somehow revealed Stacey's location. Maybe Stacey's mistake with the cell phone all those hours ago in Philadelphia had been a costly one. Or maybe we had simply blundered past one of the seven zillion video surveillance cameras in the US, and someone on Posner's payroll had placed us on a watch list of some sort.

I wondered what to do about all of this. I looked at Fix's computer and realized that I wasn't helpless. I had means at my disposal. Immoral, illegal, and highly questionable means, but that wouldn't stop me under the circumstances. I'd move mountains to save those kids.

But using the tool I had at my fingertips, a thing called Capstone, required the utmost caution. It was the cyber equivalent of the nuclear codes at the president's disposal. If I made a mistake—and there were only about a million ways to make an unrecoverable and deadly mistake—the consequences would be a hell of a lot worse than losing two dozen kids to the ghastly plan already in motion, as horrible and heartbreaking and devastating as that would be.

Capstone was definitely out. I was unequivocally *not* going to let that genie out of the bottle.

Probably.

Maybe.

Fuck, I didn't know.

But I didn't have to make that decision right now. There was another option. I had an ace in the hole. I'd sworn to only use it in life-and-death situations, but the current predicament sure as hell qualified.

"Fix," I said, "can you use your netbook to make a secure phone call?"

DAN GABLE IS ONE OF THE BEST GUYS ALIVE. WE WORKED together for many years at Homeland. Technically, I was his boss, but we were more a partnership than anything else.

Dan is built like a big cube with rounded corners and thick appendages and excessive chest hair. He's mostly muscle with a layer of simple carbs spread over the surface. He's shorter than me by about two inches, and his shoulders are about as wide as his inseam. He has big, meaty paws, which he uses to pound stubborn computer systems into submission one keystroke at a time. It's comical to watch him work, hunched over the keyboard with his sausage-fingers pounding away mercilessly. But Dan is one of the best cyber guys in the world.

Dan is also worth his weight in gold in the field. One time, a deranged Venezuelan spy with the cute little moniker of El Jerga—The Shiv—cut my body to ribbons and electrocuted me to death. As in, my heart stopped beating. Dan arrived on the scene just a moment later, scared away the madman, then gave me chest compressions until the paramedics arrived. It's therefore no exaggeration to say that I owe Dan my life, though I like to think my skill and cunning also helped him out of a jam or two over the years.

I had given the middle finger to the Department of Homeland Security a few months ago after a case went awry and they hung me out to dry. Except for Dan, nobody at Homeland had my back who *should* have had my back, least of all my superiors, and that betrayal made a dozen too many. So I walked.

Dan was still in the trenches, still hunting spies, still on the federal payroll. I shivered at the thought.

I also shivered at the thought of calling him. Our working relationship was mostly defined by me calling him at all hours with some emergency for him to drop everything and help me with. Which was precisely what I was planning to do right now.

Problem was, I was no longer Dan's boss, and Dan couldn't very well use government resources to chase after problems that weren't necessarily the government's problems.

But the government could go to hell. This was important.

Dan didn't answer, of course. I'm certain he didn't recognize the telephone number on the caller ID and he probably thought it was some robot auto-spammer calling about a timeshare or foolproof pyramid scheme. Or, more likely, some predatory health insurance company trying to score one more juicy victim.

So I waited one minute and called again. And waited one minute after that for my next call, then waited two minutes before making a third call. Then I waited three minutes. It's the Fibonacci sequence: one, one, two, three, five, eight, etcetera. We'd used this little code a few billion times over the years when we called each other at unexpected times using unexpected phone numbers.

I was confident that by now, Dan knew it was me. The question was, would he want to hear from me—particularly given the fact that it wasn't yet dawn and he and Sarah had young kids who kept them awake half the night.

"I thought I got rid of you months ago," Dan said when I called again five minutes later.

"It's your animal magnetism," I said, warmth spreading in my heart and my face breaking into an enormous smile at the sound of Dan's tired, groggy voice. I love him like a brother and I hadn't fully realized how much I missed him. "I just can't help myself."

"Well, it's been a lot less fun around the cubicle farm since you rode off into the sunset," he said.

"I don't believe that for a second," I said. "Didn't you get a raise and a new job title?"

"Guilty," Dan said. "I don't think I'll ever stop feeling like an intruder in your office."

I smiled. "Please," I said. "You were always the brains of the operation."

"And the brawn," he said. "Come to think of it, what the hell did *you* ever do around there?"

I laughed. It was beautiful to reconnect with an old friend. But a glance at Stacey's slumbering form and Fix's impatient expression told me it was time to get down to business.

"So, listen, Dan," I said. "You'll never believe this, but I was hoping to ask a favor of you."

I heard an exaggerated sigh over the static-laden voice-over-internet call from Fix's laptop. "You never call unless you need something. You're like a college kid, only calling home when you're out of cash."

"Guilty," I said. "But this time it's really not my fault."

I explained the situation to him from the beginning. Stacey staggering around in her underwear in the middle of the night; the twenty-four kids still in captivity and probably being transported from Philadelphia to who knew where; the snuff film plot; the 9 p.m. deadline; the RF cryptocurrency payment tags; Isle Royale, in the middle of Lake Superior; the third RF tag hurtling through space in the same direction we were flying.

I saved the best for last: "Philadelphia Police Commissioner Frederick Posner was one of the three."

Silence. I took it to mean that Dan had seen the evening news the night prior.

"Jesus, Sam, you didn't," Dan said after a long moment passed.

"Right," I said. "His tragic end was pure coincidence."

More silence.

"I assume you called someone else first? Maybe someone who had jurisdiction?"

"The Philly cops who responded to the rape report were under Posner's thumb," I said. "Alfonse Archer is on vacation and not answering his phone or email. And the clowns answering phones at the FBI tossed the report onto the pile of UFO sightings and fake terror plots."

Dan was quiet again, and I pictured him chewing on his lip the way he always did when his mind was working in high gear.

"The whole thing does sound far-fetched," he said.

"I wish it were. But I think it's a real thing. I think it's a whole industry on the DarkNet and I think these kids will die horrific deaths if we can't stop this."

He didn't need to tell me that this kind of thing didn't come anywhere close to being in Homeland's lane, that it was unrelated to national security, that using Homeland resources to go after these people would put him in jeopardy. I knew all of that.

But I never doubted Dan.

"Okay" he finally said with a sigh. "Tell me how I can help."

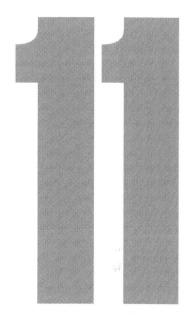

"THE MOST IMPORTANT THING IS TO GET THOSE KIDS TO
safety," I told Dan, speaking loudly over the static and jet noise.

"Right," he said. "But where are they, and who's holding them, and what
is the tactical situation like, and who has jurisdiction, and who can move
quickly enough to put a hostage team on scene?"

"Yes. All the above. I have no answers. That's why I called you. You're the
guy with all the fancy toys and the army of mouth-breathers at your disposal."

"Ease up," Dan said. "I was just thinking out loud. Let me make some
coffee and have a quick think on it. How do I reach you?"

I handed the phone to Fix, who spoke some techno-jive about using the
aircraft's satcom link to connect to Fix's laptop that Dan evidently understood,
because Fix didn't have to repeat the instructions. After a few more sentences
that were largely unintelligible to me, Fix handed the phone back.

"Something's bothering me," Dan said. "I get that Posner and his scum
needed to move the kids. They had to assume that Stacey could find the
warehouse again."

"Right," I said.

"But it seems like a huge logistical problem, moving all of those kids

51

across the country and hiding them in the middle of some frigid lake. And all inside of a day's time or so. Why go to all of that trouble? Why not just move them to some other hiding place in Philadelphia or someplace nearby?"

"I don't have a good answer," I said. "Especially considering that Posner had at least a few crooked Philly cops who were in on the scheme. They could run interference in case anyone outside the operation got wind of it and investigated. It seems like Posner and his men would have had all sorts of horsepower and brainpower and the home field advantage by staying nearby."

"Maybe Posner's death spooked them."

"I'm sure it did," I said. "But it still seems crazy to move two dozen kids over a thousand miles and then pile them all on a boat to get to some tiny island in the middle of the lake."

Dan was silent for a moment. "This feels like a decoy," he finally said.

I had considered that possibility. Maybe Thunder Bay was a red herring. Maybe these animals didn't move the kids that far from the original location after all, and a thorough search in Philly would turn up something. Or maybe the rapists left physical evidence behind at the first warehouse that could help the investigation.

"Obviously the best thing to do is to start a search around the area where I found Stacey," I said. "I tried to get this going in the first place, but the Philly cops who responded to the rape were part of Posner's posse, and I didn't get any Bureau traction because Archer is on vacation and this whole thing sounded crazy to the guy manning the phones."

"I'm sure I'll have better luck with the FBI," Dan said. "I'll call them right away. I'll mention the sensitivity of involving the local police. Hopefully, they'll keep it a federal operation. Maybe I can convince them that the perps likely crossed state lines."

I frowned. Searching the area in Philly definitely needed to be done. It was irresponsible not to do it. But it would be the proverbial needle-in-a-haystack situation. We couldn't count on anything turning up at all, much less in the next few hours.

"What if these guys are loaded for bear up in Isle Royale?" I said. "I'd love to have some help."

"Smart," Dan said. "Plus, you're a civilian these days, and you would have no legal basis to do anything at all."

He was right, of course. I would be afforded some professional courtesy given my background, but mostly I would be shuffled off to the side while the grownups handled the situation. I bristled at the thought. I knew how the 'grownups' operated, especially the ones who inhabited sleepy little jurisdictions where nothing ever happened. Not impressive.

"Details," I finally managed.

"And as an aside," Dan said, "I hope that whoever took care of the Posner problem had the presence of mind to collect her shell casings before leaving the scene."

"I don't know why you would say that," I said. "Statistically, it's very unlikely that it was a woman. Women hardly ever commit violent crimes."

"Right," Dan said.

"Focus," I said, eager to change the subject. "I need help at Isle Royale. Can you make a few unofficial calls? Maybe claim that you can't reveal your sources, but you have reason to believe, blah blah blah?"

"Yes, absolutely," Dan said. "But who the hell do we know up there, that far north?"

"Not a living soul. And anyway, I assume Canada owns the island."

Fix tapped me on the knee to get my attention. He shook his head and turned his laptop around to show me the Wikipedia page for Isle Royale.

"Scratch that," I said, squinting my middle-aged eyes to read the tiny font. "Isle Royale is fifteen miles from Minnesota and about that far away from Canada, but it's owned by Michigan. Which is fifty-six miles away."

"Any chance Michigan maintains a police presence on the island?" Dan asked.

I read more information from Fix's laptop, then shook my head. "It would be one very sleepy precinct," I said. "Isle Royale has a population of zero, and the island is completely closed to visitors this time of year."

Dan was silent for a moment. "Which would make it a perfect spot to do terrible things to two dozen kids."

"Exactly."

I ended the call with Dan so he could get to work energizing the FBI to search the area in Philadelphia where I had found Stacey, and to find someone to help us when we arrived at Thunder Bay on our way to the remote island in the middle of Lake Superior.

What the hell would we find when we arrived?

I looked at my watch. Six a.m. East Coast time. Fifteen hours left to unravel this mess. *My God, how the hell are we going to save those kids? What if we find nothing? What if I'm wasting everyone's time by flying across the country to the middle of nowhere?*

I shook my head. I had made the best decision I could make with the information available. I could second-guess until the end of time, but what better choice could I have possibly made with the information I had?

Still, something nagged. Two things, actually. I needed to talk to EvilPhuck.

I CURSED MY LACK OF FORESIGHT. I SHOULD HAVE ASKED
Evil to provide this information at the outset. This is why I can't be trusted
to use the damned Capstone password. I'm a babe in the woods with this
kind of stuff.

Fix called up the chat with Evil again and pinged her. She didn't respond.
"Probably getting ready for work," Fix offered.

"Ping her again," I said after a few eons that actually lasted only minutes.

Fix shook his head. "Impolite. We don't want to piss her off."

"Right," I said.

I reached for his laptop and did it myself.

It worked. Evil's response was rapid and to the point: "WTF?"

"Can you please collect historical location data on those three RFID tags
over the last 48 hours?"

"No."

I shook my head and cursed.

"Not part of our deal," Evil typed.

I rolled my eyes.

"How much?"

"1 more BTC."

The mercenary hacker wanted another Bitcoin for the trouble. Four thousand bucks more, on top of the twenty I'd already paid her.

I shook my head and clenched my jaw. I considered playing hardball with her. Maybe I'd threaten her by namedropping a few federal law enforcement types I knew who would want to have a conversation with her. But those threats would be idle. EvilPhuck would simply disappear into the DarkNet. And I didn't want to make an enemy out of someone who had somehow gained unfettered access to some of the most valuable information on the planet.

"OK," I typed. "But you deliver the goods first. Then I'll pay."

A long moment passed while I waited for Evil's response.

"And the RFID tag that's traveling northeast at 500mph?" I added. "I need to know exactly how close it is to our aircraft."

Evil's reply: "1.5 BTC."

I shook my head and cursed. "Deal. Hurry. Lives are at stake."

"They always are," Evil replied.

My blood was boiling a bit at the hard deal Evil had made, but I supposed that every foray into the classified system posed a serious risk for her. There wasn't much room for charity. And what else could I do? Find someone else with her kind of access? Not likely.

My mind returned to chewing on the facts. My eyes burned. I didn't remember the last time I'd slept. My thoughts fragmented. I closed my eyes, just for a moment.

And then I was back in the cabin in the mountains. The struggle. The screams, which I experienced as someone else's, even though they had come from my mouth. The pain. The opiates forced into my veins against my will. The grunting, sweating animals defiling my body, smirks on their faces, veins bulging in their necks, vague and distant pain in my innards. My inability to muster the strength or coordination to stop them. The slow dying of something at the center of me, something vital and irreplaceable.

A pair of hands on my shoulders. A face up close, talking to me. Familiar. Kind. Real and immediate, not merely remembered.

Consciousness returned in a flash. Fix stood before me, shaking me awake, his body jostling back and forth in the turbulence. Stacey looked on from her seat in the cabin, concern on her face.

"You're okay," Fix was saying. "Nothing to worry about. All good. You're safe."

I realized that I was sobbing.

It took me a moment to gather my wits. Embarrassed, tired, shaken—I was in no condition to be leading an operation like this one. Or any operation. A quick glance at Fix told me he was thinking the same thing.

"You need to level with me," Fix said. "There's something you're not telling me."

I shook my head. "You know everything you need to know."

He laughed without humor, then sat silent for a moment. "Here's the deal," he said. "I'm not an idiot and this isn't my first day on the job. Either you level with me about this—whatever *this* is—or I'm calling my boys in the front of this airplane and we're turning around and going home."

I can't say it surprised me. I was beyond strung out, probably looked like hell, and had just awakened from a nightmare sobbing and wailing. Fix and I had worked together in the past, and he knew me well enough to know that my current behavior was a long way out of character.

But I had no intention of confessing anything to anyone, ever.

I shook my head.

Fix shrugged, unfastened his seat belt, stood up, and walked toward the cabin.

I cursed to myself and balled my fists. If he convinced the pilots to turn the jet around, there was no way on Earth we would save those kids. We were following the one lead available to us, on the strength of my gut feeling that Stacey was telling the truth. But I *did* believe her. Not 100%, but enough. And if those kids died on my watch, I was not sure I could face another sunrise.

"Wait," I called to Fix.

He turned around, eyebrows raised, a small smile on his face.

"I'll tell you what you want to know."

He returned to his seat. I took a deep breath and started describing to Fix what had happened just a few hours before, in the Philadelphia police commissioner's office. Fix let me tell the story, interrupting a few times to clarify things I'd intentionally glossed over. No dummy, that one—Fix picked up on all the things I tried to hide and he forced them out of me, using those kids as leverage.

In the end, I told him everything.

FIX SAT SILENT FOR A LONG MOMENT AFTER I FINISHED recounting the previous evening's events. The murder, I mean.

"Thanks for trusting me," he finally said. "But remind me never to piss you off."

I smiled. The silence lingered. Fix said nothing. He looked troubled, conflicted.

"Are we good?" I asked, unable to stand it any longer. "Are you still in?"

Fix stayed silent for another long moment, and I feared I'd lost his help. My mind pondered other options if Fix bailed. There weren't any I could think of.

Finally, Fix spoke. "I'm really not happy about this," he said.

I held my breath. I didn't know where to start if Fix left us in a lurch. Where would we go from here? How much time would we lose if he turned the jet around? Could I convince him to drop Stacey and me off in Thunder Bay? Who could I find to replace Fix's cyber expertise? Who had Fix's connections? I had no answers.

Fix fixed his eyes on mine. "What you did wasn't smart, and you're probably going down for it. I'm definitely not going down with you as an accessory after the fact. I will watch you burn and not think twice about it."

I nodded. Yes, I murdered that man. He had it coming. Get to the point already.

"But I will not have those kids on my conscience for the rest of my life," he said. "I'll help you."

I let the air out of my lungs in relief. "Thank you," I said.

He waved his hand. "No big deal. Let's get to work," he said.

I had been asleep for an hour before my nightmare struck, and a lot had happened in that time.

Fix had heard from Evil. The RFID tag that was following us at 500mph had veered away from our flight path and slowed, and looked to be landing somewhere in the Michigan Upper Peninsula, or possibly in northeastern Minnesota.

It was a relief to know that the tag, which I was confident belonged to one of the three co-conspirators preparing for the pay-per-view rape and murder of two dozen young people scheduled to occur a mere fourteen hours later, was not somehow traveling with us on our chartered airplane. That eased my suspicions regarding my compatriots—Fix and Stacey both, and also the flight crew.

The second development also came from Evil. She reported that the RFID tag she had been tracking on Isle Royale had moved, and was now in downtown Thunder Bay, Canada.

Which was our destination.

My pulse instantly raced and my stomach filled with butterflies. We were minutes away from landing.

Fix had also heard via secure SATCOM link from Dan Gable at Homeland. Dan had contacted the FBI. In typical fashion, the suits at the Bureau wanted to have a conference call at 9 a.m. on the East Coast to "discuss the issue, inform relevant stakeholders, examine facts, and explore a way forward." Meanwhile, two dozen kids awaited a grisly death at the hands of sadistic maniacs. The bureaucratic BS made my stomach turn. It reminded me how much I didn't miss working for the government.

"There's one more thing," Fix said after he'd finished giving the rundown of everything I'd missed while I was busy having flashbacks.

"Lay it on me," I said.

Fix got a faint gleam in his eye and I could tell there was some kind of juvenile innuendo on deck, but he wisely held his tongue. Maybe the unintentional glimpse I'd given him into the disaster that was my psyche had served as a warning.

"There's a third RFID tag," Fix said.

I shook my head. "There used to be," I said. "But the first one was... destroyed. There are only two left."

"That's what I'm saying, Sam. The third one is back. Posner's RFID code is back online."

FREDERICK POSNER'S ELECTRONIC ID CODE WAS BACK
online. How could that be? I'd taken great care to blow it to bits in his
office in Philadelphia. I had decided that if the radio frequency identification
chips—also known as RFID tags—were indeed the way these animals were
expecting to secure their payment for the evening's pay-per-view atrocities,
then I would see to it that not only would these three subhumans not receive
the funds, but *nobody* would. I planned to kill the assholes, and I also planned
to destroy the payment chips.

Posner was the first. Two remained, and in what seemed like validation
of my earlier decision to follow the evidence to a frigid lake in the middle of
nowhere, both of the remaining RFID tags appeared to be converging on the
same area.

But now Evil had detected a third tag again, one using Frederick Posner's
code. I couldn't wrap my exhausted mind around how that might have been
happening.

"Fix, are you *positive* that's what Evil said?"

"Hard yes," Fix said.

"Where did she find the third code?"

"I didn't ask."

"Are you serious? What the hell is the matter with you? You didn't think we'd need to know that information?"

Fix held his hands up. "Kidding. Of *course* I asked her where Posner's ID code popped up."

I elbowed him in the gut, harder than I intended but not as hard as he deserved.

"Isle Royale," Fix said. "Right in the middle."

I chewed on this. Had Posner's RFID chip somehow survived the direct impact of the .45 hollow-point slug? Had someone inside Posner's organization fished it from the bloody goo around Posner's corpse? Maybe restored it to operating condition?

I shook my head. It really didn't seem likely. The chips are sturdy enough to withstand normal bumps and dings, but a .45 ACP round leaves the muzzle with an incredible amount of energy. No way the electronics embedded just beneath the skin of Posner's neck had survived the bullet's impact.

So someone else must have copied Posner's unique ID number into a new RFID tag and flown it up to Isle Royale. But why?

The answer came to me pretty quickly. *Insurance.* A way of enforcing honor among thieves. The payday for the heinous atrocities scheduled for later in the evening must have been quite large—large enough to entice one criminal to steal the other two shares of the take. So maybe to prevent that kind of thing from happening, they had some arrangement requiring all three RFID codes to access the payment account.

I asked Fix about this, and he said it's not common, but having an account protected by three electronic failsafe measures is not unheard of. Things can be set up so that the funds can only be accessed when all three RFID tags are present in the same room and being read by the same computer, Fix explained.

"So they need all the tags, or nobody gets paid," I summarized.

Fix nodded. "That's actually a safe bet. I mean, why else go to the trouble to recreate the first tag?"

"I was going to ask you that same question. You're the evil genius cyber criminal, after all."

Fix smiled. "I only agree with the 'genius' part of your assessment. The 'evil' and 'criminal' parts just tell me you're a victim of the brainwashing."

"I'm perfectly willing to accept that," I said. "Now focus. Is there any other reason you can think of that these guys would need to resurrect Posner's ID chip?"

Fix rocked his head back and forth a bit. "I can see them possibly using a similar protection scheme on the broadcast itself. That way it's not just the payment that's protected, but the whole show. Something happens to any of them before the show, and nobody gets paid, plus the two survivors have a mob of angry customers on their hands."

I mulled this over. It seemed a solid bet that the third RFID tag was a key to their operation. I filed it away for later.

"Hey," Fix said. "Shouldn't we be arranging transportation for when we arrive?"

I shook my head. "Absolutely not. Way too risky, given that the other two RFID tags are in the area."

"What do you mean?"

"It would be easy for Posner's men to step in as our 'transportation'. We'd be walking into a trap."

Fix nodded. "Makes sense, I suppose."

I could tell he had more on his mind. I wasn't wrong.

"Listen, Sam," he said. "I know this is none of my business—"

"Let's leave it that way," I interrupted. It came out more harshly than I'd intended. He looked a little wounded.

"I'm sorry," I said, hoping to repair some damage. "I mean, it was nothing. Just a nightmare. It happens from time to time. I'm sorry you had to see it."

He looked at me and shook his head. "It didn't look like nothing."

"Really," I said. "You were great, and I appreciate it. But seriously, it wasn't anything to worry about."

I don't think I convinced him, but he didn't press me any further.

The first officer announced our imminent arrival. I was grateful for the interruption.

Instead of buckling my seatbelt for landing, I unfastened it. Then I got up and made my way to the spot in the cabin floor where the Russian flight crew had stashed the duffel full of weapons and ammunition. I pulled away the carpet, fished in my bag for a pocketknife, and used the blade to open the fasteners. I selected three pistols, checked them, and loaded them. I tucked the best one into my belt and handed the others to Fix and Stacey.

"Try not to leave these lying around," I said. "Something tells me they will come in handy."

THE THING ABOUT CANADA IS THAT IT'S REALLY FREAKING cold. If you're thinking about going anywhere near the place during any month other than July, you're crazy. It's arctic tundra, fit only for reindeer and polar bears and hardy survivors. Maybe that's why Canadians are so polite—they're stuck indoors with each other for, like, eleven months a year.

Fix's friends in the front of the bizjet guided us to a very respectable landing. Taxiing took very little time, and before I knew it, an icy Canadian welcome had blasted into the cabin through the open hatch. I was instantly shivering.

"Dressed a little light, didn't we?" Fix observed.

I scowled at him. Wasn't like I'd had a lot of time to pack for this little adventure. Five and a half hours earlier, we had been sitting in his basement, wondering what the hell to do next.

I noticed that Stacey was looking at me with a wary expression on her face. Perhaps my little meltdown was unsettling for her. Hell, it was unsettling for me, too. I wasn't used to having an audience during my flashbacks. I had isolated myself from pretty much all human contact after my ordeal in the Colorado mountains had ended. I fancy myself the independent type, but I'm not sure that isolation was the wisest move in this case. I had been through something beyond horrific, and it undoubtedly warranted professional help.

But I wasn't there yet. I still didn't want to talk about it. I *couldn't* talk about it.

So it smoldered, and it fed the outrage and anger that drove me forward. I didn't trust the establishment to get its act together in time to save those kids. I was happy that things were happening with the FBI and Homeland—cumbersome and bureaucratic as they were—but I wasn't about to give up my search.

And I wasn't inclined to trust the system to mete out justice, if I'm being honest. Some cancers just needed excising once and for all, without all the hemming and hawing.

Hence Posner's demise. It would have been much more efficient to kidnap him and work him over for information about his other two co-conspirators instead of killing him. But that would have required a bunch of help. I'm much stronger than average, but hauling his fat ass out of the building and throwing him into the back of a van wasn't something I could pull off on my own. I couldn't exactly ask any of my friends on the federal payroll to lend a hand in something like this, especially since the "proper" authorities were already officially cognizant of the accusations against Posner and his gang. Posner's disappearance would raise too much suspicion. And Stacey wasn't someone I'd be able to rely on in a tactical situation like a kidnapping scenario.

So I did the next-best thing and removed Posner from the equation.

A Canadian customs official climbed onboard the aircraft, jolting me back to the present. He had no interest in searching the jet, which was a good thing given the contraband hidden in the smuggler's hold, and also the contraband tucked in my belt. Canadian gun laws more closely matched the rest of the world's views on firearms and differed significantly from the Wild West approach taken in the States. Also, Canada has fewer than one school shooting every year, while America has hundreds. Related? Evidently not if you're a gun lobbyist. Arm the teachers, they say, because it's easy to do the right thing in a real firefight with zero training. I'm not a bleeding heart and you'd have to pry my guns from my cold dead hand, as that annoying actor is famous for saying, but I've had hundreds of hours of tactical training and I know what the hell I'm doing. The algebra teacher does not.

Again I digress.

Pleasantries and a few forms were all the customs official was after, and his business took under a minute. "Welcome to Canada," he said on his way out of aircraft.

And then he said something that made my blood run cold.

16

"I'M TOLD YOUR TRANSPORTATION IS ALREADY WAITING for you," the Canadian customs official said offhandedly as he exited the aircraft.

This sent a wave of adrenaline surging through my system.

Transportation? We'd deliberately avoided arranging transportation. Way too easy to wind up kidnapped and gutted like a fish.

I looked at Fix. He shrugged his shoulders. "Wasn't me."

"Check with the flight crew," I told him. "Maybe they did us a 'favor'."

Fix walked to the flight deck and had a brief exchange with his Russian-speaking friends. There was back-slapping and yukking. My knee bounced impatiently. We didn't have time for the college fraternity routine.

"They said they called ahead to grease the skids," Fix said. "Don't worry, they come up here all the time for reasons you shouldn't ask about. Their guy on the ground is solid. Nothing to worry about."

Which made me even more worried.

"Look," Fix said. "We've got enough firepower to overthrow a Third-World country. I think we'll be okay."

"You've obviously never been kidnapped," I said.

"You obviously need to pick better associates," he said. "Trust is the basis of my business. Mistrust is the basis of yours."

He had a point. But that didn't slow my heart rate by much. I came by my mistrust honestly. It saved my life about a million times over the past two decades. I wasn't about to go against my intuition now.

"Tell you what," I said. "You run along with your Russian buddies. I need you to run an errand, anyway. Stacey and I will figure out our own transportation."

"You're a hard case," Fix said, shaking his head. He looked at his watch. "We're down to a little over thirteen hours. We don't have time to waste."

"Exactly," I said. "Divide and conquer. You take care of the errand. Stacey and I will work on getting us out to the island."

"Whatever. This is your kind of game, not mine."

I told him what I needed. When I had finished, I noticed that he was staring at me with his mouth open.

"Dude, what if I can't get that kind of equipment here?" he said. "This isn't exactly Silicon Valley."

"You'll think of something. Now get moving. We're wasting daylight."

Fix deplaned first. Stacey and I watched his progress through the porthole, in the relative safety of the aircraft cabin.

Maybe Fix was right, and the guy on the ground here in Thunder Bay was solid. Maybe there was nothing to worry about, and splitting up was actually a less efficient approach. Maybe I had further reduced our odds of finding those kids before the pay-per-view atrocity began in just a few hours.

But maybe not. It was impossible to know for sure. And you have to rely on *something* to help you make good decisions in an uncertain world. Twenty years of training and field experience seemed as good a starting point as any.

Fix disappeared in a beat-up king-cab pickup truck left over from sometime near the turn of the century. It was roughly the size of a small aircraft carrier. My gut tightened up as I watched him go. I had placed an enormous responsibility on him. I didn't have a plan for what we'd do if he failed.

His piece of the puzzle was pretty much everything. I was relying on his technical savvy to give us real-time intel on the location of each of the RFID tags. EvilPhuck's illicit access to that data had been helpful, but that would no longer work. Since we were getting up close and personal with these assholes, we needed instant, up-to-the-second, reliable information on their whereabouts. Also, I wasn't eager to keep paying four thousand smackers every time I needed an update.

"May the force be with you," I breathed as the truck drove away. Seemed an appropriate sendoff for our techno-geek.

A little more homework wouldn't have killed anyone, it turned out. Though the distance is less than twenty miles, traveling from Thunder Bay to Isle Royale takes an average of five hours. That would not work for us.

Also, I had the idea in my head that the Thunder Bay airport would be a small airstrip that would be easy to get in and out of. Instead, it turned out to be one of the busiest airports in Canada. Which meant that making our way from the private passenger area over to the public transportation area would be a giant hassle.

But these two things worked together in our benefit. Playing the planes, trains, automobiles, and boats game to get to Isle Royale just wouldn't be fast enough. But it was also clear that we were in the right place to solve our problem.

Our starting point turned out to be a short walk from where Fix's friends had parked their aircraft. Which was a good thing, because the weather left a bit to be desired. There was a thick, low overcast, and the ice crystals hanging in the air felt like they were shredding my lungs. Adding to the experience, the strap from the duffel full of Russian hardware was digging into my shoulder.

We passed the FedEx shipping hangar, took a right after the Air Bravo building, and found our way to the Superior HeliTours and Adventures lobby.

We were both freezing by the time we pushed the heavy door open. A door chime announced our arrival, and the desk clerk eyed us with suspicion. Who wanders around Canada in the dead of winter without a parka? We do, thank you very much, and may we please borrow your thermal underwear.

"Any chance we can get out to see Isle Royale today?"

The clerk shook her head. "Weather's too bad," she said. "None of the tours are going today."

I took a gander out the window, even though I'd just spent the last twenty minutes walking through the weather. The skies didn't look great, but Brock had flown missions in some thick soup, as he called it, so I imagined that the current problem might be a legality thing instead of a safety thing.

Brock. The thought of him cast an immediate pall over me. It had been months, but the thought of losing him still made my insides go cold. I had been over this territory a million times in my mind: maybe I only still wanted him because I couldn't have him; maybe what I really missed was the person who *I* was when we were together; maybe things weren't really as perfect as I was imagining them in retrospect.

But all of that was bullshit. I still missed him because I still loved him. And I would always love him. He was the one.

I shook my head and pushed those thoughts aside.

"What if we have a very compelling reason to head out there to the island?" I asked the desk clerk.

She shrugged. "Still a firm no, I'm afraid."

"Is that company policy?"

"Insurance company."

Right. How silly of me.

"Any chance we might talk to one of the helicopter pilots?"

She smiled and did a little ironic curtsey. "You're talking to one right now."

I hadn't seen that coming. She looked barely old enough to drive. But maybe I was just getting old, and everyone younger than forty seemed like they were wet behind the ears.

"Is there any kind of circumstance that might allow you guys to make a trip out there?"

She shook her head. "Not as a tour."

"What if we didn't call it a tour?"

"Then it would be a charter."

"That sounds better."

She shook her head. "Similar kind of problem. But now it's the owner's policy we're up against."

"Can we talk to him?"

"Her."

Dammit. Twice. When had I started buying into the patrician bullshit? "I'm sorry. Can we talk to her?"

"I would hope so. She's my mom."

MOM TURNED OUT TO BE A NO-NONSENSE KIND OF lady. She wore jeans and flannel. She had thick shoulders and strong hands. But she also had a pretty face and bright, clear eyes, plus a slim waist and an enviable ass. No ring on her finger. I imagined she probably got plenty of attention from the men who passed through her business. Maybe not all of it was welcome.

"Becca Robinson," she said over a firm handshake. "I see you've met Lizzie."

"Liz," her daughter corrected.

"I understand you're mad eager to see Royale," Becca said.

I nodded. "That's one way to put it."

"Not a great day for sightseeing."

"That's not really on our agenda," I said. "We're investigating potential criminal activity out on the island."

Becca squinted her eyes at me a bit. "Don't see a badge," she said.

"I'm not carrying one," I said. "I'm not at liberty to say much about my affiliation or about our business out here. But I can say that our work is in the public interest and is very time-sensitive."

True, but misleading. Lying with the truth is an art.

Becca nodded toward Stacey. "And this is your associate?" Maybe an edge in her voice, maybe not. Hard to tell sometimes with Canadians.

I shook my head. "Can't say much about her role, either," I said.

Another sideways squint from Becca. "You're going to have to give me something. People around here are pretty uptight about smugglers. If I were to give a ride to a couple of criminals, that could turn out to be a real problem for me."

I nodded. "I understand. Let me assure you that you're in no danger of being affiliated with any criminal activity. Quite the opposite, actually. You'd be doing a great service to many people who could really use the help. Good people who don't deserve what's happening to them."

Becca looked like she was about to speak but held her tongue.

"If this is all above-board," Lizzie said, "why are you here? Why aren't you on a police helicopter heading to the island right now?"

I nodded and smiled. "Good question, and one that I certainly would have asked if roles were reversed. The reason we're interested in hiring a tour service is that we're not yet at a point in our investigation where we can take a high profile approach."

"You don't want them to know they're being watched," Becca said.

"Exactly."

"Is this some kind of drug thing?" Lizzie asked.

I shook my head. "I'm really not at liberty to say."

A look passed between mother and daughter. I got the idea that my act hadn't been persuasive. Since I had quit my job at Homeland, I'd only rarely wished that I still carried a federal badge. But this moment was one of those times. The badge might not have pulled much weight in Canada, but at least it would have lent some credence to my story.

"Listen," I said, arms raised in capitulation. "I really appreciate your time. If you're not able to take our business today, I understand completely. Maybe you'd be so kind as to point me to someone who might be able to help?"

Becca sighed. Lizzie shook her head the slightest bit, and I thought I detected a small eye roll. She seemed to know what her mom would say next.

"Okay," Becca said, frowning. "We leave in forty-five minutes." She walked away.

Lizzie gave me the eye. "You're lucky," she said in a low voice. "She'd give a ride to Satan as long as he paid cash."

She turned to follow Becca, then stopped and turned around. "So help me, if you're taking advantage of her…"

She let the thought trail off, turned on her heel, and stomped out the door and into the hangar.

A PAIR OF EYES, PEERING OUT THROUGH A GAP IN THE window blinds in the Superior HeliTours and Adventures accounting office, a small, dingy, musty closet of an office dominated by an ancient computer and a heavy sheet-metal desk fashionable in the Fifties, observed the exchange between the four women with extreme interest.

The man pulled a burner phone from his pocket, dialed a number, waited for voicemail—the number never rang through to a live person for security reasons—and began speaking.

"You'll never believe this," he said. "They waltzed in here like they owned the place. Both of them. Let me know what you want me to do about it."

He ended the call and returned to his desk, but he couldn't concentrate on his work. His heart was pumping too fast, adrenaline upset his stomach, and his hands shook with anticipation and anxiety.

He pulled the flask from the bottom desk drawer and downed a healthy pull. The familiar burn was soothing, but not entirely. This thing was no longer merely an idea, no longer an abstract set of plans. It was suddenly very real.

Could he go through with it? It was a hell of a thing. Out there in a way that was shocking to the ordinary mind.

But his wasn't an ordinary mind. Never had been. Everyone around him had known from his early childhood that he was different. And not in a good way. That Michael Robinson, they'd say. Something ain't quite square.

He smiled. If they'd only known the half of it.

The alcohol found its mark and calmed his nerves. His optimism expanded, and so did the smile on his face. This was his last day as a lackey, as an awkward number-cruncher who needed hiding from the normal folk and especially from the paying customers, good for spreadsheets and tax returns but little else.

But no longer. Tomorrow, everything would be different.

FIX BUMPED ALONG IN THE PASSENGER SEAT OF THE OLD
pickup. He kept his hands in his jacket pockets. His left hand idly worked
loose change. His right hand fondled his cell phone.

The man at the wheel wore a long, shaggy beard, stained jeans, and a
leather jacket that looked to predate even the truck. The man had a rough-
hewn appearance with crow's feet in the corners of his eyes and smoker's lines
around his mouth.

"What's your name?" Fix asked.

"Phil," said the driver.

"You didn't ask me where I was going."

"Didn't need to," Phil said.

"How so?"

Phil shook his head instead of answering.

"Where are you taking me?"

"Won't be long," Phil said.

"Good to know. But where are we headed?"

Phil didn't answer.

A metallic taste settled in Fix's mouth, and his ears started ringing. This wasn't a good development. Maybe his Russian friends hadn't done him much of a solid after all.

"Purely business," Phil said, slowing the pickup for a right turn into the parking lot of what looked to be a disused railway shipping station. "Nothing personal. And you won't want to use that gun in your belt. It won't end well for anybody. My suggestion is you keep it tucked right where it is. Everything will go smooth and we'll all be on our way."

That's when Fix noticed the van following close behind Phil's truck. Phil stopped, so did the van, and out jumped a small gaggle of lumberjack-looking guys wielding various blunt and sharp objects.

Last out of the van was an older man, fifties maybe, with white hair and a flannel jacket and a pair of sunglasses covering his eyes, which seemed laughably unnecessary in the deep winter gloom. The man retrieved a shotgun, marched to Fix's window, ceremoniously racked the slide, and aimed the weapon at Fix's head.

"If you'd be so kind as to step out of the truck," the man said.

Fix's heart pounded in his chest. He felt a strange urge to shit himself. His right hand fumbled with the cell phone in his pocket. He desperately needed to dial 911. But the damned touchscreen made that impossible without looking at the phone. And that didn't seem to be an option.

The old man tapped the barrel of his shotgun impatiently against the glass.

"I'd get out, I were you," Phil said from the driver's seat. "Don't want to piss him off. And I'd keep your hands where he can see 'em. He's the nervous type."

"Thanks for the help," Fix said.

His hand shook as it found the door handle. He gave it a pull, but nothing happened.

"Gotta put your shoulder into it," Phil said. "Needs some grease."

Fix torqued the handle and the door screeched open. As soon as daylight appeared through the opening, one of the Paul Bunyan dudes ripped it open the rest of the way and hoisted Fix out of the truck by the jacket lapels. Fix's feet didn't touch the ground until the big bruiser set him down, three paces away from the truck and in the center of a ring of dour-faced young men.

"I can pay you," Fix said, realizing as the words tumbled thoughtlessly out of his mouth that it was a ridiculous thing to say. These men either already knew he could pay, or they didn't care in the first place. Either way, he hadn't helped his situation any, and he'd merely revealed that he was just another fearful punk who couldn't handle himself in a jam. He resolved to shut the hell up.

Which suddenly became very easy to do, because one lumberjack hauled off and punched him in the gut. The air left his lungs and his diaphragm spasmed, and while the blow was brutally painful, the pain was a distant second to the sudden knowledge that he might never again be able to draw a breath. He puffer-fished and writhed and curled himself into a ball, vaguely aware of the amused chuckles coming from the toughs.

He saw stars and thought *this is what drowning must be like,* and a part of his mind noted that it was an extremely uncomfortable way to die. And then the spasm subsided and his first breath came rushing in and the stars cleared and the panic loosened its grip on him, leaving fear and pain in its wake.

Fix heard a car engine and glimpsed a police cruiser pulling to a stop at the edge of the circle of tough-looking young men.

Salvation, Fix thought, but the goons didn't react like he expected. In fact, they didn't react at all.

The cop got out of the car and donned a dark blue wheel cap with a thick red band around its base. He too wore sunglasses.

"What we have here?" the cop said.

"New friend," the white-haired man said. "Vouched for, but we wanted to be sure."

"He resist?" the cop asked.

The white-haired man shook his head. "Got a gun on 'im, though. Didn't want to take no chances."

"Can't just gut punch everybody you don't know, Karl," the cop said. "Bad for business."

"You pick 'em up next time then, why doncha Mick," the old man said.

"Maybe I will, Karl. Then nobody would have to pay you no more. More for the rest of us. What ya say, boys?"

Fix heard a few noncommittal mutters from the gaggle of muscle, but nobody outright endorsed the police officer's idea.

"What's your name, fella?"

Fix gave the name his mother had christened him with.

The men laughed.

"Jeezuss," said the cop. "Clarence? What kinda name is Clarence these days? Never hear of nobody called Clarence any more, unless he's an old codger."

Fix didn't reply.

"So, Clarence, here's how it goes. And you can stand up for this. Can you stand up for this? Go ahead and let's stand up, why don't we?"

Fix struggled to his knees, then to his feet.

"There's that gun to think about," the cop said, "so let's see your hands at all times, okay?"

Fix stood with his arms raised above his shoulders, still out of breath, still smarting from the blow.

"So it's a terrible welcome you just got, I know, and I do apologize for that. Go ahead and look at me when I'm talking, that way I know you're not thinking about pulling out that gun and doing something really stupid. There's a good man."

A fit of coughing took hold, and Fix doubled over with the strain.

"Pretty good blow from young Terence over there, I take it," the cop said. "But never mind. Think of us as all being on the same team. Maybe like a little initiation ceremony, like on your football team growing up, right?"

Fix hadn't played football growing up.

"So here's how it goes, and we'll all be on our way. You're here because somebody we know vouched for you, but we always do a little of our own due diligence and whatnot. Not everybody in this town is as business-minded as we are. Some folks frown on some business that other folks do."

Fix's coughing fit let up and he stood upright again, hands on his hips. He glimpsed the officer's name tag. Sevier, it read.

"But that's not our way," Sevier said. "Live and let live. That's *our* way. That right, boys?"

Grunts of assent from the peanut gallery.

"But I don't want you to flaunt our goodwill. Whatever business you're here for, and I know you're here for business because like I said, somebody gave us a little introduction, and it was a favorable one which is why this is a friendly meeting and whatnot, but anyway, whatever business you're here for, you make sure you do it in a smart way."

Fix didn't know what the hell that might have meant—did they think he was planning to go about his business in a stupid way?—but he nodded anyway.

"Some folks think all the business that gets conducted around here needs to be official and taxed and whatnot. But we're a little more libertarian about things. Trevor, you understand what 'libertarian' means?"

Trevor nodded.

"No, you don't," Officer Sevier said. "You don't know any word bigger than two syllables. But your big fat buffalo of a momma loves you just the same."

Chuckles from the gang. Fix snuck a glance in Trevor's direction and noticed that the big man had a rosy-cheeked blush growing on his boyish face. But he didn't appear to be angry at the insult.

"I forget anything, boys?"

"The vat," somebody said.

Vat? Like a barrel full of chemicals or something? What the hell was that about? It sounded like something out of *Deliverance*.

"Right!" Sevier said. "How could I forget? Trevor, all your dumbness musta rubbed off on me for a sec."

More chuckles. More blushing.

"See, Clarence," Sevier said, leaning on Fix's given name to the mild amusement of the crowd, "around here, it ain't like down there in the States. We got a thing here called the VAT. That stands for Value Added Tax. It helps make sure the commons is maintained in good order. That means that the goods and services are available for all upstanding citizens and whatnot. You want to be an upstanding citizen, Clarence?"

Fix nodded. Whatever you say.

"See, the service we perform around here is this: We let you do your business and we don't get in your way. Unless you raise a big stink. Then we got no choice but to prosecute you to the full extent of the law and whatnot. So that's what I mean when I say that you gotta be smart up here while you're goin' about your business, whatever that may be, and trust me, I really don't want to know, and neither do my associates here."

Fix nodded. For the first time, he thought there might be a way out of the situation that didn't involve more bodily injury.

"But this kind of service has its costs," the cop went on. "And seeing as how you're new up here, and not familiar with the way things work, we thought we'd take a minute to explain, just so there's no misunderstanding and whatnot."

Here comes the punchline, Fix thought.

"So the VAT is fifteen percent of the total transaction value," Sevier said.

"Who do I pay?" Fix asked, surprised at how normal his voice sounded after Trevor's fist had wreaked such havoc on his gut.

"You'll know when the time comes," the cop said. "We do this little thing as a courtesy up front, just so there's no surprises down the line and whatnot."

Fix nodded. Awful swell of you, he thought. Just like a standard mafia protection racket, only with a dash of Canadian politeness. And whatnot.

"Oh, and one more thing before we wrap this up and get on with our business," Officer Sevier said. "Sometimes two guys may find themselves on opposite ends of a thing. Like, maybe they're both paying their VAT like good, responsible citizens and whatnot, but one of them wants things a certain way, and the other responsible citizen wants things the opposite way. You can see how a conflict might develop. Happens more often than you might think."

"I'll try to stay clear of anybody else's business," Fix said.

"Good man. But just in case it happens, and like I said, it seems to happen quite a little bit, at least more often than you'd hope, but anyway, over time we devised a way to deal with these kinds of situations."

Fix said nothing.

"That's where Karl and his boys come in," Sevier said. "See, we figure, the guy who should get his way is the guy who happens to be working on the bigger deal. And naturally, that's also the guy who'll end up paying the higher VAT and whatnot. You can see where we're coming from on that, and so forth. So Karl and his boys make sure that's what happens, and they make sure there aren't any hard feelings on the part of the party that doesn't get his way. Doncha, Karl?"

"We do," said the white-haired guy with the shotgun.

"I see," Fix said. "I'll try to steer clear."

"That's a wise way of going about it, and it'll be smooth sailing for you that way. Right, boys?"

Grunts of assent.

"Nice day, now," the cop said, and disappeared back into his cruiser.

Karl's lumberjacks piled back into the van. Phil jumped back into the driver's seat of his pickup.

"Ain't got all day," Phil said, and Fix got back in the truck and buckled his seatbelt.

Phil turned to Fix and smiled. "So, Clarence. Where to, then?"

LIZZIE WAS KIND ENOUGH TO TAKE STACEY AND ME TO
a local store to pick up some winter clothes, and then for a quick bite to eat.
I was a new woman after a little breakfast and some hot coffee. And it was
great to stop shivering, finally. I'd been cold since that first blast of arctic air
had invaded the aircraft cabin, and I huddled into my coat and reveled in
the warmth.

Lizzie didn't have much to say. I could tell she was wary of us, and I also
thought she felt protective of her mom. Which seemed a little unnecessary,
because Becca Robinson definitely struck me as a lady who would have no problem
holding her own in all but the worst situations. But I might have been wrong.

Stacey was also a little standoffish. I was fairly sure that my episode on
the flight up to Thunder Bay had shaken her up. She had placed her trust in
me as someone with the skill and experience to save those kids and keep her
safe, and it probably did nothing for her confidence to see me melt down like
that, even if I hadn't been conscious at the time. Honestly, the whole thing
felt damned embarrassing.

Maybe I needed to stop living out of my car, find a place to call home,
and find a good psychiatrist.

Or maybe I'd just keep wandering around like Jack Reacher. Attachment is the root of suffering, they say, though I don't think that's the attachment they're talking about.

And it was all academic anyway until we could get this situation sorted out. No way in hell was I going to walk away from those kids, no matter which authorities got involved.

Lizzie excused herself to visit the restroom and it was just Stacey and me left at the table in the greasy-spoon diner.

"What are we going to do if we find them?" she asked.

Which was a damned good question. I gave her the only honest answer. "It depends."

You never know what needs doing until you understand what you're up against. Stacey had no trouble understanding that, but I knew she needed something else. She wanted to know whether we stood a snowball's chance in hell of freeing those kids and surviving in the process.

And I sensed that she also wanted to know how we would make sure the animals behind all of this got the justice they deserved. I didn't probe her on it because this kind of thing is often best left unsaid, but I got the impression it wouldn't break her heart if none of the perpetrators survived long enough to go to trial.

I shared her sentiment. This quasi-vigilante penchant was a character trait I had exhibited on more than one occasion during my long career at Homeland, and it wasn't really a secret.

Which made me wonder yet again why an über-spy named Artemis Grange, the man who held the title known in the most powerful circle on the planet as the Facilitator, had entrusted me with the world's most sophisticated, pervasive, and invasive surveillance and intelligence network. He had showed up at the end of my ordeal in the cabin—and Grange himself had killed the animals who had abused me—then he had coerced me into taking over for him at the very top of an organization called Capstone.

Capstone transcended political, economic, and religious divisions. It was precisely the thing that conspiracy nuts howled about. In fact, plenty of conspiracy nuts howled that Capstone was a real thing, that it really existed, and that it regularly altered the course of global events.

They had it right. That's what Capstone did.

At least, that's what it had done until Artemis Grange's conscience got the better of him. He abdicated his throne and threw everything in my lap.

I was in no shape to handle that kind of power. I hadn't yet decided whether Capstone should even exist. I believed that it should never have been built, but now that it existed, there was a different problem. If one group could muster the resources and brainpower to construct something like Capstone, then what was to stop another group from doing the same thing? What if Capstone's evil twin had the goal of turning the globe into some kind of Islamic dystopia, for example? Shouldn't Capstone be used to stop that kind of thing from happening?

And wasn't there enormous potential to use the massive power of ubiquitous global surveillance—anyplace with a power grid fed terabytes of information into Capstone every second of every day—to end human suffering and make the world a better place?

In other words, I had no clue whether I should burn Capstone to the ground, turn it over to someone better equipped to handle the responsibility, or remain involved somehow.

I did know one thing for certain. I was a terrible choice to take over as the Facilitator. This little adventure was proof positive. If I got the chance to rid the gene pool of the subhuman slime that could plan and implement something this dark, this brutal, this depraved, I didn't doubt for a second that I would do it.

And I would enjoy it.

If I'm honest, a part of me enjoyed killing Frederick Posner. He needed to die, and a good bit of me was glad to have pulled the trigger.

But what if I had been wrong about him? What if he *didn't* actually deserve to die? What then? That thought brought me crashing back to reality.

You have to get rid of Capstone, I told myself. *You're a loose cannon, a vigilante at heart, and you always have been.*

Which was true. But it was equally true that I really gave a damn about justice. *Real* justice, which is not actually what the legal system delivers.

So was it possible that I knew my limitations well enough to surround myself with people who might keep me in check? Could someone sanity-check my decisions? Who?

Which opened up another can of worms entirely: when that much wealth and power are at your disposal, who the hell can you trust? And let there be no doubt: it's enough wealth and power to corrupt even the brightest shining stars.

I sighed and took another sip of coffee. It had cooled and now tasted like someone had left a dirty sock in the percolator. I grimaced, noting how exhausted the mental spin-cycle had made me. I'd been churning the Capstone question over and over in my mind a thousand times a day since Grange had left me the keys to the kingdom.

That is, I worried over Capstone when I wasn't too busy suffering nightmares and flashbacks from my torture and rape.

No wonder I was such a fucking mess.

I awoke from my reverie to notice Stacey's eyes locked onto my face once again, her brow knotted in worry.

I took her hand. "We're going to be fine," I said. "I used to do this for a living."

She managed a small smile. "Remind me never to go into your line of work," she said.

Her face darkened again. "Being this close to those men," she said, eyes moistening. "I'm really scared."

I tightened my grip on her hand. "I'm not going to let anything happen to you. I promise."

SO COLD. AND DARK. JANIE'S TEETH CHATTERED. THEY'D hosed her off not too long ago—to get rid of the funk and make her at least a little fuckable, couldn't have the clients all limp-dicked because of the smell, they said—and they hadn't bothered to give her a towel. So she'd drip-dried, shivering and miserable in that dark, hard, drafty cell.

The sedation had worn off. Janie's head felt thick and foggy. Her vagina hurt. And her anus. It had been a very, very hard few days. Her eyes burned and her skull pounded. And the fear—like nothing she'd ever experienced.

Shoulda never left home, Janie thought for the thousandth time. Not that she missed her doped-out mom or the slack-jawed, buck-toothed, unwashed, meth-addicted live-in boyfriend of the month. Those men often wanted things from Janie, young and slender and comely as she was, and Janie couldn't always count on her mom's help to keep the horny bastards at bay. She'd narrowly escaped an unwanted encounter on more occasions than she could recall, and that was no small motivation for her leaving.

Running away was how the high school counselor had put it. You don't want to be a runaway. As if the negative connotation was somehow compelling enough to entice Janie to stay in her hellish home environment, with its drugs and guns and decay. The logic was lost on Janie, as was the social worker's advice to find a friend or relative to stay with until her mom could get "back on her feet."

Because that would never happen, Janie knew. And who would she stay with in the meantime? In that part of Ohio, everybody under the age of eighty had an addiction to something. Nobody had a job, because the work had all been automated away. There was nothing for anyone to do but lie around getting high, sharing venereal diseases, and picking fights with each other.

Janie shook her head. The irony was rich. She'd run away in part to escape sex with her mom's scumbag boyfriends, only to wind up selling blow jobs at truck stops for food money and a ride out West to some big city with enough prosperity to offer a reasonable chance at building a life for herself.

And look where that landed you, she thought. Stuck in a cage like some kind of animal, forced to have hard, painful, unprotected sex with whichever disgusting bastard happened to showed up next at her cell door.

"We all have a choice," Janie's high school counselor was fond of saying. Maybe that was true and maybe it wasn't. Sure didn't seem like anybody in town would have chosen to wind up sick and addicted and broke. It really seemed like everything had disappeared right in front of their eyes, slowly at first, and then suddenly one day the jobs were all gone. Every last one of them. It wasn't as if people had stopped working hard or had suddenly forgotten how to do their jobs. The jobs simply went away.

"Learn to code" was the bitter joke popular on social media after the last factory closed down. And that's when it got really bad. Janie's friends started coming to school with their eyes glazed over. That wasn't her thing—she wanted a life and a future and a family and a career—so she dropped out of her social group and withdrew into herself a bit.

But where was she going to hang out, if not with her friends? At home, watching her mom bake herself on meth and then scuttle into the back room to bang whichever skinny dirtbag happened to stumble through the door that day? Not going to happen.

Maybe I deserve this, Janie thought sometimes.

Maybe I did *have a choice,* she thought at other times. *But it sure as hell didn't seem like it.*

She remembered the first time a trucker had asked her for favors in exchange for a meal and a ride. At first she thought he was kidding. But he wasn't kidding. And it was too late to turn down the deal—they were hurtling down the highway. Janie protested, but the man had nonchalantly set a large hunting knife on the dashboard in plain view. He didn't have to verbalize the threat, because it was right there in front of her eyes.

It was over quickly, and at least the man had showered recently.

She would never forget what he said when it was over. "Congratulations, honey. You're now a working girl. I'm honored to be your first client."

She'd run to the rest stop bathroom and vomited. Then she'd cried her eyes out.

And now this.

She heard footsteps crunching in the gravel beyond the door to her cell. Janie held her breath. *Please, please, please, pick someone else! Don't do this to me again. I can't take any more of this!*

The chain rattled, the latch gave way, and an icy winter blast froze her innards as a large man let himself into her cell. "Time to warm you up a little," the man said with a scumbag smile and an amused cackle. "Boss wants you nice and *loose* for the main event."

She couldn't stop the tears.

22

THERE'S A POINT AT WHICH ALL MY ATTEMPTS AT PATIENCE
fail me, and I wind up being the biggest pain in the ass anyone has ever seen.
I was rapidly approaching that point.

"Where the hell is Fix?" I raged. He wasn't answering his phone, and I
had no idea whether he'd been able to round up the equipment to track those
electronic ID tags that the thugs were using.

Plus, the weather was getting worse, and Becca Robinson was considering
pulling the plug on our plan to scope out Isle Royale. It was pretty much now
or never.

I made an executive decision. "We go without Fix," I said. "Let's get
rolling."

Becca and I trudged out of the operations building and onto the tarmac.
Stacey had fallen asleep on the couch in Becca's office and I had elected not
to wake her. She'd been through hell and we still had a long day ahead of us,
no matter which way you sliced it. And having an untrained girl at my side
in any kind of tactical scenario meant nothing but liability. She'd just have
been one more variable for me to control, and truth be told, I wasn't up for
the challenge.

"Went for a ride," I wrote on a yellow-sticky. "Be back soon!" I placed the note on Stacey's hip so she'd be sure to see it when she woke up. Then I shut and locked the office door on my way out.

Becca and I rounded the corner of the building and headed toward one of the three red helicopters parked on the ramp. The wind had picked up and an evil bite edged its way around and underneath my new winter clothes. Before I knew it, I was shivering again. "If I lived here," I groused, "I would move somewhere else."

Becca chuckled. She wore a light jacket and no hat. "You should come visit when it *really* gets cold," she said. It took a different breed of cat to live up here, I noted.

She made sure I strapped in securely. She tried to take my duffel bag away and stow it in the rear of the helicopter, but I wouldn't let her. I wanted immediate access to all the firepower inside the bag. She gave me a look—there was a legitimate concern of the bag impeding the flight control movement, as there was a second copy of the stick and rudders on my side of the cockpit as well—but ultimately all she said was, "Please keep control of that bag at all times."

Becca did her preflight walk-around and was about to take her place at the pilot's controls when a beat-up old king cab pickup drove out onto the tarmac. Fix jumped out of the passenger's seat wearing a backpack and carrying what looked like a camera case.

Becca situated him in no time, started the engine, and before I knew it, the damned thing started vibrating like a jackhammer and the ground slowly moved away from us. Gawd, I hate helicopters. Airplanes I understand. Helicopters just seem like a bad idea all around.

"Talk to me, Fix," I said over the intercom. We all wore headsets to drown out some of the godawful racket and to allow us to speak to each other without screaming.

"I had an interesting welcome to Thunder Bay," he said.

That wasn't what I had in mind for this particular conversation. "I don't care right now," I said. "Tell me about the RFID scanner."

"Right," Fix said. "Never mind that I risked life and limb. Let's get to what *you* want to talk about."

I turned around with a scathing rejoinder on my lips but Fix beat me to the punch. "Just kidding," he said with a smile. "I know we're up against the clock here."

He explained the rig he'd purchased as he pulled each component from its carriage bag and assembled the pieces together.

"Standard RFID scanner," he said showing me a thing that looked like a snub-nosed pistol with a calculator where the gun barrel should have been. "Problem is, it only has a range of seven meters."

I shook my head. That would make the damned thing pretty much useless for our purposes.

"But that's why you have to get two of them," Fix went on. "And you have to do a bunch of computer math to amplify and compare the signals between the two scanners."

"We don't have time for computer math," I offered helpfully.

"My dear, what exactly do you take me for?"

He was right, of course. I'd brought him along precisely because he was an expert.

"And anyway," he said, "there's an app for that."

Fix connected the two RFID scanner thingies to a USB cable, which led to an adapter that plugged into an iPhone.

"I hope that's a burner phone," I said.

He shook his head. "Jailbroken, with the cell reception and wi-fi disabled. Totally off the grid, and we're only using it as a computer."

I wasn't so sure about that, as I'd seen Dan Gable work some magic to exploit those devices in the past, but I let it pass for the moment. There wasn't any time to explore alternatives.

Becca banked hard to the left, and suddenly we were out over the water. "Just a couple of minutes to Isle Royale," she said. "Any particular place you want me to take you?"

I recalled the map image from EvilPhuck showing the location of the two RFID tags she'd located using very questionable and very classified means.

Isle Royale is much longer than wide, and the long axis runs from the southwest to the northeast. The red blips had shown up about a third of the way from the northeastern tip of the island.

"Makes sense," Becca said. "That's where all the campgrounds are. There's also a visitor's center on the northeastern end of the island."

"What kind of range can we get using two scanners?" I asked Fix.

"Much better," he said brightly. "Half a kilometer."

I'm no mathematician, but some quick calculations told me that half a kilometer is about a third of a mile.

I shook my head. Isle Royale is fifty miles long by fifteen miles wide.

"We'd be lucky to find them in a week of searching," Becca said.

23

THE ACCOUNTANT MIKE ROBINSON DOWNED HIS FOURTH
healthy swallow of whiskey and savored the burn. *Better slow down,* he
thought. *Don't want to have the stumbles later on, when things get* real.

He smiled. The alcohol had taken the edge off the apprehension and
anxiety. His wasn't a normal psychopathy, if there was such a thing. Most
people who were into the things that Mike Robinson was into had very little
fear of social consequences. The same detachment that allowed them to not
only tolerate certain activities, but in fact to enjoy them, and over time to *crave*
them, also allowed them to have unwavering faith that they could extract
themselves from any kind of unpleasant situation that might arise because of
their compulsion.

But Mike Robinson wasn't so gifted. He had all the cravings, but little
of the bravado. He had all the neurosis, but unlike other psychopaths, he felt
nearly as much fear as normal people felt. He lived his life in perpetual fear
of discovery and punishment. Hence a somewhat problematic affinity for the
drink. It gave him the necessary detachment from fear that others of his ilk
were so blessed with.

He hated them for it. And he envied them. Which was the perfect combination to make him susceptible to falling under the spell of a guru.

He'd found a guru to follow, all right. It had been one hell of a ride. Mike Robinson had found the courage and tenacity to do things he'd only dreamt of in the past.

Of course, he'd done plenty of those kinds of things on his own. The difference was that he had always held something back. No matter how far he pushed himself, there always remained some longed-for pleasure, some transcendent experience, some new way to elicit howls of pain and discover fascinating new configurations of flesh and bone and sex and sinew, that lay just beyond his ability to reach.

Or rather, that lay just beyond the boundary of his will and commitment. These were not bridges that one crossed, but were massive gates that, once traversed, slammed shut in one's wake.

Once you went there, there was no going back.

It was his fear that held him back, and he knew it. But that was a thing of the past.

Mostly.

Maybe one more drink, to make sure the nerves stayed at bay.

It would be a big night, and Mike Robinson wanted to be in the perfect state of mind.

And he had work to do. He shut down the computer in the dreary accounting office at Superior HeliTours and Adventures, the company that Becca had started with the divorce settlement money, more her baby than just a business, really, much more of an object of affection than Lizzie ever was.

Big Sis, if you only knew, Mike Robinson thought as he shoved a small USB drive into the computer's portal and turned the power back on.

The USB drive contained a computer operating system called Tails, designed from the ground up with anonymity and privacy in mind. The name was an acronym: The Amnesic Incognito Live System. It mostly served the politically oppressed, among the fastest-growing class of human in the modern digital era, but its use had spread rapidly to paranoids, tax evaders, and self-styled radical libertarians.

And criminals.

Mike Robinson smiled. These were his people.

The operating system finished booting up, and Robinson navigated to the appropriate anonymous site on the DarkNet. There was no Google down here, where the machines talked to each other and people of a certain kind shared photos of their exploits, so you had to know right where you were going. Otherwise you'd never get there.

Mike Robinson knew there was much more to the DarkNet. It was really the infrastructure that made the "white web" hum along as easily as it did. The DarkNet was the boiler room that kept the cruise ship of the Worldwide Web slicing along through the water. Even though the Dark Web had a bad name among those who knew very little about how Internet technology worked, illicit activity was only a tiny fraction of the DarkNet's total bandwidth. But those other things held no interest for him. He liked what he liked, and this was the best place to find it.

And this was the best place to *participate*, too.

"Airborne," he typed in the chat window belonging to a certain unassuming site with the unofficial name of Scream. Once you were past the security portal, there was plenty of screaming to be found. Mike Robinson knew firsthand. He'd seen all the videos at least once, many twice.

It gave him a charge to be on the other side of everything for once. Instead of getting off while other people had all the fun producing all of that compelling... *content*, this time Robinson would actually *do it*.

"Fuckin' A," he said as he clicked the 'enter' key, noticing a slight slur in his words, but deciding that maybe just one more little slug of whiskey would put him at the right vibration level for what lay ahead.

He felt excited about the contingency that had arisen. His partners—those who remained, that is—had freaked out. And justifiably so. But the *problem* that had developed, which evidently involved the redhead and the young brunette, had given Mike Robinson a big opportunity. He had taken on the added responsibility with gusto and zeal.

The response to his message came almost instantly. "Proceed as planned. Everything's in the green and on schedule."

MIKE ROBINSON FINISHED HIS WORK ON THE DARKNET
website called Scream. And in the relative privacy of his office, he took several
minutes for pleasure as well. Just to take the edge off. He hoped the release
would give him more stamina later.

It wasn't as if he *wanted* to enjoy this kind of stuff, he thought as he
cleaned himself up. Truth be told, his proclivities made his life maximally
inconvenient. But it was how he was wired. Always had been.

He knew on some level that Becca's motives for hiring her brother into
her company were complex. She felt some older-sibling responsibility for him,
undoubtedly. And she also wanted to keep an eye on him. In fact, Robinson
knew this to be the case. He'd overheard Becca having a few uncomfortable
conversations about him.

Nothing new. Story of his life. That was part of the draw to accounting.
The numbers never judged you, and you never had to affect a fake sociability
around them. Much easier than with people.

Robinson shut down his computer and headed out for lunch.

But on his way out, his plans changed dramatically. Something caught
his eye through one of the office windows. *Could it be?*

Right there in his sister's office, he saw something that was simply too good to be true. Like a gift from providence, he thought, savoring the zing of anticipation that flowed through his body. He felt suddenly giddy. He was nearly beside himself with eagerness and impatience to *get the party started.*

Calm, he reminded himself. It was dangerous to get too eager.

He walked with forced nonchalance to the operations desk. A quick look at the security camera monitors showed him exactly what he wanted to see. Lizzie had the engine cowling open on a helicopter out in the hangar, her elbows twisting as her hands worked on something deep inside the engine. The security cameras didn't have microphones, but Robinson knew that a steady torrent of curses was likely streaming from Lizzie's mouth. It might be hours before she came up for air.

Robinson smiled, and his stomach fluttered with excitement. Perfect timing.

He found the security camera monitor for the administrative section of the building, reached around to the back of the unit, which was both a real-time monitor and a digital recorder, and loosened the cable until the picture disappeared. He grabbed a sticky-note pad, scrawled a message that something was wrong with the camera feed again, and that he would be back to investigate after a quick run to the office supply store. Robinson stuck the note onto the screen.

It wouldn't seem the least bit suspicious, he thought. They'd been having problems with this video feed for some months now. No one at the office seemed to suspect that one particular individual had been behind all the trouble.

He returned to his office, unlocked the ugly metal storage cabinet, pulled down a thick accounting textbook, and placed it on his desk. Inside the cover and nestled within the book's hollowed-out pages was the primary enabler of his extremely antisocial habit: a box of transdermal Fentanyl patches. It was touted as a miracle drug, which was undoubtedly true from Big Pharma's perspective. The magic in these little patches was fifty times more powerful than pure heroin. And these were high-dose patches. Sure, governments had paid lip service to a crackdown, but it was hard for politicians to take action against their largest campaign contributors, and the pharmaceutical companies were more than happy to churn out massive profits with zero regard for the death toll. Must keep the shareholders happy. The amazing fact was that despite all the recent hubbub, the drug was easier than ever to buy.

Fentanyl was pure gold for a man of Mike Robinson's predilections.

He selected two patches—one for now, and a spare for later in case it proved necessary. He replaced his stash and locked the cabinet, walked quietly into Becca's office, and gently applied a Fentanyl patch to the slender brunette girl's exposed arm.

I GRIMACED AND SHOOK MY HEAD AS ISLE ROYALE CAME
into view. It was one of the largest freshwater islands in the world, and the
electronic search gear Fix had found would only allow us to "see" the RFID
signal from Posner's group members inside a half-kilometer radius.

To cover the entire island, we'd need to fly over it tip-to-tail at least a
dozen times, probably more like fourteen or fifteen. And we'd also have to
be very precise about our flight pattern, because it would be easy to screw it
up and cover the same ground twice, and also to leave other portions of the
island unsearched.

"We need a lucky break," I breathed.

"Maybe not," Becca said. "Depending on what kind of operation you're
looking for, and I really have no clue about that because you've kept me
completely in the dark, but parts of the island are hard to reach. If they had
to haul around a bunch of equipment, or if they needed shelter of some sort,
there's only a couple of spots they could use."

"One of them is Windigo," she went on, "which is a harbor on the far
southwestern side of the island. Maybe a half-dozen buildings. It'll take
us just a minute to rule it out. Then we can focus on the northeastern end

of the island, which is probably a safer bet. There's more infrastructure on that end, and that's where I'd go if I were trying to set up a camp of some kind."

I nodded my assent. "Let's do it. Fix, you ready?"

"Already scanning," he said.

Becca angled the helicopter to the south, flared out to the west over the frigid-looking water of Lake Superior, and started a slow, sweeping turn back to the east. I glimpsed Windigo through the fog, and it slowly came into focus as we neared. A few structures materialized through the mist. Seventies-era tract housing. Exactly like the shit you see in California coastal towns and Colorado ski resorts. It always amazed me how Americans seemed to build the ugliest structures imaginable in some of the world's most picturesque locations.

"Fix, getting anything?"

"Nothing."

"Are you sure that damned thing even works?"

He didn't dignify my insulting question with a response.

"Can we make a tight circle over the town a couple of times?" he asked.

Becca obliged, slowing the helicopter to little faster than a hover, keeping a constant left bank as we orbited the ugly little boil of a village in an otherwise unspoiled natural wilderness.

"One more time," Fix said. "I want to be 100% sure before we move on."

Fix's RFID locator found nothing on the second orbit either, so we moved northeast. He kept the device hammering away, sending out interrogation signals that would elicit a response from the RFID tags embedded beneath the skin of the two remaining assholes plotting the inhuman rape, torture and murder of two dozen young people for fun and profit.

My jaw clenched again. I was way too emotional about this situation. I was tired, strung-out, and extremely motivated to stop this madness before it went any further. I didn't fault myself for being in that state of mind, but it wasn't exactly conducive to making smart decisions.

And I was much more likely to pull the trigger and splatter these assholes' innards than to hand them over to the system. Assuming anyone from "the system" would find their way this far north before the atrocity began.

Dense forest rolled beneath us as Becca guided the helicopter toward the other end of the island. It was easy to see how people got lost and died on the island. It was a big island, and it was unadulterated wilderness. If you planned to venture out into the thick of it, you'd damned well better know what you were doing.

"Wait!" Fix hollered. "I saw a signal!"

"ARE YOU SURE?" I COULDN'T BRING MYSELF TO BELIEVE that Fix's little gadget had found a real RFID signal. We were flying over nothing but dense, impenetrable forest. The nearest human outpost was miles away. We were several miles inland from the coast, and any boat-based signal would have been out of the half-kilometer range of Fix's detector.

"It definitely pinged," Fix said.

Becca banked the chopper hard right and circled back around.

"There it is again," Fix said.

"Read me the tag's code," I said, still skeptical.

As Fix rattled off the numbers he saw on the RFID detector, I felt a surge of adrenaline in my system. The code matched one of the three tags we'd identified as being part of Posner's group. I'd written them all down on a note in my pocket, but I didn't need to fish it out. I had memorized the codes. This was definitely one of the people we were looking for.

"One more!" Fix said. "The second one has Posner's code."

Which seemed to make sense. To use Posner's RFID tag to unlock access to the payment account for the evening's live-streamed atrocities, they would likely need all three tags in the same place at the same time. So if they'd recreated Posner's tag after they learned of his death, it made sense that one of them would carry it around on his person.

"I'm getting a triangulation," Fix said. "Becca, if we could move the center of our orbit a little to the south…"

Becca's hands moved the stick a bit and she elongated one side of our orbit. She fiddled with a few knobs, and the helicopter flew itself in a slow orbit. For some reason I never trusted autopilot systems, and especially not in a helicopter.

"Right there," Fix said, pointing downward at an angle.

I looked. I'd been looking this whole time. All I saw was the clock ticking away as we wasted time on this wild goose chase. We'd been had. I was sure of it. There was nothing down there but forest. No way they could hide two dozen kids nearby.

And there was also no way the perps would have spent the day a dozen miles from the nearest road or structure. It would take them hours to return to civilization from here. There were no trails or roads for miles, and they'd have to hack their way through thick northern rainforest, both coming and going. Instead of taking serene walks in nature, those animals would be busy preparing for the live webcast scheduled to begin in just a few hours.

"Can you come to a hover and sneak us slowly to the west?" Fix asked.

Becca obliged.

"A little farther."

I saw nothing but forest.

"Almost there."

Not even a glint of metal. Not a single straight line that might give away some manmade object left behind in the forest.

"Perfect," Fix said. "We're right over the signal."

"Okay," Becca said. "Now what?"

"Can you set us down somewhere?" I asked.

Becca chuckled. "Where did you have in mind? On top of a tree, maybe?"

She had a point. There was nothing around us but dense forest. There wasn't a clearing in sight, let alone one big enough to accommodate a helicopter.

Then I saw it. My heart sank. "Back us up a bit. Ten feet, maybe."

As Becca maneuvered the helicopter using the autopilot settings and the angle of the fuselage changed, the entire corpse came into view. Unclothed. Female. Young. Legs broken and splayed at a horrifying angle. Partially eaten by predators.

"Jesus," Fix said. "They planted the tags on her and threw her from a fucking helicopter."

I CURSED MYSELF SILENTLY AS THE HELICOPTER RATTLED
and shook its way back to Thunder Bay. How much time had we just wasted?
Every second counted. Yet we had squandered the better part of an hour on
an expedition to a remote island that had resulted in a horrifying discovery
but no clues that would help us find the perpetrators by nighttime.

We'd thoroughly searched the northeastern end of the island as well,
looking for signs of recent inhabitance or human activity, but there weren't
even any tracks in the snow. "It last snowed on Sunday," Becca said. "Four
days ago. Nobody's been here since then, at least."

My mood was beyond dark when we landed. I hated being played. These
assholes were toying with us. They had figured out the RFID tag angle, and
they had used it against us. Smart move, I had to admit. It's what I would
have done. I'd known all along that some kind of manipulation using the
tags was possible, maybe even probable, but I think a part of me just hoped
we'd get a little lucky.

And I knew that regardless of what the odds were, we had no choice but
to investigate the RFID hits out on Isle Royale. There was no way around it.
It wasn't a bad decision, even though the whole thing had gone to shit.

"Now what?" Fix asked as the engines spooled down.

I shook my head. Becca had called in the body to the Thunder Bay airport control tower. They were accustomed to coordinating search and rescue efforts out on Lake Superior, and would contact the authorities to start the recovery effort and investigate the homicide.

But I had no idea where that left us. We weren't certain that the kids weren't being held on Isle Royale, but the island seemed deserted. Other than the corpse, which was now a grisly image in my brain that I knew I'd see in my nightmares if I ever had the bad judgment to fall asleep again, we'd seen no evidence of human activity out there. None whatsoever.

"Look on the bright side," Fix said. "We know for certain we're at least in the right neighborhood."

I shook my head. "Not necessarily. Remember, Evil found that first RFID tag hit over twelve hours ago. They could have packed the kids up and driven them hundreds of miles away by now. And there's no guarantee that the rest of the kids were *ever* here. Maybe those fucking animals flew up here completely as a diversion, and left the kids somewhere else, a thousand miles away. Maybe they found a local girl to bait the trap we just fell for. We can't make any assumptions."

I was hoping Fix would have a good counter argument that would lead us on a more favorable line of reasoning, but he stayed silent.

I was shivering again by the time we got back inside Becca's HeliTours operations building. Snow fell, and the gusting wind turned the flakes into icy missiles.

The building was eerily empty. The desk was unmanned. The lights were off in the administration section of the building. Becca looked a little miffed as she filled out the flight paperwork. She muttered a throwaway line about how hard it was to find good help, especially when you had to hire your kin, then called her maintenance chief to talk about a small problem she'd discovered with the helicopter.

I walked back to Becca's office to break the bad news to Stacey.

The lights were off. The door was open.

Stacey was gone.

"NO BIG DEAL," FIX SAID. "SHE'S PROBABLY JUST IN THE restroom."

But I had already checked there. And everywhere else. I'd even gone to the maintenance hangar and spoken to Lizzie. She looked at me as if I'd grown a third arm. "Why the hell would she have come out here? And anyway," she said, showing me her oil-stained hands, "I probably wouldn't have noticed if she did. It's not like I'm playing solitaire here."

Charmer, that one.

I made one more lap of the operations building. I couldn't call Stacey because I had forbidden her having a cell phone. Entirely too risky, I'd said. But now that choice was cutting the other way.

"Any chance she took a walk or something?" Fix offered.

"Sightseeing in a snowstorm?"

"Right," he said. "Not likely."

Being this close to those men, she had said. *I'm really scared.*

And what were my words? *I'm not going to let anything happen to you.*

I worked hard to keep my growing panic under control. And guilt. I'd promised her I would keep her safe.

To my eye so far, there wasn't any evidence to suggest that anything foul had taken place, but Stacey's fears weren't exactly unfounded. We had flown across the country looking for the viper's nest. It wasn't beyond reason to suspect that we'd been bitten.

I asked Becca if I could see the security camera footage. "Hell, no," was her response. "You walk in here all high-and-mighty and I rearrange my day to fly around in bad weather—looking for fucking *corpses*, thank you very much—and now you want to see my security footage when your friend takes a powder? Not happening."

I nodded. She had a point. "I'm sorry. You're right. But this really could be important. Is there someplace we can talk privately?"

"Yes. You may talk to me for as long as it takes to run your credit card for the flight."

"I'm paying cash. And I need to talk to you now."

She eyed me for a long moment. Then she walked into her office. I followed, and she motioned me toward a chair.

"I don't know who you are or what you're involved in," Becca said. "But I can't get tangled up in this. I live here. This is my business and my life. I built this from nothing. And it's hard enough to keep my pilots from running drugs and who knows what else during the off-season. I don't need trouble from… whatever the hell *you* are."

"That's fair," I said. "But this isn't about me or what I want."

I took a deep breath and explained in broad terms what had happened over the past two days. Becca was no idiot, and she had connected quite a few of the dots for herself already. What she hadn't known was that the people we were after had already victimized Stacey.

"Jesus," she said when I finished my summary. "Why the hell did you leave the girl here alone?"

That was the question that kept stabbing me in the chest. I'd left her there because I thought she'd be safe inside a locked office, inside a locked building, with a gun in her belt. The answer was rational. But it wasn't enough to assuage my guilt and anger.

"I'll have the rest of my life to second-guess my decision," I said. "But right now, I need your help."

But there was nothing on the camera feed. In fact, there was no camera feed covering the building's administrative section at all during the time in question. That feed had gone dark.

But the feed covering the operations desk was telling. It showed a middle-aged, unkempt-looking man with a limp and a strange expression on his face. The man sat in front of the bank of security monitors, manipulated one of the units, and the feed from the admin section went blank.

"Who is that?" I asked.

"My brother. He's our accountant. The security camera in that section of the building has been acting up for months now. Michael's been working on it off and on."

Working on it. That was one way to put it. I got that taste in my mouth again, the one that my body foists on me when it knows my world is going to shit, and the ringing in my ears intensified.

"Where is Michael right now?" I asked.

From her office phone, Becca dialed her brother's cell. We both heard his phone ring from where we sat. He'd left it in his office.

"Does he do that often?" I asked.

"I don't know," she said. "I never call him."

"But he's your accountant, right?"

She gave me a look. "How much accounting do you think a business like this requires?"

"You don't need a full-time accountant?"

"I barely need TurboTax. I do all the books myself."

"Why did you hire Michael?"

"Because somebody had to," Becca said.

I cocked my head and frowned a bit.

"Michael isn't like most people," she said.

"How so?"

She was silent a moment, maybe considering how much she wanted to tell me, maybe considering how she wanted to say it.

"He has no capacity for empathy," she finally said.

Alarm bells rang in my head.

"His therapist said that he does not experience compassion, kindness, or a vision of morality that normal people naturally share," she recited in a mocking singsong.

In other words, Michael Robinson was a psychopath.

I heard a door open at the far end of the hallway. The whine of aircraft engines invaded the office. An icy draft gave me a chill.

"Michael!" Becca called from her chair. "That you?"

Heavy, uneven footsteps sounded on the tile floor. A man appeared in Becca's office doorway. I recognized Michael Robinson's disheveled, middle-aged form from the security camera feed I'd viewed earlier. In his hand was a roll of electrical cable.

"Is that for the video camera?" Becca asked.

"It's acting up again," he said. His voice sounded normal. He looked at her and ignored me completely.

"I saw your note," Becca said. "Think that new cable's gonna do the trick?"

"Hope so."

Michael didn't elaborate and an awkward silence followed.

"Listen, Michael, you remember seeing a pretty brunette girl in here with Ms. Jameson earlier?" Becca nodded toward me.

Michael's eyes settled on me for the first time. Something went cold inside of me. His eyes were dead, like a shark's. I saw none of the normal things that happen when one human recognizes that he is in the focused presence of another. He observed me as if I were an object. I've been around these kinds of people many more times over the years than I cared to recall.

In fact, one of them had killed me. Thank the stars for modern medicine and defibrillators.

There was something else going on with him, too. His face was puffy and his eyes had a glazed quality to them. Maybe he'd been hitting the sauce.

"No," Robinson said, turning back to Becca. "Been in my office all day."

"She was asleep in my office when we left on our tour," Becca said.

"That so?"

"Didn't you walk past my office to get to the front desk and futz with the camera?"

"Must've done," Robinson said. "But I didn't snoop. Your office is your business, far as I'm concerned."

"You're sure?" I pressed. "It's very important that we find her."

"Sure as the tits on your chest."

"Dammit, Michael!" Becca snapped. "We've talked about this!"

"Well, jeez. I told ya no and that means no. I didn't see the girl."

Becca shook her head and waved her hand at him. "Off you go. Fix that camera. And watch your damn mouth around people."

She looked at me and shook her head. "I'm very sorry. That's why he works here. I got sick of everybody in town calling me to complain about another one of Michael's messes. He's like a child."

I smiled and shrugged. "No big deal. I've heard much worse."

My mind chewed on what Michael Robinson had said, and something didn't quite seem right. Aside from the creepy remark about my tits and the even-creepier dead-eyed, soulless look on the man's face, I mean. After a few seconds, it came into focus. I picked up on what might have been a strange choice of words. Robinson didn't say *a* girl. Or *any* girl.

Robinson said *the* girl. As if he'd known who Stacey was, despite his claim of not having seen anybody all day.

I ROSE FROM THE CHAIR IN BECCA'S OFFICE AND WALKED out into the hallway. I paced back and forth, stacking facts together, entertaining any conjecture my mind conjured about where Stacey might have gone, whether she went of her own volition, how this development might fit into the bigger picture.

The body in the forest on Isle Royale would provide a ton of clues, but there was a huge problem. Murder investigations often took months. I needed answers immediately. And it would be many hours before investigators could make their way to the remote location to work the scene. The worsening weather would only delay things further.

Another thought struck me. Posner and his vile brethren had planned to sell pay-per-view tickets to an atrocious event that he and his people were putting on at significant risk. They had boasted about how much money they would make. But wouldn't they have demanded at least a portion of the payment up front? When was the last time there had been any kind of public performance where tickets weren't available in advance? It had never happened, as far as I knew.

And for a pay-per-view setup with as much electronic security as the

"Snuff Fest" had to have—they were proudly documenting crimes that carried the death penalty in many countries around the world, for fuck's sake—there was undoubtedly an elaborate customer verification process. They had to have organized all of this well in advance.

So these men had probably already collected at least a portion of their bounty. But why all the gloating about the *future* payday while they gang-raped Stacey in the Philadelphia warehouse?

Then it hit me. The "Snuff Fest" impresarios suffered from the classic problem of doing illegal business anonymously: how the hell did you vouch for the other party? How could you be sure you weren't cozying up to an undercover police officer posing as an online thug? How could you be certain you weren't paying your hard-earned Bitcoin for a good time, only to have your name added to a federal indictment for your trouble?

The trust problem wasn't only a black-market problem. It also existed in above-board markets. And there was a particular kind of business that commanded high fees in return for bridging the trust gap between parties to a transaction. In real estate, they were called title companies. Banks often performed the same function in other business transactions. They acted as a neutral third party whose role was to ensure that the buyer had all the required funds to close the transaction, and to safeguard the buyer's funds until the sellers met all requirements for dispersal.

In other words, Snuff Fest needed a middleman. It was just too risky a venture to attempt without an escrow service.

Luckily, I knew the right guy to sniff them out. "Fix!" I yelled. "I need you!"

JANIE LAY CURLED IN A BALL ON HER CELL FLOOR. WHAT she wouldn't have given for a blanket. But they were probably afraid she'd choke herself to death with it. And they obviously wanted her alive, for the moment.

They'd at least brought her a space heater. Hypothermia would be bad for business, the man had said with a cackle. Though he was happy to have warmed her up momentarily, and she could go ahead and thank him for his kindness. Another cackle.

She had no more tears to cry. She'd never understood how a person could get to the point where they didn't care if they lived or died, but now Janie understood perfectly. She was there right now. In a deep part of her psyche, she had already given up on living. She knew that she would probably never again see the light of day. This wasn't something she spoke aloud, and her mind didn't form the words in its quiet recesses, either. It was as though she knew, but she was hiding it from herself so she wouldn't lose her mind.

There were more footsteps in the gravel outside her cell. Janie didn't stir. If they wanted to rape her again, there was nothing she could do about it.

And she had gotten used to it. She'd even learned to fake a little moan now and again. That way they were less likely to hurt her.

The footsteps stopped in front of Janie's door. She closed her eyes and clinched her fists. The chain rattled, the rusty hinges complained, and an icy wind made her curl up even tighter.

"Candyman," said a male voice. Janie opened her eyes. Another guy in jeans and flannel. But this one was older. Gray hair.

Something else was different about this one. He didn't have that lusty look in his eyes like the younger ones did. Maybe he was too old, and he couldn't get it up anymore.

"This won't hurt," he said, brandishing a hypodermic needle and syringe.

"Please, no," Janie pleaded. "No more. It hurts. Please, just leave me alone. I won't tell anyone."

The man's grip on her arm was surprisingly strong. She understood immediately what he was doing. He was getting the veins in her arm to stand out, so he could inject her.

She tried to kick and scream, but a blow to her stomach took all the wind out of her. She struggled for air and barely noticed the needle entering her arm.

It burned like nothing she had ever experienced before, as if he had injected pure acid into her vein. She cried out in fear and pain.

And suddenly, everything was...

Wonderful.

Absolutely amazing.

Blissful beyond words. She had never felt such an intense, powerful, all-encompassing sense of wellbeing. Her body flooded with warmth and comfort and contentment. This was the afterlife. It *had* to be. Everything was so *perfect*.

She looked at the man. She felt an overwhelming sense of love for him. She wanted to thank him for his kindness. She was so grateful that he had stopped by. He was undoubtedly the kindest person she had ever met. Maybe the kindest person she'd ever *heard of.* She tried to tell him so, but she couldn't find the words.

And then he left, and Janie was alone with her bliss.

31

THE BRUNETTE GIRL WAS BOUND AND GAGGED, BUT IT
didn't matter. She was comatose anyway and would undoubtedly remain that
way for most of the trip. Her limp form lay in a large dog carrier. A padlock
secured the gate to the cage. Cargo straps held it in place.

The big engine propelled the police K9 truck west on Highway 102.
Kaministiquia passed on the right, little more than a firehouse and a two-table
diner. Sistonens Corners was next, and the 102 ended at a T-intersection. The
driver turned north onto Highway 11/17, the Trans-Canada Highway.

The driver of the police K9 truck wasn't a police officer. In fact, he was
a convicted felon. At least, that was true before he officially became someone
else. As far as anyone from his former life could tell—those who cared enough
to speculate, anyway—the convicted felon had simply gone missing. Nobody
had cared to search for him, because he'd already done his time. In the eyes
of the justice system, he was rehabilitated.

Helluva joke, really. Prison was graduate school for crime. Everybody
knew it, yet they kept piling people into private, for-profit prisons, and people
kept serving brutally long sentences for bullshit offenses while judges and
politicians took bribes.

But prison was a lifetime ago. Things were different now.

Sort of. He was still in the felony business. If you needed something done, you could count on old Phil.

He was really a glorified delivery boy. Just like the job earlier in the day, picking up that Clarence character at the airport and hauling him to meet Karl's boys and Officer Sevier. There really wasn't much to it. But that suited Phil just fine. The money was good, and he'd seen too many ambitious pudknockers wind up with leaky gut syndrome or lead poisoning, as they used to say. He was perfectly content to earn six figures to obey the traffic laws and keep his mouth shut.

Of course, the unwritten rule was that if things ever went sideways, all of that money he'd taken from them over the years wasn't just water under the bridge. He'd pocketed their cash and built his life around their work, which meant that he'd damned sure better keep his mouth shut. About *everything*.

And they were serious about that rule. If word ever made it back to the bosses that anyone said even one word more than the Four Magic Words—*I want a lawyer*—comeuppance was swift and merciless. It didn't matter if you were in protective custody. They still got to you. Sometimes they even hired a cop to do it. If you ran your mouth, they would dirt you.

But Phil didn't worry about any of that. He understood the game. He'd long ago made peace with the fact that his would most likely be an early and violent death. In fact, he'd resolved that if things ever looked really messed up, he'd cap himself. Goodbye world. Thanks for the memories. He wasn't big on suffering or deprivation, and there was nobody in his life who would mourn his passing.

Still, Phil was in no hurry to get caught. Officer Sevier had told him how to disable the tracking device in the police vehicle without showing evidence of tampering, and Phil had taken great pains to follow Sevier's instructions to the letter.

He'd also been diligent about transporting the acid. Nasty stuff. Phil didn't know where they found it, especially in those kinds of quantities, but they said it was strong enough to dissolve steel. Hydro-fluoro-something.

The acid, plus Ontario's quarter-million freshwater lakes and hundred-thousand kilometers of rivers and streams, made Phil fairly confident that they could dispose of any kind of DNA evidence the evening's festivities might produce.

That shit wasn't his thing—he didn't see any need to kill a girl after you had your way with her—but who was he to judge? And anyway, the risk premium they paid him for the acid transport job had set him up pretty damn well. He knew better than to do anything flashy with the money, but he was sure as hell going to buy a new TV.

He heard a few bumps and thumps from the girl in the dog cage behind him. She was tied up good, and locked up besides, so he didn't worry about her making a break for it. Plus, that freak with the weird eyes and the strange limp had drugged the hell out of her, so Phil doubted she'd be able to do much even if she hadn't been packaged up like glassware.

He shook his head. That girl had a lot of pain in front of her. He didn't like it much, didn't understand why people would pay to see that shit, wasn't proud to be part of the whole thing.

But the girl's suffering would *have* to end at some point. It couldn't go on forever. Hell, that was the whole point, right?

32

THE CANDYMAN HAD GONE, AND IN HIS WAKE, everything in Janie's mind was sunshine, rainbows and unicorns. So much pleasance and love and joy. Why couldn't she just have found this state of mind earlier in her life? It would have changed everything for her. She saw the unity and connectedness of everything. There was no conflict. There was no struggle. Only the vast, amazing, loving symphony of life. Even her cold, dark cell seemed somehow welcoming.

The two men who came in after the Candyman were strong and handsome. Janie liked them right away. They spoke words that made no sense to her, but their voices sounded deep and masculine and attractive. Their musky scent was inviting. They wrapped her body in a fur coat. It was glorious and luxurious, and cozy and warm.

The men helped her out of her cell. There wasn't much daylight to speak of, but even the gray, dreary weather held an unspeakable beauty to Janie's eyes. Why hadn't she appreciated the miracle of clouds more fully before? Why were her eyes never fully open to such wonder and joy? Was it her mother's fault?

Janie's thoughts of her mother didn't produce any judgment or anger.

Mom had done the best she could manage under the strange circumstances of her life, Janie knew. And Janie loved her mother for trying so hard, for persevering, even though everything seemed hopeless. Janie wrapped warm, loving emotions around her mother, and formed a sincere intention to reconnect, to allow her mom to reenter her life. How could things not be different—better in every way—now that Janie suddenly knew the truth?

And such a simple truth. Everything is beautiful. Everything is valuable. Everything is precious, even the hard things. *Especially* the hard things.

"This changes everything," Janie said. Or at least, that's what she intended to say. Her words sounded foreign even to herself.

One man smiled at her, and Janie beamed back at him. He had such a strong jaw, and his shoulders were so masculine, and his eyes were so striking, piercing right through her in the best way. Janie wanted to get to know him better, and his friend too. What gods must they be? They were so beautiful and so kind.

Soon she was back indoors. There were bright lights—unusually bright. And warm. Janie wanted to take off her fur coat, and so she did, even though she had no clothes underneath, because what was there to be afraid of, and what was there to feel embarrassed about? The men smiled and applauded.

Janie heard other voices in the room. They were also hard to understand, but Janie understood on a deeper level that there was nothing but kindness and love behind the words.

They pointed her to a camera, and Janie smiled, her face beaming with joy and happiness. She waved at all of her friends who were surely watching on the other side of the lens. They would be so happy for her, for this incredible joy she had so recently discovered. Wouldn't they love to join her? Wouldn't it be amazing for them to experience this, too?

The men invited her to lie down on a soft, padded table in the middle of the room. Someone attached a heart rate monitor to her wrist. She heard the beep of each heartbeat amplified through a set of speakers. Janie thought the rhythm was pleasant and soothing.

One man poured oil on her body. He began touching her in the most exquisite way. It felt so amazing, the strength of his hands, but also their softness, and he had such skill. Her body responded instantly. The second man joined the first, and the sensations were like nothing in Janie's experience—so powerful, so exquisite, so pleasurable.

Soon a desire welled up deep within her, and it came to the surface, and her hands and her mouth and her body longed to give something back to the men. She thought of asking whether it would be okay if she touched them, but she somehow knew that it would be perfectly fine, and so she reached for them, and she found them hard and ready.

Slow and gentle at first, then faster and more furious, with a great deal of movement, and things she'd never dreamed of, strange positions that felt so wonderful. There was no pain, only pleasure and joy and enjoyment, and as her pleasure grew, one man wrapped his hands around her neck, and the pressure was intense and frightening, but in the best way, tighter and tighter, and she felt as if she might explode in pleasure, and her body bucked and rocked and stars formed in her eyes and it was hard to breathe but *so amazing*.

The pleasure went on and on and on, coming in waves, the most beautiful thing she had ever experienced. The ancient survival mechanisms were silenced at first by her intense orgasm, by the sheer, unadulterated *goodness* of the feelings filling her entire body, coursing through her entire being, but a small voice deep in her mind became louder, and more strident, *air, air, air, breathe, must breathe...*

Then came a sudden, pure, all-encompassing panic. Her body thrashed. Janie kicked and flailed, arms and legs a blur of motion, trying to reach the hands clasped around her neck, but she couldn't reach them, couldn't get them to let go, because someone else had restrained her wrists.

This lasted forever, for all of eternity, while Janie's panicked eyes filled with stars and her vision dimmed and her mind and lungs screamed for oxygen and her diaphragm spasmed and her arms and legs struggled against the men who held her.

Suddenly, there was wisdom and acceptance. *So this is death.* Janie stopped fighting its arrival. *This is the way of things, living and dying, and now must be my time.* She stopped fighting and welcomed the end, curious about how it would feel, but somehow certain that it would be okay.

Seconds later, Janie's heart beat its last.

33

IT DIDN'T LOOK MUCH LIKE A CONTROL ROOM—IT contained little more than a laptop and a portable hard drive—but that's what the production team was calling it.

Technicians quickly edited the video of Janie's death using FinalCut Pro, rendered it to MP4 format, scrambled it using 256-bit encryption, compressed the file size, and sent the file via Tor, an anonymizing web browser designed to obscure the origin and destination of the information "packets" that zipped between Internet servers all over the planet, to their guy in Belize.

The man in Belize—Castillo was his name but his online pseudonym was Reckoner—decrypted the file and verified its content. He used special software that used mathematical techniques to detect even the smallest amount of movement captured in video, such as the movement seen if a person were still breathing slowly, for example, instead of not breathing at all.

He let the software run for a full five minutes after the girl's heart rate monitor had flatlined. It was easy to fake a flatlined heart monitor. It was another thing for an adolescent girl to hold her breath for five full minutes.

Satisfied that the girl had indeed died on camera, and satisfied that the performers' faces and other distinguishing characteristics were obscured during editing, the Reckoner in Belize added the latest file to the queue. Only the last five murders were planned for broadcast in real-time. The first nineteen killings would be uploaded from Castillo's private server to a highly secure data facility in Novosibirsk, Russia. The Russian data farm would release the digital file for global enjoyment starting at nine p.m. US Eastern time.

Castillo the Reckoner had seen what was on the menu for the evening, and he knew that it would whip the audience into a frenzy by the time the last kid met her end.

Castillo sent an encrypted email to the banker in Panama. Part seven of the twenty-four-part delivery was complete and verified, the message read.

Castillo had wondered momentarily how the Panama banks had remained in business after a massive and highly publicized data breach had exposed the extent of the banking industry's involvement in global corruption, collusion, and crime. But he didn't wonder for long. Perversely, the exposure was probably *good* for Panama's business in the long run. Sure, the usual noises would be made about tighter regulation, but the trouble would ultimately just result in the banks getting away with a higher premium.

Moments later, the Reckoner in Belize received an encrypted response from Panama. Another one-twenty-fourth of the deal's total value was en route to the seller's accounts.

Back in the control room, the producers shared a round of high-fives to celebrate the news. A small vial of cocaine made the rounds, and each man bumped his buzz a little, just to keep the intensity up. There was still a lot of work left and many hours of celebration yet to come. Seven kills down, seventeen to go.

The early ones had been somewhat benign, as far as sexually fetishized murders went. Some strangulations, a bit of knife play, a broken neck—tame stuff, really, at least for people into the scene. They designed the early killings to be appetizers, to provide thrills and demonstrate bona fides, but the real fireworks were yet to come.

In fact, the demise of the next kid—a young Hispanic boy of around twelve or thirteen—would mark a real turning point. The crew members were already busy preparing the set. The main feature was a steel cage with meat hooks dangling from the ceiling. It would really be something to behold.

In back of the makeshift studio, Janie's body was being carefully lowered into a barrel made of specially formulated plastic. Hydrofluoric acid was no joke. One splash was enough to kill a person several times over. The men positioned the girl over the barrel using a winch and moved a safe distance away while the motor lowered her into the foul liquid.

As the disposal crew worked, the next performer walked past them on his way to the studio. The man was white, middle-aged, balding, and dressed in a suit and tie. He greeted the men in a clipped East Coast accent and carried a briefcase filled with sharp objects. On his face was eager anticipation.

I WATCHED AS FIX CHECKED FOR INCOMING MESSAGES
on his laptop. He was using an obscure message board on the Dark Web. I had
helped him find the right wording for the request he had sent out moments
earlier, asking for help to stop a series of killings scheduled for later in the day.

"Don't get your hopes up," he said. "The people involved in this kind
of thing are *extremely* careful about letting outsiders in. Even the customers
have no idea about the business arrangements on the back end. They just send
their Bitcoin to a certain account, and that's it. Maybe they'll get a link that
points to a secure portal somewhere, but even that will be hard to decipher."

I nodded my understanding. There was another factor working against
us. People willing to murder kids for kicks would have no qualms taking
out an informant. And the fundamental operating principle governing illicit
transactions on the DarkNet was that you were never safe. You were always
at risk of being "doxed"—having your real identity exposed by hackers or
the authorities.

Even the best hackers in the world lived in constant fear of being doxed.
No matter how thorough your privacy protection measures were, and no
matter how diligent you might be in trying to disassociate the digital artifacts

of your real existence from your online DarkNet persona, there was never any way to guarantee your own safety and security. The security game has always been an arms race, with the particularly nasty characteristic that it was impossible to know whether you were in trouble until it was way too late to do anything about it.

So there was almost no chance that anyone would step forward to share knowledge of how the Snuff Fest monsters might have engineered the financial transaction. There was probably only a handful of people who knew any of the details, and they were not at all likely to drop a dime on their companions.

Still, it never hurt to ask. Sometimes criminals make mistakes. Better to have a small army of concerned citizens—fellow criminals, yes, but not all crimes are equal, and I had to believe that there were plenty of people who had no qualms buying recreational drugs, for example, but whose stomachs turned at the mere thought of an abomination like Snuff Fest. Maybe someone would hear whispers of something, and that would lead to a breakthrough.

But we couldn't count on it. "Is there anything else we can do right now?" I asked Fix.

The normal gleam in his eyes was missing as he looked at me with a somber expression and shook his head. "I'm out of ideas."

I looked at my watch. Two p.m. Seven hours to go. All of those kids. All of those lives. The helplessness was unbearable. I wanted to explode.

35

"BULLSHIT," I SAID. "I DON'T ACCEPT THIS. WE WILL BEAT these assholes or die trying."

I started my bossy traffic cop routine. "Becca, please file a missing persons report with the local police for Stacey. And can you also please look through the security footage at the front desk and print out a still photo showing Stacey's face?"

She gave me a strange look for a second—one Alpha deciding whether to challenge the other Alpha in the room—then she nodded at me and picked up her office phone.

I turned to Fix. "Please get in touch with Evil and ask her to give me an update from her National sources. I want to know if she's seeing any additional RFID tags with similar characteristics to the first three. And let me borrow your cell phone."

"Do you want fries with that, ma'am?" he asked me.

"Hold the salt," I said.

I took his phone and dialed a number I knew by heart. I expected that I would have to use our Fibonacci code, because I was using Fix's cell phone and the number on the caller ID display might be unfamiliar, but I was wrong. Dan Gable picked up on the first ring.

"I figured it was you," he said. "Listen, I'm in the middle of something and I don't have much time, but there's something you should know. Someone pulled up a facial recognition hit on you near the police station the night of the murder."

Shit. I'd been miles beyond careful when I'd paid my visit to Frederick Posner. Paranoid, more like it. But there were so many damned cameras. It was impossible to avoid them all. "That's crazy. Must be a mistake."

"From an ATM camera in front of the building across the street from the front entrance," Dan said.

It didn't make any sense at all. I didn't use the front entrance to Posner's building, and I'd never have missed an ATM camera. I'm not the world's best at counter-surveillance, but I'm no amateur, either. There's a reason I'm still alive and kicking after twenty years in the spy game.

"That can't be right," I said. "I was never there, Dan."

Which was technically true. I was never *in front* of Posner's building.

"I'm just telling you what the Philadelphia police department reported," Dan said.

Suddenly it came into focus. "Dan, we need intel on the Philly cops. This is obviously a setup. I need to know how deep Posner's corruption reaches down to the rank and file."

"I'm on it."

I was sure that Dan knew who splattered Posner. But he was smart enough not to press me on it. And he was a good sport for playing along with me over the phone line, which I knew was being recorded. All calls in and out of the Department of Homeland Security were archived and stored permanently.

"Listen, Dan, things have turned to shit up here." I took a minute to bring him up to speed on Stacey's disappearance, the dead body we found during our helicopter search of Isle Royale, Mike Robinson's strange behavior, and Fix's recent request for intel from his business contacts.

"Sam, I'm really worried about those kids," Dan said. Translation: this situation is fucked up like polio and your investigation is dead in the water.

"Me too," I said. "I'm foundering here."

Dan was quiet for a moment. Over the phone connection I could hear his fingers drumming against his desk, usually a good sign that the gears were turning in his head.

"Sam, let me run some nodal and geographic analysis on the three RFID tags you mentioned. I'll overlay the signals on top of cell phone signals, computer wi-fi, IP addresses, rental car trackers, etcetera. Maybe we'll come up with something."

It was a long shot. That kind of analysis took enormous computational power, and it took time to set things up properly so you didn't wind up with reams of BS to sift through. It couldn't be done properly in just a few hours.

And that was assuming you had all the necessary data. But some information required a successful liaison arrangement with a few three-letter bureaucracies. Which was about as easy as passing a healthcare law.

"Thanks, Dan," I said. I could hear the defeat in my voice.

"Be careful, Sam."

I'd barely hung up with Dan when Fix tapped me on the shoulder. "Listen, I know you didn't want to hear about this earlier, but I have to tell you something."

He told me about an encounter with the tough old redneck called Karl and his band of dimwitted heavies. And he told me about Officer Sevier's entrepreneurial arrangement with any and all criminals who cared to do business in and around Thunder Bay.

Holy hell, was there anybody left on Earth in a position of authority who wasn't on the take? But I didn't see how that knowledge might help us in our current predicament, with the clock racing onward toward nightfall and our investigation stalled completely.

"Why are you telling me this now?" I asked.

"Sam, Officer Sevier just walked through the front door."

"FIX, YOU NEED TO STAY OUT OF SIGHT," I TOLD HIM AS I watched Officer Sevier of the Thunder Bay Police stride into the helicopter tour reception area. I gave Fix a shove toward the far end of the administration wing of the building. "But don't go far. I'll need you soon."

I strode quickly to join Becca and the crooked cop in the lobby.

"That was fast," Becca said to Sevier.

"I was in the neighborhood when the call went out," Sevier said. Becca eyed him with a bit of wariness. I got the sense there was some kind of history between them.

"Sam Jameson," I said, extending my hand to the officer to break up what had become an awkward silence.

He sized me up like only a beat cop can. "Pleasure, ma'am," he said, but somehow the politeness landed like condescension.

"So how long has the girl been missing?" Sevier asked.

"Just a couple of hours," I said. "But the circumstances are quite unusual."

"What might those unusual circumstances be?" Sevier's face betrayed nothing, but the word choice showed no small amount of skepticism on his part.

There were two different complications at play, I realized. The first was Sevier's personality. He seemed like a bit of an asshole. And the second was the fact that Sevier was dirty, at least if Fix was correct, and there was no reason not to believe Fix's account of his recent shakedown. Given that Sevier was on the take, I figured that he might be a source of information about what had happened to Stacey.

But crooked cops are good at covering their tracks, and they're good at resisting any kind of leverage. So I would have to use an approach that I'm not known for: finesse.

"Maybe we can talk somewhere more private?" I suggested.

Sevier made a point of looking around the empty helicopter tour office. It was just us and the cobwebs in the corners, so my request for additional privacy probably struck him as a little silly. But he nodded and smiled. "Lead the way."

But I wasn't quite ready to go to work on Officer Sevier the Crooked Canadian Cop. "Maybe Becca can find us some coffee? And I need to visit the ladies' room."

Which was not false. But neither was it completely true. I made use of the ladies' room facilities. I also sent an urgent but detailed text message to Dan Gable.

"I feel like a new person," I said as I joined Sevier and Becca in a small conference room that smelled of mildew and burnt coffee.

There was a strange look on Becca's face, and there was a hardness on Sevier's, and my intuition grew stronger about some kind of history between the two of them. Were they once an item? Had it ended poorly?

"Lucky coincidence that you were so close by," I said. "I'm really concerned about Stacey."

It was important to use her name. I wanted Stacey to be a real person in Sevier's mind. If he had something to do with Stacey's disappearance, I wanted to use every trick in the book to get information out of him.

And the *lucky coincidence* bit was actually a subtle shot across the bow. Maybe I was way off the mark, and maybe I was making an ass of myself — wouldn't have been the first time all day—but I was setting Sevier up for something and I wanted his mind to churn defensively.

Sevier shrugged. "Thunder Bay isn't that big a city, Ms. Jameson. Our response time is good everywhere in town."

"That's great," I said. "Becca, can we please see that picture of Stacey?"

I watched Sevier's face closely as he picked up the still photo from the security camera situated behind the front desk in the reception area. I thought I saw a twitch in the corner of one eye, but I couldn't be sure.

"Pretty girl," he said. "Any reason she might have taken off on her own?"

I shook my head. "None that we're aware of. And she had every reason *not* to."

Sevier arched his eyebrows. "She's young. Sometimes it's hard to know what people that age are thinking."

I nodded. "Sure. But not always."

Fix's phone vibrated in my pocket. Text message. I really hoped it was from Dan Gable, but I didn't look.

"Ms. Jameson, young people pick up and leave all the time. It's only been a couple of hours. Maybe she was hungry and whatnot. Maybe she needed to stretch her legs or something. Or maybe she was too self-absorbed and whatnot to leave you a note."

I nodded serenely and waited. It was time for Sevier to reassert his authority.

He didn't disappoint. He frowned and rubbed his chin. "And I'm not terribly clear on your relationship with the girl. Tell me more about that."

It wasn't lost on me that he didn't use Stacey's name. I took it as a bad omen. I also took his question as an opportunity to fire another shot across the bow.

"I'm not at liberty to discuss the nature of my relationship with Stacey," I said.

Sevier took it in stride. There was no surprise on his face. Which struck me as an admission.

"Maybe now would be a good time for me to have a look at your ID," Sevier said.

"Sure thing. Let me go get it."

unkemptI walked out into the hallway, fished in my pants pocket, and found Fix's phone. I'd felt the vibration of an incoming text message a few minutes earlier, and I held my breath as I looked at the screen. *Please, Dan.*

Sure enough, my man in DC had come through again. In our long tenure together at Homeland, Dan had saved my bacon more times than I could count, and I resolved to buy him a better Christmas gift this year.

"It's queued up to the spot you asked for," the message read. Then, in signature fashion: "And this better be worth the trouble."

I clicked on the link, previewed the audio, walked down the hallway and had a brief word with Fix, and strolled back into the conference room.

"I must have left my ID and badge in my other pants," I said, the *badge* part implying that I still held some sort of official status, which I definitely did not. "But I was able to find this."

I pressed the little sideways triangle on Fix's phone and turned up the volume. Sevier's voice crackled over the tiny speaker.

"But this kind of service has its costs. And seeing as how you're new up here, and not familiar with the way things work, we thought we'd take a minute to explain, just so there's no misunderstanding or whatnot. So the VAT is fifteen percent of the total transaction value."

Sevier's jaw clenched. He shot daggers at me with his eyes.

"It's a little toy called Twizzler," I said with a smile. "It doesn't officially exist, of course. But you don't have to have your phone powered on in order for Big Brother to listen to what you say."

Sevier's face reddened. "Means nothing. And we have laws up here. You can't just tap my phone."

I shook my head. "It wasn't your phone, officer."

Fix's timing was perfect. He opened the conference room door and took the seat beside me.

"Hi, officer," Fix said. "Nice to see you again."

37

HE WAS NERVOUS AS HELL, AND IT HAD TAKEN SOME convincing before he had agreed to take this risk. But I was proud of Fix. Say what you want about his chosen occupation, but the man had courage and scruples. Another reminder for me that legality and morality don't overlap as much as we think.

Fix's opener was beautiful. "I'm not sure how much our venture here will be worth," he said to Officer Sevier, "but I'm prepared to make a down payment on our fifteen percent VAT."

Sevier's face turned a deep shade of red and the veins stuck out of his neck. He was one pissed off corruptocrat.

But we hadn't finished. We were just getting to the good part. "You probably think you're safe because your boss is also on the take," I said. "But you're both amateurs. Small-time. You were in way over your heads and you didn't even know it. You left digital evidence everywhere, and you're both going away for a long time."

Sevier seethed. But he was smart enough to keep his mouth shut. I stared into his eyes and I saw the familiar panoply of emotions play out behind them. It's always fun to gut an asshole who deserves it.

As I stared Sevier down, I noted Becca's reaction in my peripheral vision. She sat shaking her head and looking at her hands. As if none of this business with Sevier was a surprise to her. She knew him well enough to know of his corruption. Maybe that's why they were no longer an item. Or maybe I was making shit up again in my head. Happens from time to time.

I could see on Sevier's face that he had conceded this round to me. But I also saw that the war had just started. That was unfortunate, because I needed his full cooperation, and the hardness in his eyes and the forward jut of his chin told me he was nowhere near broken enough for me to put a saddle on him and ride him all the way to Posner's posse.

Negotiating 101: never break the silence. So I waited Sevier out. Fix followed my lead and kept his mouth shut. Becca remained unnaturally interested in her cuticles.

"What do you want?" Sevier finally asked, his voice controlled but barely.

I told Sevier what I wanted. And everybody in the room thought I had lost my mind.

BECCA LOOKED AT ME, EYES WIDE WITH DISBELIEF.

"Jesus H.," Fix said. "You can't be fucking serious."

My demand of Sevier had caught them totally off guard.

But Sevier got it. He understood. I was speaking his language. Sevier knew where I was coming from, and that put us on terms that he could appreciate.

"Half is too much," he said. "I can't do it. I have expenses too."

"Fine," I said. "Then I want forty percent of every dime you have earned and every dime that you *will earn* on this thing with the girl."

We were negotiating, but that meant I had already won. Sevier believed he could work with me, cut a quick deal, and it wouldn't cost him his life and his family and his future. It was an out, a lifeline, and he was no idiot. The cost was nothing compared to the benefit. He'd probably already planned how he would spend that dirty money, but those plans could wait. There would be other opportunities, but not if he wound up in jail.

And what were the odds that if he were arrested and charged, they'd let him go to trial in the first place? One of his former associates would surely take him out long before he sang.

I'd made it sound like I was driving a hard bargain, but I was offering him his freedom for peanuts. It didn't take a rocket scientist to know that this was the deal of the century. Sevier held out for the sake of pride and showmanship, then nodded his agreement.

But I wasn't done. I couldn't let him suspect that he was being set up for something worse. I had to keep pressing for more.

"To be clear," I said, "I mean that you will give me forty percent of *everything* these guys are paying you. For *everything* you're doing for them. Not just for Stacey's abduction. For the whole fucking mess."

He looked at me and blinked a few times.

Fix looked like he'd lapsed into stuporous catatonia.

Becca's expression was eerily blank. She'd had her suspicions about me from the outset, and my play seemed to confirm something in her mind. I'd have to deal with that later. Truth be told, I was having some suspicions of my own about Becca.

"You're out of your mind," Sevier said, shaking his head. "I can't do forty on the whole deal."

It was not lost on me that Sevier had made no protest about the accusation that he had been involved in Stacey's abduction. Another admission. I squashed down the anger. I wanted to hurt this man.

"No problem," I said, standing up from the seat. "I just need to make a quick phone call."

I didn't make it two steps before Sevier caved. "Wait!" he said.

I turned around with raised eyebrows.

"I'll make it work," Sevier said, his jaw working. "But you gotta handle this the way I say. Otherwise you'll get us all killed."

THE MAN CALLED PHIL DOUBLE-CHECKED THE DIRECTIONS

against the map he'd pulled from the dashboard. Confused about what he saw, he retraced his steps in his mind again, following his route all the way back to the start, hoping he hadn't made a mistake somewhere along the way.

The downside of being a glorified errand boy was that if you ever fucked up one of your errands, it was hard to make a compelling argument against being replaced. It wasn't as if obeying traffic laws and keeping your mouth shut about who might or might not be strapped down in the cargo section was a high-end skill. You didn't exactly need a graduate degree. You just needed a certain willingness to live on the fringe, and that wasn't nearly as uncommon as one might expect.

"Dammit," Phil said. He wished he'd had his cell phone. That way he'd be able to call Karl and double-check everything. But the instructions were very clear: no electronics of any kind. His fancy computerized wristwatch had to stay behind, too. Pure old-school for this job. Which Phil understood. Even though Canada didn't have the death penalty, what they had was much worse: a mandatory life sentence for first-degree murder. Phil shuddered at the thought.

"Naw," he said aloud to himself after mentally retracing his steps for a third time. "This is the right spot. Has to be." Everything checked out. He had missed no turns, and he had triple-checked all the road names.

In some cases "road" was a stretch. Out here, people might use the word to describe a game trail.

Phil scratched his head. It made little sense. He was expecting a hideout, a place where they could keep two dozen kids under wraps with no one the wiser. But that's not what he saw.

In front of him lay a flat field full of brown, winter-dead, windblown grass. No structures. No fences. No signs. No hints of civilization.

What Phil wouldn't have given for just one phone call. He panicked a little. There had to have been a mistake. Would he take the blame for it? Would he miss the deadline?

Would he be replaced?

Which meant that he would be *disappeared,* too.

Relief flooded him when he heard the low growl of aircraft engines, distant and faint at first, then growing unmistakably louder.

The twin-engine turboprop cut its throttles, settled to a bouncy landing, and growled a throaty roar as it used reverse-thrust to slow down.

Phil's relief was complete a minute later when Trevor's hulking form stepped out of the passenger's seat, and the pilot joined him a moment after.

"Got something for us?" the big lummox asked.

"Maybe I do," Phil said.

ALMA GUTIERREZ WAS NEARLY BESIDE HERSELF. SHE hadn't slept in days and she wasn't eating. Her worry over Alejandro had completely consumed her life. She'd used up all of her remaining sick days at work to spend her time looking for him.

He was a good kid. That's what she kept telling the law enforcement people in Fort Worth. He got all A's and B's in school. He played the trumpet. He was on the high school debate team. He built things in his brother's wood shop. Yes, his hair was a little long and he wore jeans with holes in them. But Alejandro was straight as an arrow. He didn't run with the wrong crowd. He didn't run with any crowd at all. He was too busy with school and sports and music. Alejandro had never even been late for dinner. Not once.

So Alma Gutierrez knew something was terribly wrong. He would never just pick up and leave. And all of Alejandro's things were still in his room. It just made no sense. He would have taken *something* with him if he had run away from home, right?

"Ms. Gutierrez," the Fort Worth police officer said in a soothing tone. "Kids come and go all the time. Even the responsible ones. They're still children, and they still have a lot of growing up to do. Boys especially. You're *sure* there were no signs that Alejandro might have been unhappy at home?"

Alma Gutierrez shook her head, struggling to keep her patience. "There were none. He's a hard worker and sometimes he gets stressed out about school or something. But our family doesn't fight. We have a good relationship."

"And there aren't any new relationships in Alejandro's life? A girlfriend, maybe?"

She was thoughtful for a moment. "There was a girl he talked about, someone he liked at school. But I don't think it went anywhere."

"Could Alejandro be upset about that?"

"Officer," Alma Gutierrez said, "Alejandro has been gone for four days. He went to school in the morning and didn't come home. This is the third time I've tried to get something done about it. Maybe he *felt* upset about a girl. I don't know. But four days?" She shook her head. "No way. Not my Alejandro. He would never put his family through that."

The cop nodded. "We've already got him in the system, ma'am. Hopefully something will turn up soon. I'm very sorry this has happened, and we'll do everything we can to help you find your son."

Alejandro's mother wiped her eyes. "Thank you," she said.

"It would be helpful if you could give us a few more pictures of him. Everything goes into the computer now, and more information is better."

Alma Gutierrez nodded. She'd expected this and had brought a USB drive full of over a hundred pictures of Alejandro that she'd taken over the past couple of years. She found the memory stick in her purse and handed it over to the policeman.

"I'll get these in the system right away," the officer said. "Hopefully something will turn up soon."

THE MEN IN CHARGE OF THE MAKESHIFT PRODUCTION

studio on the Canadian tundra had strictly forbidden cell phones and other electronic devices. In fact, those items weren't allowed on site at all. All performers, and all members of the production and cleanup crews, understood the consequences of violating this order. And the organizers were serious. A crew searched everyone upon arrival, and thoroughly. The risk was simply too high.

But it took a certain set of personality traits for a person to perform in the production underway inside the studio. Leading the kinds of lives they led also required certain skills, and most of them were adept at sneaking around and hiding things, even from the people closest to them in their everyday lives. The performers in the production weren't exactly model citizens, and they weren't always agreeable to being told what to do. Even when the instructions were in everyone's best interest. Even when the rule was strictly enforced, and even when the consequences were potentially dire.

One performer had recently finished his work. He was flush with exhilaration, adrenaline, and post-ejaculatory wellbeing. He felt larger than life. Invincible. Someone transcendent, towering over the plebs and proles he shared the planet with. His session with the teenaged boy had proven yet again to the performer that he wasn't merely some office drone, puttering through life, wasting his time putting cover sheets on TPS reports and trying to look attentive in corporate meetings.

The performer was a destroyer, an angel of death.

And he wanted a memento. It was his thing. Lots of people like him collected them. He understood it was risky, but it went with the territory. He took the right precautions, hid them the right way, did all the right cyber stuff. He wasn't foolish about it. Which was to say, given the insanity and foolishness of keeping photographic evidence of the grisliest kinds of crimes, he was at least appropriately concerned about keeping the photos and videos private.

The performer had carefully read the arrival instructions and knew what to expect. He had brought none of the items that he normally used to document his conquests.

But he had brought a highly unusual item. Remarkably inexpensive. Highly innovative. A pair of clear-lens eyeglasses, purchased at the Urban Spy website for $149 USD. The video camera lens was invisible. The unit had a built-in wi-fi antenna and was Bluetooth-enabled. It looked like a normal pair of eyeglasses.

And it had recorded the entire performance from his first-person vantage point. Every scream, every howl, every crack of bone. Even the money shot.

The performer's face appeared locked in a permanent, blissful smile as he handed his soiled clothes to the cleanup crew. He cleaned his body of the young man's blood, changed into street clothes, and climbed into the van that would take him back to the airport.

He'd have loved to stay and watch the remaining performances. There were still ten of them to go, and some of them sounded epic. He would have learned a great deal that he could later incorporate into future *sessions*, as he called them. But that wasn't in the cards. For security reasons, the performers weren't allowed to lay eyes on each other. So he settled into a languorous ease as the driver guided the van through traffic, reminiscing about the magnificent, unbelievable things he had just done, things that before today he had only dreamed of doing to another human being.

It seemed like a dream, like it hadn't really happened. Was it even real? His smile broadened. *Definitely real.*

But there was a problem, the same problem he always had, which was that enough was never enough. Each *session* sated his appetites for the moment. But that feeling never lasted. There was always more to explore. So every indulgence, exquisite and satisfying as it might have been at the moment, only ended up whetting his appetite.

More. Bigger. Better.

That was part of the reason for keeping mementos. Finding an outlet for proclivities like his was fraught with risk. So the videos helped. He would get off on them a few times, and that would extend the time between *sessions*. Because sessions were risky. Each time he indulged himself, it raised the odds of his capture. Nobody was perfect, and risky as the videos were, he ultimately viewed them as insurance.

The van driver dropped him off at the airport curb without a word. Just a quick one-day trip. The wife thought he was away on business. The boss thought he was touring a local college with his daughter. Good thing the wife and the boss had stopped sleeping together, he thought, or his cover might have seemed suspect.

The performer retrieved his backpack from the Admiral Club's concierge. He grabbed a beer, took a seat in the VIP lounge, pulled his phone and laptop from the backpack, and sifted through his email.

Eric from legal was still banging on about something in the recent contract negotiations with Symington Electric. The performer thought Eric from legal would have been a perfect candidate to star in an upcoming *session*, but that would have been a foolish play. Best not to shit where you sleep, as the saying went.

In the background, while the performer fired off a few noncommittal replies to the death-by-corporate-bullshit-nonspeak messages that crowded his inbox, the Urban Spy eyeglasses recognized the performer's phone, and the phone recognized the eyeglasses, and they performed a digital handshake, after which the video footage began automatically uploading.

The phone automatically sent all new photos and videos to an online server touted to be highly secure and built around privacy, the best money could buy, so your data was safe even if you dropped your phone in the toilet and it was also safe from hackers, and multiple copies were made, all stored on redundant servers, encrypted of course, again the best that money could buy.

The performer smiled as he thought about how much fun he would have watching the video of his performance. His wife had some kind of work function and his daughter was going to a basketball game at her high school, so the evening would be his to spend as he pleased.

He knew exactly how he would pass the time.

I ASKED FIX TO MEDIATE THE CRYPTO PAYMENT FROM Officer Sevier. Fix set up a few new cryptocurrency wallets, which were really not wallets at all, but account numbers containing a public name that matched a private key.

The concept was deceptively simple. If you wanted to make a payment to someone, you really just made an announcement. It had to have a certain format, and a bunch of computer-geek stuff went into verifying you had the funds, and more computer-geek stuff went into recording your payment in a way that kept it safe from future alteration. That's where the cryptography came in, and even with my limited understanding of the specifics, I had to admit the whole thing was a stroke of genius.

On the other end, receiving payments required no effort on your part. The entire world simply recognized that so-and-so had transferred some specific amount of money to your account. The entire world now agreed that the money belonged to you. If you wanted to spend that money by paying it to someone else, you had to prove that you were the account's owner. This is where the private key to your account came in. You used it to "log in" to your account, which, as Fix explained, really wasn't what was happening. But the rest of his sentence made my eyes glaze over, and I stopped paying attention.

The important thing was that Officer Sevier was now officially in my pocket. He had paid what amounted to a bribe to keep me from revealing his long record of criminal complicity. Bribery begets bribery.

Fix knew what to do from here. He would work with Dan to follow the money. The money that Sevier had paid me was more than likely dirty money, which came from other criminals. If you could piece together the transactions, you could form a roster of associates that Sevier had done illicit business with recently.

But this was much easier said than done. Any competent criminal knows to take precautions. Digital currency transfer is permanent, and all transactions remain in a permanent and unalterable record. So covering your tracks requires playing games with the account numbers. In effect, every transaction requires laundering. Criminals split transactions into a tangle of smaller transactions sent between brand new accounts that have never been used before. Unraveling the thicket requires massive computing power and a very sophisticated approach.

State intelligence agencies were good at things like that. Most people think the impetus behind "reining in" the digital currency phenomenon is reducing crime. This isn't false—police agencies love to arrest perps, and spy agencies love to burn the other country's agents, but that's not the real motivator behind developing effective cryptocurrency tracking procedure. The real reason Uncle Sam spent so much time and effort trying to crack that code is government greed. The Internal Revenue Service wanted its slice of every cryptocurrency transaction.

And the government also wanted the ability to shut crypto down, or take it over entirely, when the inevitable currency crisis strikes. And most people in the know have no doubt that such a day is coming. Probably sooner rather than later.

Dan and Fix had their work cut out for them, and so did I. I hustled out of the HeliTours building and waited by the passenger door of Officer Sevier's police cruiser. The weather seemed to let up, at least for the moment, and that evil wind had subsided. But I hoped he would arrive sooner rather than later. There wasn't much daylight left.

Sevier arrived five minutes later. "What in the hell do you think you're doing?" He said as soon his eyes found me.

"Congratulations. I'm your new partner. At least for the moment."

He laughed. "Lady, you've got some balls. Anyway, it's against department policy."

My turn to chuckle. "Kind of like bribery?"

"No ma'am. I'm paid up. You don't get to hold it over me again and again."

I shook my head. "You made a down payment. That doesn't buy you anything but a little time. And I will be in your knickers every step of the way until we see this thing through."

He looked around, suddenly aware that our conversation was taking place in a public situation. He used his fob to unlock the cruiser and motioned for me to get inside.

"So just what do you think we will do together?" Sevier asked as I pulled on my seatbelt.

"I have all sorts of fun activities planned for us. But first on my list, you helped Mike Robinson move Stacey somewhere. I want to know where."

He shook his head. "No way. Not part of the deal. And anyway, you don't get paid if you interfere with the job!"

"Officer Sevier," I said, "that's nothing for you to worry your pretty little head about. Right now, I want you to start this car and take me to Stacey."

From the look on Sevier's face, there were a few thoughts whizzing around in his skull. But he didn't think nearly long enough or hard enough, and when he started the car and said, "Okay then," I knew that we would have trouble.

SEVIER HAD CAPITULATED TOO SOON. DESPITE WHAT HE
said, he had no plans to take me to Stacey. He might show me where she'd
been taken, but Stacey wouldn't be there.

Plus, the whole thing had a not-*that*-briar-patch vibe to it. Sevier had
worked to make my demand seem unreasonable, but he hadn't worked hard
enough. In my desperation to find Stacey and the rest of those kids, I had
stumbled through some kind of opened door, and Sevier was working hard
to disguise his glee at the sudden windfall. I felt like the jumping fish that
landed in the fisherman's boat.

My objective had to change. But to what?

And then the car was in gear and we were moving and I was officially
along for the ride.

I had no backup. Fix already had his work cut out for him, tracing the
cryptocurrency accounts that Sevier had used to pay his bribe. Was there a
discreet way to alert him I had possibly, maybe… okay, *definitely* fucked up?

The phone in my purse was Fix's phone. I could Google the HeliTours
phone number and ask Becca to put him on the line, but what would I say to
Fix while Sevier overheard my half of the conversation?

Sevier sped up well past the speed limit. We were heading east on Arthur Street, and it looked like Sevier was getting ready to merge onto highway 61 heading north.

I thought about calling Dan again. But how much could he do from his desk in DC? Thunder Bay was a couple thousand miles and an entire world away. I might as well have been on the moon.

I was alone.

I had trouble keeping my mind from flashing back to one of the worst nights of my life. I had been trapped in a car with a piece of shit named Donald John. I drove while he pointed a gun at me. His directions took us to the cabin in the mountains, where my world shattered into a thousand pieces.

My breathing grew shallow and my heart beat fast. Sevier's face took on an ominous quality. He had a taser and a nightstick and a sidearm. And he had friends with a vested interest in making sure I didn't find Stacey or any of the other kids whose lives would end in just a few hours. On my side was a Russian-made pistol that I'd never fired before—and it was buried in my purse. I shook my head and cursed myself under my breath. Had I played right into his hand?

If so, did I have any other choice?

Breathe. Think. Look around. An answer is usually right in front of you. I forced myself to step outside my growing panic.

Sevier sped up the ramp and merged with the sparse northbound traffic on Highway 61. His cell phone buzzed. He took it out, looked at the text message, worked his thumbs over the little keyboard while driving with his knees. The picture of public safety.

I looked closely at the police cruiser's interior. A small laptop computer stood on a stand bolted to the center console. It angled away from me, and I couldn't see the information displayed on the screen. Beneath the laptop was a radio.

The cruiser had a standard plexiglass perp cage separating the front and back. On the plexiglass was a bracket holding a shotgun, oriented vertically with the barrel pointing up.

It was a mistake for Sevier to let me ride in the passenger's seat. I could make too much trouble for him. But I supposed he was working the psychological angle, allowing me to feel comfortable and trusted. Maybe he hoped I would let my guard down.

But that wasn't happening.

Sevier passed cars as if they were standing still. I hadn't seen him switch on the emergency lights, but the way cars moved over for us made it seem likely that he had. Or maybe it was the Canadian politeness.

The Bright Idea Fairy hadn't yet alighted on my shoulder and whispered an elegant solution to my colossal fuckup, so I scanned the cruiser's interior again, this time forcing myself to go more slowly.

Shotgun. Locked in place with a fingerprint ID scanner. Not that it would have been much use in such close quarters.

Radio. The frequency setting was 451.31. I didn't know if that piece of information would be useful, but there it was, so I took a moment to imagine using my fingers to dial those digits on a phone pad. It helped to solidify the memory.

Computer. Some Dell piece of crap. I wondered if it crashed all the time like my computers at Homeland used to do. The display was polarized and angled away from me, so I couldn't see any of the information. But taped across the top border of the monitor was a white sticker with black lettering. TBPD0659. Thunder Bay Police Department unit 0659, I figured.

An idea was forming. It had implications, and serious ones. But maybe it was time to set aside my reservations and use the tools at my disposal, regardless of the baggage in my head. A tool was only a tool, right? What mattered was how you used it.

But that was the problem. My own tragedy motivated me far too much. I had murdered a man in cold blood because I thought he deserved it.

Hell, he *had* deserved it. But that kind of thinking couldn't be applied at scale, and if there was one thing that Capstone was good for, it was discovering—at scale—exactly who needed killing. But there was a word for that kind of behavior, using the world's most powerful and pervasive surveillance apparatus to mete out punishment as you saw fit and to hell with what anyone else might think about it. The word was tyranny.

A highway interchange came up, and Sevier took the exit for westbound traffic on Highway 11/17, the Trans-Canada Highway.

Somehow the words "Trans-Canada" were less than comforting.

One nanosecond later, we exited the booming metropolis of Thunder Bay. There was nothing in the windshield now but roadway and frozen wilderness.

Ostensibly, Sevier was taking me to see Stacey. But in reality, I was pretty sure he was taking me to be taken care of.

I had to make a move, and right fucking now.

A LITTLE TIP ABOUT DECEPTION: DETAIL IS USEFUL. THE more vivid a picture you can create in your mark's mind, the better your odds he will bite. As long as your play is believable. You can't draw a vivid picture of little green men on Mars, for example. But if you're a woman, you could easily say something like this: "Listen, Sevier, this is kind of embarrassing and the timing is not good, but I need to find a restroom."

"Really?" he said. "You went to the bathroom twice while we were talking at Becca's."

"This is a different issue," I said. "Related to the phases of the moon. Although sometimes it sneaks up on me. And if you don't stop, you will have a mess to clean up."

There was a brief and involuntary look of disgust on his face, then a reluctant nod of understanding. He slowed, used an emergency turnaround, whipped the cruiser into the eastbound flow, and dove over into the right lane, barely making the Thunder Bay visitor's center exit. He didn't squeal the tires, but it was close.

"Thanks," I said as I got out of the cruiser and hustled toward the walking path that led to the restrooms. Sevier's police cruiser was the only car in the lot, I noticed. I couldn't have asked for better luck.

The path split after twenty yards. Ladies went left, men to the right. The path curved around to the far side of a low redbrick building that housed the facilities. It was one of those outdoor rest-stop restrooms, a separate building from the visitor's center to limit foot traffic inside the center. The restroom entrance was not visible from the parking lot. Perfect for what I had in mind.

I didn't go inside the ladies' room. Instead, I flattened my back against the brick wall and side-stepped until I was directly beneath the surveillance camera mounted above the restroom entrance. I leapt and swatted the camera until it pointed uselessly toward the upper corner of the alcove. Then I ducked behind a large tree opposite the entrance and waited.

Sevier wasted no time. I heard him long before I saw him. A man's gait is distinct from a woman's, and his police-issue low-quarter shoes showed the pavement who was boss with each plodding step.

I held my breath as he approached my tree. His footsteps stopped. So did my heart.

Was I fully concealed? Had a stray gust of wind blown my red hair into view? My grip tightened around the Russian pistol in my purse.

Sevier's footsteps receded. He was moving away from the tree, and toward the ladies' room entrance. Strange place for a man to be, but the police uniform would undoubtedly stop any questions he might otherwise have received.

I readied the pistol and stole a glance toward the entrance. Sevier's back was to me. His hand reached for the door handle.

Now.

Three quiet steps brought me nearly within striking distance. I raised my hand above my head, fingers wrapped tightly around the butt of the weapon. I readied my blow, aiming for the crown of Sevier's head.

In my pocket, Fix's phone buzzed.

Sevier was fast. *Shockingly* fast. The kind of lightning reaction that only preparation gives. Like he'd known all along, and the buzzing telephone was merely confirmation of what he already suspected. His body twisted. He led with his right elbow. It would have been a beautiful strike, but it whiffed. I was already moving backward and to my right, away from his power zone.

The nightstick came next, held reverse-grip in his left hand. It cut the air as it sliced over my head. It would have changed my life forever, if I didn't die of a brain hematoma first. But it missed too, thanks to a timely reaction that was pure instinct after all those years of sparring.

Sevier was country-boy tough, but he wasn't trained. Too few hours in the gym, too many hours spent sitting on his ass in a police cruiser. He was accustomed to using the power of his uniform and badge to bully people, and it had probably been the better part of a decade since anyone had fought back.

I found myself in a perfect position for a side-kick to his kneecap. It was a little slow by my standards, and my aim wasn't as precise as I'd have liked, but it landed with plenty of gusto. With a bit of experience, you can tell right away when you've wrecked something important, and I knew that the fight was over even before Sevier's scream pierced the air.

I heel-stomped his instep for good measure—another solid bit of work that would take months to heal properly—then snatched his taser and sent a torrent of angry electrons through his nervous system. Sevier's body went rigid, every muscle contracting under the onslaught, and I liberated a few useful goodies from his utility belt while he flailed.

I did a quick scan for bystanders. Still none. I grabbed Sevier's feet and backpedaled toward the foliage, groaning against the strain. Sevier weighed two-twenty if he weighed a pound. And it wasn't two-twenty the good way. A thousand donut jokes flew through my mind, but I restrained myself.

Was that poison oak beneath Sevier's body? I could never remember what to look for. One can only hope, I decided, dragging him further into the brush.

I was relieved to find zip-ties on his utility belt. More secure than handcuffs, which have an annoying penchant for breakage when worn by the right person. That person being one who knows how to twist them in the right way to break the weld between chain and cuff. No such problem with zip-ties, and Sevier's taser-induced stupor lasted just long enough for me to secure his hands behind his back and tie his ankles together.

"I wouldn't start yelling for help until you hear somebody coming," I told him. "You'll wear out your voice for no reason. Play it cool and someone will eventually find you."

"You crazy bitch. You're going to burn for this."

I smiled. "You're cute."

"You'll wish you'd never been born."

I yawned.

"The girl's already dead," Sevier said with a sneer.

"Now you're just pissing," I said. "We both know you're small-time. You're a barnacle. You squeeze a few bucks off of the real players, but nobody takes you seriously. Because you don't have the balls to do anything real."

That vein popped out of Sevier's neck again. "Fuck you," he said.

"Many have," I said, "and they all say it was life-changing." I picked up Sevier's service pistol. "But you're not my type."

I looked at Sevier's piece. Nine-millimeter. One in the chamber. Safety off. Ready to party.

"Steady now," I said, placing the barrel against Sevier's good kneecap. "I'm a little amped up, and I wouldn't want to shoot you accidentally while you tell me where you were planning to take me."

I DRAGGED SEVIER INTO THE BUSHES, WINCING A LITTLE

with each of his cries of pain. I really don't enjoy inflicting pain on people. Even bad ones.

I turned and walked, chest heaving a bit from the exertion. "Don't run off," I said over my shoulder with a wink, welcoming back my inner bitch.

I walked nonchalantly back to Sevier's police cruiser, thinking about the destination Sevier had shared with me through clenched teeth. It sounded like a great place to be dismembered. I hoped the ploy I had in mind would work, because I really didn't want to go where Sevier had tried to take me.

I started the engine and drove over the curb onto the finely manicured lawn in front of the rest stop and visitor's center. I'm sure the lone employee, a young lady whose jaw worked a piece of gum so savagely that her exertions were visible from a hundred yards away, would probably have objected to my blatant disregard for the Keep Off The Grass Sign if she had taken the time to look up from her phone. But she did not. She remained engrossed. Score another win for social media.

I maneuvered the cruiser—not one of those hideous sedans that nobody but cops and feds would ever be caught dead driving, but a rather decked-out Enforcer version of the Ford Explorer, which despite Detroit's less-than-stellar reputation of late, was actually an attractive and well-built vehicle—until the back hatch was mere feet from Sevier's prone form.

"Surprise, Officer Sevier," I said cheerily. "You're coming along with me. It will be great."

Sevier's eyes widened a bit, and I got the idea that he wasn't nearly as excited about this development as I was. I smiled, feeling smart.

"Up we go," I said, rolling him onto his chest. "There's a good man. Now tuck your knees under your chest. Maybe fewer calories in your life would be a good thing."

Sevier howled as I gave his bad knee a nudge. "We need you in the back of this cruiser," I said. "That will require a team effort."

Sevier told me where he wanted the whole team to shove it.

I placed the taser between his butt cheeks and nudged the business end up against the man-jewels. Despite the extreme discomfort he felt in his knee, Sevier instantly became a team player.

We were both sweating and worn out from the exertion by the time I reached up to shut the hatch. "I feel like we just bonded," I said with a smirk as the tailgate auto-closed and latched.

I situated myself in the driver's seat, which required no adjustment. I'm tall for a woman, and I like it that way. Height is power.

"So off we go," I said, putting the transmission in drive. "What do you suppose we'll find when we get there?"

Sevier was quiet.

"How do you suppose I'll react if I don't like what I see?"

Nothing out of Sevier.

"As you pointed out," I said, "I *am* one crazy bitch."

Still nothing from the back of the cruiser.

"I guess we'll both just have to endure the suspense," I said. I started humming a tune.

We weren't even off the grass and back onto pavement yet when I heard Sevier's voice. It was smaller than before, like the man himself had shrunk several sizes in the past few minutes. Which I supposed wasn't far from true.

"We might want to go somewhere else instead."

I smiled. "I'm all ears."

46

THE TURBOPROP LANDED AT 4:23 P.M. THE FLIGHT LASTED less than half an hour. The ox in flannel and denim named Trevor unfastened the straps that secured the dog cage to the aircraft's cargo hold. The pilot found a cargo tug from somewhere on the tarmac and the two men wrestled the cage onto the small flatbed.

"I'm awake," the girl said from within the cage, her voice groggy and faraway but determined. "You don't have to treat me like some kind of animal. I'm a human being."

"Sorry," Trevor said. "I got my orders. Not supposed to go making changes on my own and whatnot."

He hazarded a look inside the cage. What he saw startled him, made him stop breathing almost. The girl was drop-dead gorgeous. Dark hair, perfectly symmetrical face, thin features, and the most piercing blue eyes anyone had ever seen. Like fiery ice. Or icy fire. Trevor snapped his head back around so as not to get caught staring. What he was afraid of, he didn't know. The girl was the one in the cage, after all, and not him.

"It's a short enough drive," the pilot groused as he parked the cargo tug next to a white panel van. "We could just take this crawler. I don't see why we have to lift her into the van just to go two blocks."

Trevor shrugged. He didn't see the logic either. But logic wasn't one of his gifts. Fortunately, his job rarely required careful planning or complicated reasoning. His domain was far more physical than cerebral.

He stayed out of the girl's view as he helped the pilot place the cage in the back of the van. But Trevor snuck glances inside the cage through the ventilation holes. What he saw had all manner of hormonal and biological implications inside his body. The girl was something special, magazine pretty, refined and delicate yet feral, though Trevor wouldn't have used those words. He would just have said *smoking hot*.

He wondered what Karl and Sevier were really up to.

He wondered how he would react if he knew.

I TOOK A HARD RIGHT TURN, FOLLOWING OFFICER
Sevier's strained instructions from the cargo area of the patrol cruiser. The
sound of his voice suggested the adrenaline of our confrontation had worn
off, leaving nothing but the pain of his wrecked knee and injured foot.
I questioned whether debilitating force was necessary, as I always did in
situations like this one, and I concluded that even if I didn't absolutely *need*
to set the guy up for an extensive knee reconstruction and six hard months
of merciless rehab, he probably had it coming anyway. Maybe if he'd had his
ass kicked more often coming up through the ranks, he wouldn't have turned
into one of the worst kinds of people on Earth: a crooked cop.

We were heading to the Lakehead University campus to meet someone
named Karl. Karl had information that I would find useful, Sevier had
promised. He had good reason not to lie to me. I had promised to rearrange
his other knee using his service pistol, and he had every reason to believe I
would do it. At least, he *should* believe it. Because I wouldn't hesitate.

As I drove the police cruiser, I got a good look at the information displayed
on the laptop computer bolted to the dashboard. The computer automatically
ran the license plates of every passing car.

Every. Passing. Car. Automatically.

What a wonderful thing, and what a terrible and grotesque thing, too. Every time a citizen drove past a police car, a police database tracked their whereabouts. That hackneyed old line about having nothing to worry about unless you're doing something wrong comes to mind, but Officer Sevier was living proof that it's bullshit. He was as crooked as they came, and it struck me as obscene that he had unfettered access to such a wealth of private data. I wondered if he used it to his advantage.

I shook my head. Silly question. *Of course* Sevier used it to his advantage. Humans are human everywhere. Even the ones in uniform.

Especially the ones in uniform. I should know—I was still completely in love with a man in an Air Force uniform, though he hadn't returned my calls in months.

As I perused the readout instead of minding traffic—it's amazing that more cops don't have fender-benders because of that giant screen screaming for their attention—that white sticker on top of the display kept grabbing my attention. TBPD0659. I shook it off as a distraction and tried to refocus.

"Take a left on Oliver Road," Sevier said.

My phone buzzed again. Actually, it was Fix's phone. It had buzzed just a split-second before I could complete my preemptive strike against Sevier back at the rest stop, which had kicked off our altercation. I had forgotten about the phone in the commotion. Not good. Dan and Fix were both hard at work, trying to track down the reptiles responsible for the atrocity they were calling "Snuff Fest," and I was eager for news.

I fished the phone from my pocket, hoping that maybe Dan or Fix had come up with something useful. I pushed the button and typed in Fix's PIN. The screen flashed a text message.

I read it. I couldn't believe what I saw.

I read it again.

And a third time.

Then I slammed on the brakes, pulled the police cruiser over to the side of the road, and read it again for a fourth time.

It couldn't be right. There had to be a mistake. This was impossible.

"What the hell are you doing?" Sevier said. "You can't stop here. You'll make a mess out of traffic."

I read the text message on Fix's phone for a fifth time, and then a sixth. My eyes swam and the earth shifted underneath me. Everything I thought I understood about the situation had suddenly flown out the window. It was an entirely new ballgame now.

I read the message for a seventh time, and then an eighth. Just to be sure I hadn't completely lost my mind. It still said the same thing. It still *meant* the same thing—that everything I thought I knew about this predicament was dead wrong. My heart raced, my breath came in shallow gasps, and I fought back a stranglehold of panic.

I put the transmission in park, opened the door, and ran like hell.

TO MY KNOWLEDGE, I MET THE MAN NAMED ARTEMIS
Grange only once. I say "to my knowledge" because Artemis Grange is a
legendary spy, the kind of person who can escape your notice even while
standing right in front of you, even if you're a trained and experienced spy
catcher like yours truly. Grange's ability to blend in and melt away is not a
unique skill. Many spies have near-perfect field craft. It's almost the price of
entry these days.

Most spies never transition from expert field operator to expert strategist.
This set Grange apart from all the rest. His skill in the field was equalled—
surpassed, some would say—by his skill in the back-room meetings that
greased the machinery of statecraft. Grange could get you to sell out your
own mother and feel good about yourself for doing it.

Grange tried to kill me once. He orchestrated a situation that attracted
all of his enemies—real and imagined, as it turned out, because a necessary
but unfortunate side effect of a life spent in the trenches of treachery is an
unhealthy dose of paranoia—to the same place at the same time. Then he set
off an explosion. It killed a half-dozen people. I survived, but barely. So did an
intelligence agent named Peter Kittredge. Artemis Grange disappeared into

the ether. He abandoned his work with the Central Intelligence Agency, cut all ties to the US government, and vanished.

Immediately after that episode, I quit my job at Homeland. I should have quit years ago. The job cost me my relationship with the man I'd waited my entire life to find. It had also cost me my life once. Fortunately, death didn't stick. Dan Gable kept the blood circulating through my body until the paramedics arrived and restarted my heart. But I think what finally soured me on the whole thing was the betrayal. My superiors should have had my back. Instead, they offered me up as a sacrifice to save their own asses. So I walked.

I sold my house and all of my things. They just reminded me of Brock, and that was a pain too sharp to bear. I fled to Charleston, South Carolina, where I licked my wounds for six months. But losing a love like the one Brock and I shared was not something I could get over. That tragedy was more like Chernobyl—my heart was a radioactive wasteland with a zillion-year half-life.

Still is.

I was mired in self-absorption and self-pity in Charleston when Peter Kittredge showed up in my life again. He didn't bring good news with him. Despite my attempt to walk away from the life, the life had followed me. I was in someone's crosshairs. I tried denial, but only for a few milliseconds. Denial always leads to death.

The only way out is through, we decided, so Kittredge and I teamed up and went into attack mode. We made great headway, and along the way, something sparked between Kittredge and me. He's no Brock James, but he's something special in his own right, and I think I began to love him. Not with all of me. Not perfectly. But some.

Then things turned plaid. I found myself in that cabin in the Rocky Mountain wilderness, miles from anywhere, too remote for anyone to hear my screams, my begging, my pleading.

Artemis Grange rescued me.

Mostly. I mean, he killed the men who were drugging and raping me. The men were "turning me out," making me compliant and drug-addicted and ready for their prostitution ring, and Grange put bullets through their brains. He did that right in front of me.

Then he made me an offer that I couldn't refuse. Grange had inherited a title called the Facilitator, a role that most sane and educated people dismissed as being the product of overactive imaginations and under-active prefrontal cortexes. But the Facilitator really existed.

Exists.

Kingmaker. Manipulator. Emperor of everything. All the wacky shit your crazy news-addicted cousin won't shut up about. Almost all of it is true. Minus the aliens.

Grange wanted out. He'd spent his life under the sword of Damocles, and he was ready to get out from under it. That wasn't possible as the Facilitator. He felt ill-suited for the task, and I think he also questioned whether anyone on Earth should hold that kind of power and responsibility. He questioned whether he was the right man for the job.

Plus, he didn't want to die an early death. As you might imagine, assassination is quite an occupational hazard when you control vast wealth and the most comprehensive intelligence apparatus ever assembled.

Grange made me an offer I couldn't refuse. My life for Brock James' and Peter Kittredge's lives. Both of the men I loved. *Still* love.

Only Grange didn't want to kill me.

He wanted me to become the Facilitator. To take over for him. I was beaten, battered, defiled, strung out, exhausted, and emotionally wasted, and I agreed. But I don't know that I'd have chosen differently even if I had been the picture of health and serenity. I loved Kittredge. And my heart still belonged entirely to Brock, strange as that may sound considering my feelings for Kittredge. If Brock said the word—hell, if he said *anything at all* to me—I'd be on the next flight to wherever he was. I'm still not over him, and I don't think I ever will be.

Anyway, my stint as the Facilitator had so far lasted a little over two weeks. I had spent most of that time recovering from my ordeal, and I still had no clue what to do about Capstone. It was designed and built entirely by government, military, paramilitary, and criminal labor, and it operated without official government cognizance. Capstone is a state-within-a-state. Except that it siphons electronic intelligence from every civilized nation on the planet. Which makes Capstone an empire unto itself.

It scares the living shit out of me.

I would have loved to burn it to the ground. But I didn't know enough about how it worked. And worse, the fact that it existed was proof that something like it *can* exist. So someone else—Vladimir Putin or Xi Jinping or maybe some antisocial nerd-freak at Facebook or Google or maybe some Colombian drug boss—could build something similar.

And then we would all be fucked.

I had the Capstone password stuck in my brain, but I was terrified of using it. Mostly because I was terrified of myself. I wasn't a strong enough character to manage my own fucking life. What kind of mess would I make at the helm of something like Capstone?

Which brought me back to Artemis Grange.

My legs were heavy and my chest burned in the frigid afternoon air, but I kept running away from Officer Sevier's cop cruiser, which I'd left idling at the curb with Sevier and his broken knee stuffed in the cargo hold. I ran south, past a warehouse and into the forest beyond. I stopped running when the forest became too thick to navigate safely. I ducked behind a tree. I don't know what the hell I was hiding from, but I knew I needed to hide.

I looked at the text message on Fix's cell phone one more time. *Sam, this is not what you think it is. You're walking into a trap. —AG*

Those initials—AG—were the same initials left on the note the Facilitator left me when he abdicated his throne. I knew who sent the text message. It had to be Grange.

Which meant that maybe he hadn't fully abdicated. Maybe he had maintained his access to Capstone.

You're walking into a trap.

I had to assume his intelligence was about as perfect as intelligence can get.

So maybe this wasn't just about saving two dozen young lives and preventing an unspeakable atrocity.

Maybe this was also about saving myself.

IN HIS SMALL OFFICE IN BELIZE, IN A DILAPIDATED
building that might have been condemned in most other cities, the Reckoner
worked on the latest upload. He watched the proceedings, as he had watched
all of them, with a mixture of interest, disgust, indifference, pity, curiosity,
and revulsion. It was a hell of a way to earn a buck, acting as middleman for
a transaction like Snuff Fest. He wasn't into the scene, didn't get off on the
atrocity, but neither did he have enough of a problem with it not to take part.
It came down to his addiction, which needed feeding, and cash kept him in
supply.

He kept watching. It went on and on. Terrible things. Unspeakable
cruelty. Depravity on a new level. And suddenly it was too much. Too horrific.
Too inhuman. He snatched the trash can near his desk and threw up. He
gagged repeatedly until there was nothing left in his stomach. And maybe
nothing left in his soul.

He stood up and walked with a halting gait to the filthy lavatory. He
found the sink and splashed brown, rust-laden water on his face. How much
worse could it possibly get? There were still half a dozen murders left. The
thought made him woozy all over again. People were worse than animals.

People inflicted pain on each other for pure pleasure. People were vile, horrible, nasty, and beyond hope.

And he was part of the problem.

The Reckoner shook his head, smashed another pill on the filthy countertop, and anesthetized himself with another snort through a rolled-up bank note. Maybe he would take some time off, he thought as the drug entered his bloodstream. Maybe he was working too much, not taking good enough care of himself. Maybe some time away would help.

But he was kidding himself. He had rounded a corner. He had become part of something that had already changed him forever. This he knew beyond any doubt.

The recurring suicide fantasy played again his head. A leap from the top of his office building. An overdose. The taste of the snub-nosed .38 in his desk drawer, one squeeze of the trigger, then sweet oblivion.

But the mess. And the cowardice. His little boy would know, eventually. The Reckoner couldn't live with that.

And he was already in way too deep to back out now.

He returned to his desk. The video had continued to play and had concluded in his absence. He didn't rewind it to watch. He knew that nobody could survive the damage he'd seen inflicted on the poor kid moments before.

The Reckoner took a deep breath and sent his message to Panama. Only a few more to go. Then he would get seriously fucked up and try to put all of this behind him. But he knew it was a fool's errand. Some lines you just shouldn't cross. And there are some things that you just shouldn't see.

IT WAS ALL ABOUT THE PASSWORD, I REALIZED. CAPSTONE was a repository and processing system for intelligence information leached from all over the globe, stolen from governments, businesses, and private citizens. It pilfered sensitive information from anyone and anything with a video camera, audio recorder, or text function.

Data is worse than useless without the ability to process and understand it, and without the ability to act on it. Capstone had both essential capabilities baked into its infrastructure. Capstone used some of the most sophisticated artificial intelligence algorithms in existence. Capstone also employed some of the most effective, ruthless, and dangerous humans in existence, too. They were the pointy end of the spear, as the saying went. Some of them were good at killing. Others were good at cyber attack. Still others were good at political manipulation.

But the key to unlock them all—the key to the kingdom—was the password. My password.

They all answered to me. Madam Facilitator. Because Artemis Grange had thrown it all in my lap and fled.

But I realized now that he hadn't disappeared entirely. He had remained in the picture to some extent. It made sense—I hadn't exactly been in tip-top shape when he left the whole thing at my feet. Still wasn't. He's a smart guy, and he probably knew that I had a lot of healing and soul-searching to do before I could take the reins. And he also knew that a vacuum of power—particularly *that* kind of power—was more dangerous than a nuke. In the wrong hands, Capstone could indelibly alter human society in the blink of an eye.

So maybe Grange was still monitoring things, waiting for me to step into my role. Or spying on me to figure out whether I *would* ever step into that role… or whether I might require disposal. It was a chilling thought.

I realized this must have been what Grange felt when he complained to me about the burden of the responsibility. I had known abstractly that my taking the helm of Capstone would place me in more jeopardy than I had ever known before—and that was sure as hell saying something, given my work for Homeland over the years—but this was the first time that I had *felt* the danger. It was palpable and slightly paralyzing.

I looked again at Grange's text. It was sent to me. On Fix's phone. That alone implied a level of pervasive intelligence that was difficult to digest.

I read the message again, probably because I was still having trouble believing it.

Sam, this is not what you think it is. You're walking into a trap. —AG

A trap. For what purpose? I had nothing of value.

Except the password.

I replied to the text. I asked Grange to help me. If he knew it was a trap, I needed his help to turn the tables. I wouldn't need much, because I was still damned good at this game. Just a nudge in the right direction.

The text bounced back as undeliverable. *This address does not exist*, the phone complained.

I clicked on Grange's text message and called up the options page. I wanted to place a phone call to the sender, but there was no option to place a call. The message didn't originate from a telephone.

"Son of a bitch!" I heard desperation in my voice. And anger. "You fucking bastard, Grange! You can't leave me hanging like this!"

Tears. Were those tears in my eyes? Damn it all, this was not the moment to have a moment.

"Grange!" I don't know why I yelled his name. It was irrational. Nothing around me but trees, birds, and squirrels.

Breathe, I coached myself. *You knew this was coming. You tried to deny it, but deep down, you knew it would happen. You just weren't expecting it to happen so soon. You wanted to be ready for it, to have your feet back under you before you took on your first Capstone challenger. But we don't get to choose the cards we're dealt. So harden the fuck up and play the hand you have.*

Which was what, exactly? A couple dozen kids were about to lose their lives for the sexual pleasure of the sickest humans drawing breath.

Two dozen beautiful young people. And there I sat, leaning against a tree in the middle of the damned forest, clueless about what to do next, where to turn, or whom to trust.

The phone buzzed in my hand. Another message from the same sender. *Find the devil you know,* it said.

"What the hell do you mean by that, Grange?" I knew a hundred devils. Maybe a thousand. Which one was I supposed to find? And why the hell was Grange speaking in riddles? Why not just tell me what I needed to know? Why all the fucking head games?

I tried replying to the texts again, with the same result. *This address does not exist.* How apropos, I thought bitterly.

But this mental spin cycle wasn't helping. I drew a deep, calming breath. I thought about what I knew. I thought about what needed doing. I thought about everyone I'd met so far since finding Stacey naked, alone, and freezing half to death in the Philadelphia night.

I thought about Grange's warning—*You're walking into a trap.* I didn't know if he meant following Sevier's instructions specifically, or the entire situation.

If Sevier was the trap, I'd mitigated the trouble by running. For the moment, anyway.

But if the entire situation—Snuff Fest and those poor kids—was *itself* a trap, there was no way I could walk away. And maybe that's why Grange had warned me. Because he knew I wouldn't back down. *Couldn't* back down. He of all people would know why.

And if that's what he was thinking, he was dead right.

FIRST THINGS FIRST. I WAS NOT AN ANIMAL. I WAS NOT like the monsters I was hunting. I thought of Sevier, tied up and injured in the cargo compartment of the police cruiser. When I left him, he was cursing a blue streak in the backseat. His face was pale and sweaty. I was no expert, but it looked like shock was setting in. His knee had sustained considerable damage and he needed medical attention.

I used Fix's phone to dial emergency services. 911 in Canada, same as the US. I told the emergency personnel about Sevier's situation. I didn't tell them he was a police officer. I was sure they'd figure it out on their own. He wouldn't have to invent too much about the events of the past hour to make it seem like he was the victim. Never mind my reasons—fact was, I had attacked him.

He was a bad person and under different circumstances I wouldn't hesitate to put a round or two through his heart. But these weren't different circumstances. It cost me very little to keep a bit of my humanity intact, something I desperately needed at the moment. My anger and fear were getting the better of me, and I needed to reassert some control, some agency. And anyway, this situation—whatever the hell it was—would be over long before Sevier could threaten me again.

At least, that's what I told myself. But maybe I was making a huge mistake. Maybe I would regret this small mercy.

I followed up on my Good Samaritan act by stealing a car. An old-school Toyota Camry left over from the Nineties. The paint had seen better days, and I wouldn't win any races with the hamsters under the hood, but the car had two irresistible features: no electronic monitoring system, and an old-school ignition that had to have been designed with car thieves in mind.

It started on the first try. God bless those Japanese engineers. Say what you want about German automotive prowess, but if it's reliability we're after, I'm going Japanese all the way.

And God bless Grange. Because despite the annoying riddles, damn if he hadn't given me exactly what I needed. I put the car in gear and drove as fast as prudence would allow to find the devil I knew.

I parked the stolen Camry in the handicap spot in front of the Superior HeliTours and Adventures building, took a steadying breath, and walked through the door with as much composure as I could muster.

I needed to get the lay of the land before getting to work. Nobody sat at the reception desk. I peeked into the hangar. Just Lizzie and her helicopter, greasy parts lying everywhere.

The lights were off in Mike Robinson's office.

Becca's office lights were on. I marched in wearing a jaunty smile. The look on her face told me a great deal. It wasn't just that I had startled her. I got the idea that my presence, my mere aliveness, had scared the hell out of her. Like she wasn't expecting to see me again anytime soon. Maybe ever.

And then the surprise and fear and vulnerability were gone. Instantly, just like that, as if a different person had suddenly taken over Becca's body. Her face revealed… absolutely nothing at all. It was the strangest thing to witness, and I'd be lying if I said it didn't shake me a little.

"Hi Becca," I said, doing my best to disguise what I felt. It was a tall order, given what I had just observed on her face. But you don't get good at catching spies without also getting good at playing a role.

"Any luck?"

I shook my head. "Officer Sevier had something come up," I said.

"Did he drop you off?"

I shrugged. "Higher priority emergency." Which was truthful but misleading. I should write a book someday. How to lie without lying, by yours truly.

"What are you working on?" I asked.

She shook her head. "Some bookkeeping."

"I thought you said the books kept themselves."

She gave me a bit of a look. "Figure of speech. Somebody still has to crunch the numbers."

I nodded.

"Listen, Becca, I really need to talk to Mike."

She shook her head. "I am not my brother's keeper. I gave that up a long time ago."

"But he's your employee."

Becca shrugged. "I pay his bills. He shows up, does some work, makes a mess," now with a sweep of her hand, "and leaves me to clean up after him."

Right. She mentioned this before. "It sounds like you *are* your brother's keeper."

She laughed without humor.

"Mike knows something about where Stacey was taken," I said. "I'm asking for your help."

Becca's shields slammed back in place. Her face went blank. "I learned a long time ago that Michael needs his privacy. Where he goes, what he does, that's his business. I don't ask and I don't want to hear about it."

"Why not?"

Something flared in her eyes. "Because Michael is not like normal people. Michael is a wild animal trapped in a human body."

I let a long moment unwind.

"I know," I said. "I can see it in his eyes. And you know that's why I have to find him."

She shook her head. "I'm sorry," she said. "I don't know where he is."

I leaned in and lowered my voice. "Becca, I appreciate how you've helped us. But I promise you, if anything happens to Stacey, I will hold you personally responsible."

The silence grew heavy and angry, but neither of us broke it. The blank look returned to her eyes, and I got the impression that I was the least of Becca Robinson's worries.

I left her office without another word.

My blood was pumping when I left Becca's office. I wanted to choke the life out of her. She knew where her brother had gone. Worse, she knew something about what had happened to Stacey, and she wasn't lifting a finger to help.

At least, that's what I assumed. But I had to remind myself that things aren't always as they seem. Becca's complicity might have been coerced. She did, after all, have a daughter and a business—two powerful leverage points that could easily be used against her. She might have been protecting Michael Robinson because she had no other choice.

But a girl's life hung in the balance.

And two dozen more lives, as well.

Jesus, I was running out of time. I picked up my pace. I walked past the conference room. Fix sat at the conference table with his back to the hallway windows, hunched over his laptop, speaking into a burner phone. I shook my head. His position was bad for security—anyone could have gotten the drop on him—but I was happy to have him on my side. I needed all the help I could get.

I checked Fix's cell phone, which I still had with me, for another message from Artemis Grange. Nothing. The grand wizard had evidently bestowed all the enigmatic wisdom he saw fit to share.

I found Lizzie in the same position I'd left her in before: swallowed inside the engine bay of one of the HeliTours birds.

"I know you're busy," I said, "but I really need your help with something."

Lizzie didn't reply.

"Listen, I made a mistake. I should have trusted you from the beginning," I said. "But I wasn't sure who to trust. We're in a bad situation, and we can't get out of it by ourselves."

Lizzie emerged from the bowels of the machine. "Plenty of trouble to go around. I try to mind my own."

I nodded. "Smart policy. I'd like five minutes of your time. That's it. Then you can wash your hands of this and get back to your life."

Lizzie sighed, frowned, and wiped her hands on a rag draped over the cowling. She descended the ladder in a bit of a huff. "Fine," she said. "Time starts now."

I resisted the urge to take her by the collar and cuff her. Instead, I told her Stacey's story. Abduction. Drugged with muscle relaxers to make her orifices more compliant. Sexual abuse of the vilest kind, over and over again. How she finally escaped by biting a chunk off the guard's dick, which he'd shoved down her throat until she gagged. How she'd run nearly naked through the streets until, thanks to pure luck and my trauma-induced insomnia, I saw her and picked her up.

I told her about the twenty-or-so other kids in a similar situation. And I told her about the utter atrocity, the pure abomination, that a band of despicable humans was calling Snuff Fest.

Lizzie's face turned to stone as I talked. Her breathing quickened. She wouldn't hold my gaze. When I said the words Snuff Fest, you'd have thought I'd punched her in the stomach. A single tear escaped the corner of her eye and ran down her face. She wiped it quickly, as if ashamed by the display of weakness.

"Lizzie," I said. "Your uncle knows something about what happened to Stacey. I can feel it. Your mom says she doesn't know where Michael is. I know they will kill Stacey, and all those other kids, too. People younger than you, with their whole lives ahead of them. They're going to die the most painful death imaginable, all for somebody's sick pleasure."

Lizzie shook her head. Crushing tiredness settled over her eyes. Her shoulders sagged. She shook her head again.

"Please," I said. "If you want me to beg for these kids' lives, I'll do it. There's no time, and I'm desperate for any bit of help I can get."

A long moment passed.

"Lizzie, please," I said.

She sighed. "Not here," she whispered.

"Excuse me?"

"We can't do this here. And nobody can see me with you."

52

LIZZIE AND I MET AT THE SAME DINER WE HAD VISITED earlier in the day. It seemed like an entire lifetime ago, though it had only been a few hours. So much had happened—Becca had taken us on the helicopter search for the RFID beacons, which had revealed a girl's corpse rotting in the Isle Royale forest. Stacey had disappeared. Michael Robinson had claimed ignorance, even after disabling the security camera that would have shown Stacey's abduction—if she had indeed been abducted, which seemed like the only safe bet. Officer Sevier had nearly tricked me into walking into a trap. Artemis Grange had reappeared from some parallel universe to warn me, and to admonish me to chase after the devil I knew. And I had witnessed a veil of steel closing over Becca's eyes when I asked her about her brother.

And now Lizzie sat in the passenger's seat of the stolen Toyota Camry. I sat in the driver's seat. We didn't risk going inside—too many eyes watching. The blinking of the digital clock on the car's dashboard mocked me, reminded me that time was wasting, that lives were on the line, and yet I held the silence. I sensed that Lizzie's resolve was fragile. If was afraid that if I pushed her, she would change her mind about helping me. I focused on my breathing, closed my eyes, quieted the urge to yell at Lizzie to *get the fuck on with it already*.

"I think everybody around here knows about us," she finally began. "The Robinsons, I mean."

I said nothing.

"I was maybe four or five years old. My family has a cabin out in the woods. We drove out there for some holiday in the summer. I never liked going to those things. To me they were just about burnt burgers and horseshoes and those fucking mosquitos. And my cousins. I hated my cousins."

Her eyes found mine. "You probably think I'm strange."

I shook my head to reassure her. I didn't think she was strange. I wondered where this was going, though.

Lizzie went on. "My cousins teased me, pulled my hair, pulled my panties down and tried to finger me. They were, like, four or five years older than me. I knew it was wrong, and it hurt. I threatened to tell on them, but they said they'd do it with a sharp stick next time. So I kept my mouth shut, and I avoided them whenever I could. My mom never knew why I dreaded these family things. But she's not an idiot. She had to have known something was up."

I nodded, trying to keep my face neutral, but something was boiling inside me. Why the hell were there so many fucked-up humans? Watching Lizzie and listening to her story—the weight on my heart was suddenly stifling. I had to work hard to breathe, to smash down my own memories, to keep them from surfacing. I was too tired and strung-out, and if I opened that door even a little, I was sure that I would lose my shit entirely.

"Anyway," Lizzie said. "I had to go to these things, and they scared me. As soon as my mom and I pulled up to the cabin, I would pretend to go on an 'adventure'"—Lizzie put air quotes around *adventure*—"but really I was hiding in the forest."

I nodded.

"One time," Lizzie went on, "like I said, I was probably four or five. I don't remember exactly..."

She trailed off, her eyes far away. I sensed that she wasn't seeing what was in front of her, but probably seeing things burned in her memory.

"My grandpa and uncles were big hunters back then," she said. "They built a smokehouse. I'd heard them talk about it, but I had never seen it. It wasn't anywhere near the cabin. I didn't know where it was, but I stumbled on it one day. They had built it in a small clearing. Nothing was smoking, but I could still smell that something had been burned there. I'll never forget the smell. It wasn't right. It wasn't like a pig or an elk or a deer—I wasn't a huge fan of those things, but at least they smelled like food. But this smell…"

Jesus, I thought. I don't need to hear this.

"I stayed away from the smokehouse for a while," Lizzie said. "The smell was terrible. It stuck to the roof of my mouth. But something kept drawing me back, like there was something pulling me toward the door."

Lizzie wept softly. She wiped the tears from her eyes. I put my hand on hers and gave it a squeeze. "It's okay," I said.

She shook her head and took a deep breath. "When I opened the door, I knew something was wrong. There wasn't any meat hanging up, but there were skins. Maybe six or seven of them. I saw the fur. It made me cry. These were such beautiful animals, and they had just peeled the skin right off."

Lizzie pulled her hand from mine and began picking at her fingernails. She did that a lot, I could tell. Most of them had scabs, and a couple were raw and bloody. This young woman had some demons locked inside her.

"I wish that was all, but it wasn't. I was turning to leave when I saw it," she said. "My eyes were blurry from the tears, but I knew something was out of place. Part of my brain figured it out and I jumped and screamed. I ran into the forest. I couldn't stop crying."

She drew a shaky breath and picked at her fingers.

I let a minute pass, maybe more. "Lizzie, can you tell me what you saw?"

Another shaky breath. More tears. "I saw the Robinson family disease," she finally said. "The thing that everybody around here knows but nobody has ever proven."

I didn't understand.

She stared off into the distance. "One of the skins," she said. "It had no hair. And it was pink."

I did my best to remain stoic but supportive as Lizzie told me the rest. A childhood filled with abuse. Topics that were never broached, places on the family property that were never visited or spoken of. The Robinsons passed rape and murder from generation to generation as a birthright.

If you want to build a psychopath, it's not hard to do. Just molest him when he's little. Cause pain. Visibly enjoy it while you're doing it. That kind of thing grows in a person's psyche like a cancer. When he's old enough and powerful enough, a burning need will drive him to be on the other side of the pain. Full circle.

Abuse reverberates for women too, but with different damage. Our coping mechanisms aren't as overtly violent. We pick our fingernails to bloody stumps or cut our arms with razors or become pathologically promiscuous. A woman's anger turns more inward. We're more likely to destroy ourselves, but less likely to hurt someone else. And we're more likely to seek abusive relationships and stay in them until it costs us our lives.

You should take all of this with a grain of salt. I'm not a professional. But I've run into this kind of thing enough over the years to believe what they say about abuse. It's the gift that keeps on giving.

And there's something else at work, too. Genetics. Madness may run in the family. Twins commit murders together. Separated twins commit murder separately.

Lizzie described her family as suffering from a disease, and I sensed she was accurate: it definitely ran in the Robinson family.

"Lizzie," I said, my grip tightening around the steering wheel of the stolen Camry, "Your uncle and Stacey. This sickness is happening again, isn't it?"

She nodded.

"I will protect you," I said. "A team of federal agents is on the way." At least, I hoped that was the case. I was relying on Dan Gable to make that happen, because that was a wet noodle that I could no longer push for myself. I wasn't a federal agent any longer.

"You can fly south to Michigan or Minnesota," I told Lizzie. "They will keep you safe while we sort this out with your family."

She shook her head, sadness in her eyes. "They'll find me," she said. "They always find people."

"Not if you're protected," I said. "I'll make the call right now. You'll have the best protection in North America."

She shook her head again.

"Lizzie, please. Help me stop this. I will make sure you're taken care of. You have my word."

She looked me in the eyes again. "Don't make promises you can't keep. I'm not a child."

I shook my head, completely at a loss. She was right. I'd promised to protect Stacey, too. And what a bang-up job I'd done keeping that promise.

I needed Lizzie's help. There wasn't any time for me to work things out on my own. If she didn't cooperate with me, I was afraid that those kids would suffer an unspeakable death. I thought of Stacey, of her delicate, beautiful body and face, of that spine made of steel, of all she had endured, and all that she was still to endure if I failed to put a stop to it.

Tears of anger and frustration welled up, but I choked them down. I took a deep breath and resolved to keep going, no matter what.

Then Lizzie surprised me. She gave her bloody fingernail one last tug, sighed, and said, "I know where Uncle Mike likes to hide."

I HAULED ASS BACK TO HELITOURS. LIZZIE WANTED TO drive her own car, but now that I had a solid break in the case, I didn't have the time to waste. And I was deathly afraid that if I let her out of my sight, Lizzie would think twice about helping me put an end to the madness.

My fear might have been misplaced. I stole glances at Lizzie's face. I thought I saw strength and resolve.

I parked in the handicap spot again, and we dashed into the building together. Lizzie's earlier trepidation about being seen together was evidently no longer a factor in her thinking. She had made a choice, and it didn't look like she had any misgivings.

She dashed behind the operations desk and pulled out the flight notebook for one of their helicopters. I was about to ask if I could help her prepare for takeoff when Fix rounded the corner in a rush.

"There you are," he said. "Been taking a siesta?" That boyish grin again. I shook my head at him.

He waved a small stack of papers in front of me. "Transaction ledger," he said. "From your Bitcoin payment from Sevier."

I took the papers from him. "What am I looking at?"

"This is a rat's nest," he said. "They spread the funds out over thousands of different accounts. I have to download the complete blockchain to trace each of them back."

I shrugged. "Download it, already."

"You don't understand. The complete blockchain is an encrypted record of millions of transactions. Downloading it takes hours, Sam. With the internet speed in this building, maybe days."

"Shit."

"Right," Fix said. "Shit. So it's downloading now. Has been since just after you left. Once I have all the information, I have an app that can parse it in a few minutes. But we're still hours away from having all the information we need to piece Sevier's network together."

I shook my head. It seemed like we were having a hard time catching a break. But all wasn't lost. The data delay meant that Fix was free to do something else.

"Grab your coat and a pistol," I said. "We're taking a field trip."

54

MICHAEL ROBINSON HAD *THAT FEELING*, THE ONE HE lived for, the one that proved he was still alive, that there was a beating heart in his chest, that he wasn't some emotionless automaton. He knew he wasn't alone. Others like him had the same problem. All the normal things felt utterly empty, meaningless, wasteful even. Which was why Michael Robinson and people like him did the things they did.

He felt the rare and exquisite zing of excitement hit his psyche, and it gave him such pleasure. It was so rare for him that he had to engineer elaborate scenarios to enjoy that biochemical cascade. The experience of life really boiled down to the chemicals made in the brain. And today, glory be, Michael Robinson's brain was making all the right chemicals.

He smiled. He sharpened his knives. He thought about the brunette. They'd save her for him. And there was a bonus, too. The redhead. Tall, gorgeous, athletic. Maybe a little long in the tooth, but every bit the MILF to die for. And that sharp tongue, too. Subduing her, taming her, breaking her, would be exquisite. He vowed to cherish the experience. Strays and hookers and junkies were one thing. Sure, they offered a cheap thrill in the moment, and they usually got him through his rough patches, but he had long since grown bored with them.

But quality like the redhead was rarer than diamonds.

Robinson looked at his watch. Nothing to do now but wait. It was such exquisite agony. He cherished the feeling. He cherished feeling anything at all. And today would be a day worth remembering.

55

LIZZIE WORKED ON FILING THE PAPERWORK FOR FLIGHT.
Becca had disappeared somewhere. Fix paced. He was out of his element,
doing his best to stay calm and collected, but the only cure for nerves is
experience, and Fix didn't have any operational background to fall back on.
I watched him carefully, debating the wisdom of taking him along with me.
Michael Robinson was a psychopath, and the one thing you can count on is
that psychopaths aren't penned in by normal behavioral boundaries. It could
get very dangerous, very fast.

But what choice did I have? It didn't make much sense to go after
Robinson alone.

Scratch that. Lizzie would be with us. So I wouldn't merely be going after
Robinson alone. I'd also be trying to look out for Lizzie's safety. With no
backup. I shook my head. That would have been beyond stupid.

"Hand me your weapon real quick," I said to Fix. He gave me a look and
I could tell there was a smart comment brewing, surely something tongue-
in-cheek about my picking the wrong moment to emasculate him, but he
acquiesced without a word.

I checked his piece, ejected the magazine, retracted the slide, confirmed an empty chamber, and left the empty weapon with the hammer cocked and the safety engaged. I handed it back to him. "Practice the drawing motion a few times and use your thumb to disengage the safety."

He nodded and did as he was told. Slow and awkward.

"Again," I said. It needed to be second-nature. We would never get there in the few minutes we had for practice, but at least Fix would have some recent muscle memory to work with if things turned plaid on us. When I felt slightly less uncomfortable with the fluidity and accuracy of his movement, I had him reload the weapon, put a round in the chamber, and set the safety.

"Now put that thing away before you hurt someone," I said with a good-natured smile.

"Yes, ma'am," Fix said. But I sensed he was grateful for the instruction. Shit was about to get real.

Lizzie popped her head back into the building. "Five minutes," she said as she worked the computer at the ops desk.

Watching her prepare for our flight sparked an idea. I pulled out Fix's phone, cognizant that I had been using it for far too long already, and was therefore an easy target as long as I kept it on me, but I was reluctant to get rid of it for fear of missing some piece of intel from Artemis Grange. I dialed Dan Gable's number.

He picked up on the third ring. I heard the unmistakable blare of an airport announcement in the background. "Taking a trip?" I asked.

"Hey, Sam. Yeah. Quick little no-notice jaunt to the other side of the pond."

Shit. I knew that Dan wasn't officially working on this case—it had nothing to do with his area of responsibility at Homeland—and I knew that he would have limited resources to devote to saving those kids, but somehow I was expecting to have his help for a little longer. I hadn't expected him to be pulled away to something else so quickly.

"Life of a rock star," I said, not quite disguising my disappointment. I knew he couldn't tell me where he was going or what he was working on—I no longer had an active security clearance—so I didn't bother to ask him. And there was nothing he could do about it, anyway. He had to go.

"I'm so sorry to leave you hanging like this, Sam. I feel terrible."

"Duty calls. This Canada thing was just a little fun on the side."

"Right," he said with a gallows chuckle. "Saving two dozen kids from murder shouldn't be a side gig. I really wish I could help you see this through. But the FBI got their act together, and they're airborne and heading your way. They're working the diplomatic angle to land in Canada, with a backup plan of Michigan or Minnesota in case the negotiations don't work out."

"If they can't land here," I said, "there will be nothing left for them to do but count the bodies. They'll never get here in time."

Dan let out a long breath. "I know, Sam." He sounded tired and deflated, and from his breathing, I surmised he was hustling to make his gate on time. "I damn near had to fellate the SAIC"—special agent in charge—"to get him to put a team together. But we eventually worked out our differences."

"When do they land?"

"Seven-thirty local time," he said. "Last I heard, anyway. I don't know if they've been delayed."

My heart fell. There wasn't enough time, not by a mile. If Stacey's recollection was correct, the broadcast would start at nine. Which meant that kids would die. There were no two ways about it. We still had no clue where those kids were being held. We had no on-scene intelligence. We did not fully understand what we were up against, and we had no plan of attack. The FBI could send every agent on its payroll to Thunder Bay, but we still wouldn't be able to get it done in ninety minutes.

We. I don't know why I was thinking in those terms, because I knew better. The odds of the FBI teaming up with a retired Homeland counter-espionage agent in a domestic kidnapping case were exactly zero. But it was all academic. The Bureau team would never get here in time to locate the hideaway where the kids were being held, organize a raid, and neutralize the assholes. I had been suspending my disbelief, hoping for some kind of miracle, but deep down, I suppose I knew all along.

The cavalry wasn't coming.

I was also losing my intelligence support at Homeland because Dan was about to board a transcontinental flight.

My chest constricted and my breath grew shallow. Nobody was going to save those kids but me.

"Sam, that's my flight," Dan said.

"Right. You need to go. We're all counting on you to save the world."

"Your hope is badly misplaced," Dan joked. "But I will give it the college try."

"Stay safe," I said, and ended the call.

Fix and Lizzie were right next to me, but I felt completely and utterly alone.

WE HAD THREE GUNS BETWEEN US—ONE IN MY BELT, one on my ankle, and one in Fix's belt—but still I wondered whether it would be enough. I'd brought a flashlight along on Lizzie's recommendation. We had spare ammunition, two spare burner phones, and Fix insisted on bringing his laptop. I supposed that leaving it behind would make him feel like a samurai stripped of his sword, and in this kind of game, you never really knew what items would come in handy. Catching bad guys had increasingly become about digital clues. I had a hunch we'd need Fix's expertise.

Lizzie reached into a drawer at the operations desk and pulled out a worn yellow-stickie note. I glimpsed geographic coordinates. Our destination, maybe.

Something niggled at the back of my brain, something I should have thought of much earlier. I knew it was the kind of thing that Fix excelled at. We had a quick conversation. "Sure," he said. "It'll take me less than a minute." He ambled off to Becca's office, still dark and empty, and emerged seconds later with a smile on his face. He gave me an exaggerated thumbs-up, then we gathered our stuff and got ready to depart.

Fix and I followed Lizzie onto the tarmac. The breeze was as unfriendly as ever, the sun hung low on the horizon, threatening to abandon us to the frigid wind, and I wondered for the millionth time how I had landed in yet another situation like this one.

Lizzie was efficient. She didn't waste any of our remaining daylight as she worked quickly but thoroughly through her preflight checklist. Watching her reminded me of Brock. He flew F-16s for years, and he also flew us across Europe in a puddle-jumper to escape a very dire situation that had started in Budapest and eventually spread all the way back to DC.

Thoughts of Brock always gave me a heavy heart. I still loved him. Probably always would. I understood that I had put him through a lot, probably more than just about anybody could handle. But goddamn it all, would it kill him to return a phone call just once?

The whop-whop-whop increased in speed and annoyance, and we were airborne. God, I hate helicopters. Jets, I understand. But helicopters… Flying coffins, Brock used to call them.

Lizzie took us to the northwest, over the town of Thunder Bay. It looked only slightly more substantial from the air than it seemed on the ground. Then it was behind us, just like that.

"Nobody likes going out there," Lizzie said, her voice punctuated by the rotor blade shock waves. "My mom and I haven't been there in a long time."

For obvious reasons, I thought. The Robinson family's cabin in the woods didn't sound like a happy place. People had suffered and died there.

"But Michael goes there?"

Lizzie nodded. "He says it gives him space to think."

Think being code for murder, maybe. But maybe I was being uncharitable. Maybe Michael Robinson had learned how to manage himself and his darker proclivities. As cold and lifeless and creepy as those eyes were, I had to remind myself that he was a child once, that he didn't choose his DNA or his family or his upbringing or his environment, that he didn't have nearly as much choice in who or what he became as we'd like to believe. None of us has nearly as much agency in our own life as we're deluded into thinking. Sure, we choose one thing over another, but the brain we use to make that choice is the product of genetics and experience, mostly well beyond our control.

Nice thoughts. But I knew better than to think Michael Robinson was anything other than dangerous, and probably deadly, too. It seemed to run in the family, if Lizzie's account was true.

Lizzie followed a winding river that looked exactly like every other winding river beneath the helicopter. I read somewhere that Canada might contain two million lakes, many joined by rivers and streams. A canoe was probably more useful in most places than a car.

A clearing opened up. Lizzie slowed to a hover, cleared the area to make sure she had enough space to land the helicopter, and settled us gently onto the brown scrub. The engine whine receded and the blades slowed their assault against the air. The flight had taken but a few minutes.

"I don't see any cars," Fix said over the intercom.

I looked over at Lizzie. She was looking at the cabin. A shudder ran through her.

"I imagine how hard this must be," I said, thinking of my own cabin experience two weeks earlier. "You don't have to go in with us."

Lizzie nodded. "Thanks," she said. She fished into her jacket pocket and handed me a key. "I'll wait here."

57

NEVER GO IN THROUGH THE FRONT DOOR. OR THE BACK door. In fact, never go in. That's the safest way to handle a situation like this one. But safe and effective are two different things.

Fix and I took our time, walked around the cabin, searched for signs of inhabitance. A cold breeze rustled through the pine trees and grabbed me by the face in its icy hands. The sun had sunk further. We were running out of daylight.

The wet ground had settled beneath the cabin over the years, and there was a noticeable droop to the roofline. It was a genuine log cabin. There was also a wraparound porch devoid of furniture. It looked like it was constructed in sections, expanded over the years by different people with different skills. The vibe fell somewhere between quaint and ghetto. Built by the owners, not some big construction company. It had a homespun quality to it, for better and worse.

There weren't many windows, and the ones we found were dark. We heard no sounds from within. If there was a car on the property, we didn't see it. It looked like we had wasted yet another hour on yet another dead end, but maybe we would find a clue inside the cabin even if it was devoid of people.

Fix and I donned gloves to protect against leaving our fingerprints. If this place had half the grisly history that Lizzie claimed, I wanted to leave no evidence of our ever having been here. Yes, we would undoubtedly shed skin and hair—almost nothing to be done about that without significant prior preparation—but taking steps to avoid leaving fingerprints seemed like the smart move.

I stepped quietly and carefully onto the back porch. I expected creaking boards and I wasn't disappointed. Unfortunate, but unavoidable. I put my ear against the back door and listened for sounds. Nothing but squirrels scolding us from the trees above and the occasional birdsong. No noise from within.

I handed Fix the key and took a step back from the door to cover him as he worked the lock. It took him a few tries before the latch yielded. The door was just as reluctant. It required a hard shove before it budged, which it did with a loud complaint of screeching wood. The settling of the foundation over the years had bent the door frame out of true. So much for a quiet entry.

It was dark inside. Mildew and decay wafted from within. The smell brought me back to a place I'd rather forget about entirely. My heart raced, my stomach clenched, and tears welled in my eyes.

Fucking hell, get ahold of yourself.

I shook off the uneasy feeling and turned on the flashlight, held it against the barrel of the pistol, and cleared the area around the door and a reasonable distance into the room using the light of the beam. I poised my finger against the trigger guard, ready to move instantly to the trigger if the situation warranted.

It didn't. Empty. Dark. Was there electric service out here? I searched for a wall switch but didn't find one. No outlets on the walls, either. I was glad I'd followed Lizzie's flashlight advice.

The cabin was sparsely appointed with mismatched furniture dating from the Vietnam era or earlier. There was a main living area with a small kitchen tucked in a corner, a small washroom, and two bedrooms.

One bedroom had a queen bed. The mattress sagged in the middle. Both sleeping parties would undoubtedly roll downhill during the night and wind up smashed together at the bottom of the U. The room had no closet, but an old dresser lurked in the corner. There were clothes in the drawers. Men's underwear, a handful of permanently stained wife-beater tee shirts, worn blue jeans, and a heavy flannel shirt. The man's scent was still on the clothes. Not entirely clean, but not entirely unpleasant either. I pointed at the collection of clothes and Fix nodded that he got the message. Someone came out here often enough to keep some things handy.

The other bedroom had three mismatched bunk bed units jammed in an unlikely configuration. Accommodations for six people, maybe more if the kids didn't mind doubling up. It reminded me of a few "vacations" my family had taken during that brief period when we were still a family. Pure misery. I shuddered at the recollection.

As the flashlight beam played over the room, a glint of polished wood and black metal caught my eye. A shotgun, leaning upright into the far corner of the room, incongruous in a room full of children's beds. But I reminded myself that we weren't in Kansas anymore, Toto. This was bear country, and kids probably learned how to shoot before they learned how to walk.

I grabbed the rifle and checked it. One in the chamber, ready to fire. Twelve gauge, I thought, but I wasn't certain. I didn't want to leave a loaded weapon lying around for someone to pick up and use against us, so I handed the rifle to Fix, cautioning him that it was loaded.

We continued our search. The bathroom was small and dirty. It stank, but not in the usual way, not in a way that I could place. Some kind of chemical smell mixed with something fecund, and notes of an air freshener. Plus, shit. It was a lovely combination. I wasn't eager to perform a closer inspection.

That left the great room. It was utilitarian and nothing more. This property had been in the Robinson family for generations, according to Lizzie, but there were no portraits on the wall, no family pictures in frames on the mantle, no signs that the cabin was anything other than a cheap vacation rental. That struck me as more than a little strange. Then again, the Robinsons didn't seem like your everyday family. There didn't appear to be much love between them, and there was that psychopath gene to contend with.

There were no bookshelves. There was no television, likely due to the lack of electricity (yes, my deductive powers *are* quite impressive, thank you very much). If any food had been prepared in the kitchen recently, I didn't find any evidence. The one thing the room had in abundance was seating accommodations. It reminded me of my grandmother's sitting room, an off-limits place stuffed full of sagging sofas and flowery chairs used only for the biweekly religious meetings she hosted, and the good lord help you if you parked your dirty little ass on any of the furniture. Pillar of the community, that one, at least when her vodka stayed down.

As Fix and I drew closer to the fireplace, the room seemed warmer. It wasn't purely psychological. I put my hand against the bricks, and even through the glove I could feel the warmth of a recent fire. It made the adrenaline flood through me, and it gave me chills at the same time. Someone had been here. Maybe one of the Robinson psychopaths.

I shook my head. I was letting Lizzie's stories get to me.

Or maybe I was exhibiting the proper level of alarm.

I searched all the horizontal surfaces for any bit of paper, anything with information on it, but the place was devoid of it. I couldn't decide if that was unusual or not. How much paperwork would you really need to bring with you out here? Still, I thought it might have been strange not to keep any lists. Groceries, repairs, spare parts, etcetera—you wouldn't want to make any extra trips this far out of town if you didn't have to. So maybe someone paid very careful attention to keeping the place somewhat sanitized. Thinking of Lizzie's earlier account of her family dynamics, it wasn't hard for me to imagine why.

We had nothing so far. Yes, someone came out to the cabin with enough regularity to warrant keeping a change of clothes in the drawer. Yes, someone had been here recently enough for the fireplace mantle to still retain some heat. Not exactly smoking guns.

I played the flashlight over the room again, somewhat at a loss, hoping to spot something I'd missed earlier.

It worked. I didn't catch it on the first pass, or even the second. It wasn't until the third sweep of the flashlight that the strange little rug caught my eye. Just one rug in all that expanse of flooring. Too small to be an area rug. Too large to be a doormat that had somehow migrated away from the door.

I slid the carpet out of the way with my foot, and instantly I knew the game had changed.

I nodded at Fix, and he set the shotgun on the floor and positioned himself to open the trapdoor. I trained the pistol and flashlight toward the opening, and on my signal, he heaved.

Shit, I was facing the wrong way. I could only see the first few steps, and I couldn't see down the stairwell. It fell away to the right, so I repositioned to the left side of the opening and aimed the flashlight down the length of the stairwell.

The snafu didn't seem to matter. The cellar was dark as death, and more stale air hit me in the nostrils. The stairs seemed to be in passable condition, so I waited for Fix to lay the trapdoor open on the floor and grab the shotgun before I started down, flashlight again next to the barrel of the pistol, playing the light back and forth in front of me.

The stairs creaked and the air grew colder. I shivered involuntarily. I suddenly had to pee. Goddamned nerves. Plus middle age, if I were to be brutally honest with myself. (But why start now?)

The cellar seemed smaller than the cabin above it. Stacked cinderblocks formed the walls, but they rested on bare earth below and didn't reach all the way to the ceiling above. I realized the cellar had been dug after they constructed the cabin. Why? Did the Robinson family suddenly feel the need to store roots over the winter? If so, you'd have expected signs of that—some infrastructure to organize the space and separate the varieties, maybe. But there was none of that. Only a bare, open ceiling in a cellar dug too shallow. Not so low that I had to duck my head, but I did anyway, for reasons I supposed were purely psychological. Hunkering down against the frightening unknown, maybe.

I reached the end of the stairwell and immediately threw my body into the nearby corner, twisting as I did to cover the room. I shined the flashlight beam in a back-and-forth pattern, searching for motion or people or some sign of danger. My eyes registered only barrels, dozens of them, large and blue, some made of metal, some made of plastic. How had they wrestled them down the stairwell? Maybe it was an optical illusion, but they seemed too large to fit.

The shadows cast by those damned barrels danced off the walls as I moved the flashlight beam, creating the disconcerting illusion of motion. My heart hammered in my chest, the ringing in my ears grew deafening, and I fought like hell against a sudden onslaught of fear and claustrophobia. I had spent the past several weeks driving around the country soaking in the open nothingness of the Midwest because after my ordeal in the mountain cabin, I couldn't stand to be in closed spaces. That fucking cellar was freaking me out.

It seemed to take forever before I got ahold of myself, calmed my breathing, got my heart rate to settle down a little. I would have to clear behind every one of those barrels, I realized, so I got busy.

The stairs creaked as Fix moved forward to join me in the dark, dank cellar. He smartly stayed a few paces behind me as I moved methodically through the space, moving the flashlight beam to clear the zillion potential hiding spaces created by those damned barrels.

I settled into a methodical groove. Clear nearby. Play the beam back toward the center of the room to prevent surprises. Clear behind us. Clear the next column of barrels. Repeat.

Behind the last stack of barrels on the far side of the cellar, the flashlight beam caught something that made my heart stop cold.

Shackles. Bolted to the cinderblock wall. Jesus, the reality of it hit me like a freight train. Lizzie's story, the Robinson sickness, the nothingness behind Michael Robinson's eyes—the shackles seemed to confirm the worst. I had seen enough. I needed to get the hell out of there.

"Hukkkkk," Fix said.

Then gurgling.

Warm wetness sprayed my legs and torso, and then the clatter of the shotgun hitting the hard cellar floor hit my ears, and I was turning, turning, fast as I could but still so fucking slow, *no no no no, not again* hammering in my brain, and the red spray gushing in spurts and Fix's body falling at my feet, his hands clawing at his neck, and *where the fuck is he that motherfucker* but he wasn't there, where the hell could he have gone, and then the electricity tore open my side, blue and hot and so devastating, wrecking everything, the end of the world, God it hurts, and every muscle clamped down and my back arched and I knew I would fracture my skull on the hard floor as I fell, but he caught me, stopped my fall, *that motherfucker not again I can't do this again, not so soon, I won't survive it this time* and a rag covered my mouth and the electric spasm let go and I didn't want to breathe in but I couldn't help it, then the chemicals filled my lungs and colored dots filled my vision and I needed to vomit. *Jesus it's happening again, it can't be happening to me again, I've been through way too much already,* and then I was out.

A NEW PERFORMER ARRIVED AT THE MAKESHIFT production studio. He didn't arrive in the same way as the other performers, who had ridden with the production team's driver. The latest performer arrived on foot. He wore a high-end, form-fitting latex mask, a strange creation with Richard Nixon's likeness on one side and Donald Trump's likeness on the other. The effect was unnerving, but that wasn't why the performer had chosen this mask. He had chosen it because it was an inside joke.

Very few people who would have truly understood the joke were still alive. That was an unfortunate consequence of modern realpolitik. Life as a public figure was difficult, but far more so when one favored certain... *activities*. So hard to trust anyone with secrets like that, but one couldn't exactly feed the animal desires without some kind of outside help, an unfortunate but necessary risk, but not one without side effects. People occasionally fell out of the Trust Tree, or came dangerously close to discovering the man's real identity, and soon thereafter those people became the tragic victims of automobile accidents or skiing mishaps, or more commonly heart attacks, happening at such a young age, such an unexpected tragedy, but one guessed that genetics played a large role in such things, and what was to be done other than cut back on one's sins for a while, maybe lessen the odds of a similar end?

It was truly an auspicious day. Twins, a boy and a girl, both of the perfect age, blossoming but not yet fully in bloom, would share the stage with Richard/Donald.

But that wasn't the half of it. That was something he wanted, but on this day, Richard/Donald would also get something he *needed*.

The password. The keys to the kingdom. The thing really existed, *it really did*, and the sun wouldn't rise again before it all became his. There would be no turning back. Nothing would stand in his way. No earthly desire would be off limits, no enemy would hold even the slightest sway over him, no political foe would stand a chance, no *nation-state* could unseat him. Sure, there would still be complications to handle. But he would have the right tool for the job. In fact, he'd have the right tool for just about *any* job.

Richard/Donald felt giddy with anticipation. First the two young twins. And after he'd had some time to recover, after he could get it up again, he would turn his attention to the redhead. He wouldn't get the first crack at her—an unavoidable concession, but he was more than happy to agree to Smokey's terms under the circumstances. There would still be enough fight left in her (she was nothing if not a fighter, they said) to make it not just worthwhile, but enjoyable too.

The performer looked at his watch and strode confidently into the production studio, nodding to the guard holding the door who stifled an amused grin as he took in the strange mask, but Richard/Donald didn't notice, excited as he was for what lay ahead.

STACEY WASN'T UNCOMFORTABLE. IN FACT, SHE FELT good, very much at ease. Her sanguine mood was no doubt aided by the drugs, which she had fought in vain. The men had easily subdued her and jabbed the needle in.

She allowed herself a small, ironic smile. It would all be over soon, one way or another.

Not that she was delusional. She understood the seriousness of her situation. But they must have given her different drugs this time, perhaps something to help her keep things in a healthier perspective as she awaited her fate, whatever that might be.

And was it really so bad the last time they'd had their way with her? Why had it felt like such a big deal? Some sexual things, kinkier than she'd otherwise have preferred, but it could have been much worse. Some rude jokes, sure, and some scary talk, but at the end of it all, they had gotten off and then left her alone. She shrugged. Maybe she had just been in some kind of negative headspace at the time. Not like now. Things seemed much better now.

In a quiet corner of her mind, Stacey knew she should care more about the way things would turn out, but she didn't. It didn't seem to matter. It was as if all of her thoughts, especially the unpleasant ones, remained a pleasant distance away from her true self. None of them affected her.

Suddenly, and maybe this was because of the drug coming on full-force, she was back in American Lit class at Bryn Mawr, trying to torture some meaning out of Faulkner's drunken ramblings, trying to understand what all the fuss was about, why anybody bothered reading this guy's drivel in the first place, let alone taking a college course around it.

And there was also that tortured phone conversation with her parents, both of them on the line like some corporate conference call, the pain and awkwardness heavy in the silence that followed her announcement that she needed some time off to think about things, though which "things" precisely needed pondering was something she couldn't adequately explain to her father, at least not in a way that made him less angry about wasting all of that tuition money, which at Bryn Mawr was nothing to sneeze at. She smiled at the memory, which was only a few months old, but it seemed very far away, so distant that the jagged edges no longer stabbed her heart.

She could get used to this kind of perspective, she thought. And what did it matter, anyway? What did *anything* matter? Just a strange configuration of self-aware carbon riding on a watery rock in the middle of the blackness. Everyone. Even the special ones. *So what* if she never saw her next birthday? *So what* if she lived to be a hundred? Either way, it wouldn't make any difference to anyone or anything in the long run. The notion drew a chuckle. Nihilism, her philosophy teacher would have called it. Realism, more like.

Whatevs.

Stacey giggled. *Whatevs.* Her friend from New York had taught her that word. And also how to finish a blow job properly. Just stop breathing if you don't like the taste of it. And open your throat up a little and don't be afraid of the gag reflex. Guys think it's hot, the girl had said. Did they really? She still didn't know. Hadn't really had much opportunity to practice. At least, not until she met that older dude in the bar, and then she had woken up in a cage.

The thought of the cage produced an involuntary shudder. The horror and fright of it penetrated her chemical euphoria a bit, and her smile dimmed. At least they weren't holding her in a cage this time. It was some kind of office, empty, with stained carpet and institutional lighting and one blue wall.

But warm. No screams, at least none that she heard. They hadn't messed with her recently, and that was something. So it could have been worse. And maybe it *would* be much worse in the future, but Stacey didn't feel the need to worry about it. She closed her eyes and enjoyed the pretty colors behind her eyelids.

The door opened. Not hard and fast like the other times, but gently, timidly almost, like whoever it was didn't really want to disturb her. Stacey vaguely recognized the face, but definitely recognized the rest of the man. The guy was huge, hard as a rock, not fat, strong as hell, dressed like a lumberjack. She recognized him as one of the guys from the airplane and the passenger in the golf-cart-thing they'd used to transport her from the airport.

He occupied the entire doorway for a moment, then slipped inside, did something with the lock from the outside, and closed it behind him. He offered her a bottled water. "Thanks," Stacey said. The word came out with more syllables than necessary, and her voice sounded far away and dreamy.

"Don't mention it," the man said. Was he a man? Stacey wondered. He was big enough for manhood, but there was something about him that seemed young. Something in his face. He looked very... earnest. That's what it was. And eager. And nervous?

"Come here often?" Stacey said, and she didn't know why she said it, and it made her giggle again, which made her a little self-conscious despite the drugs, and she covered her mouth with a hand.

The big guy smiled at her, a kind, lingering smile. He sat down against the wall opposite her. "Never, actually."

Stacey fiddled with her fingers, suddenly shy.

"Name's Trevor," the guy said, his eyes seeking hers. There was something in his gaze that Stacey recognized, that desperate, hormonal longing that young men had when they looked at her, bare and difficult to disguise yet somehow wholesome and genuine, too. She wasn't an idiot. She'd been pretty her whole life, and she knew when someone was into her. And Paul Bunyan here was definitely grooving on her. This guy wanted to fuck her, sure, but more than that, she thought, he probably wanted to make love to her, slow and tender. It was cute and clumsy and unsophisticated, but sweet, too, and it made her giggle again.

The moment stretched out a bit too long and grew uncomfortable.

"Is this the part where you saw off my arms and legs?" Stacey asked, definitely because of the drugs but probably also because she was fairly certain that was how the day would end and she didn't want to beat around the bush.

It must have been the wrong thing to say, because in a flash, Trevor was on his feet and out the door.

I AWOKE TO THE IMPOSSIBLY LOUD HAMMERING OF A portable generator. It sounded like it was located somewhere inside my skull. How utterly inconsiderate of someone, disturbing my slumber that way. But as my mind cleared, those trivial thoughts vanished, replaced by the worst kind of fear.

Before I could stop them, my eyes snapped open. I was still in the cellar of the Robinson's cabin. Bare bulbs hung from the low ceiling and threw off just enough light to make the place even more terrifying. I had missed them during my flashlight search, where I had failed to…

Jesus, Fix!

The memory came crashing in. My eyes darted around the cellar. Fix lay motionless in a pool of blood, one arm folded awkwardly under him, legs splayed.

I cried for him, and for me. Hot tears dripped from my cheeks onto my shirt. So much death. I couldn't take any more of it. I'd seen so many brutal, awful, horrible things. I wanted to be dead, just so I wouldn't have to witness any more senseless death.

A sick sense of familiarity settled over me as I took stock. I was on the cold, hard ground, duct-taped to one of those big blue barrels. He must have used the entire roll of tape, because it covered most of my torso. My legs were free. My forearms were free below the elbow. He had secured my upper arms against the barrel.

I shifted my weight, testing the barrel. It was full, heavy as hell and going nowhere.

Trapped.

I had been here before, several times, details maybe slightly different but with the same upshot, and that made things worse instead of better. I knew exactly what lay ahead of me. It scared me witless.

My mind flashed back to a cavernous warehouse where I was strapped against a wall. Brock was hanging nearby, also shackled, but sideways, so that his broken ankle hung at an impossible and nauseating angle. And he watched me die at the hands of a madman.

Then I was in that fucking mountain cabin again, drugged and bound and gagged and helpless and defiled.

The sobs came at me out of nowhere. I cried helpless tears of despair and hopelessness. My chest heaved and snot ran from my nose and my heels scratched at the packed earth beneath me. Why did this keep happening? Why struggle to save myself yet again if I would only wind up back in another fucked-up situation? Why not just surrender to whatever madness awaited, gut it out, and wait for death to take away the pain?

It was bitter like bile. Brock had left me because of this shit. And I had quit the life. I had walked away. Done. No more. I wanted matinee movies and yoga classes. And I wanted Brock back, wanted that more than anything.

But it was all taken away. Everything. There was nothing left of me but some kind of hollow, rotting shell. I was nothing but a ball of pain and anger and heartache.

And then I'd found Stacey, and she was exactly like me but years younger, and I couldn't ignore her pain, and I couldn't let it go. I found purpose in killing Posner and tracking down the rest of his gang of animals. I told myself it was justice, but really it was just selfish. I wanted to punish someone for my own pain, to settle my own score, and Posner was a perfect target. Maybe there was some righteousness involved, but really it was revenge. I wanted to find some asshole—*any* asshole—and make him pay for all I had suffered at the hands of others like him.

Now Fix was dead. He was a good guy, a good *man*, likable and strong and helpful and courageous. Gone now, thanks to the way I shamed him into helping us, threw him into the deep end, way over his head, and I got him killed. I looked at his twisted body, all that blood, punished myself with the horror of it, cried harder and harder until I couldn't breathe.

And Stacey would die, too. I'd promised her I would protect her. I had given her my word that I would see this thing through, that I would keep her safe and make those animals pay for what they had already done, and for what they planned to do. I would save those other kids.

I looked at my ridiculous self, taped to a fucking barrel, and my sobs turned to laughter, angry and bitter and hateful and mirthless. Look at you, sitting here, worthless, riding in to save the day like some fucking superhero, and here you are again, waiting for someone to come and rescue *you*. What a joke. Your entire life, your entire career. Some kind of sick joke. This will be a fitting end, I told myself. I would finally get what I'd had coming for years on end. I would finally prove Brock right—that I would get myself killed and leave him alone and brokenhearted.

Only I was the one who would die alone and brokenhearted.

"There, there now."

The voice made me jump, snapped me back to reality, frightened me so much that I peed a little.

Michael Robinson stepped from the shadows. The dim overhead light twisted his features, turning him into some kind of demon, eyes hidden in the shadow of his brow, his gaze holding nothing recognizably human, nothing but pain and death.

In his hand was a knife.

I closed my eyes and waited for the end to begin.

FBI SPECIAL AGENT ALFONSE ARCHER EYED HIS wristwatch and adjusted his earplugs, which he wore religiously whenever forced to fly.

The Bureau jet was all business. No frills. Like a flying cubicle with a small conference table. He wasn't happy to have been summoned back to work in the middle of his vacation—that should teach him not to stay local during his time off—but he knew that if it involved Sam Jameson, it was probably serious.

And he knew that if she'd asked for him, it probably meant she was in deep kimchi. She'd never once just called to chat. Mostly, she called when she needed saving. He thought it would end when she quit her job at Homeland, but either she had a knack for finding trouble, or trouble had a knack for finding her.

Half a dozen agents huddled around the conference table, poring over maps, missing persons folders, communications intercepts, and a synopsis of the situation forwarded by Dan Gable from Homeland.

Archer perused the list of missing persons reports filed over the past few weeks and months. Several hundred of them, all fresh cases, a drop in the bucket compared to the ninety-thousand people missing in America at any given time. Many of those people *wanted* to be missing. Sometimes disappearing is an attractive option, depending on the mess you've made.

But not all of them had chosen to disappear. Many were victims, taken from their lives by force. And sadly, most of those people didn't survive longer than forty-eight hours after abduction. Kids, mostly, and young women. Archer suspected the real number of missing persons victimized by foul play was much larger than the statistics reflected, because many victims lived on the streets, had no real structure to fall back on, and had nobody in their lives who gave enough of a damn to search for them. People assumed they died of a drug overdose, and many of them did.

"Update?" Archer said, locking eyes with another of his agents.

"New batch of digital artifacts is on its way," the agent said. "Bandwidth problem with the SATCOM link, so it's taking longer than normal." Which was already too long for Archer's taste.

"How about the dip clearance?" Archer asked, referring to the diplomatic permission from the Canadian government required for an American investigative team to set foot in an official capacity on Canadian soil.

The agent shook his head. Archer cursed, looked at his watch. According to their flight plan, they'd have to decide soon about where to land the plane. They were less than an hour out from Thunder Bay, putting their landing time at around 7:15 p.m. The forecasted headwinds hadn't been as strong as expected, and they'd made up time en route. But if they were forced to land in Michigan, Archer feared the entire trip would be a waste of time. There was no way they'd be able to save those kids with Lake Superior standing between the FBI team and the action.

There was an unspoken fatalism about the whole endeavor. The team had enough experience to know that it would have been prohibitively difficult for the criminals to orchestrate two-dozen near-simultaneous live killings. The logistics were hard enough to manage for just one killing, if the perps had any concern for avoiding instant capture by the authorities. The digital security precautions alone were immense, and hard to replicate at that kind of scale.

Which meant that the kids were probably already dying. There'd undoubtedly be a grand finale which might be a live event, but there was no way that all twenty-four murders would happen in real time. Way too risky.

So the operation was much more a recovery mission than a rescue mission. No one would ever admit that out loud—the entire team would move mountains to save even one child's life—but no one on the team had high hopes.

Archer knew Sam Jameson well enough not to write her off. But his professional assessment, based on many years in the field, was that the odds were not in their favor.

62

TREVOR DIDN'T LIKE THE LOOK ON HIS COMPATRIOT'S. Tweak, they called him, because he was always twitching and shivering like a small, hairless dog. Tweak wasn't known for his judgment, and Trevor figured it was only a matter of time before the skinny drug-addled loser caused serious problems.

"Dude." Tweak's customary opener. "Karl said no more boning the girls now. They all have to be fresh for the thing."

Trevor frowned. Yes, he was hot for the gorgeous brunette… but he wasn't a rapist. "I didn't do anything," he protested.

Tweak's face twisted into a sardonic smile. "Right. And I'm your fairy godmother. The hell you take me for? You big dumb animal."

Trevor bristled. It was one thing for Karl and Sevier to call him stupid all the time and make fun of his family. But it was another thing entirely to have to put up with that kind of abuse from a walking turd like Tweak. Tweak was below him in the pecking order, at the very bottom of the totem pole, stuck with all the dirty work nobody else wanted. Tweak was eager to improve his lot in life, and Trevor had the sense that Tweak was gunning for him, looking to replace him a few rungs higher on the ladder.

"Tweak, knock it off already. I told you, nothing happened in there."

"Then why are you blushing?"

Trevor blushed harder. Congenital. Nothing to be done about it. Fair-skinned and maybe a bit more insecure than your average young man—rough combination in a crowd like Karl's gang.

"See what I'm saying? You're lit up like Christmas," Tweak pressed. "Cuz you banged her. Huffing and puffing away with your chubby little prick." Tweak thrust his skinny hips a few times, made a slapping motion with his hands, flicked his tongue like a lizard. "Couldn't help yourself, couldja?"

"Knock it off. Someone's going to hear you."

"Surprised we didn't hear your squeals through the door." Tweak laughed, harsh and low-class. Then his face got serious. "And I'd be willing to bet Karl isn't going to be happy about it."

Trevor sensed a change in Tweak's voice. The skinny doper was planning something. "You stop saying that," Trevor said, struggling for words with more force but finding none that seemed to fit. "It's not funny. You know what Karl's like."

Tweak's smile turned smug. "Exactly. I wouldn't want Karl mad at me for humping the meat, 'specially after he went to all that trouble to forbid it and everything."

Trevor looked hard at the skinny kid, assessing. Was this a joke? Was Tweak pulling one of his typical stunts, looking to get a reaction?

"Ha ha," Trevor said. "Funny. But the joke's over. I didn't do anything to that girl. I brought her some water. That's it."

"You think Karl's going to believe that?"

"Why wouldn't he? It's what happened."

Tweak laughed. "But what if someone told him something a little different? What if Karl maybe heard a different story?"

Trevor stared hard. His face felt hot, and he realized that his fists were clenched tight as a sailor's knot.

Tweak pressed the attack. "You remember what he did to that kid from Saskatchewan. Over what? Going to the wrong address?" Tweak shook his head. "I'd hate to get caught doing something *really* wrong." That harsh, low-rent laugh again.

"It was more than just the wrong address," Trevor protested.

Tweak's eyes sparkled. "You're right. It was 'cuz he was making time with that girl, too. Somebody's daughter. After Karl told him not to. Karl had a plan for her. And anyway, lots of guys get caught because of chasing skirts. Bitches ain't nothing but trouble in our line of work. Ain't that what Karl always says?"

Trevor's eyes widened. Was this really happening? Was Tweak seriously planning to go to Karl with some bullshit accusation?

"Hell of a secret to carry around," Tweak said, a threatening note in his voice. "I'm sure it would be very valuable to you. For me to keep quiet about the girl, I mean."

Trevor's voice rose. "What are you playin' at? I'm tellin' you, I didn't do anything to that girl. This is crazy!"

Tweak nodded his head. "Totally nuts," he agreed. "A guy'd have to be crazy to commit a flagrant violation of the rules like that. What with Karl's temper and all."

Trevor's head throbbed in time with his heartbeat and there was a rushing sound in his ears. He flexed his fists.

"Where'd they bury the Saskatchewan kid?" Tweak said.

Trevor's fists tightened. He knew damn well what had happened to the kid with the bad sense of direction and the crush on that girl.

"Oh, wait," Tweak said. "I remember now. Karl hauled that stump grinder out next to the river and fed the poor kid through. The fish had themselves a little feast, didn't they?"

Trevor's breaths came short and fast.

"They'd have to try something different with you," Tweak went on. "Your big dumb ass wouldn't fit through the grinder." He cackled, long and loud, shrill and barking, maybe chemically enhanced or maybe calculated for maximum effect.

Trevor drew a deep breath. "Stop it, Tweak. I'm warnin' ya."

"Course," Tweak said with the faintest gleam in his eye, "it wouldn't have to come to that. I'm sure we could come to an agreement."

Trevor wasn't the quickest weasel in the den, but he had seen this kind of thing before. One guy gets a leg up on another, and he never wants to let go of the advantage. No matter how much a fella pays, the blackmailer always wants more. And always demanding payment at the worst times, too. It was a big reason why he never stepped out of line. He didn't want to live the rest of his days trying to live something down.

"I'm a reasonable guy," Tweak said. "And it was a simple mistake. Good fun, getting a little tail, 'specially as fine as that girl is…" Tweak trailed off, shaking his head. "Hell, I'm not afraid to admit that I was tempted, too. But I know better than to get crossways with Karl. Not worth it! No way!"

Tweak let loose with that cackle again, and maybe that was what pushed Trevor over the edge. Trevor's fist met the skinny kid's chin with the force of a freight train, shattering his open jaw and twisting his head up and back, lifting the smaller man off his feet. Tweak's skull hit the hard floor unimpeded, absorbing all the impact, sending shards of bone into his brain.

And then it was over, Tweak's limp form lying inert, face smashed, skull fractured, mouth dripping blood, no movement, no heartbeat, and Trevor realized that he was crying.

OFFICER SEVIER OF THE THUNDER BAY POLICE
Department lay on a hospital cot awaiting painkillers and a splint for his
knee. The nurse had taken one look at the knee and left the room, announcing
over her shoulder that she'd be back shortly with something for the pain. That
was half an hour ago. Socialized medicine, Sevier groused under his breath.
It all sounded like utopia until you really needed help. Better off flying to
Thailand to see a doctor.

Sevier fiddled with his phone, checking email, playing that silly game
that all the kids were playing these days. He'd downloaded it on a whim, but
it had quickly become something of an addiction. He didn't hear the man
enter his hospital room.

"Sevier," said the booming voice. "How's it hangin'?"

Sevier looked up to see Karl's large form, tall and sinewy, close-cropped
white hair, weathered face, signature flannel jacket.

"What the hell are you doing here?" Sevier fairly hissed. "Are you out of
your damn mind?"

Karl made a motion with his hands, like *calm down*. "Just checking up
on an old friend who had an unfortunate accident," he said.

"Since when are we ever supposed to be in public together?" Sevier's voice was low and mean. "You want to get us bent over?"

Karl ignored the question. "Rough afternoon you had, eh? That redhead getting away in your cruiser. And your knee. Did you fall or something?" Karl chuckled a little at his own joke.

"You need to leave," Sevier said just above a whisper.

"Course, there's lots of talk around town right about now," Karl continued. "About some kind of transaction you were party to?"

Sevier's face lost its color.

"I'm not one to believe those kinds of rumors," Karl said, his voice calm. "And maybe I got the details wrong." He looked pointedly at Sevier.

"You don't understand," Sevier tried. "I was setting her up." But the performance was weak and the look on Karl's face told Sevier that nobody was buying. He wasn't used to being on this end of a difficult conversation, and all the fear running around in his brain caused his mental circuits to short out. How the hell had they known? Who could have told?

But he knew the answer.

"Is it just me," Karl said, "or have you put on a little weight?"

Sevier said nothing, his eyes fixed on the older man's face, looking for a sign.

"You should ease up on the sugar and fat," Karl went on. "They say it's a risk factor for heart disease."

Sevier's eyes caught a blur of motion. Karl's right hand emerged from his jacket pocket like a missile, landing with a punch on Sevier's shoulder, lingering a moment, then the burning started, deep and hot, searing the inside his shoulder, spreading to his chest, and why couldn't he breathe? Why couldn't he speak? What the hell was happening?

Karl smiled, brandished the hypodermic, shrugged his shoulders. "Nothing personal, old friend," he said. "Just business. We're all going to miss you. But not very much." A brief chuckle, again amused by his own wit.

Karl slipped the needle into the sharps container hanging on the wall of the hospital room, turned on his heel, and yelled for a nurse to come quickly, because something was very wrong with his friend.

I SAT ON THE DAMP CELLAR FLOOR, BACK AGAINST A barrel, duct-taped in place, my arms bound against my torso, unable to move or breathe or think.

Michael Robinson leered, waved his knife at me, and twisted his face into a grotesque grin that made my skin crawl.

Panic drowned me. Tears and howls came out of me. I thrashed against the tape and the barrel and the cold, damp earth. My legs kicked and flailed of their own volition, trying in vain to upend the barrel or scare away the madman.

Michael Robinson laughed at me. "Not so tough now, are we?"

His eyes showed aggression, arousal, meanness. *He really gets off on this shit*, the cold, clinical part of my brain announced, the lone calm voice inside my head somehow cutting through all the hysterical shrieks and howls from my crazy ones.

I would die here, in this cellar in the middle of nowhere, next to Fix's still-bleeding body. I knew it in my bones.

But I resolved not to go quietly.

"Welcome to my humble hideaway," the killer said, arms stretched wide, a sick grin on his face, eyes cold and evil as ever. "You probably don't know it, but you're in good company right now." He laughed, a strange, high-pitched cackle that sounded like pure insanity.

In an instant, his face was serious again. "Sometimes, when you're quiet enough, you can still hear the screams."

I shuddered. Robinson saw my reaction, and his face opened up into that inhuman smile again. "Trust me," he said. "We're going to have a good time together."

He affected some kind of exaggerated sadness, the dim overhead light turning his features into some kind of freakish mask. "But not right now," he said, puffing his lower lip like a petulant child. "You'll just have to wait for the fun. I appreciate that waiting is hard, but I promise you, it will be worth it." He smiled and winked at me and licked his lips, and the hair stood up along my spine.

He moved on me with surprising speed. He slapped my mouth, then disappeared into the shadows. I heard metal on metal. Robinson reappeared with shackles in his hands. In a blur of motion and curses, Robinson slapped them on my legs, too tight for comfort, the hard edges digging into the curves of my ankles.

Another flurry of motion and the knife was out again, right next to my cheek, brushing lightly against my skin, cold and hard. I didn't move. I couldn't draw a breath. I studied his eyes, searching for some sign of humanity or empathy, but I saw nothing but infinite emptiness. The Robinson family curse.

"You're so beautiful," he said.

He grabbed my hair and kissed my mouth. His tongue touched mine before I could rip my head away. I should have bitten it off, but my revulsion was overpowering and I couldn't think, only react.

He laughed again, high and fucking crazy. "You're a feisty one, too," he said with a note of what sounded like admiration. "Not like the druggie chicks. They're so limp and boring and it's always over too quick."

I shuddered again, bile rising in my throat. I thought of impaling my neck on his knife, ending it quickly, a few seconds of pain in exchange for eternal numbness, a quick way out of the nightmare, because I didn't have the strength to survive this again. Ever.

Stacey came to my mind, young and pretty and smart and courageous. *I will protect you,* I had told her. And less than two hours later, they'd taken her.

"Where is she?" I hissed.

Anger flashed across Robinson's face, then vanished as quickly as it had appeared. His features turned strangely soft. He caressed my hair and traced the outline of my ear with a fingertip. "Let's not worry about the girl," he said, his voice low and soothing. "She's in good hands. Let's focus on us."

He licked my face.

I threw up.

He slapped me, hard. The sting brought tears and the concussion brought stars and an instant headache.

"Fucking bitch puked on me." Spoken almost to himself, with a look of surprise. "Doesn't make a man feel very sexy, now, does it?"

The stench and fear and revulsion made me retch again. Robinson cursed, disappeared into the shadows, returned with a bucket. He doused me with ice-cold water. The harsh realness of the frigid deluge snapped me back to my senses.

Focus. Take stock. Be patient. Use what's available. Find the weakness and exploit it. Phrases from training and real-life nightmares poured into my brain one after the other.

But it was no use. Robinson disappeared into the shadows again, this time returning with the rag doused in chemicals. He clamped it across my mouth and nose. I held out for as long as my body would let me, but reflex took over. Against my own will, I filled my lungs with toxic fumes.

For a brief span as the chemicals hit my brain, I stopped caring. I didn't care about Stacey. I didn't care about Brock. I didn't care about Fix.

I didn't care that I was about to die.

And then, blackness.

VIBRATION. MOTION. NOISE. COLDNESS. A SHARP PAIN IN my wrists and ankles. My head thick with fog and fear and chemicals. My eyelids too heavy to lift.

And then my stomach climbed up into my throat and it felt like free-fall. My eyes snapped open.

Helicopter.

Lizzie Robinson at the controls. Michael Robinson in the passenger seat next to her, on her left side, directly in front of me. My body strapped into the tiny backseat, cramped and cold. Gloom and gathering darkness outside, and in my fog I felt curious about how Lizzie planned to navigate without daylight, forgetting for the moment that the helicopter was fully equipped with instruments and autopilot and all the bells and whistles.

Claustrophobia struck, now of all times, and I choked back a scream.

Jesus, get ahold of yourself, I coached. *Breathe. Assess. Plan.*

I looked down. My wrists were duct-taped together. The tape pinched my skin and pulled at the hairs on my arms. But my hands were in my lap, not behind me. They had removed all the duct tape that had held me fast against the barrel in the cellar. It was probably necessary to wrestle my dead weight into the tiny backseat.

I looked forward. The cockpit seemed cramped and tiny, designed either to save money and weight or to accommodate miniature humans. Maybe both. Michael Robinson's seat was maybe two feet in front of my face. Straps from his five-point harness held him in place. The back of his head looked like any normal person's, and this strange juxtaposition—a normal looking human head stuffed full of murderous psychopathy—made me unaccountably angry.

My hands were moving before my conscious mind even knew about it. I threw my arms up and over Robinson's seat. I lunged forward. My torso slammed into the back of Robinson's chair as my arms extended over his face, then down to his neck.

I pulled back, threw my full weight against my hands, the thin edge of the duct tape digging into Robinson's neck, my back bowed with the strain, my legs pressing and shaking, the steel shackles digging into my ankles and the tape ripping the skin from my wrists.

Robinson's hands snapped to his neck. He clawed at my wrists, to no avail. The duct tape held fast, a noose of his own construction. He worked at my fingers, but I snapped them shut into a fist and pulled harder, harder still, my muscles burning and flesh tearing.

Robinson had an air problem for sure, but more troublesome, he had a blood problem. The thin edge of the duct tape pinched off the carotid arteries, one on each side of his neck, and it was only seconds before Michael Robinson shut down. His hands loosened their death grip on mine. His body grew slack and his head slumped. I didn't let up, even when Lizzie's blows landed, awkward and weak because of the angles involved. She screamed and scratched and threw wild haymakers at me that glanced or missed or crashed inadvertently against her uncle's face.

I closed my eyes and held on. I didn't want Michael Robinson merely unconscious. I wanted him off the board permanently. I remembered what they'd taught me about blood chokes: half a minute for brain damage, two minutes for death. I steeled myself and counted slowly in my head. One one-thousand. Two one-thousand.

Lizzie's blows halted. Suddenly, the helicopter lurched and heaved, and

I was weightless, then forced up against my restraints. Negative G's. I lost all purchase on Michael Robinson's neck, and my legs kicked involuntarily, smashing my shins against the metal seat pan in front of me.

Lizzie hauled on the collective, negative G's suddenly became positive, and our three bodies slammed in unison back into our seats. The angle was wrong and something gave way in my lower back.

I repositioned my body for purchase and leverage and tightened my duct-tape garrote around Robinson's neck, only to find myself pressed up against the straps again as Lizzie manhandled the helicopter's controls into another negative-G maneuver.

As the positive G's came back on, I held on tight to Robinson's seat, hoping to ease the impact of my ass against the hard seat pan. It worked, a little, but whatever it was in my lower back that had been mildly annoyed before was suddenly full-on hateful. Pain spiked, stark and catastrophic, and it took my breath away.

I knew I couldn't take another collision between my body and the hard seat. I'd lost this round. I looped my arms up and away from Robinson's neck. He was still unconscious and slumped against the restraints, and I didn't know whether he was still alive.

Lizzie was yelling something, but I couldn't make out her words over the din. I had the presence of mind to know that she was now the primary threat.

But I had to be smart. She was at the controls of the helicopter, for fuck's sake. Even if my hands were free, I'd have had one hell of a time trying to control the helicopter from back here. Impossible, really, because those foot pedals are important. They keep the crazy contraption from spinning around and around because of the torque of the main rotor. I couldn't just clock her, land the damn thing, and ride off into the sunset.

But neither could I let her take me to wherever they had in mind. There would be reinforcements, probably angry ones, and I would be right back in a deadly situation.

The thought occurred to me, stark and cold and clear, that I would probably be a last-minute addition to the Snuff Fest lineup.

I shook my head. Not happening. I would die in a fiery helicopter crash eight days a week before I'd let another man force himself on me. Enduring that again would sentence me to dying a new death every day for the rest of my life, and I couldn't handle the thought of it.

It was now or never.

I had no plan, just blind rage and fury, which blocked out the fire in my lower back. I lurched forward again, this time angling toward Lizzie's seat to my right. I swung my two fists together toward her face, but missed. My forearm slammed into the side of her seat. She shouted again, and I could just make out the curse words over the noise.

I flailed and grasped, desperate for purchase and leverage, and wound up with a handful of her hair. I pulled for all I was worth, dragging her head and torso toward me, watching her hands flail uselessly.

Her neck ended up stretched and exposed, and I made quick work of her, repeating the garrote. I stopped as soon as she lost consciousness. Even in the chaos and danger, no part of me wanted to kill this child.

I looked out the windscreen. Instant terror. There was no horizon, no sky. Nothing but cold, dark, damp earth filled the view. The helicopter was flying straight at the ground.

I DIDN'T THINK. I JUST REACTED. I LUNGED FORWARD, MY arms shooting out to grab the collective, the control lever attached to the floor between the seats in front of me.

It was just out of reach. The harness gave me enough play to strangle the people in front of me, but not so much that I could reach that damned lever.

The buzz and hum of panic vibrated in my brain and the wind noise grew louder as the helicopter sped up, nose pointed straight at the ground. My hands flew to the harness release at my chest. I clawed at the metal release mechanism, curses streaming from my mouth, twisting and pulling and hauling on the metal parts until something moved, I have no idea what, and I was suddenly free.

My body rocked forward and my hand shot to the collective. I pulled. The G forces came on strong, smashing my body downward toward the floor of the cockpit, and I lost my leverage on the collective lever.

Just as well, I realized. The attitude of the helicopter was all wrong. I was trying to pull through nose-down, like at the bottom of a loop, which was exactly the wrong thing to do, and there probably wasn't enough room below me to complete the maneuver without meeting a fiery end. I realized that I first needed to roll the aircraft to the nearest horizon using the stick between Lizzie's legs.

"Bloodyfuckinghell!" I yelled, nonsensical and foul and frightened and right on the very edge of panic.

But I channeled my inner Brock James. Among his many amazing qualities, the man I loved with all of me was the very definition of calm and collected in extreme situations. A lifetime as a fighter pilot gave him that ability. Or maybe that ability was innate and had allowed him to survive a lifetime as a fighter pilot. And in that instant, with the death-trap hurtling toward the ground and my remaining lifespan measured in seconds, I made the decision that if I somehow walked away from this mess, I would not rest until I found Brock and had a conversation with him. I didn't care what it took. He was the other half of me, and I was tired of walking the Earth with half of my heart missing.

My hand shot to the cyclic and my eyes started a search for the nearest horizon. It's a helluva lot harder than it sounds, because the windscreen was full of nothing but dark ground, and there wasn't much light left in the sky to help.

But out of the corner of my eye, up and to the left, I spied a sliver of brilliant orange. I snapped the cyclic as far left as it would go. The helicopter rolled left with shocking snappiness.

Shit, too far.

Back to the right. Just a little.

I braced myself better this time, feet planted on the floorboard, torso braced against my knees, and I bicep-curled the collective upwards.

The G forces crushed me downward again. That thing in my back protested with hot needles of pain. The aircraft shuddered. I thought the damn rotor would snap free from the rest of the helicopter. I'd heard about accidents caused by the rotor taking a sudden vacation while the helicopter was still in flight.

And something else. Hauling on the collective like that caused a massive amount of torque. That's why they have those foot pedals, which were a long way out of reach. The damned thing twirled around like a maple leaf falling to the ground. It disoriented me, left me completely at a loss for what to do next, so I just held on, kept the upward pressure on the collective lever, and held my breath.

Earth. Sky. Earth. Sky.

I saw individual trees as the thing spun around. The ground was fucking *close.*

I am going to die.

Earth. Sky. More sky. Earth again, but just for a bit.

Oh my god, the trees were getting big. I pulled harder, winced as the airframe shuddered, held my breath as the tail twirled around.

I pulled even harder on the collective. The helicopter buffeted and rattled. Was I stalling the thing? I relaxed the upward pressure on the collective, but felt instant terror looking at the trees growing ever larger in the windscreen with each rotation. I wished I could stop the damned thing from twirling around and around, but I couldn't reach the rudder pedals. I pulled harder on the collective again, but with the same result—I was afraid I would stall the rotor blades and fall like a stone. I backed off again, yelling and cursing and howling at the helicopter to please, for the love of all things holy, just fucking *cooperate.*

The wind noise lessened. With each rotation, I noticed more sky and less ground. And the trees had stopped getting bigger.

Could it be? Had I survived?

The yaw didn't stop, but it slowed down enough for me to get my bearings. Yes, the helicopter was definitely closer to straight-and-level. Maybe even climbing.

There was no way I could fly the damned thing—I could only reach one control at a time, and I couldn't reach the rudder pedals at all. I didn't even toy with the idea of manhandling Lizzie's comatose body out of her seat. Even if I were successful, what did I hope to accomplish by sitting at the controls? I might as well have been a Labrador Retriever trying to drive a car. I had no clue.

Should I try to wake one of them to land the thing somewhere?

Not a bright idea, I decided. It would be too easy for one or both of them to pull a weapon. It was a shock that they hadn't done so already, come to think of it. And how could I possibly get them to comply—land now, or I'll choke you again? Somehow that didn't feel nearly compelling enough to ensure a positive outcome.

Think. Assess. Relax.

But quickly.

I was having a devil of a time holding the helicopter anywhere close to straight or level. I needed expert help, immediately.

I scanned the instrument panel, thinking about the controls Lizzie had used, and also Becca during our earlier flight.

Right there, in the center of the console. AUTO PLT. ENG/DISENG. ATT HOLD. ALT HOLD. HVR.

English, please?

Was I looking at the autopilot controls? Or something else, something that I shouldn't touch? Only one way to find out.

I pushed the ENG/DISENG button. Several lights illuminated. The helicopter stopped yawing, entered a smooth bank, and stabilized itself heading roughly west, into the sunset.

I breathed. Then I laughed. Giggled my silly ass off. Adrenaline, fear, absurdity, and the impossibility of the situation all just seemed... funny. Crazy what a mind in distress will do.

Could I control the thing just by adjusting the autopilot settings? I tried twisting the knobs on the control head.

No, not that one. The helicopter lurched wildly.

Or that one, either. Holy buckets, this was much harder than it looked. And nothing about it ever looked easy to me.

I didn't give up. I stuck with it, and through trial and error I learned how to get the helicopter to turn to a new heading, and I learned how to make it hold its altitude.

Great, but I wanted to get out of the damned thing. Could I make it descend?

Yes, but not using the autopilot. I had to twist the knob on the collective. That seemed to control the engine speed, which seemed to control how hard the rotors worked. Or something. Not my area of expertise. Too bad the only pilot onboard was comatose, and also probably a psychopath.

I could fly straight and hover using the autopilot, and I could descend using the throttle. Seemed like that should be enough to get me down safely.

Now, where to land the damned thing?

I settled on what appeared to be a clearing just beyond a set of lights belonging to a gas station. The lights seemed to illuminate the field well enough to clear for obstacles. I didn't know how much space I needed to land the thing safely, but the clearing seemed plenty big.

I urged the helicopter forward until I felt centered over the clearing—though I couldn't tell precisely where I was because the far edge of the clearing disappeared into darkness just a few dozen meters beyond the last parking lot light.

But it felt like now or never. I engaged the HVR function and the crazy contraption came to what felt like a complete stop.

Then I gave the throttle grip a little twist.

Way too much. The thing fell like a stone. I torqued it in the opposite direction, trying to arrest the sink rate. Oh my god, why won't the engine spool up any faster? Ground rush. Bang. Bounce. My back—how can it hurt so much? Bounce again. And the damn thing started flying again!

Of course it did. I'd left full power in.

Breathe.

Reset the autopilot.

Relax.

Very tiny twist of the throttle grip. Tiny sink rate. Don't touch anything. Let it descend slowly.

Still too fast. Bang. Bounce.

But smarter this time. I pushed the collective all the way to the floor. The helicopter fell and the skids pounded the tundra for the last time.

I sat there for a moment, blinding pain radiating from my back, my breath still coming in gasps, my body wedged between Michael and Lizzie Robinson, thankful to be alive.

THE GOVERNOR OF THE GREAT STATE OF NEBRASKA
disembarked from his charter flight, fresh on the heels of a very successful
diplomatic foray into the tundra of the North. His Canadian counterparts
seemed duly impressed with his agricultural cooperation initiative, though
still somewhat confused regarding the details. But such was the game.
Policymakers set the direction, and it was up to the staff to hammer out the
specifics.

And anyway, the trip wasn't really about high fructose corn product and
maple syrup. A standard product dilution scheme, take the expensive stuff
from the tree and cut it with the cheap sugar solution from Nebraska. Profit.
Tax revenues. Indifferent consumers just liked the sweet taste and didn't look
too closely at what they shoveled down their gullets. Everyone wins.

Sure, the business was a bit unpleasant, and maybe even scandalous if you
didn't happen to put the corn juice on the ingredient label, or get the payoff
details just perfect with the Certified Organic people, but whatever. It was
enough that the governor got his initiative out there in the press. He needed
to give his salt-of-the-earth corn-growing voter base something to count on
in uncertain times. It wasn't lost on them that their fate depended on cattle

and hog markets, cows and pigs being the only mammals stupid or helpless enough to consume the inedible corn springing up from Nebraska's dry earth by the metric ton. And it wasn't lost on Nebraska's farmers that the Ogallala Aquifer wasn't too many years away from giving up its last drop of water, leaving America's Breadbasket to return to its natural state—tumbleweeds and dust devils and broken dreams.

Not that any of it mattered. Because the governor of the great state of Nebraska had his sights set on more strategic aims. A few overgrown agricultural companies were small potatoes. Lucrative ones at the moment, but entirely too parochial and provincial to hold the governor's interest.

His heart was elsewhere. Publicly, he wanted to put an end to the Liberal Scourge once and for all. He wanted good, hearty, god-fearing people back at the helm of our nation's government. He wanted to put religion back in government. He wanted to break the backs of the liberal media. He wanted to double down on the war on drugs. He wanted to double down against immigration. He wanted to fight back against the big cities and their liberal leanings. He wanted to double down on defense, to mount the required effort against those distant Muslim countries, full of theocratic idiocy and, damn it all, oil.

All of that played very well in Nebraska and the surrounding states, and so he said them with gusto and conviction. Hell, he even believed some of the things he shouted into the mic with religious fervor.

But mostly, he wanted power, kickbacks, and easier access to pubescent boys.

Every great man had his weaknesses, the governor reasoned. Even the paraplegic WWII president was getting a bushelful of action on the side. Kennedy had his drugs and women. Clinton with his blow jobs. The new guy with his mafia-like corruption.

Business as usual. Same as it ever was.

The governor smiled brightly as his minions arrayed themselves around him. He strode with purpose and gravitas to the waiting limousine. He waved to the sparse crowd of local reporters—he'd hoped for some national press, but some noise about the US president brazenly siphoning taxpayer money into his private golf course was dominating the day's cable entertainment channels—and ducked inside the limousine.

From across the limousine, his chief of staff outlined the day's remaining events. Jennifer Renner was her name. She was youngish—mid-thirties—and unusually pretty. Everyone assumed the governor was getting a little more than advice from her, and he was more than okay with that. It was a particular quirk of the staunch conservative wing that any amount of private indecency was fine as long as you were on the right team. But sweet Jesus help you if you were on the other side. The preachers and church ladies would burn you at the stake. They impeached the other team's president over a blow job, but didn't bat an eye over their guy's hush-money payoffs to faded porn stars. Imperfect vessel of the Lord's will, etcetera. Ritchey knew what all politicians know by instinct: party over principle is the only principle that matters. Pander to the base and you'll win the chase. Same as it ever was.

He hadn't hired Jennifer Renner by accident. He wanted her long legs and movie-star looks and sharp wit and toned body to make everyone assume that Governor James Ritchey was much like many of the political giants of old: not immune to the weaknesses of the flesh.

If they only knew.

Ritchey eyed his fingernails absently as the chief of staff prattled on about donor luncheons and corporate chiefs scheduled to appear at the mansion for dinner.

His heart skipped a beat. He saw dried blood beneath the nail of his left index finger. Not his own, obviously. Somehow, despite all of his precautions, he'd missed it during his thorough post-performance cleanup.

"Thank you, sweetheart," Ritchey said, failing to notice the way the patrician presumption made Jennifer Renner's face turn wooden. "That'll be all for now. I need to make an emergency bathroom stop. Something's not agreeing with me. Can you have the driver find us someplace quiet?"

He folded his hands in his lap, hoping she hadn't seen the blood.

EXTRACTING MYSELF FROM THE BACKSEAT OF THE
helicopter with my wrists duct-taped together and my ankles bound by
shackles was a non-starter. Also, there were the two comatose psychopaths—
one a middle-aged serial killer and the other a young girl maybe a few minutes
on the north side of twenty years old—strapped into the front seats to contend
with. Both were Robinsons. Crazy ran in the Robinson blood. And murder,
in the most gruesome of ways.

I didn't know what time it was, but I knew the clock was running out.
Stacey had been missing for several hours. It was sunset, and Thunder Bay was on
Mountain Time, meaning that nine p.m. Eastern was probably only minutes away.

Unless I got my shit together, two dozen kids would die in a series of fetish
killings, webcast globally for the entertainment of the world's sickest humans.

I scanned the cockpit for anything I could use to free myself. I wanted a
sharp object to help me do something about the duct tape between my wrists,
but I saw none.

Michael Robinson stirred.

Quick as a flash, I wrapped my wrists around his throat again to finish
the job I'd started earlier. The pain in my back grew intense as I pulled the

duct-tape garrote tight around his neck. I closed my eyes, focused on my breathing, and started a slow count. One one-thousand. Two one-thousand.

Robinson stopped moving by the time I reached fifteen. Just a couple minutes more, and he would be off the grid completely and for good.

But something stopped me. My humanity, maybe. I'd already murdered an unarmed man in cold blood, a police commissioner, no less. Did he deserve to die? I certainly thought so at the time. And Michael Robinson certainly didn't seem to contribute much to society. Wouldn't the world be better off without him? How many lives would I save by finishing off this cold-blooded killer?

But my life wasn't in immediate danger. Michael Robinson wasn't endangering anyone else at the moment, either, and maybe I'd be able to extract some battlefield intelligence from him to learn where the kids were being held.

I relaxed the pressure on his neck, still at a loss for what to do with him, still unsure how I would get out of the damned helicopter, and clueless about how in hell I would find the kids and stop the perpetrators before it was too late.

Not a good situation. Very high stakes. Very low odds. I felt drained, completely out of energy and will, completely out of gas, unable to think straight.

Just then, Lizzie woke up.

I snatched my hands from around Robinson's neck and tried to trap Lizzie in the same position—my bound hands around her neck—but she squirmed out of reach.

"Please!" she said. "He made me!"

I wasn't buying it. I reached forward and grabbed a handful of hair.

"No!" she sobbed. "He made me do it!"

I pulled Lizzie's head toward me, exposing her neck, and I snapped my hands around her throat again. Deja vu. How many times had I choked these two people already? I'd lost count. But I couldn't think of any other options.

But there was something in her voice. And there was that thing in my heart, imploring me to regain control of myself.

"Talk," I said, relaxing the pressure just enough.

Her hands clawed at mine. I slammed the pressure back on her neck for a couple of seconds, a warning, then let up. "Next time, I'm going to kill you," I said.

"Uncle Mike made me! I didn't have a choice."

"Made you what?"

Lizzie tugged at my hands again, aiming for more breathing room, but I held firm. "What did Michael make you do?"

"Fly you back."

"Back where?"

"To Thunder Bay. The airport."

I tried to make sense of it. Why the hell would they want me back at the airport?

"What was he going to do to me?" I asked.

Lizzie cried.

"Lizzie, I need to know. What did Michael have planned?"

Cries turned to sobs. Her body shook with their force. "Oh my god," she said, over and over again.

"Lizzie!" I snapped. "Hold it together! I need to know, right now. There is no time."

Her tears dampened my hands, but I wasn't moved. I held fast.

"I won't ask again," I said, adding pressure to her neck for emphasis.

Her sobs slowed, then stopped altogether. She calmed. But I didn't have time. "Tell me now, Lizzie, or I will choke you out and figure this out for myself."

She took a deep breath. "I don't know for sure. He was planning to meet someone there. But he wanted me to hurry. He said he wanted some quality time with you before the meeting."

I shuddered involuntarily. Quality time with another psychopath.

"Do you have a knife?" I asked her.

She nodded.

"Get it out."

"What are you going to do?" Worry and fear in her voice.

"Nothing," I said. "It's what *you're* going to do."

Lizzie cut the duct tape from my wrists. Tucked inside of Michael Robinson's pocket, I found the key to the shackles around my ankles. It took a few tries to get them to release, but they eventually yielded. Then I used them on Michael Robinson. I fastened his right wrist to his left ankle, securing the helicopter's safety strap inside the shackles. Best-case, it would prevent Robinson from escaping the helicopter entirely. At worst, it would slow him down for one hell of a long time.

You should kill this asshole, the operator in me scolded. But I just couldn't do it. Something inside of me had given way. All the death and horror should have numbed me to the whole thing, but it seemed to have had the opposite effect. I just couldn't stand the thought of strangling a comatose man to death, no matter how vile a creature he might be.

I tucked the helicopter key and the key to Robinson's shackles into my pocket, grabbed Lizzie's hand, and marched toward the gas station. The building sat about three hundred yards away. But it was always hard to tell distance at night. Not enough peripheral cues to make an accurate measurement, and the brain gets confused by bright objects, which seem to be much closer than they really are.

My feet were already wet and freezing. It was cold as hell outside, yet the ground remained a soggy marshland. Shouldn't it have frozen over?

My thoughts turned to Lizzie. The things she had said. Her story about the human skin in the Robinson family smokehouse. Something didn't quite sit right.

"How long have you been protecting Michael?" I asked.

"I don't protect him. I can't stand him. I wish he'd die in a car wreck."

"But you haven't turned him in."

"Who would I call? The cops?" She snorted in derision.

"Is there some kind of relationship between your family and the police?"

"I don't know for certain," Lizzie said. "But that asshat Sevier comes around a lot."

The Sevier link didn't surprise me. Something about Becca and Sevier had triggered my spidey senses.

"For what?"

"I've made it clear that I never want to know anything about anything," Lizzie said after a while.

"And that absolves you?" I asked.

Lizzie grew silent. We sloshed through the muck. The gas station was much farther than I'd originally thought. We slogged on for a dozen paces in silence before Lizzie answered, her voice small and weak.

"No," she finally said. "It doesn't absolve me. But it keeps me alive."

"What do you mean by that? Is someone threatening you?"

Lizzie was silent another long moment and I wondered if I had pushed too hard.

"His name was Kevin," she said after a time. "My cousin. Three years older than me."

Oh shit, I thought. *Not another Robinson horror story.*

"He saw something," Lizzie went on. "I mean, we all saw things. But Kevin…"

Another long pause. The muck sucked at our feet with each step.

"Kevin thought he would do something about it," she said. "So he talked."

I shook my head. "To whom?"

I should have been prepared for what she said next, but I wasn't. It still hit me hard in the chest.

"Officer Sevier," Lizzie said.

My breath caught in my throat. I'd figured Sevier to be a mid-level guy in a local crime organization, using his position as a police officer to leverage his side business, but I hadn't figured Sevier to be involved in murder. It was a line that very few crooked cops dared cross. There was no statute of limitations, and the dead seemed to have a way of getting their point across from beyond the vale.

"You're going to be fine," I said to Lizzie. "Everything will work out."

Which was exactly the wrong thing to say. Without a word, Lizzie ripped her hand from mine and took off into the darkness at a sprint.

MY SHOUTS FOR LIZZIE WENT UNANSWERED. I BRIEFLY
contemplated chasing after her—she undoubtedly knew more about what
Michael and his coterie of psychopaths had planned—but it didn't seem she
was in a forthcoming mood. It would take a lot of coaxing to get anything
more out of her, and I just didn't have time to fuck around with her. There
were other techniques I could use to get at things quickly, but they were
meant for hardened terrorists and I couldn't bring myself to foist them on a
young woman. In my younger years, I wouldn't have hesitated. Two dozen
lives were at stake. But as with Michael, I just couldn't bring myself to harm
her. I couldn't bring myself to harm one person to save two dozen more.
Reminded me of some psychology thing I'd learned in some otherwise-
forgettable Homeland training several years back.

I heard Lizzie stumble and fall in the frosty darkness. She cursed, righted
herself, and kept running. I didn't have a clue where she might be going, but
she'd lived in this area her entire life and I imagined that she knew some
place nearby, or planned to get away from me and then use her cell phone to
call for help.

I aimed for the gas station. It was also a convenience store, with an inventory of products to maintain, which meant that they probably had an internet connection.

Which brought me to the fundamental dilemma I'd wrestled with just about every hour of every day since I'd read the handwritten note from Artemis Grange, left in the mountain cabin for me to find. I'd read it a hundred times and the words were permanently burned-in:

> *You're absolutely right, of course. I am wholly and fatally unsuited for this role, and I reject it completely. Perhaps in my place, you will find what I have failed to find: a way forward.*
>
> *Capstone cannot be destroyed, but perhaps it can be redeemed.*
>
> *Good luck, Madame Facilitator.*
>
> *—AG*

Madame Facilitator. I shook my head again. It was a role I'd never imagined, never wanted, and hardly believed existed. With the stroke of a pen, Artemis Grange had abdicated, leaving me to head the world's most powerful and secretive organization. I could topple kings and destroy entire industries. I could kill people by the millions. I could shape events on a global scale.

And just like Artemis Grange, I felt wholly and fatally unsuited. I was hotheaded, angry, wounded, with a chip on my shoulder, carrying more baggage than an airport conveyor belt. I'd been abused, raped, shot, punctured, electrocuted, and killed. Those episodes crashed around in my psyche, and I was more than a handful for anyone to deal with. I wasn't fit for a love relationship, had no close friends, and had become more than a little antisocial. Despite my success at Homeland, I was a terrible employee. I followed my own counsel, had trouble following orders, and was difficult to get along with.

And thanks to Grange's sudden bout of introspection, I was now expected to do the right thing for everyone on Planet Earth.

Maybe I was being grandiose. Maybe I was catastrophizing. Maybe I was hiding behind artificial humility, or suffering from impostor syndrome.

But I didn't think so. Capstone really was the killer app at the end of the data revolution. Combined with advanced artificial intelligence technologies and an army of frighteningly competent clandestine operatives from all walks of life, it was the ultimate global juggernaut. Google and Facebook and Amazon were nothing by comparison. Capstone could bring them all down within the month. Capstone could sow total chaos, utterly upend the world order, start wars, leave entire nation-states without running water or medical supplies or food or electricity. You didn't have to drop a nuke to bring a nation to its knees. You simply had to disable the power grid, something Capstone could do in just a few hours.

Capstone could end civilization as we knew it.

But—and this came from a small but clear voice from deep within me—Capstone could also save civilization. It had the power to save us from ourselves. It had the power to reveal the dark secrets that held people in bondage by the billions. It had the power to bring the truth to light, to give people the information they needed to make informed decisions about their government, the market, and their lives. In the right hands, maybe Capstone could right the ship.

Maybe.

And that was the rub, right? Whose hands were the *right* hands? Certainly not mine. I wasn't emotionally or intellectually equipped. I was a complete impostor.

But maybe that was the right view to take into this kind of thing. Maybe a clear-eyed understanding of your own limitations was the only way to handle a genie like Capstone. Maybe the trick was to surround yourself with competent, hardworking people who shared a humble perspective on their superhuman abilities.

Because those kinds of people are so easy to find, I thought with a derisive snort. Where would I even begin?

And I'd have to find not just a few of those people, but a ton of them. Because it's always the unintended consequences that get you. Chasing profit gets you polluted air and undrinkable water and collapsing financial systems. Chasing oil gets you tangled up with religious terrorists. Chasing territory gets you into wars. Nothing goes exactly as planned, because everything relates to everything else. So handling a beast like Capstone, you'd have to be light on your feet, always watching for the unexpected, always ready to handle things in a pinch.

It all sounded like entirely too much to even contemplate, much less execute. Who could pull off such a Herculean feat? Who could handle the responsibility? More than that, who could handle all the details? Once you got past the moral problems with Capstone, you faced the pragmatic ones. And those scared me just as much.

I wanted nothing to do with it.

But there was a voice inside of me that wouldn't be silenced. *You must use it*, it said. On some level, I knew it. Had always known, I suppose. *Imagine the good that could be done.* It boggled the mind to think of the number of crimes that could be prevented with Capstone, the number of lives that wouldn't be shattered or lost entirely, the number of children who wouldn't lose their parents. How much suffering could be alleviated, all over the globe. It seemed the possibilities were limitless.

Carefully. Very carefully. We'd do things slowly and deliberately, doing no harm, following only certainties, stepping in when we knew we could make a difference, otherwise leaving the world to turn on its own. It could easily become global despotism, if we did it wrong.

I shook my head. *We.* Since when did I think I should let anyone else in on this little secret? And who the hell would I burden with this?

The voice came back, just as clear as the first time someone addressed me as Madam Facilitator: *You're not worthy of this.*

The voice was right. Who the hell was I kidding by even entertaining thoughts like this? It was delusional to think I would do anything other than hand Capstone over to someone with the morality and smarts and cojones to do the right things with it.

But who the hell would that be? Wouldn't it be someone with flaws? And what if their flaws were even more dangerous or destructive than mine?

I finally reached the edge of the pavement. My pants were soaked to the knee and my teeth were chattering. Walking on a flat surface felt alien and difficult after slogging through the muck. I couldn't feel my feet. I felt as though I were walking on someone else's legs.

Darkness. A gust of wind chilled me to the bone. I shivered, cursed, asked myself yet again how the hell I'd gotten myself into this disaster.

Under the Suncor gas station marquee, a clock. Six forty-eight. Eight forty-eight Eastern. Twelve minutes until nine. My mind snapped back to those kids, to Stacey. Where the hell had they taken her? When would the FBI arrive? Were they still coming at all? How deeply was Sevier involved? What if we couldn't stop Snuff Fest in time? What if we lost even one of those kids? Would I be able to live with myself?

I rounded the corner of the gas station and squinted under the light. I stopped.

This was it. Was I really going to do this? Was I really going to uncork the genie?

But what else could I do? Walk away? Give up?

I shook my head. I opened the door, barely noticed the warm whoosh, found the clerk. And before I could stop myself, I said, "I need to use your internet."

AN ALERT CHIMED IN THE DEPTHS OF WHAT MOST WOULD
consider a tiny data center in Bangladesh. Minuscule compared to the NSA's
monstrosity in the Utah wasteland, the Center for Internet Research was
nevertheless one of the most important facilities on the planet. It was privately
owned, but performed functions that were undeniably governmental and
mostly aimed at influencing political, social, and economic events in the West.
Hence the location, tucked away in a nondescript eyesore on a busy street that
formerly housed a textile concern.

A middle-aged technician awoke from a deep daydream and sat bolt
upright. His hand snapped to the computer mouse, a curse on his lips. The
alert beeped again, and the technician acknowledged the warning. A new
message. An important one.

He powered on the Xbox game console situated to his immediate left,
tapped his foot impatiently as the machine booted up, logged in with a flurry
of thumb motions practiced hundreds of times, and found himself at the Rune
of Ruins, a mystical location in the latest epic fantasy role-playing game. The
graphics were stunningly realistic, a testament to the lengths to which man
will go for novel entertainment.

The technician's avatar was a Dunmer, a dark and mysterious elf-like creature inspired by Tolkien. The female avatar before him was tall, athletic, fierce. Red hair, muscular, trim, dressed in a skin-tight battle suit, a long silver broadsword by her side. A digital representation of someone. Any resemblance to the real person? The technician couldn't help but wonder.

The technician's avatar conversed briefly with the tall redheaded warrior queen. The exchange lasted less than a minute. The Bangladeshi technician ran his hand through his thick black hair, still struggling to believe it was really her, struggling to digest the import of the conversation, but duty-bound to respond appropriately.

"Yes, Madam Facilitator," he typed.

Then the warrior queen disappeared in a flash of light and sparks, leaving wispy smoke in her wake.

"Priority communiqué, sir," said a breathless aide to his general, a US Army two-star famously short on patience. "Codeword Crush."

The general perked up, set down his coffee, donned his cold-weather gear, and followed the aide out of the headquarters building and into the frigid Alaskan darkness.

Codeword Crush. A code word for a code word. The two-star had been an official Capstone asset for the better part of a decade. In that time, over two dozen different codewords had hidden the program and helped ensure its secrecy. Crush was the latest, and it was due for retirement in just a few weeks. Secrecy was anything but convenient, but in the general's estimation, there was no asset in greater need of airtight security than Capstone. It scared him to death, and he regarded his role as a great privilege that came at a great price.

The aide escorted the general to a nondescript door in the basement of the early warning center housed in a building constructed in a flurry of panicked activity following the Cuban Missile Crisis. Several attempts had been made over the years to update its appointments, the latest occurring during the Reagan administration.

The aide wasn't allowed to follow the general into the room. Three humans knew the combination to the cipher lock, and the aide wasn't one of them.

"Thank you, Colonel Edwards," the general said by way of dismissal, then went to work manipulating the spin-dial lock on the heavy steel door. Finicky things, those X-08 locks. Early digital technology approaching the end of its service life with no replacement yet identified. The lock didn't like the general's technique on the first attempt, and it displayed the world-famous angry lightning bolt that has generated countless expletives over the decades.

The second try went better and the lock yielded. The general then swiped his badge against the magnetic entry lock, a secondary failsafe. He typed his nine-digit PIN into the keypad, the lock beeped, and the general entered the closet-sized secure room that contained an aging computer and a two-drawer security safe. He struggled for a moment to recall the mnemonic that helped him remember the safe's combination. Getting old. Synapses didn't fire with as much enthusiasm as they used to.

He opened the safe's top drawer. It contained a single removable computer hard drive. A red sticker on the face read TOP SECRET // SPECIAL ACCESS REQUIRED // CRUSH. The general inserted the hard drive into the computer and turned on the power switch. His leg bounced impatiently as the computer booted up.

Then he navigated the four-step identification process required to log into the most secure chatroom he'd ever encountered. He read the first of seventeen messages in the queue, breathed a prayer as he recognized the codename of the originator. Red.

He picked up the secure telephone on the desk, tapped in yet another authentication code, and bounced his leg with greater vigor as it rang.

"Priority patch," he said as soon as the command post duty officer answered. "Vice Chairman of the Joint Chiefs. I also need the Deputy Director of the FBI. Right now."

Yet another data center, this one in the Philippines. It occupied a warehouse that formerly stored knockoff leather purses en route to middle-class housewives who wanted to appear as rich as the fakers on reality TV. It housed ten petabytes of storage, small compared to the thirty-odd petabytes—thirty million gigabytes—of new information the NSA collected every single day, but the information stored in this facility in the Philippines was special. It housed the most pressing intelligence available at any moment in the NSA's massive database.

Off the books, of course. The pipeline between this facility and the NSA's infrastructure in the US was maintained by the clandestine efforts of two men and a woman, NSA employees based at Fort Meade who were patriots first, and who also didn't mind the extra pay they earned through their ultra-secret service to a thing called Crush, the current codeword for a blacker-than-black program referred to only in whispers as Capstone.

Two technicians in the Philippines warehouse read their instructions carefully, patched into the FBI's missing persons database, and also tunneled into three data centers owned by Google. The über-mensches at Google had detected the NSA's intrusion early on, but had elected to remain silent and compliant after the US government representative had suggested that the nation was overdue for another antitrust campaign, and that Google looked ripe for the picking. The representative had even outlined the government's plan to divide Google into seven different companies, leaving the shareholders at Google with little more than an email service.

Google wisely played ball, which meant looking the other way.

The artificial intelligence entity living in the data center's servers compared every photo in Google's worldwide cache to the missing persons database. This wasn't as hard as it seemed, since Google already condensed the photos into a series of data-laden descriptor words that the computers could digest and manipulate more easily, all part of Google's quest to produce the world's first sentient AI.

This quest fit Capstone's needs perfectly.

One of the FBI's missing persons files contained dozens of photos of a young teenager named Alejandro Gutierrez from Fort Worth, Texas, the son of a very concerned mother named Alma Gutierrez.

Alejandro Gutierrez's face was a near-perfect match with one found on a thirty-eight minute video stored in a supposedly impenetrable database in a nondescript warehouse in Rhode Island. The Rhode Island server's security scheme was state-of-the-art, which meant that the protocol contained several intentional backdoor access points inserted by the NSA, and was therefore not secure at all.

Every video produced by every recording device available to consumers—even the ones sold by so-called spy shops—contained a string of metadata that identified the make, model, and serial number of the recording device, the GPS location where the video was taken, and the date and time of recording. Some devices provided an interface with an on-off switch for this functionality, but the switch was nonfunctional. The information was always recorded regardless of the settings, and the information was always available if you knew how to find it.

Three minutes later, Alejandro Gutierrez was no longer missing. The AI updated his status to homicide victim, and triangulated the location of his homicide: the Canadian tundra, north and west of Lake Superior.

The AI also found the current location of the device that had captured the gruesome details of the last few minutes of Alejandro Gutierrez's earthly existence. A pair of Urban Spy clear-lens eyeglasses, purchased at the Urban Spy website for $149 USD, had captured the video. A clever device. The video camera lens was invisible. The unit had a built-in wi-fi antenna and was Bluetooth-enabled. It looked like a normal pair of eyeglasses. The AI searched volumes of purchase transactions to find the spy camera's owner: Steven Kwast of Severna Park, Maryland. The AI submitted an anonymous tip to Maryland authorities. Nearby patrol units received an order to investigate Mr. Kwast's residence and place of employment.

Last, the AI sent a report to someone codenamed Red, the new head of an organization called Capstone.

71

I SHIVERED, BOTH FROM COLD AND ALSO FROM NERVES.
I asked the gas station clerk to turn up the space heater that rattled in the corner. She hadn't taken her eyes off me since I convinced her to let me use the gas station's internet connection and computer, located in the cramped and cluttered office behind a split door leading to the checkout counter.

The idea of Capstone scared the shit out of me, but its implementation was even more frightening. The human interface was shockingly simple to use. Much like Google's famously straightforward home page—only a search bar and nothing else—Capstone was stunningly uncomplicated.

And *my gawd*, was it ever powerful. If Capstone were a car, it would be the supersonic kind used to set land speed records on the Utah salt flats. If it were a rocket, it would make the Saturn V moon shot look like a firecracker.

Beneath my fingers was mankind's salvation or mankind's downfall. There didn't seem to be any middle ground. It was incredibly powerful, and its reach was unfathomably deep. My hands shook and a knot formed in my belly. This wasn't just too much for one person to handle. It was too much for *all of us* to handle.

Capstone had already discovered the murder of a high school boy, evidently

253

committed nearby. The boy had suffered unspeakable pain and humiliation. Was there any connection with the people Stacey had encountered? Murders like that one weren't exactly rare on this fucked-up planet of ours, but the coincidence was just too strong to ignore.

I needed more data.

I Googled Stacey Lamontagne's name. Seventeen Facebook profiles came up, and I scrolled through them until I found her likeness. I copied the photo, dropped it into Capstone's interface, and waited less than a minute before results showed up. There were over twenty recent recordings of Stacey's likeness, most of them from the video surveillance cameras that had become ubiquitous in our world.

One hit was from Thunder Bay, Canada.

I read the timestamp on the video file. It was from just two hours earlier.

"I need your phone," I said to the clerk. Just as I said it, the damn thing rang.

"Hello," she answered without taking her eyes off of me. She listened for a second and said, "uh-huh," then, "yes."

She handed the phone to me. "It's for you."

I took the phone from the gas station clerk, dumbstruck. But I shouldn't have been even a little surprised. I was one of the most powerful humans on Earth, after all, and certain people evidently knew where to find me at all times.

"Hello."

"Do you feel the breeze?"

The voice I never thought I'd hear again. Cold, crisp, precise, no wasted syllables, his greeting an instant reference to our previous encounter. The breeze, from the sword of Damocles, swinging back and forth above my head, suspended by just a single hair from a horse's mane. From mythology. Damocles has everything—wealth, power, admiration—but the gods curse him to live his life beneath a massive sword, hanging point down. Damocles knows exactly how he will die. And he must live every moment knowing that it could be his last, knowing that his last moment will occur sooner rather than later, knowing that the horsehair can't last forever, maybe not even for the rest of the week, possibly not even for the rest of the hour.

Artemis Grange left me his position at the head of Capstone because he couldn't handle the breeze from the figurative sword swinging back and forth above his head. When you're among the most powerful people on the planet, in charge of an organization full of the most intelligent and deadly people that money and ideology can buy, you know your days are numbered.

I was more aware of that than ever.

"More like a gale," I said.

Grange's laugh was anything but soothing. Decades in the spy business had removed most of Grange's humanity and replaced it with tradecraft and subterfuge. At least, that was what I thought before our conversation in that godawful cabin in the Colorado mountains. He'd just finished shooting the subhumans who had drugged and raped me. He tried to convince me to take his place. When I refused, he forced my hand. He made me an offer I couldn't refuse: Brock's life, and Kittredge's life, in exchange for Grange's freedom from Capstone. I took the deal.

"There isn't much time," he said.

"I know." Thinking of those kids. "Why the hell are you just calling me now? If you have everything figured out, why didn't you call earlier?"

"You'll understand soon enough," Grange said. "But there isn't much time *for you*."

"What the hell is going on here?" I said.

"You are in play."

"Who?" I asked. I didn't have to elaborate on the question—who the flying fuck is after me?—because even though we'd met only once, Grange and I spoke the same language.

"Search for Janie Renee Wilson," Grange said, then spelled her name for me. "Do it now, Sam," he said.

The line went dead.

Dumbstruck, I handed the phone back to the girl and sat back down at the computer. Could things get any weirder? How in the holy hell had Grange found me? I mean, I knew the answer, but I still had trouble coming to terms with it. It really was a brave new world, Orwell and all of that, and it left me absolutely terrified.

I shook my head. I realized I'd been holding my breath. I exhaled. Focus. Janie Wilson.

I typed the name into the Capstone interface, recalling Grange's clipped speech rattling off the spelling for me over the gas station attendant's pink cell phone. Thirty seconds later, another AI-generated report: Janie Wilson, reported missing four months ago from a small town in Ohio whose name I didn't recognize. Facial recognition match with 97% confidence to a security camera video from a convenience store parking lot, eight hours ago.

In Thunder Bay.

Right across from the airport.

The pieces started falling in place for me. Stacey's last digital record, just two hours old, was in Thunder Bay. That wasn't unexpected — she was abducted from here.

But Janie Renee Wilson was another story. She fit the profile of the young people abducted and abused by Frederick Posner's gang of degenerates, at least as Stacey had described them. And Janie Wilson's likeness had been captured by security camera footage just eight hours ago, also in Thunder Bay. Which was the same place Alejandro Gutierrez had met his grisly end.

And that's when I knew.

My fingers flew into action.

NEBRASKA. CORN AND CONSERVATISM AND CRONYISM.

No place for a homicidal pedophile, the homicidal pedophile thought as he sat at his desk in the governor's mansion.

He chuckled. If the pie-faced, church-loving do-gooders who had voted him into office had any inkling of what he was really like, they'd lynch him by dawn. A deviant of epic proportions, and ambitious beyond all reasonable measure— those things just didn't fit the narrative. And James Ritchey had to admit that the things he had done, the things he *was* doing, were hard to come to terms with.

But it was all coming together. The redhead. The password. The clowns in Canada. Sevier— useful for a time, but a liability down the stretch—was now navigating the afterlife, thanks to Karl. Reliable Karl. Always there in a pinch, not one ounce of compunction about absolutely anything under the sun. Karl just got it done and cleaned up after himself, better than anyone the governor had ever seen. And you didn't get to be the governor of one of the fifty states if you didn't know at least a handful of world-class fixers. Especially not these days, when every mistake followed you around like a digital albatross around your neck. Mistakes from many years ago could be conjured at will and used against you. Yes, a fixer was even more necessary than a good campaign manager and a fundraiser's grin.

He surveyed the office. Photos taken during his long ascendancy with luminaries and dignitaries—at least, the sleepy Midwest's best approximation of luminaries and dignitaries, plus a few of the real kind, the big-city kind, the real alpha players who had taken a shine to him and helped him along the way, obviously with the requisite back-scratching and pole-polishing on his part, if you wanted to go back far enough.

The photos in his office were all double-entendres. Sure, the office was full of mementos of legitimate moments, but he also associated the photos and plaques and memorabilia with the *real* pleasurable stuff that marked his transformation from someone who just thought those kinds of thoughts into someone who really took action.

And oh, the action. Exquisite. A life well-lived, he mused, at least from one perspective.

From a different, more mundane perspective, however... another story entirely. A man like Ritchey had to become accustomed to cognitive dissonance, straddling two opposite worlds like that. And he had to develop a terrific stress-reduction regimen.

Such as the one next up on his calendar. A promising young intern for whom power was an aphrodisiac. Male, this one, with a list of fetishistic interests that would make Larry Flynt blush.

But it wasn't to be. A voice message notification appeared on Ritchey's phone. He brought it to his ear and listened.

The governor's blood ran cold. Robinson—that crazy-eyed dimwit of a psychopath—had disappeared. And the redhead was in the wind.

Everything he'd worked for, plotted for, lied and stolen and betrayed for, *killed* for... it was all in jeopardy. The blood drained from his brain and he felt woozy.

He put down his phone, his face a mask of stress and anger.

Capstone logged it all, instantly recognizing a connection related to a geographic area of particular interest to the Facilitator. The AI created a report and placed it in the Facilitator's inbox, along with a link to the audio.

I HELD MY BREATH AS CAPSTONE CRUNCHED ON MY
request. The little blue wheel spun around and around. It was the most
impressive intelligence apparatus on the planet, filtering and cross-referencing
massive amounts of open-ended data from millions of sources scattered all
over the globe, yet I sat bouncing my leg with extreme impatience as I awaited
the results of the query I'd just run.

Seven minutes till seven p.m. I was running out of time. Those kids were
running out of time. Every second counted.

I didn't have to agonize for long. It took maybe thirty seconds, and the
report was ready for me. What I read gave me a metallic taste in my mouth
and made my heart race. I felt sick. It was even worse than I thought. Even
worse than I imagined it might be. Stacey was in desperate trouble.

Something else. A little notification popped up, like when someone posts
something stupid on social media and the world thinks you need to know
about it right away. Only this notification was a no-shitter. I clicked it, read
the brief report that opened before my eyes, then re-read it, and then again
for a third time.

What the fuck have I gotten myself into here?

259

I sat back in the chair, pondering the implications, my mind racing to make the connections. Moments ago, someone had placed a cell phone call in which they used the words "Red" and "Facilitator."

And also the words "Robinson" and "RFID."

The call had originated from the Canadian tundra, thirty miles northwest of Thunder Bay on the far edges of cell tower coverage, and had connected to a mobile phone in Lincoln, Nebraska. The Nebraska phone belonged to a man with a name I vaguely recognized but couldn't place. James Ritchey. How did I know that name? Was I imagining a connection that didn't exist?

I shook that question away in favor of the more pressing concern: someone near Thunder Bay had used my codename — Red — and the title that Artemis Grange had left me holding — the Facilitator — in a phone conversation in which they also referenced Robinson and RFID.

This couldn't be merely a coincidence. No fucking way.

I told Capstone to search North American to find those RFID tags, the electronic chips that would supposedly enable the Snuff Fest perpetrators to cash in. Should have done this in the first place. How would I live with myself if my lack of courage to use Capstone ended up costing lives? It would haunt me to my grave.

Capstone found nothing. The RFID tags were off the grid, maybe hidden somewhere under a conductive shield that prevented the satellite interrogation signals from reaching them and activating their coded beacons. I cursed, wondered where the hell they had gone, and wondered what the Snuff Fest people were planning to do about their payment. Maybe they had made other arrangements.

"I need your phone again," I called to the teenaged clerk who had returned to her duty station behind the counter.

"Up here, we ask with manners," she called back.

I blinked twice. "Give me your fucking phone right fucking now. Pretty please."

Stunned silence from the clerk.

"Someone may die," I said. "I need your phone right now."

"Are you some kind of police person?" she asked.

"Yes," I said, just to get things moving. I was crawling out of my skin with anxiety for those kids, and for Stacey in particular.

And given what Capstone had just told me, I was also terrified for my own life.

I snatched the tacky pink phone from the girl's outstretched hand and dialed a number I still remembered from my years at Homeland.

FBI Special Agent Alfonse Archer picked up on the third ring. A hum of voices in the background prefaced his greeting. *Good,* I thought. *Wherever he is, he brought reinforcements.*

"You never call me unless you're in trouble," he said.

"Arch, you're the *only* one I call when I'm in trouble," I said.

"When Dan Gable is busy, you mean." A little laugh in his voice. And also a bit of hurt.

"Touché," I said. "Listen, where did your plane end up landing? Twenty-five kids are in jeopardy here."

Archer told me the first bit of good news I'd heard in a very long time. "We're in Thunder Bay. Diplomats came through."

I sighed a huge sigh of relief. My eyes welled a bit, too. It felt fantastic to have someone in my corner who could help. "I have something you need," I said after several deep breaths.

"All ears," Archer said. No wasted syllables. The speech of a career fed, moving smartly on a case and even more smartly up the org chart, a man ready for a corner office and his own secretary.

I told Archer what I'd learned from the Capstone report I'd just run. He understood right away what it meant, and what the implications were.

"Where the hell did you get that kind of information?"

"Don't worry about that now," I said. "We have to move."

"Seriously, Sam. I'd give my eye teeth to have access to that kind of intel. And you're a civilian now. Where the hell did this come from?"

"Arch, please. Let's talk about that later. Right now, I need you to help me." Silence.

I was afraid that Archer might go Bureau-stiff on me. I thought he might bitch and moan about jurisdiction and evidentiary rules and admissibility in court and other shit I couldn't care less about at the moment. "Arch," I said, "you won't be able to get convictions anyway, because these assholes are in Canada."

More silence. My leg bounced like a madman. I was grinding my teeth, too.

"Two dozen kids, Arch," when I couldn't stand the silence any longer.

No reply. I closed my eyes and summoned the patience to wait him out. I knew I was asking him to violate procedure, and I knew he was risking an international incident if he stepped on Canadian toes. But I was betting that I also knew what kind of man Alfonse Archer was.

"Don't move," he said after a million years. "I've got your cell phone coordinates. I'll have a helicopter pick you up in ten."

I was so relieved he was willing to help that I didn't even freak out about another helicopter ride.

THE DOOR TO STACEY'S CELL FLEW OPEN. THE BIG GUY
again. The shy one who wanted to get in her pants, but do it the right way,
with flowers and awkward silences first, and maybe no nookie until the third
date.

"Left or right?" Stacey asked. "Which leg do you want to chop off first?"
The drugs hadn't worn off.

"Quiet." With his finger raised to his lips in the universal sign for shut
the hell up.

He moved with a purpose. In an instant, she was in his arms. He lifted
her as if she weighed nothing.

"I've been swept off my feet," Stacey slurred, "but I've never been swept
off my ass!" She laughed like a loon.

The big guy put his hand across her mouth. "Shh! I'm not supposed to be
here. You're up next. They're going to kill you."

"Where are you taking me?"

"To the washroom," he said.

"But I just went." With a giggle.

"You'll find a change of clothes and an unlocked window and whatnot. Climb on top of the commode and open the window."

"It's too cold," Stacey said. "You smell nice."

"Thank you," he said. "My name's Trevor." Then he blushed, as if embarrassed by his own name.

"Trevor is a nice name for a lumberjack."

Trevor banged her head against the doorjamb on the way out of her cell. He checked the hallway again, then dashed toward the restroom.

"You're a clumsy lumberjack, Trevor." She giggled again.

"Quiet."

"I'm Stacey." The drugs made her name sound funny to her and she laughed. "You should just let me walk," she said as her head bounced off Trevor's boulder-like shoulder.

"You can barely sit," he said.

Trevor sprinted down the hallway and ducked into the women's lavatory, using his back to push open the door, repeating the maneuver to open the toilet stall. He set her down on her feet, but her legs were wet noodles and she wound up in a heap on the dirty tile floor.

"Up," Trevor said. "Get up on the toilet. Quickly."

Nothing was happening quickly in Stacey's world. "My legs aren't working right," she said. Understatement. Muscle relaxers, and plenty of them, administered to facilitate what the men had in mind for her.

"Please," Trevor said. "You have to climb out of the window. Otherwise…"

Stacey made a sawing motion with her hand. "Off with her legs, mateys!" in her best pirate voice.

Trevor helped her to her feet, squared her shoulders to the toilet, and hefted her to a standing position on top of the seat. But there wasn't any rigor in her legs as he released his grip, and she folded at the hips and knees.

"This is a fun game," Stacey said dreamily.

"Christ on a cracker," Trevor said, straining under Stacey's dead weight. "This isn't going to work."

"You're damned right it's not."

Fear seized Trevor. The blood froze solid in his veins and an electric zing of terror sizzled down his spine at the sound of Karl's voice.

"Thought you'd save this one for yourself, did you?"

Stacey's weight pressed down on Trevor, and he wrapped his arms around her torso and lifted her down from atop the toilet seat.

"It ain't what it looks like," Trevor tried, but he knew it was futile.

"Tell that to the crackhead," Karl said. "The one you stuffed behind the furnace."

It was strange how quickly the fear went away, replaced by a sad acceptance. Trevor knew that his life was over. He'd risked everything for a girl he'd spoken to twice. And he'd come up on the short side of the odds.

But he would not take it lying down.

"Run!" he screamed to Stacey. His big, powerful body was already in motion, hands already up to seize Karl by the neck, legs pumping.

Karl disappeared behind the stall partition.

Trevor charged out of the stall, all adrenaline and no forethought. He thought to duck just as his head passed the threshold, but it was already over. The butt of Karl's pistol caught him square on the bridge of his nose. His limbs went limp. His momentum carried him into the tile wall. The crown of his head took all the force. The collision fractured his skull and broke his neck.

Stacey fell to the floor, smacked hard against the tile, heard the sickening crunch of steel on cartilage, and raised her head just in time to see Trevor's inert body slump to the floor, his neck at a tragic angle.

"Oh no ohhh no no no." Stacey wailed.

"Stupid fucker," said a gruff, low voice. Then a deafening *crack*, like a firecracker.

Stacey screamed and covered her ears.

Crack! Crack!

She scooted backward into the stall until the commode stopped her. Her feet continued to push and pedal, fear in the driver's seat now.

Oh god so much blood leaking from him it's all over the floor there's no place to hide from it I can't hide oh shit the toilet oh god oh god oh god.

"In here," the gruff voice said again.

Pounding feet.

Stacey scrambled, the fear real now, penetrating through the drugs, pushing her forward, but her limbs didn't cooperate. She flailed and slipped and fell and screamed and sobbed.

Laughter. Low and harsh and male, cutting through the ringing in her ears.

She looked to its source. Tall, white hair cut short like a sailor, broad shoulders, lines on his face, and as he stepped into the toilet stall, Stacey saw something beyond cold in his eyes.

"We got a runner in here, boys," he said with a mirthless chuckle.

Panic returned and Stacey's fists and heels flew in wide, wild arcs, crashing into the tile floor and the stall partition but landing nowhere close to the man.

"Feisty!" he teased as he crouched near her on the floor, easily dodging a wild swing and fully absorbing another one without apparent effect. "Just like I like 'em." He laughed long and loud. "There we are! Going to have some fun with you!"

Stacey didn't register the rapid movement of his arm toward her body, but it wouldn't have mattered. The gray-haired man was quick and strong. His grip on her neck was unbelievably strong, his massive hands closing off her air, dragging her across the hard tile floor, out of the stall and into the waiting arms of two more men. They were all flannel and facial hair and body odor, and they were all business.

One pinned her shoulders to the floor. The white-haired man straddled her waist. His weight settled on her pelvis. Her legs kicked wildly, missing everything but the hard floor, the incredible pain in her heels registering in some deep part of her mind.

A third man stretched out her arm. He flattened out her hand and pinned it to the floor with his knee. He wrapped his hands around her arm just above the elbow and tightened his grip.

"Hold her there, boys," the white-haired man said. "Just a second now."

Stacey screamed and sobbed. Her head thrashed back and forth. Her legs kicked wildly. But it was futile.

She felt the needle enter her arm.

"Damn it all," the white-haired man said. "Hold this child *still*. The hell do we pay you for?"

"Sorry, Karl," said the man holding her arm.

Another prick.

"Slippery little vein," he said. "Third time lucky, maybe."

Prophetic. The needle entered her vein. She fought, but the men were heavy and strong and it was no use. *Oh fuck it hurts so much my god it fucking burns how can it possibly hurt so much?* It sizzled all the way up her arm. The drug crawled up her veins with an unbearable sharpness, like acid or liquid fire or some satanic potion never before seen on Earth.

The pain was incredible, terrifying, all-consuming. How did people survive this?

And suddenly, just when Stacey was certain her life was ending, the burning didn't matter. The drug in her veins still hurt like nothing she'd ever experienced before, but she didn't care any longer. Because her mind had backed away from reality, a sudden detached giddiness marking the drug's breach of the blood-brain barrier.

Stacey calmed. She stopped fighting. Her limbs relaxed. Her sobs ceased all at once. Her jaw slackened, and her eyebrows raised, and the terror in her eyes gave way to angelic tranquility.

She looked at the white-haired man. He was... *beautiful*. Incredibly so. And the shark-like emptiness had gone. Stacey saw through to his soul, light and airy and open and welcoming. His voice now just sounded masculine and strong and gorgeous, maybe the most amazing person she had ever seen, and could that feeling be... *love?* It was so strong and pure and primal, like the center of her had suddenly recognized the center of this man, this beautiful, kind, incredible man.

"That's a girl," he said, the laughter around his words no longer sounding menacing and terrifying, but welcoming, joyful, full of love.

The other men, too. So strong, powerful, yet somehow so kind. Stacey could see straight through to their souls, vulnerable and human, and she saw all the goodness and light.

She welcomed their touch as they lifted her up from the floor and carried her into the hallway. She didn't know what lay in store for her next, but she had a very good feeling about it.

ARCHER DIDN'T BRING A HELICOPTER.

He brought four.

Each one was full of men armed to the gills, dressed in black Kevlar.

I don't know how he had pulled it off. I always gave the Bureau guys endless grief over their plodding, bureaucratic ways, but Archer had gotten things *done* tonight. He had pulled together a tactical team, flown a thousand miles, and somehow commandeered four helicopters in a foreign country where his only official status was 'tourist.'

"Back to the airport," I hollered over the noise. Archer and one of his men hoisted me into the rattling death trap, wrenching my back in the process. My breath caught in my chest and my eyes watered. What the hell had I done to myself in Lizzie Robinson's helicopter?

The whining and rattling and whomp-whomp-whomp grew intolerable and the silly thing vibrated away from the earth. I strapped in as gingerly as I could manage, wincing with discomfort. I could see why people with back pain often became drug addicts. It was unbearable.

"Are you ok?" Archer asked, alarm on his face, nodding toward my jacket.

I looked down at my jacket for the first time since Michael Robinson attacked Fix and me in the cellar of that cabin in the woods. It was stained dark red. Fix's blood, arranged in an arterial spray pattern I had seen many times. From Fix's carotid artery, severed by one slash of Michael Robinson's blade.

My responsibility, said that unhelpful voice in my head, but I knew it was true. I had dragged Fix out of his element, subjected him to unreasonable danger, failed to protect him, and my failure cost him his life. Another good man and a good friend, lost on this fucking miserable journey to nowhere. I bit back the sudden urge to vomit.

The chopper lurched in turbulence, and the pain in my lower back took my breath away.

"Arch," I said, shaking away the hot knives stabbing my back, "I need you to divide your forces. We have two targets."

He did a double-take. "Two?"

I nodded. "And one of them might be a red herring. Or it might be a warehouse full of kids. I don't know which."

"How did you…?"

I shook my head. "Don't worry about that now. I know the risks, I know what I'm asking you to do, and it has to be done. If it goes to shit, I'll take all the heat."

Archer paused a beat, then laughed out loud at me. "You'll take the heat? In your capacity as a retired Homeland agent with no official standing, along for the ride on an unauthorized FBI op in a foreign country?"

"Yes. Whatever. Shoot me at dawn if it all goes sideways. You'd be doing me a favor. But we have to do this. *Two dozen* kids, Arch."

He stared hard at me a moment, the laugh entirely gone from his eyes, chewing his lip, working his jaw, muscles flexing in his thick neck. He sighed, closed his eyes, shook his head.

Then he thrust his hand at me, palm open. "Coordinates," he said.

I breathed a sigh of relief. "I texted them to you before you picked me up. What do you take me for, some kind of amateur?" I winked.

He frowned, shook his head, fished out his phone, chuckled a bit, then keyed the radio. "Listen up," he said into the mic. "Change in plans. Choppers Charlie and Delta, standby for new target coordinates. Bravo, stay with me.

Orders are to secure a perimeter and prepare to breach. Use extreme care. Two dozen minor civilians, unknown number of suspects."

He completed the briefing to his team, then sat back and rested his head against the side wall of the helicopter. I admired his command presence and efficiency. Archer was no slouch. I had really lucked out all those years ago when our paths crossed by mere chance.

My mind chewed on the facts. Not one Snuff Fest crime scene, but two. Or maybe zero.

Maybe Thunder Bay was a dead end, an elaborate ruse concocted when Frederick Posner and his army of assholes first realized that Stacey had escaped. Or maybe Posner's posse concocted it after they heard about his untimely cranial aeration event. Maybe the Snuff Fest organizers moved some of the kids up here to parade them in front of security cameras—not in an obvious way, but subtly, so I wouldn't suspect they were wise to me—to distract my investigation from the *real* filming location.

I shook my head. If that was true, there wasn't anything I could do about it now.

But I didn't think it went like that. Capstone had put together a ton of information in a matter of minutes, and the information was astonishingly complete. And it made a compelling case—we were in the right area. I wasn't sure of it, but I put the odds pretty high.

My mind kept returning to the Snuff Fest ringleaders. Three of them, according to Stacey, snorting cocaine and violating her in the Philadelphia warehouse, bragging about Snuff Fest, the payday, the disgusting and unthinkable cruelty they were about to commit.

Three men.

Posner was dead.

Where were the other two?

Who were the other two?

Where were their RFID tags? Two of them had been planted on a girl's corpse and thrown out of a helicopter into the wilderness on Isle Royale. But what if that was a diversion, rather than just a sick power move? What if they had another copy of each of the tags? The payment would proceed as normal. Snuff Fest would continue as planned.

There had to be an electronic footprint associated with a worldwide internet broadcast in real time. How could I use Capstone to break into it? I had no clue.

I needed Dan Gable. But he was over in Europe, cleaning up another disaster created by the schizophrenic presidential administration. I shook my head. Damn the luck.

I couldn't worry about that now. I had a solid lead and a team full of professionals to help me chase it down. It would have to be enough.

Still, the whole thing bothered me. The picture in my head of how the Snuff Fest operation fit together was frighteningly incomplete. An operation like this often took months to bust. Sometimes years. Yet we would have to get it done in an evening. My chest tightened and my stomach clenched. It had all the makings of a disaster.

Someone keyed the intercom and gave Archer an update in a twangy drawl. I didn't pay much attention to whatever the guy was saying.

But suddenly, something he said grabbed my full and undivided attention. Because one of the final pieces had just fallen into place.

STACEY'S DREAMLIKE STATE HAD ONLY INTENSIFIED SINCE the episode in the bathroom. She recalled the sickening angle of Trevor's neck and the pool of blood spreading on the tile floor beneath his face, but the horror of it didn't penetrate the wellbeing that pervaded her thoughts. Ashes to ashes and dust to dust, just as it should be, and everything would be fine in the end. Everything seemed too perfect in her current state for there not to be some kind of afterlife or heaven or some amazing place waiting for all of us after we shed our mortal coils. She had a hard time believing all of that religious stuff before, but somehow it made perfect sense to her now.

She didn't resist when they removed her clothes and strapped her to a medical bed, arms and legs splayed wide open, breasts and genitals exposed, bright lights in her eyes, death-metal music screeching and pounding her eardrums. Men moved with a purpose, businesslike expressions on their faces, but also other kinds of looks, full of lust and malice, but in her drugged state, Stacey saw only their interest in her and not its character. She felt curious but not afraid, not even a little alarmed, because everyone was full of such innate goodness and kindness, walking manifestations of the universal brotherhood of man. We're all in this together, she thought in some preverbal way, and even though the strap on her left wrist was too tight and it seemed unusual that so many men were eyeing her nakedness and commenting on her lack of recent grooming, she didn't feel any danger.

The blaring music stopped and a voice announced that there were fifteen minutes until showtime.

Stacey felt excitement and joy. She loved shows. What was this one going to be about?

TURBULENCE STRUCK, THE HELICOPTER LURCHED, AND my back howled in protest. The pain made my eyes water.

The pilot pulled the chopper into a wide arc. Beneath us, acting as the anchor point for the pilot's left turn, lay a dilapidated warehouse. The remnants of long-idle railroad tracks were visible by the light of the street lamp on the far side of the building. The roof had collapsed in spots. Weeds had overtaken the asphalt. Broken glass shimmered under the helicopter's searchlight. There wasn't an intact window in the place, it seemed.

On the other side, my right, lay the Thunder Bay airport. Bitterness and anger rose in my chest. I was right back where we had started, hours before. We had landed the Gulfstream jet only walking distance away from the first Snuff Fest site. We had spun our wheels, racked our brains, floundered around, and all the while we had been closer than a mile away. Maybe that was how Sevier had responded so quickly to the missing persons report we had filed from the HeliTours building.

It was only hours ago, but it felt like a different millennium. Stacey was now missing, and Fix's body was now leaking the last of its blood onto the hard-packed earth in the Robinsons' cellar. And the rest of Fix's blood was all over me.

I shook my head. What the fuck is wrong with humanity? Why the fuck am I still alive? What's the fucking point of all of this insanity?

There is no point. No reason. We just do what we decide to. And I had set on a fool's errand, trying to right a wrong that could *never* be righted. I am a fool and an ideologue and a hopeless optimist.

Or maybe I just have anger management issues. My middle finger is always in the raised position.

"Thermal," Archer said over the intercom.

Another voice chimed in from a man wearing a set of massive, silly looking thermal goggles. "Roger," the man said. "Aside from friendlies around the perimeter, nothing is registering. No signs of life inside the building."

Archer nodded. It wasn't unexpected. Infrared cameras can't see through walls or roofs.

"Update me on the friendlies," Archer said.

Another voice this time, the same twangy drawl I'd heard earlier, when I'd had that sudden lightning bolt. "Four black-and-whites, eight officers, more on the way."

"Thanks, Tex," Archer said.

"Who called them?" I asked, reminded of the stunning realization I'd experienced just moments before. It was possibly the key to the whole damn thing.

Archer shook his head and shrugged. "They were already scrambling to the scene when we called them."

"Didn't that strike you as odd?" I asked.

Archer shook his head. "Not really. It's their turf."

He had a point. Maybe I was imagining things.

But maybe not.

I needed help to exit the helicopter. The muscles in my lower back had spasmed and drawing breath was an unpleasant experience. Moving between sitting and standing positions had become excruciating. Leaning forward at the waist even a bit resulted in a sharp stab of pain that took my breath away.

I was pretty much useless. Archer didn't have to tell me to stay out of the fray. But he did so anyway.

"Maybe leave this one to us," he said, noting my ginger steps and the look of agony on my face.

I nodded. Good advice, given my pain and exhaustion. Plus, I didn't have a firearm, and Archer wasn't about to give one to me. That would be a level of culpability he couldn't possibly survive if this thing went wrong.

And I had a bad feeling that the situation was already a long way toward wrong.

Archer and his men took a position in front of the Thunder Bay cops, but still two hundred meters away from the disused warehouse. They huddled and conferred. They pointed toward various spots on the warehouse's exterior as they strategized. A loud disagreement broke out, quickly quelled by a quiet word from Archer. "Let's prepare," I heard him say. "Get in position."

They looked worried about the enemy in front of them, holed up in the warehouse.

I worried about the enemy behind us.

I turned to face the line of Thunder Bay police. I scanned the faces, looking for someone familiar, not surprised when I didn't see Officer Sevier among their ranks. I'd wrecked his knee, and I imagined it would be a solid six months before Sevier was fit for patrol again.

The Thunder Bay cops were a motley bunch. Two fat ones. Lots of close-cropped hair and ill-advised mustaches.

Short hair, military-looking. Cheesy mustache. Sounded familiar.

Was I on the right track here? Was my hunch correct? Had I put all the pieces in the right places?

I moved toward them with my hands open at my sides. I didn't want to spook them. There was little danger of my making any sudden movements, anyway, because my back had launched a full assault. Pain zinged up my spine and down my ass every time I took a step with my left leg. I shuffled like a stroke victim toward the cops. I couldn't help contorting my face in discomfort.

The officers straightened up as I approached, hands on their belts, which sagged under the weight of all the cop things strapped aboard. They sucked in their guts and puffed out their chests. They raised their chins and flared their arms. I fought the urge to roll my eyes. Men are like children, only more so.

"You part of this?" asked one of the older ones.

No, I'm a tourist with blood all over me and a helicopter full of federal friends, I didn't say. I just nodded instead, then introduced myself. Firm grips and wary glances all around. They didn't ask, but I was sure they wanted to: What's a middle-aged MILF doing here?

"A citizen called it in?" I asked, getting right to the point. "Or did one of you guys sniff something out?"

They shook their heads. "No idea," said the nearest guy, who sported multiple chins and narrow-set eyes. Smitley, the name tag read. "Just came out over dispatch."

I nodded. I was afraid of that. The Thunder Bay police department evidently employed more than one crooked officer, I surmised, and at least one of them was probably higher up the food chain than any of the beat cops in front of me.

"You guys going on this raid?" I asked, noting the nonchalance with which they stood around picking their noses.

Officer Smitley shook his head. "Perimeter only." I looked at them, clumped together, jawing with each other, doing anything but securing the perimeter around the building. Something wasn't right.

Motion caught my eye. Archer's men fanned out, taking positions across roughly ninety degrees of arc from the main entrance of the warehouse, weapons drawn. On his order, they marched forward.

I wondered how things were going at the second scene and wished I had a radio so I could listen to the tactical chatter. I felt naked and useless.

I heard tire noise behind me. A large mobile command post vehicle came to a stop twenty paces away from the gaggle of police officers, a full three hundred meters from the warehouse. The door opened. Out stepped a distinguished-looking senior officer. Close-cropped hair. Mustache. Military looking. He scanned the scene. His eyes came to a screeching halt when he spotted me.

Something ancient and biological happens when people see someone they recognize. Certain circuits light up deep in the brain. Their face changes.

You can see a mixture of surprise, plus the base emotion that underpins their relationship to you — love, hate, like, dislike, respect, contempt. Whatever it is, they can't hide it. It's among the most reliable and important human reactions we know about.

The man recognized me. His eyes hardened, just for a microsecond, just long enough.

Artemis Grange's warning flashed in my mind: *You are in play.*

It sure seemed like the warning was on the mark. But if I was in play, then so were Archer and all of his men. I had dragged them into this. I needed to warn them.

But first, I had to know if my hunch was correct. I shuffled painfully toward the senior police officer. He had regained control of his facial expression and had assumed a power pose, hands on hips, surveying the scene, working hard to ignore me as I approached.

My senses were on full alert. This is a stupid idea, I chided myself. But what choice did I have? Kids' lives were at stake. Archer's life was at stake, and the lives of his men. Fix had already paid the ultimate price in his effort to save those kids. I couldn't let a little fear hold me back. And I couldn't sound the alarm unless I was certain.

So I had to be certain.

I inspected the man's face as I neared him. Hard edges. Military haircut. Mustache.

Just like Stacey had described.

There was no way to know for certain. And there wasn't enough time to do much legwork. I needed to know right away. Was this guy one of the Snuff Fest conspirators? Did he have one of the RFID tags? Was he one of the men who had raped Stacey in that Philadelphia warehouse? At that moment, I could think of only one way to find out.

The man wore a white police shirt with a red patch on the shoulder and dark blue epaulets. Three stylized gold figures that looked like asterisks adorned the epaulets, along with a crown. The uniform flair was elaborate. This guy was up there in the ranks. It made sense with everything else I knew. So I made the only play at my disposal.

"You would be Smokey, then?" I said.

His lips parted in a pained grin, his eyes dead and wicked.

I saw his hand move. I tried to dive and roll out of the way, but my body wasn't listening. The searing pain in my back stopped me in my tracks.

The taser's hooks embedded themselves in my skin. Every muscle in my body contracted at the same time. The electricity was intense beyond words. The cold, wet asphalt smashed into the side of my face. An instant later, I was bound and gagged and thrown into the command post vehicle.

The door slammed and the engine revved. Tires rumbled beneath me. My entire body tingled painfully like a waking limb. The vehicle hit a pothole and the stabbing pain in my back brought tears to my eyes.

So this is how it ends, I thought.

THE DEATH-METAL MUSIC STOPPED. THREE MEN STEPPED forward out of the darkness and into the blinding television lights. They were nude and hard. They had been preparing themselves for their big performance.

Stacey's restraints dug into her wrists and ankles, but she didn't mind. Everything was so beautiful. If she noticed the men or their swollen state, she gave no sign. Her attention was captured by what sounded like a helicopter flying overhead. Was she near an airport? Wouldn't it be great to take a trip somewhere special? Cancun maybe? Sun and beaches and fun drinks with the little umbrellas? Maybe with some of the beautiful people she'd met here. They seemed like people who liked to have a good time. But then, what kind of person *didn't* like to have a good time? She giggled at her silliness.

Something bright and shiny flashed, and Stacey turned her head to look. She saw a naked man, muscles bulging, veins slashing through his every body part. In his hand was a very shiny blade. Was it made of chrome? So shiny. Why doesn't chrome get any respect? Silver and gold and that other metal that looks just like silver—they get all the glory. But no love for chrome.

A hand touched her opposite shoulder. Stacey turned her head to look. Wasn't this one nice? Such a fun smile on his face, and those piercing eyes were to die for. But he was very hairy. Harry, she decided to call him. "Hello, hairy Harry." She giggled again.

Harry's hand moved from her shoulder to her breast. Stacey closed her eyes and reveled in the soft, sensual touch. He gripped her breast with more force, and Stacey let out a gasp of pleasure. Who *was* this man with the magic touch?

That's when she felt the third man move between her legs.

His touch was anything but soft. She screamed in instant agony.

"Charlie and Delta are in position." The voice crackled over FBI Special Agent Alfonse Archer's headset.

Archer had a decision to make. It was one thing to take an FBI team on an evening helicopter ride in full gear. It was another thing entirely to raid a warehouse on foreign soil with no jurisdiction. The locals were already on the scene. True, they were traffic cops with little training or experience in hostage situations, but they were the law in these parts. Archer couldn't just waltz in with night vision goggles and assault rifles and start banging away as if he owned the place.

But time was wasting. The Snuff Fest hour had come and passed. Whatever the criminals had planned to do was probably already underway.

Those kids... How many were already suffering? How many had already died?

Archer took a deep breath. The cold bit his lungs. He raised his gaze to the night sky. Stars shone brightly, plus that planet. He could never remember which planet, Venus maybe, but it shone like a beacon, bright and unafraid, throwing its light into the darkness without care or concern for what savagery might be underway on a distant watery rock.

There were a thousand procedural reasons to stand down and hand the situation over to the Canadians. Archer had nothing to gain and everything to lose. Same with his men. They knew the laws and procedures as well as he did, and they took turns casting inquisitive glances at him, awaiting the order.

But it took just one brief glance into his own soul for Archer to know that there was no decision to make. He would risk his life and his career to save those kids, eight days a week and without batting an eye.

"Men, you understand the jurisdiction issue. I order you to follow your conscience, whichever direction it leads you. Either way, you will have my full support, come hell or high water."

He looked around at the men. *His* men. Steadfast, well trained, highly motivated, loyal. He loved them all.

"My conscience won't let me walk away from those kids," Archer said.

Every one of Archer's men broke into a smile. "Let's go get 'em, boss," drawled Tex in his signature southern accent.

Archer nodded to Tex and surveyed the rest of his team, looking for dissent. He found none. He gave the order via radio to the units at the other Snuff Fest site: "Rescue those hostages."

Stacey screamed. The drugs had blunted the pain, but not nearly enough. The euphoria was a distant memory. All of those good feelings, all the goodness and light and love, they were all gone. In their place was pain unlike anything she had ever known.

She was in mortal danger. She knew that now. She would die strapped to this table, camera shoved in her face, tortured and fucked by monsters. Death would come as a mercy.

Tears streamed from Stacey's eyes. "Help me! Somebody! Please help!"

But she knew no help was coming.

Archer and his men melted into the darkness. The team's thermal imaging goggles made flashlights obsolete and offered a huge tactical advantage in most scenarios. This one included.

Archer looked left and right to check the alignment of his squad of agents. Satisfied, he clicked the mic twice. They advanced quickly but quietly toward the warehouse.

The first gunshot took Alfonse Archer by surprise. Archer's body hit the ground, his reflexes taking over before his conscious mind even had a vote. He took stock. Nothing hurt. He wasn't hit. He shouted a command. He looked over his line of agents advancing on the warehouse. Right side looked intact. He turned to the left and—

Holy shit, what a mess. Barnes, the man to Archer's left, was down. Blood shone brightly in the thermal goggles. The splatter was everywhere. Barnes lay motionless.

Archer sprinted to offer first aid, but there was nothing to be done. Barnes had died before his body hit the ground.

"Retreat to cover!" Archer commanded over the radio.

79

I COULDN'T BELIEVE IT WAS HAPPENING TO ME AGAIN.
Bound, gagged, injured, tasered, hauled around like luggage in the back of a
van. Only this time, calling the cops wouldn't help. I was at the mercy of the
Thunder Bay police.

I was facing the cargo door. I couldn't see anyone or anything of interest,
so I had to reposition. Easier said than done with arms and ankles bound.
It took several tries to get enough momentum to throw my legs over toward
the front of the van.

As my legs passed over center, my bound hands acted as a fulcrum against
my lower back. Once again the pain took my breath away. Something in my
lower back was seriously wrong. I hoped the injury wasn't permanent, then
frowned at the thought. My remaining lifespan might be mere minutes if I
didn't get something figured out.

A bulkhead separated the cargo compartment from the cab. Through
a wide window cut in the bulkhead, I could see the driver's shoulders but
nothing else. I couldn't see a passenger. Was it just me and Smokey, party of
two? I liked those odds a lot better than any other scenario I could think of.

Not so fast. The van stopped. The passenger door opened, and another man climbed in. The van shifted under his weight. The cargo window was only wide enough for me to see his left shoulder. Not a cop. At least, not in uniform. The man wore a red flannel shirt.

"What's going on?" Smokey asked.

The passenger was slightly out of breath but spoke calmly. "They're getting started with the last round. I've told them to speed it up. Ten minutes at the most. Then we need to burn it to the ground."

"You've given the order?" Smokey asked.

"The fuck do you take me for?" the man replied. "All set to burn, just waiting on me to give the final go-ahead."

"Good man," Smokey said. "Any leads on the leak?"

"You mean other than Sevier? None yet. There was a bit of a mutiny, though. That dumb shit Trevor wanted to save one of the girls for himself. But that's taken care of, and she's in the theater with the performers right now. She's going to be the grand finale."

"Which girl?" Smokey asked.

"The brunette girl Robinson brought us."

Stacey! My blood froze.

I had failed. Stacey was being victimized in horrible, unspeakable ways, right this very fucking minute. I bit back a scream of anger and guilt and sorrow. My body tensed and shivered with useless angst. My fists tightened into balls. Tears came out of my eyes. *I will give these men what they deserve if it's the last thing I do*, I vowed. *I will walk to the end of the earth to find them and kill them all.*

The passenger spoke again. "News on Robinson?"

Smokey grunted. "Idiot. The redhead got him. But not before he gave us another body to handle, wouldn't you know?"

The body was *Fix*. I had suppressed the memory. That sickening gurgle came back to my mind and the hot spray of Fix's blood. I shuddered, fighting a tsunami of panic and revulsion and fear. How had I handled this kind of shit all the time for so many years? I supposed the only honest answer was that I didn't really handle it very well at all. I'd scared away the man I loved more than life, and in the end, I'd walked away bloodied, bitter, and alone.

"Where's the redhead now?"

Smokey's thumb came into view, pointing through the window toward the cargo compartment. A moment later, the passenger's face appeared. Mid-fifties, close-cropped white hair, hard face, an air of ruthless efficiency.

"Jesus, Smokey, what the hell are you thinking?"

"Relax. She was on the helicopter that just landed. Had no choice."

"In front of the fucking FBI and every beat cop in the city?"

"I said *relax*, Karl," Smokey said again. I noted the other man's name. Karl. Might be useful later.

"What the hell do you think you're going to do with her?"

"Deliver her. As promised."

"What are you talking about?" Karl asked.

"Side deal," Smokey said. "Don't worry. You'll get your cut."

"Side deal?"

Smokey was silent.

"Jesus, Smokey," Karl said. "There's another player involved here? What the hell are you thinking? Everything we've done for security, and you go and bring another fucking player into this?"

Smokey was quiet for a moment. "I don't like your tone," he said in a low voice. "Remember your place."

Karl appeared to accept the rebuke. I didn't hear him respond.

"And anyway," Smokey said, "Wait till you see the payoff. The redhead is worth more than the original deal."

"Are you serious?"

Smokey grunted.

Karl whistled.

"Still upset?" Smokey said.

"I should have been consulted."

"Don't be a bitch about it."

The men fell silent, leaving me to chew on the substance of their conversation. I was a side deal worth more than the Snuff Fest take. Why? What would a retired Homeland agent possibly offer a bunch of criminals?

There was only one answer that made any sense. The password.

I closed my eyes and thought of the middle-aged man with the aquiline nose and the monk-like bald spot who had rescued me from a fate worse than death in that mountain cabin, only to throw me into the fire as the Capstone Facilitator. Bitterness and bile crawled up my throat. *Fuck you, Artemis Grange.* Now that I knew exactly what was at stake, I also had a sense of the lengths they might go to extract from me what they wanted. Everything I'd endured in the past—and it was a lot for anyone to survive—would pale in comparison to what they would be willing to do to me now.

And in the end, everyone breaks. No one can withstand a concerted effort to extract information. Torture works. I would eventually give up the password. I would eventually betray the entire fucking planet.

I resolved to never let it get to that point. I would not let them strap me down and go to work on me. I would gain my freedom or die trying.

ARCHER AND HIS TEAM DIDN'T STAY PINNED DOWN FOR long. It took less than a minute for them to locate the shooter. For all of their apparent cyber sophistication, the criminals lacked basic tactical skill and equipment.

"Marking," the team's sniper called out on the radio. "On the roof, near the center," he amplified.

Archer looked up and searched the middle of the roofline for the bright infrared laser spot from the sniper's sight. The spot was invisible to the naked eye and nearly all commercial night vision devices, but it shone like a beacon in Archer's specialized night vision devices, and he found the spot in no time.

Rendered in artificial shades of green was the silhouette of the warehouse building. Sharp edges defined the roof and the various dilapidated pieces of ventilation equipment. Conspicuously different was the rounded outline of a man's head, peering around the edge of an old fan housing. A long, thin object in the man's hands shone a brighter shade of green. The rifle that had killed Barnes, still hot from its recent discharge, panning back and forth through the darkness.

"Engage," Archer commanded.

The sniper rifle boomed and the rounded shape on the roof blossomed into a fountain of bright green liquid in Archer's goggles.

"One more on the east side," said another voice in Archer's earpiece, barely audible over the ringing in his ears from the sniper rifle's concussion.

"Two more on the west."

"Cleared to engage," Archer said.

The firefight was brief. Fewer than five shots rang out. Three human forms fell and lay motionless near the warehouse.

"Check in," Archer said. As his team members reported their status via radio, he exhaled with relief. Everyone was accounted for, and Barnes remained their only casualty.

What now? Archer looked behind him and saw the Thunder Bay police officers in positions of cover behind their cruisers. Armed with pistols and shotguns, they wouldn't be much help, except to apprehend any suspects who might somehow make it through his team's perimeter. Low odds, Archer assessed. The criminals weren't tactically trained, judging by their performance so far. Good huntsmen, probably, but things were much different when your quarry could shoot back.

His brain ticked through the options available to him. Each had branches and sequels, and there was no procedurally clean decision from this point forward. He would have to answer for every word he spoke on the radio, every order he issued, every round expended by his men, every Canadian casualty.

But Archer's conscience was clear. The years of FBI bureaucracy hadn't fouled his moral compass. He knew there was only one choice that he could live with for the rest of his life.

He checked his radio settings to make sure everyone on his team would hear his next transmission, both at the warehouse and at the other location northwest of Thunder Bay.

He keyed the mic. "Breach and neutralize," he said.

THE POLICE VAN'S ENGINE WHINED. THE SUSPENSION
didn't do much to dampen the potholes. My face burned where it had smacked
the pavement after the taser shot. Probably road rash. The steel floor drained
the heat from my body. On top of everything else, my muscles were tightening
up in the cold.

And my pocket buzzed.

Off and on. Buzz. Pause. Buzz.

Had the crooked Thunder Bay cop not bothered to search me? The events
immediately following the taser shock were a blur, and I couldn't recall much
about how Smokey had gotten me inside the van. Had he done it alone?
Hadn't he had time to search me? What if I'd been armed? Did he think
tying me up and cuffing my hands behind my back meant that I didn't pose
any further threat?

Could he *really* have left a cell phone in my pocket? It seemed out of
character for someone involved in the Snuff Fest operation. Very cyber-savvy,
covering their tracks at every step. It had taken the world's most powerful
intelligence apparatus to breach their security. They knew what they were
doing.

But that didn't mean that everyone involved in the operation was a cyber expert. In fact, the more I thought about it, the less probable it seemed that a senior police officer in a sleepy northern port town would have had any real motivation to dive deeply into cyber operations and computer surveillance. Sure, Thunder Bay had automatic license plate recognition and logging, and probably a few other shiny objects from enterprising tech contractors, but how much electronic surveillance expertise could I really expect among the rank and file?

My pocket buzzed again.

The last person to use this number—the number belonging to Fix's burner phone—was a very special individual. I wondered if he was trying to get in contact with me again. Maybe to warn me. Too little, too late. I was on my own.

My attention turned to the cuffs binding my wrists together behind my back. I moved my hands a little. I needed to know what kind of handcuffs they were. Officer Sevier hadn't carried handcuffs, opting instead for zip ties, which are much more secure. Why hadn't Smokey switched to zip ties as well? Dinosaur, maybe. An old cop stuck in the old ways.

I moved my hands more, and my heart leapt with joy when I heard the familiar jangle of a chain. These cuffs weren't state-of-the-art. New handcuffs—where cuffs are still used, which is a dwindling number of places—are bound together by a sturdy hinge. They're far less susceptible to the technique I was about to use.

I squeezed my wrists together, which pushed the links of the short chain together. The ends of the links overlapped, which drastically reduced the amount of twisting motion the chain could support. The links bound against each other.

It had been a long time since I'd practiced this, but it wasn't something a person forgets how to do. Much like riding a bike.

Smokey braked hard and threw the van into a sharp turn. My body rolled and bumped and slid with the momentum change. That knife of pain stabbed me in my back again. My wrists moved involuntarily against the cuffs, stretching the chain back into shape again.

Smokey stood on the accelerator and the van surged forward. My body rocked backwards toward the tailgate, and I had to hop a little to get my bodyweight off of my wrists. It took me two painful tries, but I managed to reposition my body to afford my hands maximum leverage. It wasn't much leverage at all, but I hoped it would be enough. Without the use of my hands, I didn't see how I could fight off two burly men who were probably accustomed to using lethal force.

Another pothole spoiled my second attempt to position the handcuffs.

The van slowed. "Get ready," Smokey said to Karl.

"We need to give the order," Karl said.

"Do it."

A moment passed, then Karl's voice: "Burn it down."

Adrenaline surged through my body. I tested the cuffs, played my wrists to get them in the right position, found the resistance I was looking for, took a deep breath, and twisted my forearms in opposite directions.

Immediately my right shoulder seized in a painful cramp. I tried to breathe into the pain, wiggled my arm to release the cramp, but there wasn't much relief to be had. The muscles just weren't used to the weird angles and the strange forces. I would have to gut it out.

I worked to reset the position of the handcuffs, but the links weren't cooperating. I applied a twisting force again, aiming to overwhelm the last little segment of the last link of the chain where it attached to the handcuff on my right wrist, gritting my teeth against the angry protests from my shoulder.

Didn't work. The links just slipped past each other.

My breathing was shallow and my heart beat fast. The exertion and stress had warmed me, and my brow felt damp with perspiration. I tried again. Wrists together. Links overlapping. Twist. *Motherfucker.* They slipped again.

The van stopped. Smokey put the transmission in park. Karl's door opened, then Smokey's. The van rocked as they exited. The doors slammed in succession. Their booted heals clumped on the ground. I followed them in my mind's eye, my hands working the cuffs furiously, as the men rounded to the back of the van and stopped. The latch rattled and the lock turned.

I fought panic. *It wasn't supposed to end like this.*

"THREE. TWO. ONE. GO!"

One kick from the lead FBI man and the personnel door gave way. Archer hoped the other half of his warehouse team had similar good luck. And he hoped that the men at the other Snuff Fest site weren't hitting much resistance.

The lead man shot out the overhead lights. They found themselves in a narrow corridor. It was disorienting, because the building was a warehouse, not an office building. But a warren of afterthought cubicles and shabby offices greeted them.

They raced through the corridor, smashing in office doors as they went.

"Clear right!"

"Clear left!"

The offices were empty.

Up ahead, the narrow hallway took a ninety-degree left turn. A flickering glow painted the corner. An acrid smell burned Archer's nostrils. He looked under his night vision goggles and knew immediately that the situation had just turned desperate.

"Fire," he said into the mic. "Stay tight. No one splits off. We move as a group."

They rounded the corner and motion caught his eye, furtive and quick, just a shadow in the brilliant light of the flames. There was too much light spoiling the image in Archer's goggles. He slapped them away from his face and immediately saw the outline of a large man, standing without cover and taking aim. Archer loosed two quick rounds, then a third. The figure dropped. The loud clatter of a semiautomatic rifle crashing against the floor sounded above the low roar of expanding flames.

"Over here! To the left!"

The corridor opened to a vast space. In its center stood a raised dais, surrounded by television lights. Judging by their faint glow, the lights had only recently been shut off.

In the center of the dais was a bed, covered in white fur, stained crimson in large, sickening patches.

A girl lay strapped to the white fur, motionless, face sallow, hair strewn, an impossible amount of blood covering her body.

Archer didn't have to give the order. Three men fanned out to secure the perimeter around the dais, and two others joined him in a mad dash to the girl. The first man to reach her checked her pulse, then jumped on her comatose form and started chest compressions.

Archer's heart sank. Were they too late?

He couldn't worry about that now. They had to get her outside, away from the flames, or she stood no chance. None of them did. A wave of heat blasted the group, and from the corner of his vision, Archer saw a ring of flames encircling them. The criminals had used an accelerant. Fire sealed off Archer's escape route. The only way out of the flames was through them.

Gunfire echoed. The other half of Archer's team had found more shooters.

"Smartly, now, boys," Archer said. "It's gotten a little more interesting." The gallows humor of a seasoned operator up to his eyeballs in the shit. The cool understatement was calming and grounding, and his men responded. They moved quickly in a swarm of coordinated, silent activity.

Archer's razor-sharp knife made quick work of the thick leather strap binding the girl's left wrist. He moved to the girls' face, brushed her hair away, gave her two quick breaths of air. As he pulled away, he looked closely at the girl. He recognized her from Sam's pictures. Stacey Lamontagne was her name. It was her assault in the Philadelphia warehouse that had ultimately blown the entire Snuff Fest operation.

"She's loose," said the man at Stacey's feet.

"Lift on three," Archer said. "Fireman's carry. Slow is fast. Don't fuck it up."

Coughs sounded. The smoke was getting thick. Flames blocked the way. Archer wheeled around, looking for a hole in the flames that they might sneak through. There was none.

Which way had they come in? If they had to charge through flames, they had to make damned sure not to fight their way deeper into the burning building. They only had one chance.

"Got you, boss," said a drawling voice over the radio. Tex. Archer realized instantly that the man was part of the contingent that had penetrated the building from the other side. They'd fought their way through the warehouse and had found the center dais. "Hold your breath—I found an extinguisher," Tex said.

High pressure chemicals blasted the base of the fire to Archer's left. The flames yielded just a little. Archer thought of that old myth about the sea parting. "Walk!" Archer commanded. They couldn't afford to rush. Falling down could mean certain death.

They moved as a pack through the momentary hole in the flames. "This way," called the man with the fire extinguisher. "It's quicker out the back."

A deafening crash assaulted their ears and shook the floor beneath their feet. The old structure was giving way under the heat's relentless assault. A loud groan, then a screech, then another crash. A piece of heavy equipment had fallen from its stanchion, its weight suddenly too much for the melting metal brackets that had held it fast for decades.

A scream pierced the air. Archer saw the fire extinguisher on the floor. Tex was buried up to his pelvis under the massive cube of rusted steel. Jesus, it was bad. If Tex somehow survived, he would surely wish he hadn't. Without a word, the men set Stacey's naked, comatose form on the hard concrete and took positions around the massive steel machine. It had few handholds. The men grabbed it from underneath and pulled.

Even with the adrenaline-fueled surge of strength, there was no hope.

It was just too heavy. Tears streaked Tex's face. Tears blurred Archer's vision as he regarded Tex's mangled form. He shoved his shoulder into the machine, screaming at his men to move that fucking thing right fucking now goddammit. More men joined the struggle. "On three!" Archer yelled as flames encroached.

Seven men now, lifting in unison, and the hunk of metal finally moved. Tex let out a howl of pain that stopped Archer's heart. But they had no choice but to continue. The men rocked the giant metal cube off of Tex's destroyed legs.

One of the men doused the flames that had attached to Archer's back. "We gotta move!"

Three men grabbed Tex. In the roaring heat and brilliant orange light, Archer saw the man's legs sag and fold nauseatingly, then Tex and his rescuers were gone, receding into the flames.

Archer scooped Stacey's limp form onto his shoulder and followed at a stumbling shuffle.

His lungs and eyes burned. His skin burned. He couldn't breathe, but he couldn't hold his breath. They were all going to die here, in this fucking warehouse in this godforsaken town in the middle of nowhere.

Metal groaned and screeched. Supports gave way. They were out of time, Archer knew. Theirs would be an unthinkably painful death, but they wouldn't go without a fight. They charged forward, forward, ever forward, hitting a wall, following it to the left, feeling for an opening, pounding and kicking against the wall in a vain attempt to punch through, mouths open in silent screams of oxygen-deprived panic, tears streaming from burning eyes, lungs in full revolt.

And then cold, fresh air.

It washed over them. Their feet found cold, damp earth. They charged forward, coughing and sputtering, lungs filling with clear, sweet oxygen, suddenly crazed with joy, suddenly laughing, the greatest moment of their lives.

They had made it out alive.

THE VAN DOORS OPENED AND A COLD WIND HIT ME WITH malice aforethought. It was wicked and brutal, and it didn't give a shit. The icy blast wicked the sweat from my forehead. It felt like my guts had frosted over. Jesus, it was cold.

I wrestled with the cuffs. Futile. Four hands grabbed me at once. The two slime balls hefted me out of the van. They spoke, low and gruff, but a deafening whine sounded in the darkness and drowned out their words. Few sounds like it in the world—piercing, unbelievably loud. An aircraft power unit starting up.

Not good. If they managed to get airborne with me, there was no chance in hell that Archer could find me in time to spare me from whatever disgusting fate they had in mind for me. The fear gripped my gut.

Pain shot from my lower back as the two men jerked me from the police van and shuffled across the tarmac. I noticed that I was suddenly crying. Fear, pain, cold, exhaustion, futility. It all felt overwhelming. I'd been in terrible situations before—I'd even been killed—but this felt different. For some reason I can't specify, it really felt like my time had run out. It wasn't that I didn't have the strength to fight, though I was definitely less than 100% in that department at the moment. It was more that I didn't have the courage. Or the will.

I didn't struggle. No point. My wrists and ankles were still bound, and the pain in my back was unreal. That little joyride in the Robinson's helicopter must have done some real damage.

The two men hauled me up the narrow stairs to a small business jet. They had to duck to fit inside the hatch, and that brought Smokey's face near to my own. His scent was masculine and pleasant and there was something else, something that transported me instantly to another time and place, like only a smell can do. He smelled a little like Brock.

My heart broke all over again. I'd lost him, the man I'd waited my whole life to find, gone forever, lost because I couldn't walk away from the life that nearly destroyed me, and now I would die alone and afraid at the hands of a man who smelled like Brock. Holy hell, you can't make this shit up.

"Don't cry, sweetheart," the other man said with an ironic smile on his face. Smokey had called him Karl. I studied him. White hair, rough skin, hard edges, fit, trim, handsome, but pure evil. I knew the type well. "We're going to take great care of you."

"Karl, I'm going to kill you slowly," I told him. But my voice croaked weakly and the threat sounded exactly like the bullshit it was. Both men chuckled.

"You're a spicy one," Smokey said. "Makes me sad I won't be joining you on your little trip."

"Do you have to get back to serving and protecting, officer?" I jabbed, my voice a little stronger now.

I saw the backhand coming from a mile away, and I let it land. Smokey's hand hit my face with a loud smack. I saw stars and my lip stung, undoubtedly bloodied, but I managed a laugh. "That's all you got? Your dick must be the size of my little toe."

Karl's fist hit my gut with a vengeance. Again I was ready—he might as well have sent me a singing telegram announcing his intentions—but even with my abs flexed tight, the blow knocked the wind out of me. I doubled over, only partially acting, and they shoved me into a leather captain's chair. I stayed doubled over, fighting for space between my back and the chair. I needed to give my hands room to manipulate the cuffs.

I thought Smokey might be the kind of guy who felt the need to defend his own honor, and I wasn't wrong. This time, he didn't slap me. He hit my face with his fist. More stars, instant headache, probably a black eye if I managed to live long enough for the hemorrhaging and swelling to set in. I didn't laugh at him this time. I couldn't. It really fucking hurt.

I took advantage of the pain. I moaned and leaned forward again, scooting a few inches forward in the seat as I did so. The men forced my torso upright and cinched the lap belt across me.

I moved my hands behind my back, testing. Plenty of room. The small victory was hard won, but my gambit had worked. I pressed my wrists together, twisting the chain, feeling for tightness and leverage.

Karl disappeared aft of me in the cabin. Smokey exited the plane without a word. Then a tall, skinny white guy with an oversized nose and an undersized tie folded himself through the cabin door, shut and locked it behind him, and turned toward the cockpit. He changed his mind and turned back toward the cabin for a moment, with a look on his face like he'd forgotten something.

I recognized him. It was Fix's friend, the Russian-speaking one who had "donated" the flight up to this frozen hellhole. I figured as much. I wondered if he knew Fix was dead. I also wondered if he had been the one to fly the kids from Philadelphia to Thunder Bay in the first place.

I shook my head. Trust no one. *Not even the people you love most.* Thinking of Brock, whom I loved more than life, who had left me alone when I needed him most.

Focus. I would probably die, but I could at least make it difficult for them. I got back to work on my handcuffs.

A sharp sting hit my shoulder. I whipped my head to see a hand with a hypodermic. My eyes followed the arm to his face. Karl wore a vicious smile on his lips. But I suddenly didn't give a damn. I didn't have a care in the world. I felt amazing. Then I felt amazingly dizzy. I thought I might vomit, but instead I passed out.

ARCHER'S COUGHING FIT SUBSIDED JUST LONG ENOUGH to allow him to vomit. Nothing but bile came out, and his stomach cramped. Carbon monoxide poisoning from the fire, he knew. It would get worse before it got better. He couldn't take a deep breath without inciting another coughing fit, but he couldn't get enough oxygen into his battered body. So he breathed in shallow gasps, trying to stay calm, waiting for his turn with the paramedics, and waiting for a report from the other team at the Snuff Fest site north of town.

It came a few moments later. All FBI agents accounted for, with no casualties. Three suspects killed, one apprehended, one escaped on foot. One of the choppers had just taken off in pursuit.

Only two kids were rescued. One was in critical condition. The other was unharmed but in a catatonic state of fear.

Archer's heart sank. Had over twenty young people already been tortured and killed? Were there only three survivors, or was there a third site Sam didn't yet know about, where others might still be alive?

And where was Sam? She was nowhere in sight, and Archer found himself deeply concerned for her.

The ambulance pulled away with Tex's shattered body inside. To Archer, it felt like an indictment of his choice to violate procedure. If he'd followed the book, Tex wouldn't be looking at life as a double amputee.

But if he *hadn't* made that choice, Stacey Lamontagne would surely be dead. Instead, she was clinging to life beneath a swarm of paramedics. Archer knew that Tex was a big boy who knew what he was volunteering for. But that thought was little consolation for Archer. He still felt responsible and he dreaded trying to look Tex's wife and kids in the eye.

"For you, boss," a team member said, handing Archer a phone.

It was the deputy director of the FBI. "You are ordered to stand down immediately, gather up the remainder of your team, and get your asses back here as fast as possible. If they detain you, you are not to speak to the Canadian authorities. You are to refer them to headquarters without further comment. Do you understand?"

Archer understood. These weren't difficult tea leaves to read. This would hurt. It might even mean the end of his career. And if they looked at the whole thing in just the right way, and if they wanted to make an example out of the situation, Archer could see how they could come up with some very serious legal charges as well. Nobody can destroy a life as thoroughly as the feds, as Archer knew better than most.

He looked again at Stacey Lamontagne's inert form, the paramedics now lifting her into a second ambulance, and he smiled a little. *If you didn't have the balls to put it all on the line when it counted*, he thought, *then they wouldn't have hired you in the first place.* It might cost him everything, but he felt it was a pittance in exchange for a young girl's life. He'd make that choice every time.

He rose unsteadily to his feet and started thinking about the logistics for their return to the US.

I HAD NO CLUE HOW MUCH TIME HAD PASSED. I WASN'T in an airplane. I was in a bed. The sun was up and blazing through a window. The handcuffs and ankle restraints were gone. I moved a little, and my lower back screamed in agony. I must have been heavily sedated before, because that kind of pain would sure as hell have kept me awake.

I was wearing a gown of some sort. A terrible feeling curdled my insides and my heart slammed against my ribs and my hands shot to my crotch. *Had I been raped again?*

Thank God, no. At least, it didn't feel like it. I lay there, breathing hard, realizing for the thousandth time that my assault had jacked me up well and permanently. I would never see myself the same way again. I would never see life the same way. People who say that's an overreaction must not have ever been through it themselves, because being violated in that way had cracked something at the very center of me.

I needed a bathroom and I needed it now. I looked around the room. Farmhouse Americana decor, ill-advised a decade ago and no better for the wear since then, furniture clean but worn, with a smell that reminded me instantly of harried visits to the Midwest to see my grandmother when I was a child.

The far wall contained a door leading to a small room, white tiles and yellowing grout on the floor, bright flowers on the wall. I hoped it also contained the plumbing I needed.

Getting out of bed took a full minute, maybe more. Something felt catastrophically wrong with my back. I never understood back pain before—it sounded like an excuse to get out of work or receive a little extra disability pay—but *oh my bloody hell* is it ever life-changing, and not in a good way. I breathed in shallow puffs and shuffled my feet toward the bathroom. Getting on and off the toilet was a religious experience that took the better part of an epoch.

This is not good. I didn't know where I was, who was holding me, or what might be necessary to get the hell out of there. I just knew that in my current condition, I'd have had real trouble fighting my way out of a paper bag. I looked at myself in the mirror. The black eye had come in nicely. It was a good bit of work on Smokey's part. The opposite cheek also had an impressive patch of road rash, probably from when I'd fallen on the asphalt after being tasered.

I was sweating by the time I shuffled out of the bathroom. As a rule, I didn't take painkillers. I'd been sober for a long time and I wanted to keep it that way. But damn, I was seriously reconsidering that policy at the moment. Not that I had any drugs available to me but the idea sure sounded nice. I was in agony.

I found my clothes folded neatly on a wooden chair in the corner. They had been laundered. The blood stains hadn't come clean. On my shirt was the faded purple remnant of Fix's life-essence. It turned my stomach. My thoughts turned to Stacey, and the promise of protection I had utterly failed to keep.

Tears attacked me out of nowhere. I leaned against the wall for support as I sobbed quietly.

And then it passed, leaving a new calm in its wake. The toxic pressure lifted momentarily from my heart. But I knew it would be back. It had come every day since Brock left. It wasn't getting much better. I wondered why I cared anymore, about anything at all, but that was a dark pull into a spiral of despair that I didn't indulge.

I disrobed, my borrowed floral gown collecting in a heap on the floor, and set about the shockingly painful task of dressing myself. I couldn't put on my socks or shoes. It just hurt too much. At some point during the process, I remembered the cell phone in my pants pocket from earlier. I scanned the room, but it wasn't there. My captors had confiscated it.

Someone knocked softly on the bedroom door.

An attractive blonde woman dressed in a tight red skirt, knee-length, and a matching blazer, perfectly tailored, stepped into the room. She wore librarian-style glasses that worked well with her beautiful face. Smart, hot, young, professional.

"I'm the governor's chief of staff," she said. "I hope you slept well?"

Governor?

"Where am I?"

"You're a guest of the governor's," she said.

"Governor of what?"

This took her aback, and she looked at me a long moment. "Nebraska," she said.

Nebraska?

"What does the governor of Nebraska want with me?"

Another blank stare from the governor's chief of staff. "Are you okay, ma'am?"

"Not even close," I said.

"Are you going to be able to make the appointment this morning?"

I shook my head and shrugged. "What appointment?"

Her eyes narrowed. "Nine a.m., national security discussion, just you and the governor," she said.

I frowned. A national security meeting with the governor of Nebraska? It made about as much sense as an appointment with Tom Cruise to discuss theology.

We looked at each other for a long moment. "What's your name?" I asked.

"Jennifer Renner," she said.

"Jennifer, I need to ask you a favor. I've hurt my back and I need you to help me put my socks and shoes on."

Blink. Stare. Blink. "I would be happy to help," Jennifer finally said.

"And maybe something to eat."

"No problem."

"And I'll need my phone back."

"Is it not with your things?"

"Why else would I ask you to give it back to me?" Maybe I wasn't my most patient self at that moment.

She looked at me again, then knelt wordlessly at my feet to help with my socks and shoes. The whole thing felt surreal and absurd, like a Twilight Zone episode, at least until the first shock of pain hit me as I tried lifting my left foot off of the floor. That felt real as hell.

"Maybe I should sit." The words barely came out.

"Almost done."

I was shaking by the time she'd finished.

She ushered me down the hall and into a large office. She stood at the door and didn't follow me in. She didn't even look inside as she closed the door behind me.

I looked around. Big desk at one end, the usual male overcompensation artifacts hung on the walls, though these were far less impressive than the kind you normally see in offices in DC, and at the far end of the space was a door hanging ajar that led to an executive lavatory. Near the door was a large conference table with a continental breakfast elegantly arrayed on a lace tablecloth. I hobbled toward the food.

I reached the spread on the conference table, fruits and pastries and yogurt and granola and coffee. My stomach growled. But I had a sudden flash of clarity, and I made the hard decision not to eat. I'd already been drugged and kidnapped. I didn't care to repeat the experience. I found a sealed bottle of water and downed it in one try. I just looked longingly at the fruit and pastries. I would eat later, I told myself, only partially believing that there would be a 'later' worth looking forward to.

A side door opened. In walked a tall, wholesome-looking man in his forties. Bespoke suit, silk tie—red, of course, given the territory—and a practiced, almost-human smile on his face. The man instantly gave me the creeps. But maybe recent events in my life had soured me on all things patrician.

Or maybe he really was a fucking creep. Jury was still out.

"Welcome, Ms. Jameson," he said, his voice deep and even silkier than his tie. "It's an honor to have you here," with just a hint of grease in his voice, and as my skin crawled a bit, I wondered how people like the one in front of me ever got voted into office.

I just looked at him.

"Please, have a seat."

I shook my head. "Back pain. Thanks anyway."

"You don't mind if I sit, do you?"

He didn't wait for an answer. He sat lightly on a leather sofa with unfashionably ornate wood armrests. He leaned back and crossed his legs.

I had a billion questions for this asshole, and even more angry barbs, but I kept my mouth shut. I was only there for one reason: he needed something from me.

He didn't bother to introduce himself. Power move. He was such a big deal that I was supposed to know who he was without being told. But I couldn't have told you the name of the Nebraska governor if my life had depended on it. Fortunately, at the front of his oversized desk sat an oversized name plaque. James Ritchey. Governor.

That name again. *James Ritchey.* I'd seen it recently, and it had seemed familiar then, too. But I couldn't remember where I'd run across it. My mind struggled to find context for the name, even a setting in which I'd heard or seen the name recently, but I was hungry and in pain and still plagued by a thick mental fog after my heavy sedation. Nothing came to me.

My eyes returned to his face. He smiled again. This time, it wasn't a practiced politician's phony baby-kissing smile. This time, it reminded me of smugness and menace, as though some seething, festering thing deep within him had clawed its way to the surface for the briefest of moments. Then a millisecond later he was back in control, firmly grounded in his role as governor of Nebraska.

He looked at his right hand, which fussed over something small and shiny. His fingers twirled it repeatedly. It slipped, caromed off the leather cushion, and dropped onto the burgundy Persian carpet. He scooped it up again before I could see what it was.

"It's an election year," he said. "And of course not much real work gets done in an election year. You have to apply for your job again. The way it should be, of course, nothing I'd ever trade to make it easier. But it does make for a terribly busy schedule and of course the work is almost totally unrelated to the things the good citizens of Nebraska happen to care about."

I blinked a few times. Was this some kind of joke? Some men just can't get to the fucking point. First they have puff out their chests and measure their tiny dicks.

"And we often find ourselves in strange situations during an election year," Ritchey went on. "Just yesterday I went to Canada, for example." His eyes flashed meaningfully at me.

"What do Nebraska and Canada have in common?" he asked rhetorically. "Nothing. Not a damn thing. Wouldn't have been there, except it's an election year. Big deal, big campaign donor, obviously not directly because foreign companies can't contribute to US elections, but their US subsidiary can stroke a check like there's no tomorrow." A hearty laugh.

Nothing about what he said sounded even a little funny so I didn't join him in his merriment.

And my patience had worn out.

"Mr. Ritchey," I said, "what the hell am I doing here, and what the hell do you want from me?"

He looked at me. His fingers twirled the object in his hand. I still didn't know what it was. It looked to be about the size of a credit card cut in half the long way. Light gray, with dark gray lines arranged in concentric squares. Looked a little like the underside of a circuit board.

I looked again in his eyes. He had a strange look on his face, as if I had amused him in the way a child might, or maybe I was the butt of a private joke.

Let him stare. My mind worked on his name: *James Ritchey*. Where had I seen it? So much had happened in so little time, and I was sleep-deprived and traumatized and running on fumes. I was a long way from being my best self, but I knew it was something important.

"I appreciate that you might not have planned to be here at this moment," Ritchey said, "but I hardly think that's any reason for unpleasantness. Have we not taken good care of you?"

He recrossed his legs, right over left now, and sprawled his right arm across the back of the leather sofa. His fist had covered up whatever he had been fidgeting with. I wondered what it was.

James Ritchey. Where, dammit?

My mind suddenly returned me to the small office in the back of the gas station convenience store outside of Thunder Bay. Something I had read or heard.

"Miss Jameson?"

My visualization stopped and my eyes saw him again. But I didn't answer.

"Thought we'd lost you there for a minute. Wouldn't be at all surprising given the day you've had."

He was back to twirling the thing in his hand. He dropped it again. It bounced all the way to the floor again, and when it hit the fine Persian carpet, it split into three. Three long, thin, identical-looking sheets of gray with dark gray lines etched in a concentric pattern.

Three of them.

James Ritchey.

The back office in the convenience store. I had been reading the computer screen in the convenience store office with the clerk looking on in annoyance, popping her gum. James Ritchey's name had shown up on that computer screen.

Which meant that he was mentioned in a Capstone report.

I looked again at the three objects on the floor and a tidal wave of adrenaline slammed my guts. I suddenly knew what they were.

MY HEART RACED AND MY NERVES MIXED WITH THE lingering after-effects of sedation. My stomach felt queasy and my legs threatened to buckle.

"By now, of course," Governor James Ritchey said as he leaned forward to collect the three objects from the floor, "you must realize that there's more involved here than just a bit of deviant fun."

A door opened and in walked an overstuffed suit with a bald head and an earpiece. Corn-fed for sure, with a telltale underarm bulge.

"Where are the others?" Ritchey asked the guard.

The bald bodyguard looked puzzled. "They left for the airport already. I was just checking to see if you needed anything before I joined them."

"Why the hell are you going to the airport?"

More confusion on the bodyguard's face. He blinked a few times. "Your emergency trip back to Thunder Bay?"

Ritchey turned red. "What are you talking about?"

"Jennifer told us to get to the airport right away."

"She told you that?"

The bodyguard nodded. "In a text."

Ritchey clenched his fist. He looked at me and his eyes narrowed. *"You did this."*

I hadn't done anything. But I thought I knew who had.

"I'm afraid I'm even more confused than you are," I said. Which was a lie, because I was thinking of Grange's words. *You are in play.*

Ritchey turned to the bodyguard and barked orders to retrieve the other members of the security team and get them back to the mansion immediately, if not sooner. The guard left in a hurry, muttering under his breath.

I took stock. I didn't think I was in any condition to win a physical altercation. But I was also in no shape to withstand any coercive techniques. And I owned the most valuable password in the world. It unlocked power that could turn an ambitious backwater psychopath into a global player. It could also feed and enable his disease for the rest of his life, at the cost of countless more lives.

I took a deep breath and put a smile on my face. I shrugged my shoulders and laughed a little. "Last time I was awake, I was the guest of your friends Smokey and Karl. I was in cuffs, and Smokey gave me a black eye. Then Karl stuck a needle in me, and nighty-night. I woke up in Nebraska as a 'guest of the governor.'" I made air quotes. "I must admit that I didn't expect such warm hospitality—Jennifer is a gem, you should give her a raise—but I don't know what you want from me and I really just want to go home."

Ritchey sneered. "Home to your studio apartment in Charleston?"

I didn't say anything. His verbal punch had confirmed Grange's warning that I was indeed in play, and had been for a while.

"Miss Jameson, you have something that I need. You will give it to me, one way or another."

So the games were over and it was down to business. "When did you first meet Frederick Posner?" I said in a bid to take control of the conversation.

Ritchey shouldn't have been surprised, but I caught him off guard and he did a poor job of hiding it.

"Frederick who?"

I smiled. "How about Karl and Smokey? When did you meet them?"

Ritchey dropped the guile. His face turned from faux-innocent to cunning and mean. "Police convention. Philadelphia. I heard the nightlife was to die for, so I made it a priority. Plus it's an election year, you know. Important for me to be seen as tough on crime and all that."

He smiled. There was no remorse, no shame, no guilt, none of the human emotions one would expect from someone who had done what Ritchey had done. There was just entitlement and evil.

My heart thudded and my fists balled. "You killed a kid yesterday, didn't you?"

His smile broadened. It looked genuine, maybe also proud. "Not just one," he said.

Bile rose in my throat. Not just because of the heinous crimes he had committed, but also because I knew that he wouldn't be confessing unless he planned to kill me.

But the bodyguards had left. It was just me and the governor of Nebraska. We were alone in his office. When would they be back? It could be any minute. The remaining guard did not need to drive to the airport to retrieve the other two. He just needed to make a phone call. He might walk through the door at any moment to give Ritchey an update.

I cut to the chase. "What happened to Stacey Lamontagne?"

He shook his head and shrugged. "Is that a name I should recognize?"

"Did you kill her?"

He shook his head.

"Where is she?"

He shrugged again. "I'm certain I do not understand who or what you're talking about."

I seethed. Smug bastard. I wanted to harm him, to inflict pain, to hear him cry and beg. I couldn't help but wonder if that made me just like him. I wondered if I had become a psychopath.

"How did you find out about me?"

He thought for a moment. "That's the trouble with spies, isn't it? You never really know where their loyalty lies. Capstone has the same problem all such organizations have."

Capstone. Hearing the word in this context somehow made it more real. More terrifying.

"You're not equipped to manage it effectively," Ritchey said. "You lack the will and the conviction. You won't do what needs doing."

I knew he was right. I'd known since the moment Artemis Grange threw the fucking thing in my lap. But still my shoulders sagged and all the air left my lungs. My eyes felt heavy and my mind felt thick with deep, crushing exhaustion.

"I want the password, Miss Jameson. I *will* have it. You *will* give it to me. That is inevitable. Everyone breaks eventually. Even you." He snorted with derision. "You can't even tie your own shoes. How long do you think you'll last before you beg me to stop?"

My eyes closed. I nodded slowly. I felt the sudden urge to cry. "Not very long at all." My voice sounded small and weak. I leaned against the conference table for support.

I looked at the floor. Thoughts bombarded me. Drawing breath seemed to take more energy than I had available. My eyes unfocused. Fix flashed in my mind, lying on the cellar floor, blood pooling. And Stacey. I knew she had suffered unimaginable pain and degradation at the hands of people who didn't deserve the air they breathed.

I felt small and defeated. "I have nothing left. No love. No career. No friends. All the fucking pain and suffering. The... rape."

My voice broke but I didn't care. "And all the fucking torture and death. It stole me away from myself. I don't know how many years it would take for me to even start feeling normal again."

My eyes welled up and my throat tightened. I was hollow, alone, hopeless. I looked at Ritchey. "And I don't have the will to try."

A long moment passed. I stared at the floor. Ritchey watched me. When I looked into his eyes again, I didn't see empathy or sympathy but I saw understanding. He nodded. "I can make it painless," he said.

I looked out the window. Spring was taking over for winter. Life was renewing itself. If hope has a color, it must be the bright green of new leaves on brave saplings. The display of unreasonable optimism on the manicured lawn seemed foreign, unattainable, part of a world that no longer existed for me. A world that *could* no longer exist.

Was it really coming down to this? My thoughts returned to Brock, to a summer morning we shared at the Outer Banks, cool breeze stirring, coffee in his hand, hair mussed, shirtless, naked, face still flushed from our lovemaking, that transcendent sparkle in his eye and a sideways smile on his lips.

A tear spilled from my eye. When I lost him, I lost everything.

I took a deep breath.

"Okay," I finally said, my voice shaky. "Give me something to write with."

WITHOUT A WORD, JAMES RITCHEY WENT TO HIS DESK
and retrieved a notepad and pen. I straightened up as he approached. The
movement brought sharp pain and once again my breath stopped short. Not
much longer, I thought to myself.

Ritchey held out both hands. In his right hand was the notepad. At the
top was a stylized drawing of the state capitol building. Below that, *From the
desk of Governor James Ritchey,* the header announced. I looked at it for a long
time. I couldn't imagine what a man like Ritchey would do with all the power
that Capstone offered. It would be utterly disastrous.

Maybe worse than if a hollowed-out shell of a person like me stayed at
the helm.

It didn't matter. Ritchey's sickness was not my problem. There were a
million others out there just like him. What I had told him a minute ago was
100% true. I wanted out of humanity. I wanted a quick and painless exit. I
wanted all of this to end.

But not today.

I gently took the pad from his left hand and the pen from his right. My
left fist closed around the pen, point down. In a flash, my other hand dropped

the notepad and seized Ritchey's outstretched arm. I stabbed the pen into his left forearm, then ripped downward toward his wrist. A three-inch gash opened up. It filled instantly with blood, pulsing and streaming.

Ritchey's other hand shot to his forearm. I gritted my teeth and kneed him in the balls. It connected with an audible thud as my knee crushed the soft tissue and slammed against his pubic bone. Maybe the best ball-blow I've ever landed in my entire life. He fell in a heap on the floor. As he writhed in agony, I fell to my knees behind his back, placed my thumbs on his spine, and curled my fingers around his neck, stopping just shy of his windpipe. I squeezed, just hard enough, but not so hard that I'd leave marks.

The blood choke took mere seconds. Ritchey's body stopped thrashing. I held the choke for another fifteen count. Not long enough to kill him, but enough to keep him unconscious while he bled out through the wound in his wrist.

People who slit their wrists often try multiple times before working up the courage to do it for real. I jabbed at his forearm twice more, barely breaking the skin, taking care to avoid getting his blood on me. The forensics obviously wouldn't all point toward suicide, but I wanted to make it as convincing as possible.

I wiped my prints from the pen and stuck it in his right hand, closing his fist around it. I released the pressure and let the pen fall to the floor.

I used the conference table to hoist myself upright, wincing and groaning with the shocking pain in my back, but aware enough to avoid the growing pool of Ritchey's blood near my feet.

I hobbled to the executive restroom and threw up in the sink. I rinsed my mouth, splashed water on my face, and shuffled out of the lavatory, my hand on the wall for support.

Just then the office door opened and the big, bald bodyguard returned. Confusion registered on his face.

"Oh my god, come help him!" I shouted.

The bodyguard dashed to Ritchey's inert form. He performed CPR, but the compressions just pushed the blood out of Ritchey's wrist faster. It was over.

I hobbled toward Ritchey's desk, moving past the leather couch and the three RFID tags Ritchey had collected from the floor and left on the coffee table. That little mystery was solved. Ritchey had double-crossed everyone by making copies of the three RFID tags. It was his tag that had followed us at 500 mph on our flight to Thunder Bay the day prior. Either he had made counterfeit copies of the other two RFID tags or he had somehow stolen them from Smokey. He had probably already used the three tags to collect the Snuff Fest payment. I wondered whether the funds would ever be recovered.

I stopped at Ritchey's desk, picked up the phone, and dialed 911.

THE LINCOLN, NEBRASKA POLICE DEPARTMENT WAS

thorough and competent, but the FBI soon arrived in force, and their people behaved as FBI people always do: methodical, efficient, thorough, diligent. The very definition of professionalism. They couldn't afford not to be. A governor was dead.

From the beginning, the Bureau team addressed me as "Special Agent Jameson," a sign of professional courtesy, and also a sign that they had done a bit of homework before the interview started. But I wasn't under any illusions. The FBI exists to produce convictions. Nothing more, nothing less.

Still, I told them everything.

Almost.

I didn't tell them about Capstone.

I didn't tell them I had murdered Frederick Posner.

I also didn't tell them I had killed James Ritchey. It was premeditated self-defense, which wasn't really a thing as far as the law was concerned. Manslaughter would be the best I could hope for in those circumstances. A murder rap would be on the table, and might be very attractive depending on the state attorney's politics. And I knew in my bones that I couldn't handle going to prison. I needed to be free to take my own life if it came down to it. I wouldn't survive being locked up forever with no sharp objects or shoe laces, imprisoned with only my demons for company.

I changed the order of events. I said that I had confronted Ritchey in his office with what I knew, that I told him I had already informed the FBI, and that the Bureau had already opened an investigation. I told the investigators that I had been distraught from the disturbing conversation and sick from the sedation, and that I had gone into the bathroom to throw up. I told the FBI agents that Ritchey had taken his own life while I was in the lavatory. I felt confident that nothing the bodyguard had to say would contradict this version of events. And in my injured condition, there was little reason for the investigators to believe that I had won any kind of altercation with Ritchey.

I also didn't tell the FBI investigators that a man named Artemis Grange had probably hacked into Jennifer Renner's phone and sent the text to Ritchey's security team that had undoubtedly saved my life. Sending them on a goose chase to the airport was a stroke of brilliance, and I was grateful. Sort of. Grange had thrust me into this mess. Thinning out the opposition was the least he could do on my behalf.

Still, it was something. There was still some humanity left inside of Grange. At least, I hoped there was. I wasn't in any condition to do anything good with Capstone at the moment, and somebody had to mind the shop while I licked my wounds and decided what the hell to do with the terrible responsibility that had been thrust upon me.

My story was implausible, but not impossible. That a sitting governor, a police commissioner, and a number of senior police officers in two North American cities might be involved in a murder-pornography operation was shocking to the collective conscience. But none of the details I offered seemed to surprise them, and I figured that Archer must have reported enough information back to the home office to get the FBI wheels turning. They had probably already confirmed at least a few of the clues I had provided to Archer courtesy of the Capstone report.

Ritchey's men had drugged and kidnapped me, I said. The blood tests I consented to would confirm it. I lied and said that I didn't know why Ritchey didn't just kill me when he had the chance. I could connect all the dots and help build an extremely ugly case against him, I said, so it made little sense that he didn't just add me to his list of victims.

Except that it made perfect sense. He wanted the Capstone password. But Capstone didn't officially exist, and the last thing I wanted was for information about its existence to leak. If I thought I had problems at the moment, they would be nothing at all compared to what might happen if Capstone became public knowledge. It wasn't just outrageous; Capstone was a legitimate threat to the fabric of society.

I asked the FBI agents about Stacey Lamontagne. They wouldn't answer at first, but I told them I would not cooperate further until they at least told me what had happened to her. They finally relented and told me she was in critical but stable condition in a Thunder Bay hospital, under armed guard but not yet awake. I breathed a sigh of relief. It was the first bit of good news in an eternity, and as good an outcome as I could reasonably hope for, though I sure as hell wondered who was standing guard over her. Was it another crooked Thunder Bay cop? I shook my head and tried not to think about that.

They asked me if I knew anything about the Posner shooting. I told them it couldn't have happened to a better guy. I said that if they could figure out how to bring him back to life, I would happily volunteer to kill him again. They glanced at each other but said nothing.

Their questions turned to the Robinsons. How long had I known them? What was our relationship? I said they might want to take a close look at Becca Robinson's computer. Fix had installed a key logger and some other spyware before our fateful trip to Michael Robinson's cabin. I wasn't sure how deeply Becca was involved in the atrocity, but I felt certain she had helped to hide heinous crimes. I also suspected that it was one of her helicopters that had dropped the nude corpse into the forest on Isle Royale. "Look for a coercion angle," I said. "Becca has a daughter."

The agents nodded. "You think they made threats against Lizzie? That's why the mother kept quiet and cooperated?"

"Seems a safe bet," I said. "Definitely worth a close look."

I also told them about the bitcoin account information Fix had assembled after Sevier paid me the blackmail money. It would take some time to analyze, but I felt confident the web of accounts involved in the complicated transaction would eventually implicate other Thunder Bay officials.

"Sevier will be a great source of information," I said. "He seems like the kind who might turn state's evidence."

A long pause.

"Sevier died in the hospital yesterday," the lead agent told me. "Heart attack."

I pursed my lips. It made sense. "Check the cameras," I said. "See if he had any visitors."

"A gray-haired man in jeans and flannel paid him a visit."

"Flat-top haircut?" I asked.

They looked at each other again. "How did you know?"

"Probably goes by the name of Karl," I offered. "Real nice guy. If you ever find him, be sure to castrate him for me."

"You seem to know quite a bit about this case," the lead agent said.

"Old habits. I used to sit on your side of the table."

"But you don't anymore."

I nodded and shrugged. "What would you have done?"

They made marks on their notepads.

I asked about Alfonse Archer and his men. After a brief pause, they told me there were three casualties, including one fatality. One survivor had lost both his legs. My eyes teared up when I heard the news.

Archer himself was on administrative leave pending a full investigation. I expected as much, but part of me had held out hope. The news landed heavily in my heart. Archer's ordeal had just begun and would last a very long time. I couldn't account for the guilt I felt—he was a smart professional and made his own decisions, and the man I knew wouldn't allow himself to make any choice other than the one he made. But I still felt somehow responsible.

"Please do your best to take care of him," I said. "He's an honest man, and he has courage and principles. And I owe him my life."

The interrogating agents blinked at me a few times. I got the impression they'd never seen or heard anything like this. I wasn't surprised—it was crazy as hell and half the time I didn't believe it myself. I couldn't imagine how the headlines might read. I wondered how many months and years it would take for the investigation to wrap up. I wondered how many countries it would eventually involve, how many people would ultimately be caught.

Then I asked the question that had been burning a hole in the center of me. "How many kids did they rescue?"

Their expressions grew pained. They really didn't want to answer.

"Please," I said. "My friend died for these kids. So did your fellow agent."

Their faces took on an expression of exhaustion and weariness. They looked at each other and seemed to come to a silent agreement. "Three," the lead investigator finally said.

Just three kids had survived. Out of two dozen.

I fell apart. I cried uncontrollably. Sobs wracked my body. I rocked back and forth. I wanted to stop living on this planet. I wanted no part of our species.

It was dark again when the FBI agents released me on my own recognizance. Don't take any vacations, make sure we can reach you, etcetera. But they were kind enough to give me a ride to a nearby hotel in town.

When I got to my room, I lay on the bed and cried quietly until sleep overtook me.

I awoke at midnight. The pain in my back was unbearable. I asked the hotel clerk to arrange transportation to the emergency room. An hour and a half later, I was seen by a harried doctor. She looked at the x-rays. No broken vertebrae, but things weren't right with the alignment. I had probably slipped a disc, but an MRI would confirm it. They would be happy to schedule one, but it would be two weeks from now. I politely declined. I didn't know where I would be in two weeks, but I knew I wouldn't be anywhere near Lincoln, Nebraska.

The doctor was sympathetic. "If you don't want painkillers, is there anything else I can do for you now? Do you have a safe place you can go?" She looked at my black eye with a concerned expression on her face.

Tears came again. I was breaking down, I realized, having real trouble keeping it together. I pushed the words out through my tightened throat. "I think I need to talk to a psychiatrist."

There was concern in her eyes, and understanding. "There's one on call. She can see you tonight."

"I'd like that," I said.

The doctor left me alone in the examination room. I closed my eyes and waited, thinking of what I had said to James Ritchey. *I don't have the will to try.* I've never spoken truer words in my life, I realized.

I don't know how much time passed before I heard a knock on the exam room door. It opened, and an older woman with a stooped body and gray hair and a kind, grandmotherly air stepped into the room. She did a double take when she saw my battered face. "Oh, sweetheart," she said. "I'm so sorry this happened to you. But you're safe now."

I knew that she was wrong. I knew that I was anything but safe, but I decided to suspend my disbelief. I also decided to accept any help she could offer. There was nowhere to go but up.

Maybe tomorrow would be better.

We hope you enjoyed this story from USA Today Bestselling Author Lars Emmerich.

The saga continues in DEEP FAKE. Tap the image or links to secure your copy at a special Author-Direct Discount!

What will Sam decide to do with Capstone?
What happened to Brock James?
Will Sam and Brock reconcile?
What will become of Artemis Grange?
Get DEEP FAKE and be among the first to find out!

Click here to order DEEP FAKE at a special Author-Direct Discount!

READY FOR WHAT'S NEXT?

Get the latest book in the million-selling Sam Jameson
series, and catch up with USA Today Bestselling Author
Lars Emmerich, over at Lars' shiny new store:

store.ljemmerich.com

ABOUT THE AUTHOR

When Lars Emmerich was twelve, he went to an airshow. An F-16 flew over the crowd, low and fast and impossibly loud. Something stirred in his chest and tears formed in his eyes. It was love at first sight. Lars and the F-16 went on to enjoy fifteen incredible years together.

While Lars was a young lieutenant in Undergraduate Pilot Training, he read a Tom Clancy novel. It was his first exposure to the espionage and conspiracy thriller genre, and again it was love at first sight. "I will write stories like this one day," he vowed solemnly.

He's still trying to live up to that promise.

ABOUT SAM JAMESON

Sam Jameson catches spies for Homeland. Not a traditional female career path. But Sam's not really the traditional type.

She has great aim and a bad temper, and they don't always mix well. She also has the dubious distinction of having died once in the line of duty.

Sam is the star of the Sam Jameson series, which now boasts over 1,000,000 fans in 17 countries.

"This is the best writing in decades. Move over, Lee Child."
- Steve Harrell

WHY LARS 'FIRED' AMAZON

Once upon a time, Amazon decided not to pay Lars his royalties.

Lars was frightened and confused. Authors have children and must buy groceries, after all.

"Why, oh Amazon, have you done this thing?" Lars cried.

But the Amazon humans were too busy to answer, for Lars was not yet famous enough for their attention.

Only the robots took the time to reply... though the robots gave him no answers.

This taught Lars something important: **authors cannot rely on Amazon**.

So he learned how to connect directly with readers and fans, and it is the best decision he ever made.

Get the latest book in the million-selling Sam Jameson series, and catch up with USA Today Bestselling Author Lars Emmerich, over at Lars' shiny new store:

store.ljemmerich.com

ACKNOWLEDGMENTS

Lars wishes to thank the most important person in his business:

YOU.

Because of your enthusiasm, patronage, and support, Lars is blessed with the incredibly rare opportunity to pursue a lifelong dream.

Thank you.

Thank you.

Thank you again.